G000082462

THE VEN[ETIAN] DETECTIVE

REDEMPTION

Michael White

PEACH PUBLISHING

About the Author

After graduating from King's College, London, Michael White became a member of the '80s band the Thompson Twins. He later lectured in Chemistry at d'Overbroeck's College, Oxford and in the '90s worked as a journalist, including a stint as Science Editor at GQ and as a columnist for the Sunday Express.

Michael's first book (co-authored with John Gribbin): *Stephen Hawking: A Life In Science* was a global bestseller. Since then, he has published 39 books in 35 languages including the award-winning *Isaac Newton: The Last Sorcerer* and *Rivals: Conflict as the Fuel of Science*, short-listed for the Aventis Prize.

His first novel, *Equinox*, published in 2006, was a Sunday Times bestseller. He continues to write highly acclaimed fiction. More recently, he co-authored a thriller with James Patterson, *Private Down Under*, which reached the Top Ten in the UK charts and the New York Times bestseller list. His latest thriller, *The Venetian Detective* was recently optioned for film/TV.

He emigrated to Australia in 2002 and lives with his wife and four children in Perth, WA.

Copyright © Michael White 2016

The right of Michael White to be identified as the Author of the Work has been asserted by her in accordance with the Copyright, Designs and Patents Act 1988.

This book is sold subject to the condition it shall not, by way of trade or otherwise, be copied, lent, resold, hired out, or otherwise circulated in print or electronic means without the publisher's prior consent in any form.

ISBN 978-1-78036-305-9

Except where actual historical events and characters are being described, all situations in this book are fictitious and any resemblance to living persons is purely coincidental.

Published by
Peach Publishing

For my five best friends:
Lisa, India, George, Noah and Finn

Chapter One: Bread and Wine

Venice. Ten Minutes Past Midnight,
10th of November, 1592.

The masked and black-cloaked figures moved slowly, keeping to the shadows as the flirting light of a full moon reflected from the water of the canal. The water lapped on stone, a rhythm older than Venice itself.

On nights such as these, nights when he could smell blood before he saw it, the taller of the two men would assume the name Saviour. He thought it entirely appurtenant. The smaller man called himself what he was; Sin Eater.

Down the passageway they headed, away from the water, their footfall dampened by practice.

Turning left, then right, the two figures in black emerged onto a cobbled square surrounded by flat-fronted buildings. Abstract shadows formed a distorted checkerboard across the ground. In the centre of the square stood a stone font, a gossamer-thin layer of ice sealed a dirty puddle of water under a three-foot tall statue of Pan.

How appropriate, Saviour mused. Pan, the God of the Wild. God of shepherds and flocks, of Nature, the God of mountain wilderness, of hunting and rustic music. Felicitous then that Pan should preside over the place to which he and Sin Eater were heading; the brothel known as Alfonzo's where the selected victim, the prostitute, Antoinette Perugino plied her trade. Singularly apposite indeed; even if the mighty Pan had been reduced to a three-foot tall ineptly-crafted stone statue perched in a puddle.

The two men slipped to the side of the square and stopped. They could hear the sound of music, voices and shrill screams spilling from inside the bordello, and they watched as a pair of men emerged, struggled for a moment before the elder of the two stumbled off into the night and the other returned inside.

It was cold, but Saviour and Sin Eater felt nothing. They could have stayed silent and still for hours if they had needed to; but then, less than ten minutes passed before a new burst of sound came from Alfonzo's. Saviour caught his companion's eye and put a finger to his lips. The door had opened and a young woman emerged, alone. The sound from inside the bordello exploded, then dampened almost to nothing as the door closed behind her. Antoinette pulled a shawl about her shoulders. Shivering, she started to turn left when a tall figure, featureless in the shadows, stepped in front of her out of the darkness and the two hidden men heard the woman yelp in surprise.

"What are you doing here?" they heard Antoinette say.

They could not discern the man's reply.

"What do you mean?" the girl said.

Again came a deep-throated unintelligible response and the tall man gripped the girl's arm making her cry out. He had a cane in his spare hand and as he started to raise it to strike Antoinette, from the side of the square, a second dark shape rushed towards the couple. He was a squat man, and as he entered the pale red light from one of the bordello's windows, Saviour and Sin Eater, still in the darkest recess of the campo, could see his face, but he was unknown to them.

"Antoinette," the smaller man hollered, his voice rough and common. The girl and the tall figure spun round together to see the burly fellow charging towards them. The tall man released her arm and twisted to face the newcomer as he stampeded forward like a bull let loose in the ring. Antoinette screamed and slipped back as the tall man raised his cane above his head. For a fraction of a second, the top of it glinted in some stray beams from Alfonzo's, then it came down, missing the other man as he swung to his left with surprising agility.

A dozen yards away, Saviour and Sin Eater glimpsed the terror in Antoinette's pale face. Then her expression slid into a peculiar blankness and she swung round, ducked out of sight for a moment, before running south, away from Alfonzo's, crossing striated moonlight and slipping from view. She quickly reached a narrow passage that led to the water beyond and the two watchers slithered away into a parallel lane, moving speedily over the cobbles.

She was a tall woman and she walked quickly. Some fifty feet along the passage, she heard something unusual. She didn't break her stride, but quickened her pace, tightening the shawl about her shoulders. Turning left, Antoinette entered a narrower lane and glanced behind her. She saw nothing.

The pain came as a complete shock. It rippled along her left temple, down her cheek, splaying out across her shoulder. She stumbled, and collapsed onto her right side. The two men were on her. She caught only glimpses of their faces, a slice of chin beneath Saviour's mask, a flicker of black pupil, a wisp of the other's hair. She jerked away and tried to pull herself free as Sin Eater landed a second blow to the back of her head. She went to scream and a hand pulled at her trembling lips, distorting her face and drawing blood. A tooth snapped, falling white and red to the moonlit cobbles.

Saviour got behind her, pulling her up onto her haunches. She could not understand what he was doing. She felt as though she had stepped out of the flow of time, but then warm liquid started to run down her neck into her cleavage, and she saw the red spray, the ground quickly peppered with dark gobbets.

2

She could not move. Saviour lowered her onto her back and her warm blood arced, raining onto her face, her neck, her hair. She saw Sin Eater's masked head. He was leaning over her holding a small chalice and a piece of white bread.

Passing his hands over the dying woman, the man began to recite in Latin, his voice shrill, slightly effeminate. "*Ego facultate mihi ab Apostolic Sede tributa, indulgentiam plenariam et remissionem omnium peccatorum tibi concedo et benedico te. In nomine Patris, et Filii, et Spirtus Sancti. Amen.*"

Antoinette stared at him, a mist forming before her eyes, her own blood blinding her. A terrible pain cut through her and she shook, went to cry out, the sound clamped into silence by Saviour's big hand.

Sin Eater poured wine from the chalice and watched it sprinkle onto the woman's pale face, mixing with her blood. He leaned down and ran his tongue over Antoinette's skin, across her cheek to her nose, to the tip of the nose, across her lips down to her neck and then onto her bloodied breasts, slurping the wine and the blood from her nipples.

Sin Eater heard the woman gasp. He looked up into Saviour's obfuscated face and ran the bread into the blood that gurgled from Antoinette's ripped neck. Lifting the soaked bread to his lips, he tilted back his head, let the bread slide between his lips, then he swallowed and offered another incantation: "I take your sin, my child. You shall know paradise."

The two men looked down at Antoinette and saw that she was dead.

Chapter Two: Two Ships

Venice, Forty hours earlier.

To Lord Niccolo Celsi, the view from the large windows, shutters pinned back to the wall, was at once familiar yet always fresh; but today it was startlingly altered. At the foot of the vista lay San Marco, flags unfurled. To the east stood the Basilica and the Doge's Palace, while almost directly ahead a throng stretched back into the square itself and pressed up against the doors of the Basilica. Two ships had dropped anchor, gangways were lowered down to the quayside and servants scurried around shouldering bags and pushing carts laden with boxes and crates.

Niccolo Celsi surveyed the scene silently, the sound of the crowd rising from below. Leaning on the sill, he let his long black hair sweep unheeded around his angular features. He felt a chill breeze vibrate about San Marco, and from behind him, he could hear the woman stirring and pulling the covers about herself. Ignoring her, he studied the flag of Saint Mark, the emblem of the Republic atop the mast of one of the galleys. The galley was from the Doge's royal fleet, sent to convey a special traveller from Athens. Approval for this honour had been passed by the Council of Ten, of which he, Celsi was a member. He had pointedly abstained in the vote, but it had passed regardless; a fact that still irked him. The other, smaller ship had already lowered its flag.

He turned back to the room and saw the woman stir. She pulled up from the bed, brushing her hair from her face. She had a strikingly beautiful face, high cheek bones and large, dark eyes. There was something of eastern heritage about her in the almond shape of her eyes and the tone of her skin. Her heavy, dark-nippled breasts swayed as she moved.

Celsi turned back to the window. The crowds had parted as a small group moved towards San Marco and he could just make out the faces of the new arrivals. There at the front was the man he had loathed since they were both youngsters, rivals, but so very different from each other, contenders for the same woman (whom neither had secured for his own).

The man moved with a familiar gait, a confident walk. He was dressed in what to Celsi seemed completely outlandish garb, a silk top over baggy pants, a colourful cloak, and topping off the ensemble, a bright red felt hat worn in a jaunty fashion. About his left shoulder hung a large, worn leather bag and on his belt he was armed with nothing more than a dagger, the hilt just visible. It was Doctor Francesco Sagredo, the man he had hoped never to see again, an exile recalled at the insistence of the Doge.

Alongside Sagredo there were none Celsi could call a friend. Beside the new arrival walked Lord Pinelli, an elder from one of the great families, but a known heretic and occultist. Three members of the Council of Ten, Marchese da Fontina, Lorenzo Arturi and Gian Deivo walked close behind Sagredo; they looked gay, expectant, and to him, sickeningly smug. He would do all he could to wipe that look off their ugly faces.

To Celsi's disgust, the crowd was clearly thrilled to see Sagredo. He had been away for fifteen years, yet regular word had reached the Republic of the many adventures into which he had been drawn, the many noble exploits in which he had engaged, and none of it had come from the man himself; it was all hearsay, word of mouth, and to Celsi, most of it was of dubious pedigree.

He felt fingers running down his spine. Turning, he saw the girl beside him, wrapped in a sheet.

"What's the fuss?" she asked, her voice dreamy, heavy still with sleep.

Celsi barely acknowledged her and flicked his shoulders to stop her tracing her touch down his back.

"That, my dear, is *the great* Francesco Sagredo."

"Oh, I've heard . . ."

Celsi snapped round.

"Is that his entourage? The girls are calling him the new Marco Polo."

Celsi exhaled loudly. "It is the man's welcoming committee. He always travels alone, apparently. But, so much has been made of his exploits, who knows?"

The girl peered out at the view, then began to worm her way in front of Celsi trying to distract him. With an impatient hiss he pulled her aside and gaped in disbelief at what he now saw through the window.

A small group had emerged from the second ship. At the centre of the party was a man in cardinal's robes. A clutch of priests and a few dignitaries stepped onto the quay. Hardly anyone noticed them and the men looked around slightly bemused.

"Fuck!" Celsi exclaimed. "It's the Papal Nuncio! Sagredo has arrived late and the envoy from the Vatican is early. Christ above!"

The girl giggled and bit her lip. "But, Francesco Sagredo does look very dashing."

Celsi whirled on her. "Get dressed and get out."

"Nicci . . ." Antoinette looked hurt.

"Get dressed and get out, I said. I'm needed at the Palace."

•

5

Five hundred yards to the west, a young woman, Niccolo Celsi's sister, Sofia stared through a massive window contemplating a busy Grand Canal. Across the room, lounging on a couch and reading a letter was her elderly mother, Violetta.

"The waters are busy this morning, mother," Sofia said without turning. The old woman ignored her.

"I don't think I've ever seen so much traffic except during carnivale."

"What, dear?" Violetta Celsi said, absent-mindedly.

Unseen, Sofia rolled her eyes. "The canal . . . it's busy, mother!"

"Well, we have Francesco Sagredo to thank for that."

"Of course! I'd forgotten. I've heard all about him. Apparently, he is very handsome."

Violetta bridled. "The man is a vile creature! You should not believe what you hear, Sofia. Remember the word of the Scriptures, daughter: 'For such men are slaves, not of our Lord Christ but of their own appetites; and by their smooth and flattering speech they deceive the hearts of the unsuspecting.'"

Sofia turned back to the window silently mimicking her mother.

•

Niccolo Celsi strode into the western anteroom leading from the Senate Room of the Doge's Palace and saw that the Papal Nuncio, Cardinal Severina was seated with his assistant, Father Beringhiero Gessi standing beside his chair. The priest snapped to attention as Celsi paced over.

"What is the meaning of this!" Gessi barked. "You have kept His Eminence, the Apostolic Nuncio waiting for almost an hour!"

Celsi ignored the priest and stared straight into the cardinal's eyes. "Your Eminence, please accept our sincere apologies."

The skin about Severina's cheeks was as taut as a canvas on its frame. He rose from his seat. "Addressing yourself now in the first person plural subjective, are we Celsi?"

"I'm here on behalf of the Doge and the Council."

"Ah, and I am not insufficiently important to be granted a personal visit by the Doge?"

"His Serene Lordship the Doge has been very ill for some time. Were you not informed?

"No," Severina said coldly. "I was not."

"There was a great commotion outside," Father Gessi said.

"Yes, a mishap," Celsi deigned to address the priest. "Another visitor who arrived very late. It has caused some considerable confusion."

The priest exhaled through his nose, but Severina was more magnanimous. "Very well, let us make up for lost time. Who speaks for the Doge while he is incapacitated?"

"I do, Your Eminence. Welcome to Venice. Will you please join me in my office?"

The cardinal bowed slightly and followed Niccolo Celsi while Father Beringhiero Gessi, haughty and indignant still on behalf of his master, walked a respectful two paces behind them.

Chapter Three: Doge

The younger ones among you may perhaps be forgiven for being unfamiliar with the details of my first investigation, but, for those of you living in this city almost nineteen years ago, there is little excuse because the events of November 1592 have been etched into the history of the Republic. And although I wish it had been through other circumstances, I cannot help but feel honoured that I played some small part in thwarting a presence I still perceive as being that of a very sick mind.

Becoming a solver of crimes was the last thing I expected when I arrived back in Venice after spending most of the past fifteen years of my life travelling through the Ottoman Empire, Persia, India and the Orient, and it was certainly not a job I had canvassed for. Instead, it was thrust upon me by a set of strange and unexpected circumstances. For, without me knowing it, stories of my adventures had preceded me so that when the Doge's personal galley dropped anchor at the Molo, San Marco and a crowd of well-wishers had gathered at the waterfront to welcome my arrival. I was both amazed and delighted.

Having travelled so long and so far, mostly alone, I found the hordes of people almost overwhelming. I heard my name chanted as though I were a returning war hero fresh from victory on the battlefield. Women thrust their babies under my nose, and if it had not been for the burly guards on either side, I believe I could have been easily crushed.

Beside me as we made our way across San Marco was my old friend, Lord Gianvincenzo Pinelli. Like all of us, he had aged in the decade and a half I had been away from home, but that day he was filled with an almost preternatural energy and a great and genuine delight in seeing me. More than once he commented how there had been many times he had resigned himself to the belief that he would never set eyes upon me again.

More guards parted the way up the steps to the Doge's Palace and I was led along the colonnades to a small room far enough away from the entrance so that the sound of the crowd was almost totally quelled. Soon, Pinelli and I were alone; two guards stood the other side of the doors to the room.

My friend held me at arm's length, gripping each elbow and staring into my eyes. He was at least five inches shorter than me, and I suspected that under his cap, his hair had gone entirely. "We have been asked to tarry here for a while, so you may catch your breath and the Palace flunkies can prepare," he said. "Heavens, Francesco! You look rather overcome. Not at all surprising!"

I shook my head and lowered my bag to the floor. "I had no idea," I replied, easing myself into a chair and putting my hat down upon a low table. "What awaits me here? The official message said the Doge was ill and wished to see me urgently."

"I have not seen him, but I am told it is serious."

I looked at him gravely. When I left the Republic in 1577, Doge Pasquale Cicogna had been merely a successful businessman, but I had of course heard upon my journey that my old friend had been made Doge in 1585. I had been close to the Cicogna family since the Battle of Lepanto in 1571 ,when I was a young man not quite twenty-one, and still a student of Medicine at Padua. Through a complex succession of events, I had played a part in saving the life of the future Doge's son, Tomasso. The family had never forgotten this. I had been drawn into their circle and Tomasso had become my closest friend.

"Tomasso is with him?"

Pinelli sighed. "They rarely speak, and Tomasso has . . ." He avoided my direct gaze for a moment. "He is often in his cups, Francesco. He is, I sense, suffering some great internal anguish. I don't see him as often as I once did and I know he is mixing with some rather . . . colourful types."

"I see. And the Doge? What ails him?"

"No one knows. The physicks have flapped about, leeching and bloodletting as is their want, but he seems no better than when he first fell ill."

"Which was when?"

"Several weeks since."

"And you think my recall home is simply because Doge Cicogna believes I can cure him where others have failed?"

"It would appear so, my dear Francesco."

"I am flattered, but not completely reassured."

"Understandable."

"I received fragments of news on my travels. I heard of the passing of Doge da Ponte of course, and word of the wonderful new Rialto Bridge, but it was all piecemeal and sporadic."

"Much has changed of course, and not all of it for the better."

"No doubt the same old power struggles, money grubbing and vanity."

"Indeed, Francesco, and much of this may be placed at the door of your old favourites, the Celsis."

"Nothing changes. So, what have they been scheming?"

"Violetta Celsi remains the powerhouse of the clan. She is just as greedy and belligerent as ever. She grows old, but she is still venomous. Much of her

9

spite is channelled through her children, most especially Niccolo. He becomes more strutting and arrogant by the day. The family hate the Doge; Violetta has never recovered from the loss of her husband and believes Pasquale Cicogna is only Head of State by default."

"But Adamo Celsi died at Lepanto, over twenty years ago! I knew she was bitter back in the late '70s when I was exiled, but still?"

"That bitterness drives her, makes her disputatious, Francesco. It is a terrible thing to be consumed by hatred."

"It is," I said. "And what is this I hear that the philosopher Giordano Bruno has been imprisoned here in the city? That is shocking news."

"It is indeed, my friend. Bruno was arrested some six months ago and has been held in the Doge's prisons since then."

"Bruno is an extremist, but I was brought up in this fair place believing that ours is the most liberal society in all Italy. Things must indeed have changed if that philosophy is no longer sacrosanct."

"As I said, they have; but listen, Bruno is a subject for another time and I cannot help but notice you have not mentioned the one person I know you wish to learn about most." Pinelli gave me a sly smile.

"I had to cut Teresa from my thoughts when I was forced to begin a new life."

"I'm sure you did, but the two of you were so deeply in love."

"How is she, Gian?"

"She is back in the Republic."

"Back? I had no idea she had ever left."

She was married, my friend. Her family insisted she wed Marquis Louis Damas, French ambassador here and right-hand man to King Henri. They moved to Paris."

"And after Henri died? What happened?"

"So you heard how the king was assassinated?"

"Yes."

"Louise Damas died with His Majesty; trying to disarm the mad monk who carried out the crime."

"And Teresa returned a widow, shortly after?"

"And a mother. She has son, Piero; a fine young man."

I fell silent. Emotions I had not allowed for a long, long time were awoken. I caught myself observing them as though I were merely a spectator.

"You look pale. You should rest a while, Francesco," Pinelli said.

There was a knock at the door. One of the guards opened it to admit two young servant boys. The first was carrying a silver bowl; steam rising from it, a towel over his arm. The second bore a tray, a jug of pink liquid and a goblet.

"Ah, excellent timing," Pinelli said and stepped forward, instructing the boys to settle the tray and bowl on a side table.

"I shall leave you to freshen up, Francesco. Someone will come to fetch you in a while."

I ran my fingers over my forehead.

"Are you not well?"

I produced a thin smile. "Just a little dazed, Gian. Nothing a glass of watered wine and a steaming bowl will not cure. I shall see you later."

To me, the walk from the anteroom was as familiar as my face in a looking glass, and that, by the way is an accurate metaphor because I had not seen my own reflection clearly for many years, but I knew instinctively that if I were to now look upon my own countenance, it would be at once recognisable and strange; not entirely as I remembered it to be.

I was met by a single servant in red livery and we passed back through colonnades, morning sun bold and surprisingly warm, then we ascended the grand staircase, Scala d'Oro. At the top we turned left towards a set of double doors; the entrance to the Doge's apartment rooms. As we approached, one of the doors opened outwards; my guide bowed low and turned away silently. In the doorway stood a man I knew well, Niccolo Celsi.

His expression was little different to the last time I had set eyes upon him, a smirk blending contempt and bitterness. I often used to think that it was the most natural pose he could strike, for I rarely saw him without it. He was a tall man, an inch above me perhaps, slender still and I have to admit he wore clothes well, they seemed to drape on him in a way that would please any tailor. He had black, shoulder-length hair, parted centrally, a beard that was flecked with grey and his black eyes gave him a saturnine appearance. He did not look greatly different from the man I met last so long ago; his cheeks were a fraction more hollow, his eyes more tired, his high forehead more lined. He could have still been a handsome man if only he possessed a disposition even a fraction softer, kindlier.

"So, Sagredo, is this the latest fashion in the Court of the Moguls?" He looked me up and down.

"You like it, Lord Celsi? I'm sure if I gave your tailor some guidance he could run you up something similar."

Celsi exhaled noisily. "I'll bear it in mind if ever I decide to join a troupe of travelling performers. Follow me. The Doge is ready to see you."

As you may tell, Niccolo Celsi and I were not on the best of terms, nor had we ever been. Indeed, the man was the prime mover in bringing about my expulsion from the Republic in the first place, and our mutual enmity harked back at least twenty years. It would, I was sure, accompany each of us to the grave.

11

I followed Celsi into the anteroom. "It seems a strange task for you," I said. "Escorting me to the Doge."

"Much has changed in the time you have been away. I am Lord Cicogna's right-hand man, ranking second in the Republic. I have been running the government in his absence. He trusts me implicitly."

I gave him a sceptical look and raised an eyebrow.

"I did not vote for your recall, Sagredo, but the old man ensured the Council bent to his will over the matter."

"I imagine your opposition was well received."

He ignored the barb. "I would not concern yourself with such things. Instead, it might be prudent, I believe, to look to yourself, doctor; care for your physick and your surgeoning. For if you fail to cure the Doge, I will be happy to bear your head on a pole and hang it from the palace for the entertainment of all those fickle citizens who have greeted you so fondly today."

The Doge's bedchamber stood at the end of a long, poorly-lit corridor. Celsi tapped on the wood and in a while the door was opened by a man I vaguely recognised, Antonio Derretti, a court medic who had served the government for many years before I left the city.

It was a large square room, but oppressive, the drapes drawn; a musky stink hung in the air. Dimly illuminated, the place felt funereal. Doge Cicogna was sitting up on heaped pillows, a man dressed in a black gown attending him; another man in the same garb stood watching at the end of the massive four-poster bed; Derretti joined him.

I walked over to the Doge and his face lit up when he saw me. "Francesco, my dear boy." He made to sit up further, but the man in the black robe tutted and held his shoulder gently.

"Lord Doge." I bowed. "I wish we were meeting under better circumstances." I leaned in and kissed his ring. "Please tell me your symptoms."

"You had best speak to my doctors here … not that any of them know what they are doing." He gave the men at the end of the bed a scornful look.

"Where is your pain?"

"My head and my stomach." The Doge touched his left temple.

I edged the doctor aside and pulled back the covers, lifting the Doge's bed shirt. He looked frail and much too thin. "Let us find the centre of the pain, my Lord," I said and gently prodded, then used two fingers to tap at the Doge's abdomen.

He winced. "Ah, there."

I pulled up the covers. "May I see your tongue, sir?" I turned to the medics and caught a glimpse of Celsi standing, stiff-backed by the door. "Why is the room so dark?"

"To calm the humors, of course, Doctor. Sagredo," Derretti said.

12

I shook my head, paced over to the windows and threw back the drapes. Natural light flooded into the room. I then pushed away the shutters.

"What are you doing?" One of the two doctors close to the bed strode over purposefully.

"Letting in some fresh air. It's like a tomb in here."

"Are you mad?" a second assistant medic joined his colleague.

"Let it be," Doge Cicogna snapped.

"But Lord!" It was Derretti.

I came back across the room. "Doctor, I think we need to talk."

He nodded and glanced at his juniors. "Leave us."

The two men looked affronted, but did not argue. They left and Celsi came over to talk to the Doge while Derretti and I retreated to the back of the room where a table had been set up and arranged with a cluster of bottles, vials and small mounds of brightly-coloured powders. Next to these stood a jar of leeches and a set of implements for bleeding. At the end of the table, there was a silver bowl filled with blood.

"What treatments have you tried, Doctor Derretti?" I asked.

He seemed to find it hard to meet my eyes. His face looked drawn and tired. He was clearly unhappy about me being there, but knew he could say nothing about that.

"Everything one would expect," he replied flatly. "The Doge took to his bed over a week ago. We have bled him, twice daily, and began with the leeches on the abdomen two days ago. We have applied several remedies of my own concoction."

"And what do these contain?"

"I cannot divulge . . ."

"The primary ingredients?"

"For the first three days I used a mercury-based blend given orally. I then applied a compress of horse excrement on His Lordship's stomach."

"Then?"

"*Salt of alembroth* leavened with *Acidum levis.*"

"More mercury!" I ran a hand over my forehead. "Very well. Thank you."

Celsi was speaking quietly and stopped abruptly as I approached. He straightened and gave me his usual look. "Well? Any great insights, *doctor?*"

I ignored him. "Lord Doge, may I speak with you privately?"

"I am privy to anything . . ."

Cicogna raised a hand and Celsi fell silent.

Derretti had joined us and stood close to my side.

"Gentlemen." The Doge sounded weary. "Please leave us."

"But, My Lord!" Celsi protested.

"I would like some time alone with my physick."

Celsi bowed and retreated without meeting my eyes. Derretti slipped behind him silently.

I pulled up a chair close to the bed.

"It is so very good to see you, Francesco. So very good."

I smiled. The Doge found my hand and squeezed it. "Fools, all of them."

"I was surprised to see Lord Celsi, My Doge."

"That family has clawed its way to great power. They will soon be an unconscionable threat."

"Keep your friends close and your enemies closer?"

He gave me a puzzled look, then smiled. "Yes . . . exactly, my wise fellow."

I sat back and folded my arms. "You are not ill, are you Lord Doge?"

He looked down, entwining his fingers. "I didn't think I would fool you for long."

"But why?" I asked.

He took a deep breath. "It's Tomasso."

"I heard he is troubled."

"Hah! That's one way to put it. He is lost to me, Francesco and I'm afraid he will soon be lost to us all. He no longer speaks to me, but my spies tell me my son is in terrible debt, that he is killing himself with drink, that he is gambling and mixing with the very dregs of society."

I nodded. "Pinelli implied as much. But, I don't quite understand what you think I can do about it."

"You are as close as brothers."

"We were, My Doge. But you are forgetting that I have been on my travels a very long time."

"He loves you, Francesco. He respects you, looks up to you."

I gave the old man a doubting look. "I have not spoken to Tomasso in fifteen years."

Pasquale Cicogna fell silent and looked at his fingers again. "Well, that is why I recalled you."

"And it is an order that I should try to halt Tomasso's decline?"

"If it needs to be."

I could see the inner steel, the fire in the man's guts that had made him the most powerful person in the Republic. His expression softened. "But I would rather you helped us out of love."

"There was no need for such deception," I said. "You only had to ask. I would have returned for love of both you and dear Tomasso."

"It was a political expedient, Francesco. I wanted to keep the real reason veiled. My enemies would love to take advantage."

"But surely Tomasso's problems are well known?"

"They are, but I did not want to give anyone ammunition to criticise you, or I. I think you know to whom I refer." He glanced towards the door. "I also wish to try to recompense you for the foul treatment meted out all those years ago."

"Recompense, My Lord? I need none. My exile was a loathsome thing for me at the time, but I have benefited greatly from it. My travels took me as far as China and the islands south of that vast land. I travelled through India, Persia and crossed the vast deserts. I have lived a thousand lives."

"But you just said it yourself, Francesco: It was a loathsome thing at the time, and I wish to make amends. A vacancy has just come up and I shall see to it that you are elected to the Council of Ten."

Chapter Four: Old Friends

I could go into some detail about the Eighth of November 1592, my first day spent back in the Most Serene Republic, but to be honest, I believe it would slow things unnecessarily and keep us from getting to the heart of this story - the bizarre events that started soon after my return. Instead, I shall give you a brief recounting, for it has to be said that that day flashed past so quickly and was filled with so much, I do not believe I could anyway do justice to a more detailed account.

After seeing the Doge I was obliged to spend at least two hours with a succession of dignitaries, officials and government ministers before a palace guard escorted me to my modest old house on Campo S. Maurizo. And as we walked, it hit me immediately that of all the places I had visited in this world, the grandiose and the tranquil, nothing could come close to the power Venice exuded. I had been born and raised here, but returning, I felt an almost overpowering sense of excitement, a thrill no other place on earth could give me. Its beauty was beyond question, but it was also alive, fermenting, a menagerie of colour, odour, both the splendid and the sordid. For it was not all gorgeous architecture, bright light glinting on water, the wondrous asymmetry of the place, it was the contradictions: the gold leaf and the beggars, the smell of church incense and bilge, the gaudy ladies of high society and ragged children playing in the street, swearing and shouting at one another with untamed energy as they kicked a football around. It was the winding lanes and the houses flat-faced and daubed in a beautiful cacophony of colour, the maze-like routes from one point to any other, the market stalls and shops stinking of fish or blood-dripping poultry. And running through the city's wildly beating heart, the aortorial Grand Canal with its ferries, gondolas and the vessels of tradesmen and delivery services; each bank was lined by palazzi, the homes of the Republic's finest, ancient nobility alongside the newly-minted rich, men who had made their mark in the world of commerce and banking.

My house had been closed up for the past fifteen years and only opened, aired and cleaned by palace staff a few days before. My luggage had been taken there and left in a neat pile in the main room. I wandered the empty rooms, a large living area dominated by a plain fireplace, a pair of bedrooms, and downstairs, a basement which I had once used as a laboratory cum preparation room, for this house had doubled as my medical practice during the years immediately before I left the city. The place was dusty still and the smells of disuse resisted the fragrance of lavender bunches left by the cleaners.

It felt strange being alone again after such an intense few hours. I found I could not quite come to terms with the realisation that I was back in the place of my birth, the place in which I had spent the first twenty-eight years of my life. I cannot emphasise how difficult it was to absorb this. For much of my time abroad I had travelled alone or in small groups. I had spent time in both big, bustling cities and in isolated camps, settlements hundreds of miles from the nearest markings of civilisation. But during that time, I had been completely self-contained, free to follow my own whims. If I chose to stay in a particular place for a while, I would; if I desired to move on at a moment's notice, I could. Things were entirely different now. I was home, I was once more the servant of other people's exigencies and expectations. I had gone from almost unlimited freedom to the strictly contained parameters of life in Venice.

I tried to distract myself by starting to unpack, but soon grew restless and knew the only way to deal with the confusion in my mind was by confronting it head-on: I would seek out Tomasso.

Appropriately perhaps, I met him at an inn close to the Ghetto. Walking there, I was the subject of much gawping and double takes and several people insisted upon stopping to shake my hand and to wish me well. I was touched by how happy people were to see me and I welcomed it, for I knew I would not get anything like this reception from the old friend I had not seen for so very long.

It was a noisy inn and it took me a while to spot Tomasso sitting alone in a booth towards the rear of the place where a window overlooked a tatty courtyard.

"Someone told me this was your favourite watering hole, Tomasso."

I looked down at him as he lifted a tankard to his lips. He appeared confused for a second then nonchalantly swallowed and took a second gulp of ale. "Heard you were back."

I was quietly shocked by the change in my dear old friend. Although he was still lean, he had put on weight about his face. He made the most of things, wore well-tailored, expensive clothes, and I noticed his fine, soft leather boots. But it was all show. I could tell that under the veneer of sophistication and exquisite taste that had not left him, he was a mess.

I pointed to the chair opposite him. "May I?"

He simply shrugged and I stayed standing.

"It's good to see you, Tom. You look well."

"Don't lie. I look fucking terrible!"

He emptied his tankard and called over a maid, ordered for himself, and the girl turned to me. I asked for a watered wine and she left us to an uncomfortable silence.

17

"Do you wish me to go?"

"Not one letter, Francesco. Not one fucking letter."

I started to reply, but Tomasso cut over me.

"It was as though you had vanished from the Earth."

"I'm sorry."

"Sit down."

The drinks arrived and Tomasso immediately downed half the tankard.

"Why?" he asked. "Why cut me off?"

"I regret it, Tom. I regret it, now that I am here again. But you have to understand, I had my reasons."

"And what were they, pray?"

"Self-protection. I believed I would never return. You can accept that, can you not?

"And what of us? We may have held hope in our hearts, you know. We fought to have the exile order rescinded, Francesco. We struggled to get you home."

I was jolted by that. "I had no idea."

"We did not give up, not for a long time. But then I realised you really had gone and that there was nothing I, nor anyone else could do to defeat the powers behind your expulsion."

"Tomasso, I did not know. I have not known so many things. But all I can say in my defence is that I had to believe I would never lay eyes upon you again. I had to convince myself that my old life was now ash, that if I were to survive I had to look to the future, to the world beyond the Republic. Staying in touch would have been too painful to bear."

It was quiet between us for several minutes. I sipped at my drink and stared at the table with no idea what more I could say. Tomasso studiously avoided eye contact.

"The pain you bore," he said, and I looked up. ". . . that would have undone a weaker man."

"Perhaps. But really, I had no other choice. I was either to go on, to make something good come from the calamity, or to give in to it and allow myself to be broken, to end up a starving beggar."

"And so, Francesco, you are home . . . to stay?"

"I honestly don't know, Tom. Your father recalled me personally."

"I heard he had been ill."

"But you haven't visited him. I was saddened to hear that."

"Were you?" He paused and let out a heavy sigh. "He and I have not spoken for a long time. Besides . . . was he really ill?"

I could not disguise my surprise.

"I know the old bastard well! I know his ways. I suspect his motive has far

18

more to do with politics than sickness."

"Perhaps."

"My father has many enemies and many whom he pretends to call friends."

"The Celsis."

"There are others, but yes. Niccolo Celsi and his old fuck of a mother. They have half the trade of the Republic under their control, and I don't need to tell you . . . money buys *anything*."

I had quite forgotten how by force of habit Tomasso so frequently sprinkled his speech with casual profanity. "I had suspected that the Doge wanted me here to somehow thwart Niccolo Celsi," I said. "He is putting me into the Council of Ten."

Tomasso looked startled. "Satan's cock, Francesco! Now, that is a surprise."

"It's ridiculous."

"No it's not, it's perfect."

"If you don't mind being used."

"Oh come on! It has its compensations. And you can really stick it up Celsi's arse. He must hate you even more!"

We both laughed and Tomasso called the maid back over.

"Not for me, Tom," I protested. "I've got a lot to do."

"Such as?"

"Unpack, for a start. I haven't had a moment."

"Okay, here's my offer," he said. "One more drink and I'll help you. Oh, and by the way; your outfit looks fucking ridiculous!"

•

Thirty minutes later we were sitting on the bare floor in the main room of my house surrounded by trunks and boxes.

"You've kept the old place . . . I would've thought you needed something a little more lavish, more appropriate to your new, lofty position . . . like a palazzo on the Grand Canal!"

I gave him a withering look and threw open the windows. "I love this old house. It's been closed up all these years."

"Smells like it. And fuck, Francesco! What's that other stink?"

Grinning, I walked over to the fire close to where Tomasso was sitting on the floor. A pot dangled from a tripod straddling the flames.

"I got here earlier; picked up the key after seeing your father. I prepared a curry for a late lunch."

"A what?"

I ladled the food into two bowls and handed one to Tomasso. "It comes from India. Staple diet there, like beans and meat is to us. Try it, it's delicious."

Tomasso tasted it timidly and I watched his face contort. He spat it back into the bowl. "Blood of Christ, Francesco! Are you trying to poison me?"

I wolfed down the curry, making appreciative noises. "It's an acquired taste."

"I believe you," Tomasso said, getting to his feet. He pulled over a chest and levered back the heavy lid. I finished eating and started on the nearest container.

"So what's the plan?" Tomasso asked. "Apart from attending the Council, what do you intend to do? You're back for good, I hope?"

"As I said at the inn, who knows?" I replied. "When I was recalled I thought I would only stay a few days, but now, well. I honestly haven't had time to think."

"Have you considered reopening your practice?"

"Maybe."

Tomasso was pulling an intricate-looking object from a box and giving me a questioning look.

"Careful with that."

"What is it?"

"It's a clever device for seeing tiny things."

"What?"

"Things you can't otherwise see."

"Surely, if you cannot see them, they don't exist!"

"I'll show you later," I said.

"You must have experienced some wonders, Francesco. A part of me envies you." He stopped unpacking and gave me an admiring look.

"Yes, I've learned much, experienced many, many things." I paused for a moment. "Some of them I wish I hadn't seen."

"You've not missed much here, I can tell you."

"Oh, I don't believe that."

"Unless that is you count things that would bore anyone to tears. People marrying, dying, coming and going. The treadmill of life."

"You sound very weary of it all, Tom."

"I am weary, Francesco . . . fucking weary. I am simply existing . . . going through the motions."

I paced round to where he stood, taking him by the arm. "Sit. Talk to me."

"What about?"

"Well, to start with, when I left here fifteen years ago, you and your father seemed to be on good terms. What's happened?"

"Not now, Francesco. Perhaps some other time. It's . . . complicated."

"I've got time."

Tomasso opened his mouth to answer when there came a rap on the door.

20

"Damn it," I exclaimed. "Who is that?"

I opened the front door and saw a rotund man, a garment draped over his arm.

"Lord Sagredo? Milos Daniella, the Doge's tailor."

I stared at him, confused for a moment.

"Your suit for the ball?"

"Ah, yes," I said. "Please come in."

Tomasso wandered over.

"This is your father's tailor." I waved a hand towards Daniella. "He is making me a suit for tonight."

"Tonight?"

"The Doge's idea. He wants to celebrate his dramatic recovery. You're coming, yes?"

"No! I wouldn't be seen dead there, Francesco." He nodded towards the garment on the tailor's arm and tapped my stomach. "Hope it fits after all that curry!"

The tailor took my measurements and left, followed by Tomasso. Alone again, I looked around the room and at the clusters of chests and trunks. I could not find the energy to carry on with the unpacking, and within the hour, Milos Daniella was back with the altered suit.

The Doge's party was held in Sala del Maggior Consiglio, otherwise known as the Great Hall. I had been in this room many years before, but it was different now. The place had been gutted by a terrible fire in December 1577, just eight months after my expulsion from the Republic. It is said the new, but extremely old Doge, Sebastiano Venier, who died shortly after the fire, had expired from a broken heart: and it was easy to understand why, the room had been one of the most beautiful in all Christendom. Sala del Maggior Consiglio was still undergoing restoration work, but it was now close to its former splendour. The portraits of no fewer than seventy-nine Doges lined three of the walls, beginning with Doge Obalario degli Antenovi from the early ninth century and ending with the eight-fourth, Francesco Venier. Soaring high overhead, the ceiling, painted by the elderly Tintoretto and his son, Domenico, constituted the largest oil painting in the world.

The place was already well attended by the time I arrived. I felt uncomfortable in my new set of clothes. I had not worn anything so grand and formal since visiting the Court of the Uzbek ruler, Abdullah Kahn II, last of the Shaybanid dynasty in the Khanate of Bukhoro, four years earlier. The occasion had been the celebration of Abdullah's fifty-fifth birthday, and the traditional couture was far looser-fitting and much more to my liking. But at least now I merged in, because, to be honest, I was already growing a little weary of sticking out from the crowd and being something of a spectacle. Even so, I received plenty of curious stares; but then His Serene Majesty entered the room with an entourage that included half the government and patriarchs of the most wealthy and venerated Venetian families, and all eyes turned to them. The Doge walked with the aid of a stick, which made me smile inside knowing what an affectation it was. Draped on Pasquale Cicogna's left arm was his beautiful young niece, Clarissa, and to his right strutted Niccolo Celsi, looking for all the world like a human peacock.

The Doge was seated on a stage and a string quartet began with a jaunty dance piece. Catching the gaiety of the occasion, or perhaps knowing what was expected of them, straight away couples began to dance. I had slipped close to the back of the reception room and was watching quietly when I felt a gentle tap on my arm. I turned to see a young woman. She had a lovely face framed by auburn curls, her skin possessed a porcelain fragility while her dark eyes softened her pallor.

"Lord Sagredo?" she said. "Would you dance with me?"

A middle-aged nobleman, Frederico Getario, who had been standing close to me quietly observing the festivities raised his eyebrows and gave me a friendly nudge.

"I would be delighted to," I said. "But for two things. First, I need your name, and second, a promise that you will only refer to me as Francesco."

The girl beamed. "It is agreed, Lord . . . Francesco. My name is Caterina Sereneta."

"The daughter of Lord Benneto Sereneta?"

"Yes. You and my father fought together at Lepanto."

"I know we did! Where is he? I would love to know what he has been up to."

The woman's smile dissolved. "Papa died in '87."

"Oh, I'm so sorry to hear that, Caterina. Your father was a great man and a friend. Having made such a faux pas, am I still invited to dance?"

Caterina nodded graciously and I was about to lead her towards the other dancing couples when a voice boomed across the room accompanied by the harsh rap of wood. It was the court steward, Amando Puti standing towards the front of the stage, his staff raised ready to knock on the floor again.

"Ladies and gentlemen, Lords and Ladies. His Serenity, Doge Pasquale Cicogna."

The Doge pulled himself from his seat, aided (unnecessarily) by his niece. Spreading wide his arms, he revealed great swaths of golden cloth hanging down like wings.

"Most welcome guests. It is with true delight that I can be with you here tonight. And it would have been quite impossible if it had not been for one very special man, a man who has not lived amongst us for a long time, a man whose presence in our Most Serene Republic I have sorely missed . . . Francesco Sagredo."

The guests all turned towards me and began to applaud. I moved slowly and approached the stage, the audience parting before me.

"As all of you will of course know," the Doge went on as I took the two steps at the side of the raised platform. "Doctor Francesco Sagredo was exiled by a predecessor of mine, Alvise Mocenigo. It has been our loss, for the doctor is a man of great learning. Some of this wisdom was used to draw me from sickness."

The Doge turned to me as I stood a few feet to his left, hands clasped in front of me, head dipped humbly. "For his great service, I shall always be grateful, and as a symbol of my thanks, I have decided to make Francesco Sagredo an Honorary Councillor, to be elevated to full membership of the Council of Ten after a probationary period of two months."

I heard a murmur run through the audience, turned to the gathering and gave a small bow as they applauded. Stepping back to the group of dignitaries at the edge of the stage it was then I saw Teresa, willowy-thin, her long black hair unbraided, burnt umber eyes, her skin butter-soft. She was standing close to Niccolo Celsi and he was holding her hand protectively. For only a second, our eyes met. No one had told me about this.

I heard a voice close to my ear. "Oh! Did you not know, Sagredo? Teresa Dumas is betrothed to Lord Celsi."

I turned and saw that it was a young nobleman, Guiseppi Mantini, who would have been but a babe when I was exiled. He gave me a cold grin.

For the next ten minutes, I was required to partake in small talk with a stream of well-wishers and sycophants. Finally, I managed to break away, find a servant with a tray of wine goblets and retreated to the back of the room again. I had barely sipped at my drink when, turning to place the goblet on a side table, I swung back to see Lady Violetta Celsi standing a few inches from my face.

"Lady Celsi!" I said, pulling back instinctively.

"I imagine you think you are very clever, Doctor Sagredo."

"Not at all . . ."

"You always were a schemer and a charmer . . . not to mention your dubious *interests*."

She stared straight into my eyes. She had the same sneer as her son and I recalled how Adamo Celsi, her long-dead husband had been such a mild-mannered person by comparison. He must have lived a hellish life with this termagant, I thought. I hadn't seen her for a long time of course, but she seemed to have become corroded by her own excoriating vitriol. Her skin was tauter across her vulture cheekbones, and her eyes had a mistiness to them, a filmy greyness I knew to be a sign of ill-health. Her teeth were almost all gone, replaced by painted wooden dentures, but she still carried herself with a haughty nobility that worked especially well in her finery. I simply peered back at her, dumbstruck.

"I would not be surprised to learn you had put an enchantment upon the Doge."

I couldn't help smiling at that. "Lady Celsi . . . really. Your imagination is working overtime!"

"Don't you dare try to patronise me, you devil's spawn," the old harpy snapped. "Your necromancy is well-known in our republic."

A few people nearby had started to pay attention and I saw them whispering amongst themselves.

"Madame . . ." I said calmly.

"Let me tell you, Doctor Sagredo," she cut across me. "You shall soon regret ever having returned to *my* home." She spun on her heel and marched off.

Although I think I managed to maintain an outward show of calm and placidity, I was actually quite shaken by the level of Violetta Celsi's hatred. She utterly despised me, and although part of me could rise above it and feel pity for the woman and her perversity, I couldn't help a sense of shock that, after all this time, I elicited such terribly negative emotions in her. It was almost as though my return from exile was a physical slap in her face.

I decided I needed some air and found my way to an anteroom connected to the Great Hall. A pair of doors opened onto a broad balcony. I walked over to the parapet and looked out upon the splendour of Venice, a view approximately west, across San Marco and the lanes and houses beyond. It was dark save for a canopy of stars; the illumination of the moon casting a white gossamer over the roofs, and a few lights in windows and along the banks of the Grand Canal. From inside, the strains of music drifted to me through the night air.

"Francesco," I was startled by the voice and swung round to see Teresa Damas standing in the doorway leading from the anteroom.

"Teresa. You look . . . very well."

"And you don't look a day older."

"Oh, don't lie, Francesco!" she giggled.

I suddenly felt very uncomfortable and glanced towards the doors.

"I feel I should explain," she began.

"There is no need."

"I would like to."

"Teresa, I was away a very long time. You had a life to lead . . . and you have a future to consider. I'm told you have a son."

24

She looked surprised by that. "Yes."

"Piero?"

"Yes."

We fell into an awkward silence, then we heard a horn sound - a ship somewhere across the Lagoon.

"I understand you married the French ambassador, Louis Damas."

"It was arranged for me, Francesco. He was a good man, and he treated me well."

"I am glad to hear that. You deserve the best life can offer."

She tilted her head to one side. I remembered that characteristic as though the last time I had seen her do it was yesterday; and without thinking, each of us took a step closer. "Oh, I'm not sure any of us deserve that," Teresa said.

"And so now you are betrothed to Niccolo Celsi."

"Yes."

"When is the big day?" I could not keep a brittle edge from my voice.

"No date yet. But you, Francesco! The Council of Ten, no less."

"It's absurd!"

"Why do you say that?"

"From exile to member of The Ten?"

"I think you will have a great many things to offer the Republic. You must have experienced so much on your travels. I have heard some of the stories."

I felt myself blush and could barely believe it of myself. I was about to reply when the doors opened and Niccolo Celsi emerged from the anteroom.

"Stay safe, Francesco," Teresa said with true feeling before walking away towards Celsi. I watched the man's face, and in the stark moonlight, saw smugness personified.

I escaped the party soon after that and walked home alone, and hollow, noticing almost nothing around me.

Just about the only room in my house that was halfway organised was my laboratory in the basement. I had unpacked crates of chemical equipment, animal specimens preserved in jars and operating utensils, along with several dozen volumes of leather-bound learned works. These had been arranged on a long narrow table in the centre of the room and a few placed carefully on shelves. Several unpacked chests and wooden boxes lay scattered around close to the stairs up to the main room on the ground floor overhead.

I pulled up a stool close to the table and stared around trying to gather my thoughts and emotions. I remember I started talking to myself; something I had not done for a long time. 'What have you done, Francesco?' I said aloud to the room. 'Something tells me this is all a mistake. Things have moved on here, moved on without you. Old friends have died, or become drunks. Old enemies hate you even more than they once did. Old loves have found new loves. The actions of the Doge have just stirred up jealousy, enmity. You fool! You should have stayed away.'

I stood and walked towards the back of the room. There were more shelves there, mostly empty but containing a few dusty boxes that had been missed by the cleaners. I picked up the first. It was filled with parchments, now faded, detailing old bills of trade, official documents and letters. I shifted the box to one side and lifted the lower one, blew away a layer of dust and swept aside a mat of cobwebs. Lifting the lid, I knew immediately what it contained . . . old letters from Teresa.

I could not resist. I took the box upstairs, found a comfortable chair, pulled over to the dying embers of the fire and started to read.

Within moments, I was back in the days of my youth, the year after the terrible plague that had killed more than one in three of us, including my parents and my younger sister, Rosa. Teresa's family, the Alleganzas and my parents had been friends for many years, so I had known Teresa since we were young children. We had both been spared by the dreaded disease, and in its aftermath, as survivors in our bereft city; we had clung, each to the other.

I had been a practicing medic for three years before the plague had struck, and I had stayed in Venice throughout its onslaught, tending the sick. For a while, Teresa had helped me. Her family had been liberal and forward-thinking. They had encouraged her to study medicine. She was not allowed to attend medical school, but she had been tutored by a family friend, an elderly Milanese physick who had lived in the Republic for two years, leaving only when the Pestilence began its hideous in-creeping. When the Alleganzas died within days of each other, I insisted that Teresa should isolate herself, and so she set sail for to an island close to Murano where the family owned a small property.

The Celsis had fled quickly, in the summer of 1575, escaping to their country estate. Most forms of commerce and business in the Republic had ground to a halt. No ships passed in or out of the Lagoon save for emergency food carriers which were subjected to the most rigorous quarantine regulations. What little trade continued was handled for the Celsis by proxies. But by the end of 1576, when the disease had done its worst and there were no new cases for six weeks, people had begun to return, to pick up the pieces of their former lives, and as soon as the Death had passed entirely, the Celsis returned to their former power base. It was then that Niccolo Celsi begun his machinations against me.

He will tell you that the feud between us stemmed from my approach to treating the sick during the Pestilence. I will not deny that I clashed with more experienced and more senior medics over the best way to respond to the disease; and then later, I had the temerity to publish a learned volume offering my theories as to the cause of the illness and how to curb its propagation; but

26

this was not the real reason for Celsi's vendetta against me. It was because of Teresa; or more accurately, the love Teresa and I had shared. Celsi wanted her. He had always wanted her, and he could not bear to suffer seeing Teresa and me together.

By 1577, two things had become clear. First, I was about to propose to Teresa, and I knew in my heart that she would say yes simply because she had hinted so often that I should make an honest woman of her! The other matter to become apparent was the degree to which Niccolo Celsi's feelings for Teresa and his hatred of me would drive him to exert his considerable power and influence in Venice to entrap me, to have me falsely charged with heresy and then exiled.

Reading the letters Teresa had sent me as she lived in isolation close to Murano while I did my best to save as many souls as possible, brought back bitter-sweet feelings. I could once more taste Teresa's mouth on my tongue, her supple body moving under me, her soft, olive skin against mine, her breath, her words of love; and I suddenly felt sick inside. I felt old, jolted by a terrible sense of loss: and in that moment, as much as I had been putting on the bravest of faces and had told my questioners that I had lived many lives and that I would not change my past were I to be given the strangest of chances to do so, I knew that I was lying.

Chapter Five: As The Dove Flies

On the morning of the Ninth of November, the dawn of my second day back in Venice, a bird, a dove let us say, if it might fly low, see through roofs and walls and be aware of human speech, would have witnessed many things of value to our story; things I only learned about later during my investigation into the evil that was about to befall us.

For our purposes, let us imagine that if such a bird ever were to exist it would be one of those that lived on the roof of the Celsi Palazzo on the Grand Canal, a most salubrious abode for any avian, I think you would agree. And this dove, along with its co-inhabitants was especially fortunate for it was greatly loved by Niccolo Celsi, a man who cared more for his birds than he did his fellow man.

Niccolo's mother, Violetta and his sister, Sofia knew of the birds and the way Celsi loved them, but no other living sole was aware of his penchant. Celsi would never allow anyone other than his close family to learn of what might be considered a weakness, a chink in his armour of indifference.

With loving care, Celsi removed the bird from its roomy cage shared with three other doves. The bird cooed contentedly, and as the nobleman opened his hands, he muttered words of affection and encouragement, wishing the animal a fair flight, and off the dove soared.

What sights it would have seen. The mosaic of water and stone, a winter's crisp sky through which to fly. Swooping low over the palace this dove with all-seeing eyes would find the Doge readying himself for the day's vicissitudes while being dressed by his valet. Turning a little south-east, the dove would follow a line towards the Church of San Giorgio Maggiore, the newly-completed building, flame red and pearlescent in the light reflected from the water all around it. Descending, Celsi's bird might catch a glimpse of Tomasso Cicogna, recently back from his favourite bordello, Alfonzo the Spaniard's. Tom was laying on his back close to his bed, but not quite on it, unconscious and fully-clothed, his shirt front encrusted with vomit, some of which was not his own.

Feeling the wind under its feathers and the fishy brackish air filling its senses, the bird would chase the vortices of air, up and down, to left and to right to follow the curving, twisting line of the Grand Canal, the city beginning to awaken with fervent life, human commerce, daily pain and small glories. A short way south sat Teresa brushing her long, black hair and remembering past days of love and loss. And last, the bird would spot a gondolier and his young assistant preparing for work. A little tired from its exertions, the bird would perhaps come to rest upon a stone pillar close to a tributary of the Grand Canal.

There, the gondolier, Carlo Perugino and his apprentice, Tito are cleaning their boat in preparation for the day's business. The boy runs along the canal path to fetch brushes. Two loud young men, gondoliers who know the boy and Perugino, turn the corner without seeing either.

"So, Alfonzo's bordello? Good, eh?" the first man asks with a grin.

"Fuck, Luigi! Antoinette's the best girl there. Such tits as you've never seen . . . and her quim . . . !"

Luigi laughs loudly, slapping his friend on the back. "I believe you, Dante. I've heard she's everyone's favourite. Don't think you're the first, my friend!"

Luigi spots the boy, Tito; then Dante notices Carlo Perugino, Antoinette's father, and they immediately clam up.

"Shit!" Luigi hisses.

Carlo looks up; he has only just noticed them. He knows these two, knows they are cocksure youngsters and he gives them a suspicious look as they offer a wary 'hello' and walk on. Tito returns to his master with the brushes.

"Those two looked like they've been up to something."

"Out all night, I think, sir . . . a place called Alfonzo's."

Carlo pulls up from the boat, hands on his hips. His eyes narrow. "Oh?"

"Going on about some girl there . . . Antoinette. A great fuck, they reckon!" Tito smirks, but Carlo's face droops into a mask of fury. Moving with stunning speed, he grabs the boy and slaps him hard across the face sending him sprawling.

The dove, seeing everything but understanding nothing, pulls up from the stone pillar and flies off.

Chapter Six: The Ten

I did not hear the servant Isabella Dioli until she entered the rear courtyard of my house through the side entrance and let out a small gasp. I was dressed in a loincloth, meditating and seated cross-legged upon a small mat placed on the frost-dusted ground. I opened my eyes, and saw her startled and slightly frightened expression. Unfolding my limbs, I stood and walked over.

"Isabella. Hello," I said. "It's been a long time."

The elderly woman, who had served my parents since I was a boy looked uncomfortable and I gave her my warmest smile.

"I was meditating. A habit I picked up . . ."

"I'm sorry to disturb you, master," Isabella began and I waved away her apology.

"Come, you look half-frozen," I said. "Let's get you inside."

She followed me through the rear entrance that took us into my laboratory and then up the short flight of stairs to the large main room. Isabella looked around nonplussed at the chaotic state of the place.

"Still unpacking . . . as you can see," I said.

The servant walked around eyeing the mess. "It's been a long time since I stood in this house, master."

"Please, Isabella, don't call me that. You knew me as a small boy. My name is Francesco. You used to dress me, remember?"

Isabella flushed. "I couldn't . . ."

"That's an order."

She tried to ignore me and paced across the room into the my bedroom. She stopped to stare at a wooden tub, bemused.

"It's a bath tub," I said. "It comes from Turkey. Which actually brings us to the first job of the day. I will need a pitcher of hot water from over the fire in the main room."

She looked at me blankly.

"To take the chill off the bath."

She still did not seem to understand what I was saying.

"It's for bathing, Isabella. I immerse myself in water to get clean."

The old woman screwed up her face, sighed heavily and walked out.

Half an hour later, Isabella was helping me to adjust my chain and straightening the line of my official robe.

"That's fine, Isabella. I shall me late."

But the old lady would not let me go just yet. "It's not right, master . . . Francesco. Here, give me that." She took my hat and pulled it into line. "Better."

"I'm going."

She stood back at last and I was out on the campo.

Almost late, I nodded to the guards at the main gate to the Doge's Palace as they straightened their pikes and snapped to attention. I took the stairs three at a time, hitching my robe to my knees. I must have looked quite a sight!

I reached the landing on the second floor and paused to take a few breaths. Turning into the corridor, I saw the pair of guards at the entrance to the meeting chamber, the Sala del Consiglio dei Dieci. The doors were closing, the last of the Council members just visible a few yards into the room. The guards held open the heavy oak doors, allowing me to slip inside.

I have never cared much for this room. Quite a few of the ceiling paintings were done by Paolo Veronese, who I consider heavy-handed, and I found the wood panelling oppressive. I'm sure that when I was a younger man I would have been fine with it all, but my tastes had changed. I handed my cloak to a servant and found my seat close to the double doors.

The Doge was seated on a platform almost directly opposite me, each member of the Council had taken their places around the edge of the room. I caught the eye of Niccolo Celsi. He seemed a little flustered. Catching me staring, he scowled. That made me smile.

The Doge had turned eighty-three a few months earlier, but he was still full of energy. Before he had taken office he had been a successful businessman and procurator and his reign had begun shakily. He was notoriously miserly and instead of casting the traditional gold coins to the poor during his coronation procession through San Marco seven years earlier, he had dispensed silver. In fact, it is fair to say that at first Cicogna was perhaps the least popular Doge in Venetian history. Things quickly improved though. He turned out to be a fair and just leader. He had sanctioned the building of our magnificent Rialto bridge and gave the work to an unknown local architect, Antonio da Ponte instead of more famous foreigners, and he had stood up to the Pope by championing Henry of Navarre's legitimate claim to the French throne after the untimely death of Henri III just over three years ago. He was seated in a large, ornately carved chair with a broad, high back. Dressed in red and white robes, he had a heavy, ermine-collared cloak about his shoulders Reading from a scroll handed to him by one of his clerical assistants, Doge Cicogna began: "The first matter on the agenda." His deep, musical voice rang around the chamber. "...is the sale of three properties in San Polo. Our esteemed colleague,

Conte Celsi has proposed the purchase with the intention of demolishing the buildings to make room for new homes. Several of you have objected."

One of the Councillors to my right stirred and rose slowly. It was the octogenarian, Paolo Cortini. Compared to the Doge, a close contemporary, he looked about two-hundred-years-old, and had to be helped to his feet by the Councillor to his right, Marchese da Fontina. He then rested his weight on a cane, and started to speak, his voice so quiet I had to strain to hear.

"This sale is an outrage," he began. My esteemed colleague has an eye for a profit, that may not be denied." The old man looked around at each of us. "But he is stealing from the owners by offering them well below market value."

I suspected that Celsi was not only conning the residents of the houses in San Polo, but that his men had threatened them with violence if they did not accept his terms. I knew he had done this sort of thing many times before, but somehow he had always succeeded in getting away with it.

"Is what our esteemed colleague Conte Celsi has to say true?" the Doge asked.

Niccolo Celsi stood and paused rather theatrically.

Now of course I could be accused of bias, and if pressed I would have to admit to it; after all, I had been in love with this creature's betrothed, but even to this day I remain convinced that Celsi was one of the most repugnant men who had ever grown up in this most glorious city. I cannot deny that he was neatly coiffured and immaculately dressed. He did not wash, but used copious quantities of scented water about his person and his clothes. But that was just it; he spent a great deal of time and effort on making himself look fair on the outside, but paid sparse attention to what lay beneath, within his soul . . . if that is, he possessed such a thing.

Celsi broke into a calculating smile and spread his arms wide. "Gentlemen, the honourable Conte Cortini, I'm really at a loss as to where these claims originate. I am paying a very fair price for the three houses on Calle Paradiso. Indeed, I heard only this morning that the current residents have confirmed in writing their willing acceptance of the latest offer I have made to them."

A low mumble passed through the gathering. Cortini was speaking again, but no one could hear him above the commotion.

"Gentlemen," the Doge called. The chatter continued.

"Silence!" His voice boomed around the room and everyone shut up.

I glanced at Celsi. He still wore his well-crafted smile.

"I know for a fact that the residents have been coerced into agreeing," the old Councillor said, his words falling heavily into the silence.

Celsi stared at the Doge, the epitome of calm.

"Can you prove this?" Cicogna asked.

"It is widely known."

"But can you *prove it*, Conte Cortini?"

"This *person* has a long history of making money by exploitation," the elderly statesman responded, stabbing a finger at Celsi. Immediately, the hubbub started again, but louder this time. Celsi stood and still saying nothing, he let the storm break over him.

"Gentlemen." It was the Doge again.

Cortini was waving his cane at Niccolo Celsi and declaring something that was completely drowned out.

The Doge rose from his seat and gradually the noise subsided. He surveyed the ten of us seated in a semicircle around the perimeter of the room. "One more word," he said, very calmly. ". . . and I shall dissolve this Council, and none of you." He paused to take a deep breath, ". . . shall serve in public office while I live. I deem this matter now closed," He returned to his seat and nodded to Celsi, who gave a little bow and sat down without a word. The old boy, Conte Cortini remained where he stood for several long moments. Then, to everyone's amazement, he turned and walked slowly to the double doors. Reaching them, he rapped on the wood with his cane, they opened and he walked out.

I watched the Doge's face, noting a mere flicker of surprise before he looked down at his papers, the sound of rustling cutting through the silence. He cleared his throat. "The second item on the agenda is the proposed tariff on citrus fruits."

There was a tap at the door. We all turned and the doors opened. A man in the full-length red gown of a cardinal came into the chamber followed by two men dressed in black, each clutching a Bible.

"I hope I'm not too early," the man said.

Perhaps I should explain. We had been expecting him. It's just that we had become so enwrapped in our conflict that each of us, aside from the Doge of course, had forgotten, so that when Cardinal Santoro Severina entered with almost regal poise I for one was taken aback.

The cardinal had arrived here in Venice the previous day. Severina was the Pope's trusted legal advisor, and he had travelled here to bring to bear Vatican influence in what was probably the most important judicial case anyone in the Republic could remember.

Depending upon your viewpoint, the man called Giordano Bruno, was either the Devil incarnate, or a man of learning who had some valuable things to say. But he was now unable to speak publically because he languished in the prisons of the Doge's palace four floors beneath our feet.

So who was this man? Well, he used to be a priest, but in his youth he became convinced that the Church was corrupt and deliberately misguiding

33

the laity to keep it under control. He also embraced the teachings of Nicholas Copernicus who had stated in his book, *De revolutionibus orbium coelestium* that the Earth orbits the sun and is not, as Church Doctrine would have it, seated at the centre of God's universe. He went on to teach these views and had evaded capture as a heretic for some two decades.

About a year ago rumours had begun to circulate amongst my intellectual friends that Giordano Bruno was in Germany and had established a new Church of which he was the figurehead. Then, in March this year the man had turned up in Padua not twenty-five miles from here. The next anyone knew, he had appeared in Venice itself to take up with a nobleman called Giovanni Mocenigo.

I knew Mocenigo vaguely. When I was young our paths had crossed a few times in the small world of Venetian society. I had taken an instant dislike to the man and would not have trusted him an inch. But it seemed as though Bruno was deliberately courting danger. His followers in Venice had started to wonder if the man had finally gone mad, but hoping quietly that instead, he had some clever plan up his sleeve. Events though had soon proved my assessment of Mocenigo to be correct. He had betrayed Bruno. The philosopher had been arrested in May and imprisoned.

This though was where things became entangled. For centuries, Venice had been loyal to Rome, but at the same time it had remained fiercely determined to maintain the right to govern itself, to make its own judgment on the behaviour of its citizens and those visiting the Republic without any ecclesiastical interference from the Vatican.

But just as soon as news had reached Rome that the arch-heretic Bruno had been arrested in Venice, Pope Clement VIII had written to Doge Cicogna insisting the prisoner be bound over to the Roman Inquisition so that he may be placed on trial before the Curia. Pasquale Cicogna had bridled at the suggestion, and for most of the late summer and into the autumn, the Republic and the Vatican had engaged in an increasingly heated exchange, all couched, of course, in polite diplomatic language.

You see, although Rome accepted that Venice was an independent sovereign state, the Pope believed that spiritual matters transcended simple worldly concerns and His Holiness fell back on the claim that the Doge was really just a corporeal leader of men who should leave spiritual judgments to the highest earthly authority on this subject – the Pope. Needless to say, Cicogna thought very differently.

And it was not as though the bite of the pope would be a toothless one should it come. Twice during our long history Venice had been excommunicated by the Head of the Church. Clement V had deployed his most powerful spiritual weapon in 1309, and then, almost exactly two centuries later, in 1510, the same punishment had been meted out by Pope Julius II.

And this threat was not to be taken lightly. For the faithful, excommunication of the entire Republic was a terrible thing. Not only did it mean the closing of churches and the Vatican forcing all other Christian states to terminate trade links with the city, it meant the laity could not take Holy Communion. Even worse was the fact that any Venetian who died whilst excommunication remained in place would spend their time in Purgatory until they could pass on to Heaven or ... well, you get the picture.

Anyway, I digress. Cardinal Santoro Severina was here in Venice to represent the Pope in the latest stage in the tussle between the Republic and the Vatican. Clement had persuaded the Doge to allow his right-hand man to witness the trial of Giordano Bruno and to report back what he observed. The Doge could not have refused without implying that there was some impropriety concerning the procedures of the Venetian legal system.

We all stopped talking and rose as the cardinal entered the room. Servants scurried around and found a suitable chair for Severina close to the Doge, who did not get up. They positioned the chair on the floor rather than on the raised dais next to Cicogna's seat, and for the first time, I had a chance to see this man up close.

As you will have gathered, I have no personal love for the Church. I could never admit such a thing of course, for such an admission would carry with it a death sentence. I was once a reasonably faithful Catholic, but one of the many great treasures I had brought back with me from the East, indeed, perhaps the greatest, was the learning I had found on my travels.

We Venetians are justly proud of our culture, our skills as architects, engineers, mathematicians and philosophers, but ours is not the only centre of culture in this vast world. And besides, much of what we call modern learning is nothing but a reheating of knowledge such men as the Florentine, Cosimo de Medici had brought to our lands from Greece, the Ottoman Empire and beyond. Being exposed to other cultures, other religions, and different, often quite alien ways of thinking, has made me question the religious views I was handed down as a child. So let us just say that I did not consider the cardinal with anything like the same reverence that many others did in the room. I like to think this enabled me to appraise the man objectively.

He had a long, narrow face, crease marks about his lips, a furrowed forehead that spoke of thoughtfulness, perhaps inner turmoil, secrets that would probably never be revealed. But, overall, Severina had a pleasant face, perhaps even, in the eyes of some ladies, a handsome one. He wore well his robes of office, he was slim, but muscular; tall, straight-backed. As I said before, he appeared almost regal. His hair was white at the temples, his red cap covering the rest of his head. He had striking green eyes and a strong Roman nose.

Sitting calmly, his fingers held loosely a large crucifix on a gold chain that hung to his waist. His were long slender fingers, well manicured; a large ring with a prominent blood red stone sat on the index finger of his right hand.

"We are delighted to have you here today, Your Eminence," Cicogna declared.

Severina dipped his head slightly. "I hope I have not interrupted anything important."

"We have settled our discussions."

We all sat down, silent.

"Lord Doge, I thank you again for allowing me to visit the prisoner, Giordano Bruno. And, having spoken to the poor man at some length this morning, I feel even more keenly that you and your advisors . . ." He surveyed our semicircle with a gentle smile. ". . . allow the Holy Father to take the heretic off your hands. I know His Holiness feels shame that the man washed up on your shores and that he has burdened you with his presence when it is the responsibility of the Pope and *his* advisors, including myself to cleanse the man. Indeed," and he bowed slowly. ". . . I share His Holiness's shame."

"You should not feel this way, nor should the Holy Father," the Doge replied, shaking his head slowly. "Having such a man as Giordano Bruno in our midst is indeed a burden, but it is one we feel we should bear as the wretch did indeed 'wash up on our shores', as you put it." He paused for a moment. "Did our prisoner not open up to you, Your Eminence?"

"I'm sorry to say, he did not. He is a tortured soul, possessed so thoroughly by the Devil that I, a mere cardinal, could never bring such a man back to the Light of the Lord God. Which is why we need him in the Vatican. Only there may his damaged and suffering soul be cleansed, his sins forgiven. Only there may he be absolved."

I raised a hand and the Doge nodded to me. Standing, I took a step forward, my hands clasped together in front of me.

"Your Eminence, it is a great honour to meet you," I began. Severina held my eyes with a peaceful, almost serene look. "I must though ask a question of you that may not seem to have an obvious answer. You are assuming that Giordano Bruno is guilty, yet his trial has not yet begun. Do you not trust our own judiciary to learn the truth about the man, whether he be a heretic or not?"

I heard muttering from behind me and assumed it would be from the mouths of the usual suspects.

"I suppose," the cardinal responded. ". . . that this is really the crux of the matter." He produced a smile only slightly less sincere than his earlier one. "You see, we are certain of the man's guilt. We have ample evidence to support this, which we have presented to the Venetian government. For us it is not a matter of a judicial process, as such. For us it is the urgent matter of saving Bruno's soul."

"But if his soul is not unclean?"

"God's teeth!" Celsi hissed.

Severina had moved his hands from the crucifix, bringing his fingertips together under his chin. "You are Francesco Sagredo, yes?"

I nodded.

"Do you question the opinion of His Holiness, Pope Clement VIII, Patrizio Sagredo?"

"I am not a Patrizio, cardinal. A mere 'Doctor' will suffice."

One of the semicircle produced a stifled laugh.

Severina went to speak but the Doge cut across him. "Francesco Sagredo did not question Papal judgment, Your Eminence. He simply called upon the basis of all law in Christendom, that every man must be proven guilty before they are punished."

"We do not wish to punish Giordano Bruno."

"I understand that," Cicogna replied sharply. "But we have to follow due process."

"And you do not think that due process is practiced in Rome?"

"That was not the Doge's implication," I said, and Severina glared at me.

"Indeed, that was certainly not what I meant, Cardinal," Cicogna said.

"Lord Doge," Severina took a deep breath. "We seem to have reached an impasse . . . again,"

"Indeed we do, Your Eminence."

The cardinal rose slowly, nodded to the Doge, surveyed us Councillors and held my eyes for a second longer than I might have wished for.

'I've made an enemy today,' I thought.

•

Back out in the corridor, I headed for the stairs. It was very quiet now with everyone about their business. I had said nothing to anyone (because, as a member of The Ten, even a probationary member, I had no need to) but I had decided while listening to the alarmingly charismatic cardinal that I would pay our celebrated prisoner, Giordano Bruno a personal visit. 'Why?' you might ask. Well, the simple fact was that although I had heard a great deal about the man, and I had even read one of his works, *The Expulsion of the Triumphant Beast*, I was not as familiar with him as were many of my old friends in Italy. More importantly perhaps, I needed to know how he fitted into the scheme of things. What had really pushed Pope Clement into sending Severina?

I met the warden at the main entrance into the prison complex that covered three floors to the rear of the palace. He was a morbidly obese man with short legs, a ruddy alcoholic's face, his nose and cheeks red and interlaced with fine blood vessels. His name was Marcel Fabone. A Frenchman by birth, who had been brought to Venice as an infant and had never left.

It took a moment for him to recognise me. "Sir." He looked me up and down. "What brings you here?"

I could smell distilled spirit on his breath. "I've come to visit a prisoner, the heretic, Giordano Bruno."

Fabone looked startled, then a little pained. I could see his mind working. He knew that I was a member of the Council, but, like everyone else in Venice, he was aware that I had been promoted to the position only the previous evening. Understandably, he would have considered me first an explorer, an adventurer and not quite one of the ruling class. "May I ask why, My Lord?"

"Do I need to give a reason?"

"Well, no sir, of course not." He gave me a curt nod. "I'll take you to see him."

I could see why Fabone had turned to drink. He had been warden here for many years, spending most of his days within the same confines as the Republic's prisoners, breathing the same air, existing in limbo, between the living and the dead. He could walk out, of course, but he rarely did. He occupied rooms on the first level. They were comfortable, well-lit and spacious, but pervaded by the stink of the incarcerated.

He walked ahead of me filling half the passage with his considerable girth and bearing a flaming torch that cast light in a pallid sphere around the two of us. As we descended to the lowest level, the air became fetid. I felt sweat break out on my skin making my back itch under my tunic.

We passed along another low-ceilinged corridor where I could see a row of small grills to my right and bare stone wall to the left. I counted the grills until we reached the seventh and I could see that the corridor ended abruptly a short way ahead. Next to the final grill, a metal bracket held an unlit torch. Fabone plucked the cone from the holder, lit the fresh brand and handed it to me.

"You'll have only this for light," he said. "The prisoners are allowed to speak for no more than five minutes. I shall return then. I hope you understand, sir." He leaned forward, conjuring a large ring of keys from his tunic. With practiced fingers, he found the correct key and fed it into the lock of the cell door.

I lowered my head to pass under the lintel and realised I would not be able to stand upright inside the cell, the ceiling was no more than the height of an average twelve or thirteen-year-old boy. I heard the door close and the key turn in the lock. In spite of the sticky heat, a spasm of irrational fear chilled me and I felt the hairs on the nape of my neck stand erect.

My eyes had adjusted as Fabone had taken me along the dingy corridors, but at first I could make out little of the form in the corner. Only gradually was I able to distinguish the outline of a man slowly unfolding his limbs and moving towards me through the murk, his face rearing up close to mine.

He was a tiny fellow, I could tell that straightaway. His head was considerably smaller than the average and his face was covered with an unruly beard, and wisps of curly, dark hair lay matted to his cheeks and forehead. I held the torch steady, saying nothing, and he stared back at me, wild-eyed.

"Who are you?" He had a surprisingly high-pitched voice.

"My name is Francesco Sagredo."

"I don't have many visitors."

"I am a member of the Ten. I took it upon myself to come."

He looked confused, screwed up his eyes. "The Ten? So you are here to take me to torture?"

I produced a wan smile and shook my head. "I am an admirer, a sympathiser." I knew we could not be heard beyond the cell and believed that honesty was paramount.

He studied me in silence. I could read, or at least surmise his train of thought. It would be entirely natural for him to feel suspicious, to assume the worst of me, to read into my words a trap.

"Admirers and sympathisers may be men of truth, or they may be snakes. What should I take you to be, Francesco Sagredo?"

"I like to think I am not a snake, Giordano Bruno. We share some friends, Gianvincenzo Pinelli, Paolo Sarpi. I have only recently returned to Venice after many years of travel, but I understand you visited Lord Pinelli often."

His eyes lit up. "You are the traveller from the East! Of course! Yes, word of your return filtered down even to me here, in this stinking dungeon. I did not recognise your name. I am honoured, Master Sagredo."

He relaxed back on to the floor and I moved to sit cross-legged opposite him. The floor and walls were damp and the stench of the cell was sickening, but in those days I had a strong stomach and I had been in places almost as bad.

"Tell me, Giordano . . . may I call you . . . ?"

"Of course you may," Bruno replied, and I saw his brown and fractured teeth as he smiled for the first time.

"Why are you here? I said. "Did you not believe it would be dangerous coming back to Italy . . . even Venice?"

"You are assuming," he said. ". . . that I was somehow tricked into returning. But that is not so. I knew exactly what I was doing. I am reaching out to something I could not hope to hold within my grasp any other way."

I was confused, and I must have shown it clearly in my expression because the prisoner tilted his head slightly. Sparse shadows flickered across Bruno's face, the light catching his large brown eyes.

"I planned every aspect of my journey here. The man who claims to have alerted the authorities to my 'evil' presence in the Republic, the rich fool, Giovanni Mocenigo, was nothing but my puppet; he danced to my every tug on the strings."

"But why?"

"So that I might be arrested and imprisoned, of course. So that I would be put on trial here. So that I would once more draw the attention of the Vatican. I learned only today that the Papal Nuncio is here in the city. *His Holiness* took the bait."

And at that moment, looking into that ravaged face, I realised for the first time that everything was not right with Giordano Bruno's mind. There was something indefinable in the look he gave me that sent the touch of icy fingers along my spine. He was, I realised, poised on the edge of sanity, barely maintaining control. He spoke in a rational, even reasonable tone, but there was an undercurrent to his words. I couldn't quantify it at first, but then I grasped what was wrong: he was talking about the most ridiculous notions with the same sort of conviction any sane person might employ when discussing the blandest of ideas. The Papal Nuncio had been sent by Clement specifically to snatch him from the Venetian judicial system and to take him in chains to Rome so they could burn him alive, but Bruno spoke as though such horror meant nothing to him.

"You *want* to be taken to Rome?"

"Of course."

"But Giordano, why?"

"I need to give guidance to His Holiness."

"Guidance?"

"Oh come now, Francesco Sagredo! You are an educated man, a man who has experienced so very much. You know Truth, you know lies . . . do you not?"

I said nothing. He looked down at his lap, sighed and met my eyes. "The Church I love has been disembowelled. It must be made whole again. The Pope needs guidance because he has been misled by evil men in the Vatican. Perhaps he is part of the shame too, in which case, my task will be that much more irksome; but I *shall* meet with him. I will teach him, make him understand where the True Church has been perverted, and how he may heal it."

I was formulating my response when I heard the sound of scrapping and realised Fabone had returned; the time had flashed by. The door to the cell opened and the burly warden stood in an oval of light cast by his torch. "It is time, Lord Sagredo," he said.

"I shall return when I am able, Giordano," I said and turned away, leaving the tiny, stinking room to its former abject darkness.

•

Descending the steps before the Doge's Palace with my head down trying rather unsuccessfully to clear from my mind the cloying horror of the dungeons, I almost collided with a man rushing towards me. He caught my arm saving me from falling backwards.

"Sir, I'm terribly sorry," the man said. He steadied me and I took a breath. He was a ruddy-faced and jowly young fellow with striking hazel eyes and unusually fair hair. "My name is Titus, Titus Rinilto," he said, still gripping my arm.

I looked down at his hand and he withdrew it with an embarrassed smile.

"I am . . ."

"I know who you are, sir! All of Venice knows who you are."

I didn't quite know what to say to that.

"I was actually on my way to make an appointment to see you," Rinilto said.

"You were? Well, fortuitous, then. If you can tell me what I can do for you between here and my house on Campo S. Maurizo, I'll do my best to help."

We stepped out onto San Marco. A shimmering frost encrusted the stones, our hot breath billowed about us in the cold.

"Have you heard of the *Notizie Scritte*?" Rinilto asked without preamble.

"*The Daily Notices*? Well, yes. I had forgotten about it, but like many people, I used to read it to keep up to date with what was happening in the world. My father was very keen on it and bought it every day."

"Well, it is without doubt a venerable publication, Lord Sagredo. But perhaps a little dull?"

I produced a small laugh. "I cannot comment. I haven't read it for fifteen years."

"Trust me, my newssheet is far better."

"Your . . . ?"

"Yes, *The Republic*."

"Go on."

"My first edition appeared three months ago and I'm gradually building a readership."

"What is this newssheet?"

"Why, a weekly publication . . . printed and distributed by a small team

41

of helpers and sold for five soldi. My late uncle was a master printer, and I inherited his printing press. *The Republic* gives news of anything within the city that might be of interest, not just politics and military news like *The Daily Notices*."

We reached the far side of San Marco and had begun to weave through the lanes. "A very original idea," I said. "And a daring one!"

"I do not have official sanction for it . . . yet," Rinilto said. "But I believe the People should be informed."

"Those who can read," I said. "About five per cent of the population!"

"It is a beginning."

"So what has this to do with me?"

He looked at me as though I were making light of him. "Lord Sagredo, you are the most famous man in Venice. If I could put your story in my publication I would triple my readership immediately."

"I see."

"There are the official accounts and the rumours about you. I would like to interview you, have you tell me your story in your own words."

"All to be squeezed into a newssheet?"

Rinilto produced a nervous laugh and stopped in his tracks. "I would like to spread it over several weeks."

"You've rather surprised me," I said. "I have never heard of such a thing . . . although, I have to say, it sounds intriguing. You will allow me to think on it?" I started to walk on.

"Of course, of course." The fellow reminded me of a young puppy, his enthusiasm almost running away with him. "The next edition is out tomorrow. It contains a short piece about your arrival and a brief taster for my readers."

"A little presumptuous!"

"Oh, no, Lord Sagredo. It is a self-contained item. I would not dare . . ."

"I'm teasing," I said, smiling at Titus Rinilto's contrition.

We rounded the corner into Campo S. Maurizo and I could see the door to my little house. I stopped and turned to the young man. "How may I reach you, Titus?"

"My press is on Via Pisato, sir."

"Very well. I shall be in touch."

"You shan't regret it, Lord Sagredo. This is the future."

"If you say so," I replied, gave him a nod, and strode across the campo.

Chapter Seven: A Letter To The Pope

That afternoon. The Vatican Embassy, Venice.

Cardinal Santora Severina sat in a velvet upholstered, gilt chair. His assistant and amanuensis, Father Berlinghiero Gessi stood immediately to his right. Severina's face was dark with fury; a vein throbbing at his temple.

"That nobody! That pig!" he fumed. "I have heard of his heresy. Francesco Sagredo, you'll curse your mother for giving birth to you." He clicked his fingers and Gessi leaned in. "Take a letter."

The priest pulled up a chair to a writing desk, readied a quill and paper and Severina started to dictate.

"Your Holiness. Things here do not begin as well as we had hoped. I have allies in the government, but as we feared, there is an undercurrent of resentment. The Doge himself is resistant to efforts to transfer Bruno into your loving embrace, and there are other influential members of The Ten who barely keep veiled their opposition. One such is a man named Francesco Sagredo. You may have heard of him. He has been elevated far beyond his right by his friend, the Doge; and he is now a member of the Council.

"Sagredo is believed to be steeped in occult practices and I shall move to expose these. In the meantime, I beseech you to do all you can to apply further political pressure on our friends here. As you are of course well aware, Your Holiness, we cannot lose Bruno."

Severina turned to the priest. "Show me." He scanned the letter and nodded slowly. "Get this in the next dispatch to Rome."

Gessi started to retreat.

"Wait! I want two men watching Sagredo. I want them watching the man every minute, every hour. I want a daily report - everything he does. If the bastard farts, I want to know about it. You understand?"

Gessi bowed.

"Well what are you waiting for? Go!" Severina bellowed.

There was a timid rap on the door.

"Who in the name of Christ is that?"

Gessi hurried over and opened the door to a servant.

"What?"

"A message for His Eminence, Father."

Gessi gave the man a black look and ushered him in.

"Your Eminence," the servant's voice was shaky. "There is a man here to see you . . . the prison warden, Marcel Fabone. He says it's urgent."

Chapter Eight: Schemers

That Evening.

The Celsi mansion, the Palazzo Arragio on the Grand Canal, was said by some to be the most lavish and most beautiful in the Republic, but, as with many things, such an opinion was really a question of taste. The view that it was so fine a home was held almost exclusively by those with little education, who came from the furthermost end of the social spectrum from the Celsis, by those who fantasised about what it must be like to have almost unlimited wealth and on what they would spend those riches. To their peers and neighbours however, the Celsis were considered rather vulgar.

At the appointed hour, guests begun to arrive on the water close to the imposing doors of the palazzo. Teresa and her teenage son, Piero disembarked from a gondola and were helped ashore by their gondolier.

"I'm dreading this," Piero said. He was dressed formally, accentuating his height and his broad shoulders. A boy, more handsome than pretty, he had his mother's nose, well-defined cheekbones and black eyes. He wore his hair shoulder-length as dictated by the fashion of the time, and it suited him.

"Please, Piero," Teresa replied. "I expect you to be on your best behaviour tonight."

"Why, mother? Just to please that vile man and his dried up old prune of a mother?"

Teresa stopped and turned towards the boy gripping his shoulders.

"I know how you feel about Lord Celsi, but you also know that he and I are betrothed and that he will soon be your father."

"*Step-father*, mother; there's a big difference."

"And you know why I'm doing it, don't you, Piero?"

Teresa noticed two servants approaching. She raised a hand to indicate she wanted privacy. They stopped obediently and Teresa returned her gaze to her son. "You do understand?"

The boy nodded.

"Why am I doing it?"

"For me."

"Yes, Piero, for you. Please don't think for a moment that it is for love! I thought I had explained this to you."

The boy looked pained. "You did, mother . . . I'm sorry."

"Good. So, best behaviour . . . yes?

Less than one hundred feet away, a second gondola, this one carrying Cardinal Severina and Father Gessi, approached the quay close to the Celsi's Palazzo as Teresa and Piero took the path to the doors and the waiting servants.

Father Gessi turned from pondering the rushing water against the hull. "With respect, Your Eminence, I really don't understand why you have to put yourself through this nonsense."

Severina had his hands clasped in his lap. "I too wonder sometimes."

"Then why?"

"Because the Celsis are the most powerful and influential family in the Republic."

" And you are the Apostolic Nuncio to his Holiness. They should be grovelling on their knees before you, Your Eminence.

"That's as may be, Father, but I cannot wield Ecclesiastic Law here. The Venetians are very sensitive about their so-called religious freedoms. So, we need to be nice to people like the Celsi family and other nobles in this God-forsaken city. It is the only way to get Giordano Bruno to the stake."

"It's a disgrace."

"It is, but it is also a fact of life in this modern world, Berlinghiero. At least we may comfort ourselves in the fact that one day these people shall all burn in the eternal flames of Hell."

Before the meal, the cardinal and Father Gessi mingled with the small group of guests who were enjoying fine wine and dainty hors d'ouevres served by beautiful liveried boys. A lutist played one of the more famous Spanish pieces which Severina recognised as Luis de Milán's *Pavana Il del ter Sagredo y quarto tono*; the performer, the cardinal decided, was not of the highest quality and he pushed the sound to the back of his mind as the mistress of the house, Violetta Celsi spotted the clerics and came over.

She walked with a confident gait. She was slender, her pale grey dress flattered her and softened her white hair and harsh facial features; eyes too small, a watery grey, a similar shade to her dress, lips too narrow, nose too angular.

"You have come a long way since we last met, Cardinal," she said as Severina took her hand, smiled and gave the woman a small bow. She pointedly ignored Gessi.

"Thank you, Lady Celsi. I seem to recall you gave me words of encouragement back then when I was a lowly priest about to begin my time as advisor to His Holiness, Pope Pius."

"I know talent when I see it."

Severina gave the old woman a small bow. "May I introduce my assistant,

Father Berlinghiero Gessi. I believe he too is a promising theologian."

The priest nodded, unsmiling and Violetta looked him up and down. "Cardinal, you will stay a while after the other guests leave this evening, won't you? There are some matters my son and I would very much like to discuss with you."

"It would be my pleasure," Severina replied.

As well as Violetta, Niccolo and his sister, Sofia, there were six guests: Teresa and Piero, the cardinal and Gessi along with Guiro Pastolo, a merchant from Naples and his nubile bride, Stephanie.

At dinner, Teresa found herself engaged enthusiastically by Stephanie Pastolo, who appeared to be obsessed with every detail of gossip about Francesco Sagredo and had absolutely no idea of his earlier life in Venice, nor his relationship with anyone at the table. Guiro Pastolo tried in vain to begin a discussion with Gessi, but the priest was having none of it and acted the prig throughout, speaking in monosyllables and only when it was absolutely necessary. Ever the experienced professional charmer, Severina at least managed to keep up polite discourse with Niccolo Celsi. Piero Damas looked on, utterly miserable.

As one might expect, the meal was a sumptuous affair; but although Severina and Gessi were accustomed to good living and luxury, they had simple culinary tastes and shunned rich food such that by the time it was over and the party had moved to a living-room of velvet drapes, mustard damask sofas and subdued light spilling from a fourteenth century French chandelier, they were relieved. The hosts and guests were far too socially nuanced to comment upon the fact that the clerics had eaten, with appropriately biblical restraint, a sliver of fish, two slices of bread and three pieces of fruit between them.

After an hour of small talk, Teresa made her excuses and slipped away with Piero and Father Gessi claimed that he had to leave early to catch up with some very urgent work. Niccolo Celsi escorted Teresa and Piero to the front doors and returned to the lounge as a servant entered pushing a cart carrying a silver jug and a set of delicate cups and saucers. He handed round the cups and brought the jug around to the guests, serving the ladies first. When the boy reached Severina, the cardinal put his hand over the cup and shook his head slowly.

"Oh come now, cardinal," Niccolo Celsi said from where he sat next to his guest. He turned to face him. "Have you not tried this delicious drink?"

"What is it, my dear Niccolo?"

"Coffee, cardinal."

He looked puzzled momentarily. "Yes, yes. I have heard of it. Brought back from the New World, is it not?"

"It is." Celsi nodded to the servant and Severina slowly withdrew his hand.

"Just a small drop." He lifted the cup to his lips and took a sip.

"It is a strange taste at first."

Severina pulled a face. "It certainly is!"

Sofia, who was seated the other side of the Cardinal, giggled. Her mother gave her a reproving look and the girl's face fell. "I'm so sorry . . ."

"No need to be, my dear child." Severina gave her a winning smile. He turned to Violetta. "I'm sure it is an acquired taste, Lady Celsi. I will obviously need to get used to it."

The last to leave were the Pastolos. Stephanie had been plying her husband with alcohol all evening, and the man could barely stand as he leaned back to counter-balance the bulbous hemisphere of his gut. Signora Pastolos made a recherché attempt to look pained, but was clearly untroubled by the fact that her husband would be quite incapacitated until morning. Sofia wished the cardinal, her brother and her mother a good night and left them alone in the grand parlour with the servants out of earshot.

"You are aware of course, Your Eminence that we are entirely supportive of your mission here," Violetta said with typical forthrightness.

Severina graced her with a slight dip of the head. "Of course; as any right-thinking Christian would be, madam. But I welcome your words anyway. I fear there are some in this Republic who do not feel the same way; some who I would not call good Christians."

"I did not have a chance to describe the performance of Francesco Sagredo in the Council chamber this morning, mother," Niccolo said, turning towards Violetta, his face contorted as though he were sucking on an unripe lemon.

"You have no need to, my son. I can imagine readily enough."

"Tell me about this man," Severina said. "You obviously know him well."

"Francesco Sagredo is an insidious influence and if I had had my way, he would never have been allowed back into the Republic," Niccolo Celsi said.

"Why was he exiled in the first place?"

"Heresy, Your Eminence."

"Really? I was not aware of that. Explain."

"Niccolo played no small part in ridding us of the man back in '77," Violetta commented.

Niccolo leaned forward, elbows on knees. "He trained as a medic, but thought himself above all authority. During the terrible plague years, he constantly flouted regulations about containment and had the temerity to disregard the advice of his betters."

"And how did you come into conflict with him, directly?"

Niccolo was quiet for a moment. He could feel the cardinal's eyes boring into him and it made him uncomfortable. There had been many reasons for the birth of hatred between him and Sagredo, many reasons why that hatred

48

had festered. He had no intention of mentioning the key reason, that was far too personal, and besides, he had won the old battle, he had the woman, or almost had the woman who had come between him and his old enemy.

"I lost a good friend to Francesco Sagredo's ineptitude," he said. "It was soon after the plague began its terrible reign, the summer of 1575. Sagredo had a practice in San Samuele and worked for a short while at the off-shore hospital, the Lazzaretto on the island of Nazaretum. One night, in September of that year, he was called to the home of Lucio Magonna. He did not arrive until the middle of the following morning, by which time my friend was more in need of a priest than a medic. Lucio died before Sagredo left the house. When quizzed about his tardiness, he freely admitted that he had been tending Jews in the Ghetto."

Severina looked suitably outraged. "And you heard this from whom?"

"A servant of Lucio's. We." He nodded towards his mother. ". . . had escaped to our estate in Verona as soon as the first cases were reported."

"And your relationship with the Doge?"

"My family have been at odds with the Cicognas for a very long time," Violetta said. "As you are aware, Your Eminence, my husband, Adamo had been groomed to take over the Dogeship. He was favoured by Doge Alvise Mocenigo, but then my dear husband was slain . . . Lepanto." She stopped, her face drained of colour. "Pasquale Cicogna was Adamo's great rival in business and in politics. When my husband was taken from us, Cicogna was given an opportunity he could never have acquired otherwise. After Doge Mocenigo died in June '77, Cicogna was passed over twice, but he somehow managed to win on his third attempt seven years later."

"And in the meantime, the Cicognas and the Sagredos had become close?" Severina raised a questioning eyebrow.

"Sagredo is supposed to have saved the life of Pasquale Cicogna's only son, Tomasso, at Lepanto. The two youths became inseparable friends and Sagredo won the favour of Cicogna senior," Niccolo explained. "Francesco Sagredo lost both parents and a sister during the first year of The Death. He and Tomasso Cicogna are the same age and a year younger than me. The Cicogna family took Sagredo under its wing."

"And he was exiled in '77. Is that right?"

"Yes, he was. Alvise was in his final months as Doge. He had never liked Cicogna and I could see that if we were ever to be rid of the Sagredo creature, I would have to make the right moves as it was possible even back then that Pasquale Cicogna might succeed the ailing leader – he was already gaining popularity." Niccolo glanced at his mother who wore a sour, defiant expression.

"He didn't win then though, did he, son?"

The cardinal ignored her. "But how did you influence Sagredo's conviction on charges of heresy?"

"It took little effort from me, Your Eminence. He had gained a reputation for unorthodoxy during the plague years, but after the last traces of the Pestilence had gone, Sagredo published a book in which he declared that the cause of the plague was not divine, that it was a disease produced by some unknown factor, and that one day, we would understand it and beat it. He was invited to give a series of lectures on his theories at the University of Padua. The Doge, who, as I said, never much liked Sagredo, heard of this and had him arrested. My mother and I." He turned towards Violetta who was staring fixedly at her son, managed to pull some strings and . . ."

The cardinal nodded. "Well, as you know," he said. ". . . this man and I have already exchanged words."

"The insolence of the bastard!" Celsi said and exhaled loudly through his nose. "I could not believe my ears this morning, Your Eminence."

"I think he is a very dangerous individual. And so." Severina paused, running his hand over his chin. "I would like you to do everything within your power to thwart him now that he has returned. It is of the utmost importance that he does not interfere in the Bruno case. He clearly sides with the prisoner. He visited Giordano Bruno after the Council meeting."

Violetta looked thunderstruck.

"It does not surprise me in the least," Niccolo remarked coolly. "They are like two peas in a pod."

"Indeed," the cardinal said.

"You may of course count on our help in whatever way we can provide it," Violetta said. She gave her son a furtive glance. "May I, Your Eminence, beg a small favour in return?" She took a deep breath, gathering her thoughts. "You are of course aware of our many business interests in the Republic and beyond? We are finding the trade in certain substances that come this way from the East very lucrative. You understand, Cardinal Severina?"

"Of course."

"We have learned that regular supplies of these substances are not getting through to other regions, especially . . . we hear . . . Rome."

"I would not know," Severina replied carefully. "But I will take your word for it."

"We would like to offer you a business opportunity; a chance to meet the demand in Rome."

The room was incredibly quiet.

"That would be a very difficult offer for me to accept," Severina replied. "In my capacity as Papal Advisor, I am constantly under surveillance from spies of my enemies, as well as spies working for His Holiness. You do realise this?"

"Of course," Niccolo interceded. "But, as my mother said, the trade is very,

very lucrative and ripe for expansion. You are one of our most trusted friends."

"We do go back a long way, Your Eminence," Violetta added.

"Yes, we do." The cardinal held the old woman's eyes for a moment. "I will have to talk to a few . . . associates."

"It is imperative that as few people as possible know of what we have discussed."

"Naturally." Severina produced a thin smile. "As you said yourself, Niccolo, I am one of your family's most trusted friends. Now . . ." He brought his palms together. "I would like a proper cup of that excellent coffee. Your other guests have left us in peace, so I have no need to be quite so abstemious; now do I?"

Chapter Nine: Alfonzo's

The Ghetto District. Close to Midnight.

Alfonzo the Spaniard's was the most popular bordello in the whole of Venice, a dubious accolade but impressive since the Republic was known throughout Europe as the greatest adult playground since the most debauched days of the Roman Empire some fifteen centuries in the past.

Alfonzo Castello had opened his establishment after arriving in Venice a decade earlier. To some he was a fascinating character with a seemingly endless stock of tales in which he played the starring role. There were yarns about how he had walked across Europe to reach Venice back in 1582 and stories of his travels to the very tip of Scotland during the worst winter in anyone's memory. There were confessions about how he had married four times and had loved dearly each of his wives. And when he had been plied with sufficient drink, Alfonzo would claim that he had deserved none of his women and they were far better off after he and they had parted company. On other occasions he boasted that he had fathered no fewer than twenty-four children. Each of them now lived with their mothers in Spain and he clothed, housed and fed them from his earnings as the bordello's owner.

Alfonzo Castello was a large man, entirely bald, with a patch over his left eye to cover an empty socket – all that remained after he had been gouged by a bull during the *encierro* or 'running of the bulls' in northern Spain. But the man's most striking characteristic had nothing to do with his physical being: it came down to personality. He was little more than a wealthy pimp and owner of a place for drunks, drug addicts, gamblers and users of prostitutes; he existed in the twilight world of easy violence, decadence and jeopardy, a place drenched in tears and blood, where murder was commonplace and few questions were ever asked; yet Alfonzo was famous for his gentle demeanour.

Of course he could protect himself and those he cared about. He had to deal with cutthroats and some of the slimiest of pond life in the Republic, but he was rarely riled, maintained an almost Zen-like patience and stillness and was known to barely ever raise his voice: indeed, in all the time he had spent living in the twilight, he had never once killed a man, nor had he ever ordered anyone's murder. No one dared cross Alfonzo because he exuded an impossible-to-define power, a power that was sensed by everyone who met him, but never once tested.

The bordello was on Via Esconti close to a narrow tributary of one of the main waterways of the Ghetto, Rio di St.Fosca, and it was everything one would expect of such a place. During the daytime it was empty and reeked of ale and wine, tobacco and bodily fluids. By night, the place heaved with human beings; it was filled with screeches and moans, laughter and shouting, dance music from Bohemia, and Romany melodies.

The night of the Ninth November, 1592 was, at least at first, little different to a thousand others in the Ghetto and at Alfonzo's. In the ballroom, patrons milled around drinking, gambling and fondling the young women who worked there. Money changed hands, insults were thrown, declarations of undying love, slurred. Girls on drinks duty took orders and delivered trays laden with ale, and Jimito the dwarf took coats and hung them in a small anteroom close to the bar. In the upstairs rooms, customers in a steady stream of arrivals and departures, and in various states of inebriation, were serviced by the girls on Alfonzo's payroll.

Barely recovered from the hangover that had kept him in bed until earlier that evening, Tomasso Cicogna was again heading speedily and inexorably towards another drunken stupor as he propped up Alfonzo's bar. To his left and to his right beautiful girls, heavily painted and scantily dressed, draped decorously, each trying to persuade him to take them upstairs, before growing irritated that he seemed to be far more interested in ale than girls.

At twenty minutes to midnight, Antoinette Perugino, whom some considered to be the most beautiful and pneumatic prostitute not only at Alfonzo's but anywhere in the Most Serene Republic of Venice had finished her shift. Dressed still in a flimsy lace red dress and platform shoes, she descended the wide curving stairs that dominated the centre of the bordello, and was crossing the floor when she almost collided with her boss.

"Shit girl, what are you . . . ?"

"Ah, just who I wanted to see," Antoinette said holding out her hand.

"Finished already?"

"It was over just as soon as my last customer came!"

Alfonzo grinned and was about to guide Antoinette across the room to his office when there came a commotion from their left, close to the entrance.

"What is it?" Antoinette asked, but Alfonzo was already striding across the room, his customers parting before his considerable bulk. A shout cut over the music, a man's voice, bellowing a single word. "Antoinette!"

Antoinette could just see her father, the gondolier, Carlo Perugino standing, legs slightly parted, his face flushed red with alcohol and fury. As she watched Alfonzo approach him, Carlo started to sway, putting out a hand to steady himself. He knocked aside two tables, along with a collection of tankards that clattered across the floor.

The music stopped abruptly and the room fell quiet just as Alfonzo and his assistant, Stefano Vanenti reached Perugino. From the bar, Tomasso had a clear view of the scene.

"Where is she? Where's my daughter?" the gondolier hollered. Regaining his balance, he picked up a chair and charged towards Alfonzo and Stefano, screaming "Antoinette! Anto . . . in..ette."

Stefano was the first to reach Carlo. The gondolier swung the chair, missed the youth by two feet, and fell into a cluster of tables. Before he could get to his feet, Alfonzo was on him, grabbing his arms and pinning them behind his back. Stefano landed a heavy punch into the man's guts and Carlo fell to the ground, vomit spewing from his gaping mouth. Stefano went to kick him. Antoinette rushed over.

"That's enough!" Alfonzo stepped between Carlo and Stefano and felt Antoinette pulling on his arm. "Leave us, girl!"

Antoinette, her face the colour of washed entrails, backed off.

"Stefano, get rid of him," Alfonzo said calmly.

"No!" Antoinette cried as Stefano started to drag the semi-conscious man to his feet.

"Let go, Antoinette," Alfonzo ordered.

She spun on her heel. "Don't hurt him."

"Just see him on his way, Stefano." Alfonzo turned back to the girl. "You. In my office. Now."

The music started up again. Outside, Stefano pushed Carlo Perugino hard up against the wall, tugged on a pail of water close to the doors and emptied it over the man: Perugino came round immediately. Stefano drew a knife from a sheath at his belt and jammed the blade close to the gondolier's throat.

"I'm not as nice as my boss," the younger man said. "Not even close. In fact, I like nothing better than hurting cunts like you. So, I would happily slit open your throat, but, well . . . I want to keep my job . . . I'll say this just once." He leaned on the blade and it moved a fraction of an inch, piercing Carlo's neck and causing a bead of blood to slip onto the metal. "Fuck off, and don't ever come back."

As Stefano stepped aside, Carlo stood motionless for a second. Then he spat on the ground between the bouncer's feet and stumbled off.   Stefano watched him disappear into the nearest dark alley.

"So what's this all about?" Alfonzo was leaning back on his desk. Antoinette stood just a few feet in front of him.

"I'm sorry, boss. I . . ."

"What did he want?"

Antoinette looked down and shook her head.

"The last thing I need is protective fathers!"

"I'm sorry. It won't happen again."

"Is that so? Look at me."

She lifted her beautiful face. "He gets drunk and . . .

"All right, calm down," Alfonzo said. "Where are you going from here?"

"Why?"

Alfonzo shrugged. "Just protecting my investment."

Antoinette allowed a small smile. "A party."

"This place not lively enough for you?"

"I have friends."

"I thought *we* were your friends."

She started to speak.

"Here," Alfonzo said, handing her some coins. "I've added a little extra tonight. People keep thanking me for having you here." He winked. "Go on . . . off with you!"

Chapter Ten: Redemptionis

Venice, 10th November, 1592.

I awoke with a start, bad dreams lingering. The house was silent except for the sound of my housekeeper, Isabella snoring softly. I felt parched and found a jug of weak ale close to the stove. Taking a long drink, I surveyed the room lit dimly by a pre-dawn grey-blue.

I needed to clear my head. Out on the campo the air was crisp, a tang of salt blended with the usual sewage stench. I crossed to Calle Caotorta; brooding moonbeam shadows bisected the street. Pulling into a narrow laneway where lines of washing flapped overhead, I traversed a bridge before turning left onto Calle Giotto. There was no one about at this time of the morning. From far off I could hear dull thuds and male voices carried across the sleeping city from the docks where the ships lay at anchor waiting to be unloaded and restocked.

It was icy cold, a patina of frost on the cobblestones, and I had to watch my footing. It took me no more than five minutes to reach the Grand Canal. Keeping to the shadows, I wrapped my winter cloak about me and lingered for a few moments just staring at the water and feeling lonely, still half in a dream. At moments such as these I almost wished I were once more walking a desert road or waking in a strange lodge with the brooding mass of the Himalayas beyond the curtained window. At these times, I was angry with myself for simply letting things happen to me during my brief time back in the city; for so quickly gathering unto myself responsibilities, and fresh desires.

Walking away from the water, I steered a course east without really thinking where I was going. Such is this home of mine, this Most Serene Republic, a labyrinth of lanes and waterways like the vascular system of an animal Master Leonardo may once have drawn. In some ways, Venice felt to me like a living, breathing creature. Nourished by shiploads of merchandise arriving from all directions of the compass, it excreted its waste into the Lagoon; it grew, its tendrils stretching across an empire.

I was so lost in thought it took me a moment to realise I was hearing a real sound and not just the monologue of my thoughts. It was a yell. Then came another. A man's voice, strangulated. I reached the end of Calle Vallaresso, no more than a hundred yards from the western perimeter of San Marco. Looking along the lane I could just make out, at the far end close to the water, a group of moving shapes, fluid against the grey buildings. There were four men, one on his knees trying to pull himself up. A burly figure kicked him and

56

he collapsed again to the ground, a blur of white.

I didn't stop to think, just bolted towards the figures, shouting as I ran. I almost slipped over on the icy ground, but reached the shapes in a few seconds. Pulling at the closest man, I caught his elbow, he whirled round and swung his fist. I grabbed it, twisted him about and sent him tumbling backwards, tripping over his own feet. Keeping my balance, I shifted round a little so that I could slam my right foot into the back of the nearest attacker. He fell to one side but caught my shoulder with a flailing arm.

The victim in white was now sprawled on the floor face down and the third man kept kicking him. I went to grab the thug, he spun round and landed a boot in my groin sending a ripple of pain up my spine. I punched him hard in the face. He crumpled, landing badly, his head slamming against a stone step. The first man was pulling himself up. I moved to face him, a thick-set beefy fellow with malevolent black eyes; but he had had enough. He ran.

The man in white groaned and half-turned, struggling to get up. I leaned down and only then realised who it was. "Tomasso!" I said. His face was smeared with blood and his right eye had already puffed up. "What in the name of the Lord ... ?"

Blood dribbled onto his ripped shirt and a slender web of long black hair lay over his sweaty face.

I hugged him and heard him groan. Stepping back, I held him by the shoulders. "You're hurt." I touched his chest. He recoiled with a yelp. "Stay still, Tomasso," I ran my fingers along his collar bone. Turning him, I felt around his back. He cried out. "You have at least two broken ribs."

Then it dawned on me. We were standing on Calle Vallaresso, one of the most notorious streets in Venice, infamous for its gambling dens. Glancing at the building to our left I saw the door and a plaque carrying the image of playing cards and dice.

"You fool," I hissed. "You've been gambling again!"

"Fuck! Francesco, don't lecture me: Not now!" He winced and doubled up in pain.

"Let's get you home."

•

Tomasso had an apartment on Riva Degli Schiavoni with a perfect view onto San Giorgio Maggiore and the newly-built church. I suggested I find a gondola to take us there, but he had vetoed the idea saying he did not want anyone else to see him in his present condition. And so it took us almost twenty minutes to cover the four hundred yards to his home and five more to ascend to the second floor.

A servant girl was at the door as it swung open. She looked horrified. Then an older woman appeared. It was Adelina, Tomasso's housekeeper. She dashed onto the landing and helped me get my friend through the door and on to a couch.

"Not again!" she exclaimed as she pulled up from Tomasso. He gave her a harsh look. The woman turned to me and scowled.

"Heat some water, please, Adelina," I said as she retreated to the scullery.

I managed to make Tomasso comfortable and bound his torso with a long strip of cloth soaked in hot water. I used some wine to clean his wounds and found a bottle of port. Heating a cupful, I spooned it between his lacerated lips.

"Not again?" I said. "How often has this happened?"

He dismissed the question. "Promise you will not breathe a word of this to my father, Francesco."

"You know I won't," I said quietly. "But why, Tomasso? Why are you doing this to yourself?"

He looked away, closing his eyes for a moment. "It crept up on me. I dabbled a little, lost, dabbled some more, lost some more."

"And you've worked up a debt?"

He did not need to say anything.

"Well, as your physician and your friend, let's deal with this when you are feeling better. For now you have to rest and drink lots of weak wine or beer. I will come back later today with a poultice and change your bandages."

I called Adelina and she came in with the young girl in tow. I gave them explicit instructions and headed for the door. Tomasso was already snoring.

I felt bruised and battered myself. My testicles ached and I had a stabbing pain in my side. The wind off the Lagoon bit as I stepped out onto the waterfront and I swear the temperature had dropped several degrees just in the time I was attending Tomasso.

The light had changed too. The eastern sky was now slashed with orange and red, the low clouds brimming with colour. The fronts of the buildings close-by were lightening. I rubbed my hands together, blew onto them, bowled them close to my mouth and stomped off feeling the treachery of the ice underfoot.

It was still remarkably quiet, but soon the area would be alive with morning traders, gondolas in their scores, business people rushing to appointments, food stalls opening, every strand of Venetian society, from beggars to bankers would begin to go about their daily lives.

I had just reached the Molo. To my left, a sprinkling of first sunlight caught wavelets. To my right, a few people were crossing San Marco, a troop of palace guards marched through the gates into the Doge's palace. I glanced back at the water and saw a bright glint. It was like a spark igniting and as quickly dying. I squinted. It happened again and I realised it was the sun reflecting from a shiny surface. It was only then I made out two gondolas hard up against the edge of the quay. Both gondoliers were crouching in their boats and studying something in the canal. A commander of the palace guard wearing a brass chest plate stood a few yards back from the water. Two uniformed soldiers were stretching down over the stone wall of the waterfront. I started to walk towards the group and saw the two close to the water arch back as they hauled something heavy onto the stones of the quayside.

At first, the object looked like a large, white fish. It was only as I came within a few yards of the group that I realised the two men had dragged a dead body from one of the gondolas.

The two tugging at the body had not seen me, but the commander reached for his sword. "Be on your way," he growled. I put my hands up, but he suddenly recognised me and snapped to attention. "Apologies, sir . . ."

I ignored him, took two steps towards the water and crouched beside the body as the two soldiers plopped it onto the cobblestones. One of them glared at me and I heard the captain's voice. "Stand back Montani . . . Fruelli."

The two soldiers straightened. I caught the eye of the man closest to me. He looked as though he was about to vomit.

"Did you find this body?" I called to the nearest gondolier.

He nodded and pointed west across the Grand Canal towards the finger of land marking the edge of the Dorsoduro district.

The body was that of a young woman. All colour had gone from her skin except for a clutch of black bruise marks along her left temple. Her eyes were open, a creamy film over the pupils. A red silk dress clung to her. It was ripped and stained and her left arm was out of the sleeve. There were black marks along her arm which I could tell had been caused by nibbling marine life. She wore a garter about her right thigh. Her black hair was matted with seaweed and slurry, and the skin under her dead eyes was speckled with sand. It was clear from her clothing the girl was a prostitute.

The wound across her neck had been washed clean by the waters. It was a grey opening the span of my hand and an inch thick. The flesh of her throat hung bloated with water and swelling out over the edge of the deep laceration. And then there was the word. Across the poor soul's forehead, cut deep into the flesh and down to the albumen bone, I saw a shaky line of letters: REDEMPTIONIS.

Chapter Eleven: Accusations

By the time I reached home, I was exhausted. It felt as though I had already lived through an entire day. Isabella was up and busying herself about the house. I boiled some water over the fire and found a pouch containing some seeds of Kariyat, a plant I had first spotted in the foothills of the Himalayas years before. The plant was a ragged little thing with delicate white flowers, but the seeds were famous among the local Tibetans for their power to invigorate a tired body.

I crushed a dozen seeds to powder in a pestle and mortar and stirred them into the boiling water. They gave off a heady aroma, citric and sharp. I sipped at the liquid and felt it slither down my throat. The effect was almost instantaneous. I then washed, applied a hot poultice to my wounded side and dabbed at a cut under my eye with the remnants of the Kariyat infusion. Isabella had laid out my official robes and I changed, clasped my best fur-lined cloak over the top of my jacket and tugged on my hat. It was not quite nine o'clock and I knew the day ahead would be a demanding one.

We were all silent in the Council Chamber, waiting for the Doge to lift his eyes from some papers in his lap.

"The first matter today is this," he said and waved a document in front of him. "Another official request from His Holiness the Pope via his ambassador here, His Excellency Buto Testa, to allow Giordano Bruno to be transported to Rome. It was handed to me personally by Cardinal Severina this morning. It apparently arrived from the Vatican by messenger in the early hours."

A member of the Council, Lorenzo Arturi, an eloquent and well-educated man who had been a friend of my father's raised a hand, and at a nod from the Doge, he stood.

"My Lord Doge. Is there anything new in this latest missive?"

"I shall read it to you: 'Your Most Serene Doge and members of the Illustrious Council, I . . .' Ah, here's the meat. 'Giordano Bruno is no simple heretic, but a leader of heretics, a seditionist of the first order. He has consorted with Protestants, he is an apostate monk who has openly praised the heretic queen, Elizabeth of England, and has written occult works that attempt to undermine the sanctity of the Mother Church. I urge the Council to act with all haste in this matter. We have a boat ready to transport the prisoner immediately if you approve of this action . . . as I most sincerely hope you shall.'"

Several of the Council members started talking at once.

"Gentlemen."

Celsi raised a hand and stood. "Lord Doge, do you not think the time has come to accede to the Vatican's request? Are we not simply delaying the inevitable and creating growing resentment?"

"But Bruno has not yet been tried," Councillor Arturi responded. "The legal process has not run its course."

"Lord Doge, can we seriously deny the correctness of the Pope's claims in this document?" Celsi commented.

"With respect, my most esteemed colleague is being ridiculous,' Arturi said. "These claims made by His Holiness have not been ratified by Venetian Law. They are mere hearsay."

Celsi turned slightly towards the rest of us. "Is my respected colleague denying the fact that Bruno has published occult works? Are you claiming he did not live in London for two years and was in the service of the Great Whore, Elizabeth?"

"Facts are facts, but intent and the purpose of Bruno's actions are open to question," Arturi replied. "It is a fundamental law of our state that a man's guilt or his innocence, shall be demonstrated by legal procedure, not merely because it has been decreed so . . . by anyone . . . not even His Holiness, the Pope."

The Doge raised a hand and the two men sat. "I am inclined to agree with the honourable Lord Arturi, at least for the moment," he said.

Celsi was on his feet almost before the Doge had finished speaking. "But Lord Doge, time is pressing. The trial has been delayed repeatedly. We have the Papal Nuncio here in the Republic, and surely I am not the only one to sense growing impatience on the part of the Vatican."

Lorenzo Arturi sprung out of his seat, fuming. I could contain myself no longer; I too stood and the Doge nodded towards me.

"I feel I must ask the honourable Councillor, Lord Celsi," I began. "Would he have us kowtow to Rome? Are we not an independent people?"

The seated council members raised their voices again. Celsi waited a moment for them to calm down. "It is not a question of kowtowing, it is a matter of diplomacy."

"Enough," the Doge snapped. "This is clearly a very sensitive matter and one that requires careful consideration. I suggest the formation of a sub-committee comprising four Councillors and myself. This committee shall include Lords Celsi and Mendoso from one side of the argument and Lord Arturi and Lord Deivo on the other." He nodded to a man in his sixties, a distinguished politician and renowned lawyer, who had, at one time or another, served on most government councils; and then to a second, younger man, Gian Deivo.

Celsi exhaled noisily.

"Do you have a problem with this decision, Lord Celsi?" Cicogna asked.

"No, Lord Doge."

"Good. Then we may move on to the second item on the agenda, the curious discovery this morning of a dead woman in the Lagoon."

Celsi raised a hand.

"Yes?"

"My Lord Doge, I'm sorry I have obviously missed something. I have not heard this news."

"I also am unaware of this," another Councillor, Ricardo Sfortona commented. He glanced to his left and right and I saw a couple of confused expressions amongst the other members.

"Perhaps the honourable Francesco Sagredo should explain," the Doge replied.

I stood. "The body of a young woman was dragged from the Lagoon this morning close to San Marco."

Celsi made a strange sound in the back of his throat. "Hardly a matter for the Council, is it?" he said, turning from me to the Doge. A couple of the men near him murmured in agreement.

"Normally I would concur," I said. "But this unfortunate girl was murdered."

"And how can you possibly know that?" Celsi sneered.

I paused for a moment and caught the Doge's eye. He appeared curious. I realised he also knew very little about the incident. "The woman had her throat sliced open from ear-to-ear."

Celsi exhaled through his nose.

"She had also been disfigured."

"Disfigured?" said one of the younger Councillors, Marchese da Fontina.

"The word 'Redemptionis' had been cut into the flesh of her forehead."

"Unfortunate," Celsi said.

I gave him a cold look. "Certainly so for the woman and for those who loved her."

"I really don't see what this has to do with us." Celsi looked to the Doge.

"It was clearly a vicious murder and the perpetrator was obviously making a statement," I shot back.

"What are you talking about, Sagredo?" Celsi said, "I assume the woman was a whore?"

"Does it matter?" I exclaimed.

Celsi laughed and a couple of the others chortled. The Doge remained silent, looking from Celsi and his friends to me. "Was she a prostitute, Doctor Sagredo?" he asked.

"I believe from her clothes that she was, Lord Doge, but . . ."

Cicogna had raised his hand. "It is all right, Sagredo. I agree with you." He turned to Celsi. "I believe this is a matter for the Council. Our island is small, Councillor."

"But Lord Doge, surely it could have been the result of a domestic dispute?"

"It could," I interrupted. "But I think that we should investigate nevertheless. I could suggest some ways we might find clues."

"More of your Eastern nonsense, Sagredo!"

I ignored him and kept my focus on the Doge. "Most Serene Prince," I said using the formal term of address for our ruler. "I would like permission to examine the body."

A low murmur came from the others.

"May I explain? I believe that a close study of the corpse could offer some indication as to how the woman died."

"Hah!" Celsi retorted.

The Doge glared at him.

"A close look at the wound," I went on. ". . . may show signs of the type of weapon used. I might even be able to ascertain when the murder took place. I would further wish to examine the dead girl's skin, her hair, under her fingernails and toenails. But, the most useful information would come from an autopsy."

"Lord Doge!" It was Celsi, of course. He took a step forward, his fists balled at his sides. Pasquale Cicogna glared at him and he pulled back. "Which is?"

"An examination inside her body."

"This is verging on necromancy," Celsi hissed, and turned to glare at the others. "I cannot stand here and accept this, and I certainly will not be implicated in this evil." Several of the members of the Council grunted their tacit agreement.

"I am a doctor," I retorted. "Autopsies are common in other countries; in Holland and parts of the Holy Roman Empire."

"And in far off China, no doubt," Celsi said acerbically.

"I see," the Doge said and paused for a moment to look down at his lap and the sheets of paper resting there.

"As much as I appreciate your professionalism and your considerable learning, Doctor Sagredo, I'm afraid I could not sanction such a thing as an autopsy. I find the idea personally repugnant, as do most of our colleagues, I feel. But I also believe it is not something that would, at this sensitive juncture, be looked upon kindly by the Church."

I started to protest.

"I know . . ." And he had raised a hand. "I know that such things are accepted in other lands, but it is not something I can permit here, not with the

63

eye of the Vatican upon us."

Celsi started to clap gently and nodded approvingly towards the Doge, and I was gratified to see our leader give the worm of a man a very black look.

•

"Francesco."

I was the last to leave, just behind Councillor Marchese da Fontina, and had reached the corridor leading away from the Sala del Consiglio dei Dieci. Hearing my name, I turned to see the Doge, the door to his office opened a crack. Noting da Fontina disappearing from sight, I paced back along the corridor.

Pasquale Cicogna was alone. He had removed his hat and his hair stood up in fine white wisps. Lowering himself into a chair, he looked thoroughly enervated. He pointed to a seat opposite his. I walked over and sat.

"You seem to enjoy courting danger, my young friend."

I exhaled through my nostrils and peered down at my lap for a second. "It has long been a habit of mine."

"This business with the young woman dragged from the Lagoon. You know I had to rule against . . ."

"My Doge, you have absolutely no need to justify anything; certainly not to me."

"But you really do believe you can learn from her body?" He looked slightly disgusted.

"The dead may indeed speak," I replied.

"That sounds like tenebrous nonsense, young fellow." He laughed. Then very seriously, he added. "I do find the notion personally offensive, as I said earlier."

"That is your prerogative, My Lord."

"But I also know that you are garnering suspicion from all quarters, Francesco. That vermin, Celsi is the source of many vicious rumours that have reached even my ears."

"I understand," I said.

"But what do you mean, the dead may speak?"

I stared at the Doge and realised there was more to his question than simple curiosity. He was a pious Catholic, a man of genuine faith, and I knew that his current wranglings with Rome were causing him personal anguish, but he was also a man of flesh and blood and, like all of us, he was afraid of death, his terror growing stronger as the Grim Reaper strode ever faster his way.

"I am not the first to have these ideas, not by any stretch of the imagination, Lord Doge. Master Leonardo dissected bodies in Rome a century ago, and closer to home, the greatest innovator in my fraternity, Andreas Versalius, examined the inside of human bodies two decades ago in Padua not ten leagues from this room. And of course, in the countries I have visited, dissection is a practice that holds no fear; attracts unto itself no stigma."

He ran slender fingers through his long white beard. "I have heard of these things. But, I cannot sanction it here . . . not least for your own good, Francesco."

I nodded in acquiescence and wondered why then the Doge had called me in.

"But," Cicogna went on. "I do wish to know who is behind the death of the girl. So, I sanction you to do your best to find out in other ways . . . no dissections." He grimaced. "Do nothing that evil minds may twist into claims of sorcery. And it is my unofficial warrant of course. You understand that?"

I nodded. "I do, Lord Doge."

"Now, what of my son?"

I was thrown for a moment.

"I think the bad things you hear about him are exaggerations."

"You're not a very convincing liar, my boy."

I paused for a second, looking down. "He is the same old Tomasso, sir."

"Yes, I feared as much! But you are watching over him now, now that you are back with us in the bosom of the Republic. And that helps me sleep at night."

I was a little shocked. "Thank you," was all I could say.

•

At the doors facing onto the Molo, an expanse of perfect, icy blue sky stretched before me and a kit of pigeons swooped barely a foot above my head soaring to the top of the palace. I walked home wearily through the winding lanes. Turning the key in the lock of the front door and stepping inside, I was startled to see Teresa seated with another woman close to the fire.

"Well, hello," I said, a little confused.

"Please pardon us, My Lord. Your housekeeper, Isabella let us in," Teresa said.

Isabella appeared and nodded to me before heading off to my bedroom to busying herself.

"Lady Damas. What brings you here?" I held her eyes a fraction longer than was perhaps polite, but I could not help myself. I had felt a thrill pass through me the first moment I saw her there. It was a sensation I had experienced only once in fifteen years; the last time I saw her, just thirty-six hours ago at Cicogna's celebration at the Palace. I glanced at the strange woman seated beside Teresa.

" Lord Sagredo, this is one of my servants, Romia Perugino. It was her daughter, Antoinette who was murdered."

The woman was dressed in a tatty, grey and shapeless coat. As I came closer and pulled a chair up I caught her odour and watched her dab at her eyes. She looked haggard, her cheeks etched by grief.

" How have you heard about..?"

" The news is all over the city, sir," Teresa replied. "Romia here heard in the worst possible way . . . third-hand."

"I'm sorry to hear about this, madam." I turned back to Teresa. "But, why are you here? What is this to do with me?"

"You are an important man, My Lord, and well . . . I have heard that you know many arcane secrets. We." And she gestured towards her servant. ". . . hoped you might help track down the poor girl's murderer."

"You make me sound very grand!"

"Is it not true?"

"Tell me about your daughter, Romia," I said to the servant.

The woman started to sob. I found a handkerchief in my pocket and passed it to her. More tears welled up and rolled on to her cheeks.

"Sir, I'm sorry to burden you."

"Don't be silly. I would like to help you."

"There is nothing anyone can do for my Antoinette! " She bit her lip and lowered her head. "I apologise, sir."

"Romia? Could you tell me everything you can about Antoinette?"

"She was a beautiful girl, but . . ." She choked back a sob. "She was led astray.

"Antoinette used to work in my household," Teresa said. "She was a good, hard-working girl."

"But then she started at one of the bordellos?" I said.

Romia nodded.

"Did your daughter work in any particular one?"

"Alfonzo the Spaniard's."

"I see. And for how long did she work there?"

"Not long, a few months. Before that, she served drinks at taverns on the Lido. She was lured away from my mistress's house by money, My Lord. As I said, sir, she was a beautiful girl. Alfonzo took a personal liking to her, apparently. Makes me ill just to think about it."

"I understand. And when did you last see Antoinette?"

"Two evenings ago, about seven o'clock, perhaps half past the hour. She had found a room in the Ghetto."

"But your family is not Jewish."

"She has a friend, a Jewish girl, Anica Rosen, who also works at Alfonzo's. Antoinette was sharing the place with her; it was cheap and close to work. And ..."

I waited for her to go on.

"My daughter moved away from home two months ago, after she and my husband, Carlo had a terrible row. We're separated now, Carlo and me. He also left."

"What does your husband do, Romia?"

"He is a gondolier, Lord Sagredo, a fine, respectable man and regarded as one of the best in the guild."

"I see."

"Sir, I know a moment ago, I said nothing can help Antoinette. She is in the hands of the Lord now, and I know she was a good soul in spite of what she was paid to do. But I must know who killed my little girl, and why."

I fell silent for a few moments, thinking things through. "I will try to help you," I said. "Do you know the address of the room Antoinette shared with Anica?

"Calle del St. Scuro. Next to a synagogue. It is on the top floor ... I am most grateful to you, sir," the woman said and glanced at her mistress.

"You go on home, Romia," Teresa said pulling up from the chair. "I have some things to discuss with Doctor Sagredo."

Romia stepped forward holding out the handkerchief I had given her. It was wet with tears and snot.

"You keep it."

As the door closed behind the servant, Teresa and I just looked at each other wordlessly.

"I'm glad to see you again, Teresa," I said. "But should you be here ... alone?"

"You mean as a betrothed woman, Francesco?" She laughed.

"You haven't changed."

"My future husband may be adding my estate to his, but make no mistake, he does not have my heart to go with it."

"I'm relieved to hear that." I studied her face, the lines of her fine cheekbones, the almost flawless skin of her face and neck.

"I'm sorry to have put upon you with my servant. Was that unfair of me?"

I took a step towards her. "Not at all. But I'm really not sure what practical help I can give. The matter came up in the Council meeting this morning."

"Oh?"

"I suggested a close study of the corpse; posited the idea of an autopsy . . . You don't seem shocked?"

"Why should I be?"

"Forgive me. I forgot for a moment you studied medicine in your youth."

"I didn't study medicine exactly! I read widely, Francesco, and had a few months with a tutor."

"You never forget such things."

"Perhaps not. But really? Did you actually expect people to approve the idea of you conducting an autopsy?"

"No. And guess who was most vehemently opposed? I was accused of necromancy no less!"

"Well, he has ulterior motives, doesn't he?"

"Do you know where the girl's body is being kept?" I asked.

"Yes, but . . ."

"You asked me to investigate, didn't you?"

"But not if it will cause you trouble." Teresa held my gaze and broke into a smile. "Ah! I remember that look. You've got the bit between your teeth, Francesco!"

•

We went straight away to the Church of the Sacred Virgin in the San Samuele district where the church sisters were looking after Antoinette Perugino's body until it was ready for the burial arranged for the following morning. It was a well known church and very old, built, some said, around the time of the earliest crusades to the Holy Land. It was though, well-preserved and the nuns received money from several wealthy and pious patrons, including, I had heard, Violetta Celsi.

The door was opened by an elderly nun, the Mother Superior. Staring at Teresa, she seemed to recognise her vaguely. Then the woman looked me up and down questioningly and not in an altogether friendly manner. Teresa drew the nun aside and I could only catch the odd snatch of their conversation. After a few minutes, I saw Teresa hand the woman a couple of gold coins and the two of them came back across the hall.

"I am Mother Superior Helene," the nun said, her voice surprisingly low in tone. "Lady Damas tells me you wish to see Antoinette Perugino's body."

I nodded. "Yes, I am a medic . . ."

"I know who you are, Doctor Sagredo. But I don't really understand what you might want with the dead girl."

"I simply wish to try to ascertain how she died."

She looked mildly puzzled. Hers was an intelligent, strong face, her eyes searching, questioning. "Very well," she said and turned towards a narrow corridor at the rear of the hallway.

Antoinette lay in a small room off the north transept of the church. A single white sheet covered her naked and battered form. Teresa and the Mother Superior took me there and then left quietly.

I pulled down the sheet. Antoinette's hair had dried and lay under her shoulders and about the sides of her arms; a few stray hairs had stuck to her flesh. Her skin looked darker than it had that morning, her torso and extremities were covered in patches of black and brown. The body had been washed and anointed with oils, but the unction had failed to completely smother the smell of the sea and the stink of decay; the latter, a deceptively sweet odour not unlike overripe fruit.

I inspected the victim's neck, noting the character of the wound, observing that the incision was raised slightly to Antoinette's right. I pulled back the variegated flap of flesh and saw that the blade had cut very deep, slicing through the cartilage at the front of the neck. I moved her head back at an angle and caught a glimpse of her vertebrae. Next, I began to study the letters cut into the woman's forehead. They were jagged and, I surmised, written hurriedly. The lines of the letters had been cut to different depths, some down to the bone, others reaching only a short way beneath the skin. As I was about to make a close examination of the bruises over Antoinette's torso I heard raised voices coming from the nave.

"You cannot go in there!" I heard Mother Superior Helene say.

I just managed to cover the body with the sheet and duck out of sight into a small curtained alcove. I watched as a stocky man in black hose and a dark tunic burst in. Sister Helene and another nun ran close behind him. I saw the Mother Superior tug on the man's sleeve. He swung around and I could see he was about to strike her when he suddenly seemed to realise what he was doing and stopped. The nun let go of the fellow's arm and he walked over to where Antoinette lay. Pulling back the sheet from where it covered her face, he froze. I could see his face clearly, a backdrop of candlelight casting peculiar shadows around his features. He had a blackened eye and a badly split lip. Without warning, he made a terrible sound, fell forward onto the body and wept openly. Out of the corner of my eye, I saw the nuns back away.

"Oh, my darlin' baby ... What 'ave they done to you?" he said, and I realised it was Antoinette's father, the man from whom the dead girl and her mother, Romia, had become estranged. Carlo Perugino lifted his head and saw me. I pulled in front of the curtains and stepped over to him.

"Who in Our Lord Christ's name are you?" Perugino spat. I could see the wet tracks running down his cheeks. He gave them no heed.

69

Before I could answer, Sister Helene returned with Teresa beside her.

"He is a doctor, come to check on the girl's body," Teresa said.

Carlo wiped his face roughly and straightened his back. "A doctor!" Then he turned to me. "I think my daughter's beyond your care, medic." Then the man's face crumbled again and he quickly raised a hand to his mouth.

"I'm investigating Antoinette's murder."

"Investigatin'? What do'ya mean?"

"Inspecting the body for clues."

He produced a disgusted look. "Oh no, medic! Oh no! You don't lay a finger on 'er. You get that?"

I took a step towards the prone body, but Carlo misread my intentions. He leapt on me like an enraged animal. I was caught off guard and propelled backwards halfway towards the curtained alcove. The gondolier was on me, gripping my throat. I hooked my hands under his arms and thrust upwards. Then, shifting my balance, I pushed back, catching Carlo far from his centre of gravity. He flew across the room. Just in time, the nun and Teresa stepped aside and I rushed Carlo, gripping his arms around his back completely immobilising him. Leaning forward, I tried to calm him and heard the poor man's ragged sobs as his entire body shook with frustration and the terrible pain of a father bereaved.

•

The address Romia had given me for the rooms her daughter had shared with Anica Rosen was for the last house in a short row, and just as she had described it, the place lay closest to the old foundry and next door to a synagogue. I looked up to see the domed addition made to the building and recalled how residents had been forbidden to build places of worship within the Ghetto, so they had circumvented the law by adding a floor to an existing building. This had also met with the condition of their faith that there should be nothing between the place of prayer and the Heavens.

Calle del St. Scuro, where I now stood, was the oldest part of the Ghetto, the area set aside for all Jews in Venice almost a century ago, during the reign of Doge Leonardo Loredan. It had been a place I had frequented during the days I ran a medical practice. I had seen many a family die there during the plague years.

I cannot say I approved of the setting up of the place by our ancestors. They had been paranoid really, scared the Jewish community would steal business opportunities and hoard profits. One cannot doubt that the Jews are master money-makers and businessmen, but they saw themselves as Venetians and did not deserve to be forced to live in a tiny part of the Republic, a few hundred square yards in the least pretty part, close to the site of a disused foundry where once cannons had been forged for the navy.

The Ghetto was surrounded by water and there were only two entry and exit points. These were gated and guarded by armed Christian soldiers. After dark, the only Jews allowed beyond the gates were those with special dispensation. The guards recognised many of the people who lived there; but just to make sure, all people of Jewish faith were forced to wear red hats and a red badge to be kept in clear view at all times. Christians, though, could come and go through the Ghetto as they pleased.

The house was not in the best state of repair. It was probably owned by a man cut from the same cloth as Niccolo Celsi, I thought, as I looked up at the cracked windows and the crumbling plaster façade. The front door hung open half off its hinges.

I was about to step into the hall when I was approached by a young boy of about nine or ten. He was holding a sheath of paper over his arm and stopped in front of me as I turned, blocking my way to the entrance. He wore a big grin; four of his front teeth missing.

"*The Republic*, sir?" He held out a rectangle of paper.

"The what?"

"Newssheet," he said. "Latest news."

I looked at the thing waving in the breeze between his grubby, outstretched fingers and remembered Titus Rinilto telling me the next edition would be out today.

"Only ten soldi, sir."

"Really? I heard it was five."

The boy looked affronted, which made me laugh. I gave him a twenty soldi coin and he was gone almost before I had the newssheet in my hand. I folded it, put it in my pocket and pushed inwards the door to the front of the house where Anica was supposed to live. Stepping immediately into semi-darkness; the only light, a remnant of afternoon sun, came from the lane beyond the door. The hall stank with the fetor of terminal decay. I fancied I could pick out the scent of semen, several different varieties of mould and damp, and the putrid undertow of human excrement. A rat scurried over my boots and dived into a hole in the wall two feet to my left.

I saw no one on the stairs, a fact I was pleased about. Reaching the top floor, there was only one door. It stood slightly ajar. As I advanced warily into the hall, I detected a new aroma, one I had not encountered for a long time, a redolence I had left behind in Persia.

Inside, the walls dripped with damp, and the stink of mould almost overcame the other smell. Turning a corner, I came upon a living area. A

71

young woman lay on a cushion. She was alone, drawing on a long pipe. She saw me and reacted very slowly as she pulled herself up.

"Anica? I mean you no harm," I said quickly.

Her eyes were black circles in the dim light. She was clearly experiencing the effects of a powerful drug. Its perfume was familiar to me, the scent of the poppy. I had sampled opium in India, but had found no liking for it.

"Why are you here?" she slurred.

"The door was open." I glanced back towards the entrance. Antoinette's mother gave me your address."

Anica swayed, closing her eyes for a moment. Then she just shrugged and flopped back down on the cushion.

She was only half-conscious. I sighed and thought how terribly ill she looked. She had the slenderest build, her tatty clothes hung off her; she had no breasts to speak of, bruised calves, grubby bare feet and dirty toenails. Her face was gaunt. Black rings lay under dark eyes; her long, dirty, black hair clawed her sweaty face.

I came close and lowered myself cross-legged beside her, found a coin in my pocket and held it out.

"So, you looking for business?"

"No Anica. I seek information. Are you able to answer some questions?"

She grabbed the coin from my palm. "What sort of questions?"

"I'm trying to discover what happened to Antoinette."

"She was killed." The girl made a strange sound at the back of her throat. It turned into a sob and a tear slithered slowly down her cheek.

"I was one of the people who found her body."

She straightened a little and seemed to be struggling to break out of her drug haze.

"She was disfigured." I added in an effort to rouse the girl some more.

"What do you mean, sir?"

"She had the word 'Redemptionis' scored into the flesh of her forehead. Do you know what that means?"

Anica held my gaze and I watched her jaw bones move as she swallowed hard. She shook her head.

"It was some sort of message from the killer. It means 'Redeem'. It must be a statement about what Antoinette did for a living . . . what you do for a living."

"Are you from the palace guard? You don't look like a soldier. Who are you?"

I decided not to give her my name, or any other information about myself. "That is not important, Anica. Besides, I'm the one asking the questions." I nodded to her hand grasping the coin I had given her. "I have another if your answers help me."

"Give me it first."

I shook my head. "No."

Anica lifted the pipe and I snatched it. She gave me a poisonous look and deflated like a lanced boil.

"We were both working at Alfonzo's last night."

"When was the last time you saw Antoinette?"

She paused to think for a moment. "It was about midnight. She'd finished and came to tell me she was going to a party."

"Outside the Ghetto?"

She nodded. "You know she weren't a Jew?"

"So she could leave through the gates any time she chose to." I took a breath. "Did she leave with anyone?"

"No. I saw her with Alfonzo. He paid her and she was gone." Her voice broke on the last two words.

"Anica, did Antoinette have any special men? Anyone who saw her more than was usual?"

She looked down at her filthy feet. "Can I have the pipe back, My Lord?"

"When we have finished." I tried to be as gentle as possible, but I felt my patience draining away.

She exhaled heavily. "Antoinette was very beautiful, very popular."

I waited for more.

"Most of us have men who see us each week. She had one such. A tall man, quite fair of face actually. I do not know his name. In any case, it would probably have been a false one."

"Please, go on."

"He spoiled her, she told me once. He's rich, you see; owns property; a nobleman maybe. Oh, Lord in Heaven . . . I do not really *know*."

"Did he ever come here?"

"Once or twice."

"And what about this?" I flicked a glance at the pipe in my hand. "Was Antoinette . . . ?"

"I think I've said enough."

"I do not."

She swallowed hard again and clammed up. I knew I would get nowhere by treating the girl roughly. I relented and handed over a second coin.

"We all use the poppy," Anica mumbled. "How do you think we go on night after fuckin' night?"

I nodded.

She had sobered up a little and eyed me with a bitter look. "Oh . . . you can patronise, sir . . . whatever your name is. But how would you know? Your

73

kind are the men who come to us. Antoinette was not the first prostitute to be murdered and she won't be the last, neither."

I realised the drug was exaggerating her mood swings, but she was also very upset and scared. There was a great deal she was not telling me, I was sure of that.

"How do you get your hands on the poppy?"

"How can I tell you that? Fuck! Do you take me for a crazy person?"

"I'll triple the amount you have in your hand," I said.

I caught her eyeing the pipe yearningly. "And you can have this back. A name, that is all I ask of you."

She glared at me.

"I'm trying to find out who killed your friend, Anica. Do you not wish to know? You are frightened, that much is clear."

"You know nothing about me!" she snapped and made a grab for the pipe.

I pulled several more coins from my purse and dropped them into her outstretched palm, but held back with the pipe. "A name, Anica, and I shall be gone."

"Eriador, the Alchemist," she said very quietly.

I handed over the pipe, stood and looked down at her. "Thank you. I am grateful."

She ignored me, drew on the stem of the pipe hungrily and fell back into the cushion.

Chapter Twelve: The Alchemist

After interviewing Anica, I headed straight for Tomasso's place on Riva Degli Schiavoni. I took the first flight of stairs through the light-splashed entrance that led onto the dim interior of the hall and almost collided with the last person I expected to see coming down from my friend's apartment; Niccolo Celsi. We made an almost comical study in ignoring each other as we passed on the landing. He then descended to the street and I took the final set of steps to the front door.

"What on Earth was he doing here?" I asked as Tomasso led me into the living area.

"Oh please, Francesco! No hectoring! Not today!" He had a hand to his forehead and wore an agonised expression, wincing as he lowered himself onto a couch. Save for the bandage I had wrapped around him earlier, he was naked from the waist up.

I sat opposite. "I'm not hectoring ... but *that* man?"

"It was business."

"Everything Celsi does is business. But, please Tom, don't tell me ..."

"Tomasso was shaking his head. "No, I didn't borrow from him, if that's what you're thinking. I'm not quite that stupid."

"I never imagined you were. But ...?"

"If you must know, I was planning to invest in one of his building projects, but I've had to pull out. He's not happy."

"Not the properties in San Polo?"

Tomasso scrutinised me. "Why?"

"I imagine I shouldn't be telling you this, but it was discussed in Council yesterday."

"Celsi said the scheme has been approved."

"Forced through, more like. It's another of the man's swindles."

Tomasso sighed and pulled a pained expression again. "Good job I didn't get involved then, eh?" He gave me an acerbic look.

"Look, Tom, I didn't mean to cast aspersions."

"But you always do, Francesco. You treat me like a stupid child, a kid brother."

"Well, I am a month older than you."

"Not in the mood," Tomasso grunted.

"Sorry."

"Oh, that's all right then! Fuck! You come to my apartment and immediately jump to the worse possible conclusions about me. Who do you think you are ...Councillor? My moral protector? I did perfectly well here for fifteen years without 'big brother' interfering."

"I said I was sorry, Tomasso."

"But that's just it. You charge in, get everything twisted arse up and apologise ...you haven't changed a bit. You always used to do that."

I stood. "Perhaps I had better leave." I was halfway to the door when Tomasso sighed loudly. "Oh fuck it, Francesco. Sit down."

I paused, with half a mind to leave him to stew, but came back over and crouched down beside him. "Here, let me check the damage," I begun to unbind his bandage. The bruising had come out now and Tomasso's abdomen was mottled with black patches. I had earlier concocted an amalgam based on a famous Greek remedy called Theriac; a blend of Wolfsbane, Valerian, Germander, desiccated viper flesh, white wine and treacle. I smeared it liberally over my friend's torso, trying to ignore his yelps and protestations.

"Oh do shut up, Tomasso!"

"It fucking hurts."

"Of course it does. Stop being a baby."

Binding his abdomen with a fresh bandage, I warmed some wine and watched him drink it as I told him all that had happened since I left his rooms early this morning, but consciously omitting the meeting with his father.

"By the blood of Christ, Francesco! You've had quite a day! So you're thinking this poor girl, Antoinette was murdered because of some connection with the poppy?"

"Not necessarily. If that were the case, why would the killer have marked her with the word 'Redemptionis'?

Tomasso shrugged. "Do you not think it may be more to do with Alfonzo's? The fact that she was a prostitute?" He stopped suddenly and stared into space.

"Did you say the girl's name was Antoinette?"

"Yes."

He rubbed his head and looked pained. "That name. I've heard it before. At Alfonzo's, last night."

"What are you talking about?"

"You said the last anyone saw of her was about midnight at the bordello. That's what the girl ..."

"Anica."

"Yes, Anica told you." He stared past me again for a second. "I was there last night."

"At Alfonzo's?"

"Yes. There was some sort of trouble. I ..." he rubbed his head again.

"Tomasso."

"Sshh." He had a hand up. "I'd already had a few drinks. I was at the bar. A man came crashing into the ballroom." Tomasso paused again as though trying to retrieve a long-forgotten memory. "The man was shouting and yelling the name Antoinette."

"What did he look like?"

"Short, but muscular. A bald, ugly brute. He was even more inebriated than I."

It was my turn to fall silent.

"Does that help?" Tomasso asked.

"It must have been her father, Carlo Perugino. Fits his description."

"But . . . ?"

"According to Antoinette's mother, Romia, the man was mortified that his daughter was a prostitute."

"Well, he was pretty upset."

I took a deep breath. "We mustn't get side-tracked, Tom."

"We?"

I ignored him, my mind racing. "Do you think one of the regulars could have been obsessed with her?"

He shrugged. "Now I can put it together, I remember her. She was pretty gorgeous."

I looked at him askance.

"Not so much now, I imagine," Tomasso added. "You said Anica knew there was someone special who Antoinette was involved with. Maybe they became jealous?"

"Mere guesswork. There are no clues or anything to prove blame."

"What could there possibly be, Francesco? For Lord's sake, the woman was dragged from the Lagoon, you said."

"I think I need to speak with the people Antoinette knew. Alfonzo, and this alchemist, Eriador."

"And it would be helpful to know who this enthusiastic customer is, wouldn't it?"

"It would, but I have almost nothing about him to go on. A wealthy land-owner and frequenter of brothels. That does not help much in this city." I felt a sharp pain run across my forehead and yawned.

"Hope I'm not boring you."

"Sorry," I laughed. "I think the day is catching up with me. Do you know either man personally? Alfonzo and this Eriador?"

"I've barely ever spoken to Alfonzo," Tomasso replied. "I've met Eriador on several occasions." He is one of my . . . circle. He is a wise man, a highly regarded bookseller and a serious alchemist."

"You know how I feel about most alchemists, Tomasso. My experience tells me that 'serious' and 'alchemist' may not be used in the same sentence."

"Eriador is a knowledgeable man. But . . ."

"But what?"

"I would not be too surprised if he supplemented the meagre earnings from his bookshop by selling some of his chemical creations."

"Ah, turning drugs into gold?" I quipped.

"Something like that. He has a very sophisticated laboratory hidden away. We all know that poppy seeds pass through the Republic like flour through a sieve. It is inevitable that some of it would be syphoned off. And where would it most likely end up?"

"Places like Alfonzo's."

He nodded.

"If only I could have been allowed to examine the dead girl."

"Even I find that idea odious," Tomasso said.

"You never cease to amaze me," I replied. We served together in the navy, fought together at Lepanto. How many men did you see blown apart or sliced open with a sabre during those days of torture and turmoil? Yet, you're squeamish about examining the dead body of a murder victim."

"It is against natural law, Francesco."

"Oh really? And this from you . . . I assume from the mention of 'your circle,' and the fact you know this man, Eriador personally, you are still interested in the occult?"

He shook his head. "It's not the same. Besides, my learned fellow, what possible benefit could come from poking around a dead body?"

I did not feel inclined to explain. Instead, I stood up and reached for my cloak.

"You're going?"

"I need to speak to Eriador," I said. "While I still have the energy."

"I'll come with you. I know him, I can introduce you. Besides, he may not like you and things might turn nasty. I could protect you."

"Hah! What? Like this morning?"

"Those three took me by surprise. *And* I was badly out-numbered."

I couldn't help smiling. "You need to rest, Tomasso."

"Francesco, I'm fine. Surely, as my physician, you would agree it'll be good for me to get some fresh air. No?"

"Very well. But wrap up warm. It doesn't trouble me, but it's cold enough to freeze the balls off a Himalayan mountain goat out there."

•

The gloaming, the busiest time of day; people returning home from their labours, stalls closing up, traders packing away. Night would soon be closing in, torches were being lit along the Grand Canal and around San Marco, and the palace guard was changing over to those on night duty. We were lucky to find a gondola at the waterfront.

"I assume this Eriador character is quite new to the Republic," I said as the gondola scythed the water. "I had not heard of him until today."

"He keeps a very low profile. But he was not here when you lived in the city before your travels. He is a German. It's said he worked for Rudolf II himself, at the Prague Royal Court."

"The Holy Roman Emperor? Good Lord! I have heard rumours that Rudolf is interested in the Hermetic Tradition, but . . ."

"The rumours are quite true, His Court is perhaps the most liberal in Christendom. Bruno was there before he decided to come back here to Italy. The fool should have stayed put!"

"Does Eriador know Bruno?"

"I'm not sure; but I would not be surprised."

I put my hand into my pocket and touched the folded newssheet I had bought before seeing Anica. I had quite forgotten about it.

"What's that?" Tomasso said as I opened it out.

"It's called *The Republic*, some sort of newssheet."

"Yes, I've heard of it."

I studied the single page. It was made from cheap pulp paper and the printing was of poor quality, but I had to admit that it was eye-catching. Across the top, the words: *The Republic* were printed in heavy type using red ink and it was packed tightly with many lines of text bunched into boxes, with bordered areas the like of which I had never seen before. I scanned down the paper, and there, close to the centre, was a heading: HERO, LORD SAGREDO RETURNS.

I started to read. Tomasso seemed content to watch the canal bank grow closer and relax to the rhythmic sound of the gondolier's pole dipping and resurfacing.

I made a dismissive sound and shook my head.

"What?" Tomasso asked.

I did not reply for a few moments, but carried on reading intently. "Oh, honestly!" I exclaimed.

"What?" Tomasso asked again, this time more irritably.

"And I thought the young man had promise."

"Who? Which young man?"

"Titus Rinilto, the person behind this." I waved the newssheet in front of me as though it were a particularly odious fish. "He's made me out to be some swashbuckling adventurer returning as a hero! Listen to this: 'Lord Sagredo cuts an impressive figure; a larger-than-life character who engenders the envy of all men, and over whom the ladies swoon.'"

"Well, that's how the public perceives you, Francesco. Although I'm not sure *every* man envies you. I think quite a few hate you!"

I shook my head again and tapped the paper hard. "This is . . . this is such utter nonsense!"

"Oh come now," Tomasso said, grinning. "I wish someone would write such things about me. I like the idea of making the ladies swoon."

"Tomasso, this is defamatory."

"Stop being so fucking serious. It's a piece of fluff. No one takes it seriously."

"And the man had the cheek to ask if I would agree to a formal interview; to tell him my story, so he could print it in this . . ."

"I think that might be a good idea."

"Are you mad?"

"Wouldn't it be better to have *your* version of *your* story out there for people to read, rather than all the rumours and hyperbole?"

I did not know what to say to that and we fell silent for a while. The gondolier pulled to the bank of the canal and we turned onto a narrow tributary. Ahead, we could see the crumbling façade of the Church of San Barnaba, rendered iridescent by the last of the evening light.

The gondola tucked into the quay; we paid and crossed the campo, pigeons flapping away before us. Tomasso, limping slightly, led the way into a maze of narrow alleyways and passages to the north-side of the church. Passing a tradesman pushing a cart half filled with sacks of what may have been flour, we stopped at a weather-worn, brown door. A rusted iron ring hung in the centre. There was no bell to be seen. Tomasso rapped on the splintered wood. We both strained to hear a response, but there was nothing. He knocked again, harder this time. Still nothing.

"Curse it!" Tomasso exclaimed, and just then, the door opened an inch.

"Eriador? It is I, Tomasso Cicogna. I am here with a good friend. May we?"

We heard a shuffling sound and a chain being released. The door opened an inch or two and we saw a single dark eye studying us suspiciously. Recognising Tomasso, the owner opened the door further to let us in, sweeping a swift glance around the campo as he closed the door behind us.

An elderly man stood in the dark hall. He had a narrow face and huge blue eyes. His skin was as pale as ivory, almost pellucid in patches, and his thick, perfectly straight, white hair fell to his shoulders where it clung to a black velvet robe.

He locked the door behind us. "What do you want?"

"May we speak with you for a few minutes?" Tomasso said. "It is important."

The old man looked furtive. "Later. Come back later."

I sniffed the air and started along the hall.

"Stop," the old man snapped.

I ignored him.

"You don't have any right."

"Do not worry, Master Eriador. I'm not here to . . ."

I walked into a dark, smoke-filled parlour lit by scores of candles. I had the impression that natural daylight rarely troubled itself here; that the candles worked hard. Two sofas hugged the far walls. Half a dozen young people lay on the floor and the couches, passing around a long-stemmed pipe. Two naked women rolled around passionately on one of the sofas. One of the young women on the floor stood up unsteadily and walked over. It was the prostitute, Anica.

"What is it you want?" Eriador was yanking my sleeve.

Tomasso stepped into the room behind us, squinting. "Eriador, may we speak with you somewhere . . . private?"

"No, Lord Cicogna, you may not. Who do you think you are, barging in . . .?"

"Very well, alchemist," I hissed. "Don't talk to us." I started to turn. "You won't mind if I have a few words with my colleagues, though? I know some people who would be very interested to hear about your flourishing business."

The old man's face stiffened. "Come."

Eriador walked quickly and led us into an adjoining room where more candles of all shapes, sizes and luminosity stood in holders scattered about the place. The low ceiling, I noticed, was blackened. The alchemist indicated a couple of chairs and we sat while he stood in front of a small fireplace, orange flames licking the stonework. He scrutinised Tomasso.

"So, Tomasso Cicogna, what brings you here?"

"This is my friend, Francesco Sag . . ."

"I know who he is." He gave me a curt nod.

"Sir, I think we got off to a bad start," I said. "We are not here about your . . . business, exactly. You have heard about the murdered girl?"

He gave me a hard stare. "I shall not take any blame."

"I was not accusing you of anything, Master Eriador."

"But you clearly know that I sold her refined poppy. Why else would you be here?"

I glanced at Tomasso who was wincing and holding his side.

"I am not ashamed," Eriador went on. "I believe in the poppy. I believe it can free the mind. We could all learn from it."

"I assume you know that is an heretical suggestion?"

"And I'm surprised to hear you make such statements, good doctor!"

81

I smiled and the atmosphere relaxed a little. "I understand what you are saying. But I have no interest in such false roads to enlightenment."

"You are entitled to your opinion, Francesco Sagredo. I happen to hold a different view. I am convinced that Nature has provided us with means to speed up the journey to Realisation. This is the basis of my philosophy: the seed of the poppy is one of the great elixirs. There is, I believe, more than one Philosopher's Stone. Our Republic stands at a crossroads of course, and not only silks and spices pass through this city. The base materials for my blends arrive in sacks alongside bags of cumin and bundles of fabric from the Orient transported along the Silk Road. From India there is the leaf and stem of *Cannabis sativa* and *Cannabis indica* which produce a similar effect to the refined seed of the poppy."

"I am aware of all this, but your views are radical, even for one of your fraternity," I said.

"We are straying from the point," Tomasso interrupted.

"Eriador? What do you know of the murdered girl?"

"I met her just twice. She has only recently become interested in what I refine and sell. Many of the girls who work in the brothels use substances I and others of 'my fraternity', as you put it, produce here in Venice. I do not think the slaying of this poor woman is linked with the fruits of my work, or that of my scattered brothers. Perhaps, instead, it is yet another sign of the coming apocalypse."

I saw Tomasso flinch. He went to say something, but I cut across him. "What do you mean by that, Eriador?"

He studied our faces silently for several seconds, and I noticed him wring his hands together. "Perhaps I should not have ..."

"Master Eriador, you have nothing to fear. You are aware that I am no friend of your enemies. I may not share your liking for the ways of alchemy, but I respect your dedication and the desire to think in a new way. So please ... go on."

He swallowed hard and rubbed a hand over his face, pulling on the flesh of his cheeks, scraping his snowy beard. "Very well. I believe we are fast approaching the End Times, long prophesied. Giordano Bruno is the herald. The struggle now being waged over his fate is merely the prelude to the Great War, the Final Conflict between good and evil, right and wrong."

I must have shown my surprise because the old man gave me a faintly cynical smile. "Not what you expected to hear, Master Physician?"

"I must say it was not. How much do you know of this?"

Eriador held my stare then touched the side of his nose. "I know of many secret things, many dangerous things. But there are some concerns about which I should not speak."

"This battle? Do you believe it will be fought here, in the Serene Republic?"

"Well, Master Bruno is held captive here, is he not?"

"But The Apostolic Nuncio, Cardinal Santoro Severina is in our city right now trying to persuade the Doge to abjure all responsibility towards the prisoner so that Bruno may be taken to Rome to meet an inevitable fate."

"Inevitable indeed," Eriador snapped and looked from me to Tomasso. "I know of this man, this cardinal. I know he is an obsessive creature, a close associate of that devil, Roberto Bellarmino, who revels in the epithet 'Hammer of the Heretics'. Severina is one of Clement VIII's most respected advisors. But there are forces railed against that vile and unholy triumvirate of Bellarmino, Clement and Severina."

"Forces?" I said, and sensed Tomasso shifting uneasily in his chair.

"There is a group, a confederacy of the like-minded called the Resistance." He paused, then took a deep breath. "Perhaps I have already said too much."

I understood his uncertainty. He was still not sure if he could trust me. I decided silence would be best, and it worked.

"There is a band of Bruno supporters who will resist Severina. They have clandestinely challenged the evil of the Vatican for many years."

"But what possible chance does this Resistance have? When compared to any other state in Italy or Spain, our government may indeed be liberal, Eriador, but the Doge and the Council certainly have no love for heretics. Lord in Heaven, some of my colleagues consider *me* a heretic! I have to walk a very narrow path."

"Indeed, I know of this." And he gave me an admiring look. "Why else would I consider allowing you a single moment in my home? Let alone admit to what I have just told you?"

I regarded Tomasso, who was following the exchange silently.

"There are many who will support Cardinal Severina," Eriador went on. "And they will do so for many different reasons. There are two members of The Ten known to be sympathetic towards Pope Clement. There are also those who have other, far more prosaic reasons to want Bruno spirited away to Rome."

I exhaled loudly through my nostrils. "Niccolo Celsi?"

"He is known to be taking money from the Pope in exchange for exerting his influence over the Doge. He has already dined with the cardinal. He thinks of nothing but making his earthly life more comfortable."

"You don't need to convince me of this, Master Eriador. I have known Celsi for a long time and had the measure of him many years ago."

Tomasso tapped me on the arm. "Time is moving on," he said. "You have not forgotten Gianvincenzo's dinner tonight, have you, Francesco?"

I just looked at him blankly, then, through my fatigue, I remembered that our mutual friend, Lord Pinelli was hosting one of his extraordinary dinners this evening. I could not let him down.

"You have been invited to Lord Pinelli's?" Eriador said, brightening. "That is serendipitous. I am expected there also. I understand the guest of honour is the new Professor of Mathematics at Padua, Galileo Galilei."

"I have heard of him," I replied.

Tomasso nodded. "Supposed to be a very clever man."

"Well, I very much look forward to seeing you there again tonight," the alchemist said. "There will be in attendance many who share our sympathies, as you would of course expect of Lord Pinelli. Indeed, I have heard talk that, before his arrest in May, Giordano met with Professor Galilei several times and they got on famously."

"Really?" I replied. "Then I think Galileo Galilei should tread very carefully."

Chapter Thirteen: Lord Pinelli's Palazzo

I had only been home for a few minutes and was trying to catch my breath when there came a knock at the door. I ignored it and let Isabella deal with it. She tapped gently at the door to my bedroom calling me. In her outstretched hand, she held a letter. I followed her through to the living room, found a knife and slit open the envelope.

I recognised the handwriting immediately, the florid script of my old friend Conte Gianvincenzo Pinelli. On the expensive paper were written just two words: 'Come early.'

Pinelli's family had originated in Milan and they owned vast tracts of land in the Levant, Mestre and in Florence and Padua. Gian could trace his ancestry back to the twelfth century, making his dynasty one of the most ancient in Italy. Although he lived for much of his time in Padua, he maintained one of the grandest palazzi in Venice, a four-storey house built some three centuries ago on the Grand Canal close to where the waterway turns north-east.

Gianvincenzo Pinelli was a man of leisure, but unlike many who inherit splendid fortunes, he used his time wisely. He was famous in Padua and Venice as a man of great learning who owned one of the largest libraries in Europe. He was interested in every facet of the world. He cultivated exotic floral species in a specially-designed greenhouse on the roof of his ancient Paduan palazzo and he spent many hours with natural philosophers and engineers devising machines and tinkering with lenses. He was the true embodiment of the modern European spirit of intellectual curiosity.

Feeling a little rattled from all that had transpired during this arduous day, I decided to walk the short distance to my friend's home knowing I needed to clear my mind. So much had happened, it made my head spin.

I was met at the main doors by the head of Pinelli's Venetian household staff, Ajith, an Indian who had worked for Pinelli for some quarter of a century. He wore a huge smile as he greeted me, his teeth pearlescent; his eyes the colour of burned walnut darted mischievously. I had known the man for many years and held him in high regard. Contrary to his lowly social status, he was a wise man who had learned to read and write and enjoyed a unique relationship with Pinelli who understood his servant's natural intelligence and had given him permission to use the vast library in the palazzo whenever he wished.

"The air is chill this evening, sir," he said as I stepped through the heavy oak doors and into the hall. "I think we may soon expect the first snow of the season."

Pinelli was descending the grand stairs, his hand extended. He was wearing a splendid jacket and breeches made from purple velvet intercut with gold-gilt wefts. In his left hand he held a potted flower. It was an extraordinary bloom, a purple only a few shades paler than my friend's tunic; perhaps the most perfect orchid I had ever seen anywhere.

"You see this, my most honoured friend?" Pinelli said. "It was grown from a packet of seeds sent to me by an acquaintance living in Goa."

"My Lord, how wonderful," I exclaimed.

He placed the flower on a side table. I thought he looked unwell in spite of his fashionable dress and his joviality. Perhaps, I mused, it was the light, but his skin had a greyness about it, his eyes appeared rheumy.

We shook hands. "Are you well, my friend?" I asked.

"I have felt better, Francesco." His voice sounded a little croaky and there was a sore edge to his usually mellifluous baritone. "I think I have caught a chill. But come, I need to talk to you."

We turned and I saw a flash of bright colour as a parrot swooped down from the mezzanine following the course of the gilt handrail of the stairs. The bird hung in the air for a second and then perched itself on Pinelli's shoulder, its claws gripping the sumptuous fabric.

"Ah! Henri," Pinelli said, turning as the parrot leaned forward to give his master's nose an affectionate little peck. "You want to join in the conversation, do you?"

I leaned forward and ran a finger over Henri's head feathers and he pushed back against me. "Buonasera," he croaked.

A wide passage led from the hall and at the far end high double doors opened onto Pinelli's library. Floor-to-ceiling walnut bookcases lined two sides of the big room; a fireplace in which a pile of logs burned dominated a third. The fourth wall was taken up by an expanse of glass, a window overlooking the Grand Canal. In the bay of the window stood an arrangement of chairs and sofas. To the left of these, a large rectangular desk was strewn with papers and piles of leather-bound books.

Lord Pinelli's library was said to contain more than five-thousand volumes. Many of these were extremely rare, tomes he had managed to acquire from the most obscure sources. In this room I had held in my hands an illuminated manuscript copy of Homer's *Iliad* dating from a millennium past. Gian owned first editions of works by Erasmus and Chaucer, whilst the prize of his collection was a handwritten, annotated edition of *The Divine Comedy* from 1320 simply entitled *Comedià* as it had been known originally. This copy was said to have been owned by Dante Alighieri himself.

I had been in this room many times but I never grew tired of it. Each time I saw it, the room was cast in a different light. Sometimes the sun would be low on the horizon lighting everything with its effulgent glow. At other times, on a winter night such as this one, the canal appeared as a ribbon of black velvet. We sat and the Conte tugged on a silk rope close to the arm of his chair. Ajith appeared in the doorway and strode over.

"Could you please fetch us one of the bottles of the Chianti that arrived this morning, Ajith?"

Pinelli turned to me, Henri the parrot flapped a little and moved to the back of my friend's chair. "This is exquisite. It comes from our family winery near San Gimignano."

"I think Pius would like to serve you, will that be to your liking, sir?"

Pinelli grinned at me. "Of course. Where is the rascal?"

"In the kitchens, sir."

A few minutes later, Ajith was back in the doorway with Pius beside him stretching up with his ridiculously long arms to take the tray from the servant. "Please be careful," Ajith said quietly.

Pius bared his teeth and made a high-pitched squeal in the back of his throat, turned on his heel and came towards us, the tray steady in his hands.

I had known Pius almost as long as I had been a friend of his master, many years before I had been exiled from the Republic. He was an orang-utan who had arrived on a ship delivering cinnamon from India, and had, according to his previous owner, come originally from a place called Borneo. Nobody could explain how he had been living in Ceylon, and sadly, although he was a very intelligent beast who possessed some uncannily human characteristics, he did not possess the power of speech, so perhaps we will never know.

My friend, the Conte had named the ape Pius as a little irreligious joke and claimed to trusted friends that his hairy servant was more intelligent and better-looking than the last Pius in the Vatican, Pius IV, who had died some thirty-seven years earlier. Gianvincenzo had spent many hours training his pet and Pius loved the attention. Indeed, he appeared not to see himself as a 'pet' at all.

For Pinelli, this effort was more than an idle pastime. He was fascinated by the intelligence of the orang-utan and planned one day to write a treatise about him. We often talked about how some animals have almost human intellect and pondered how it was that certain species far exceeded the mental capacities of others. After much discourse, we had narrowed it down to a simple matter of brain size.

Pius waddled over with what on a human face would have been a cock-sure grin. Arriving at a small table between our chairs, he placed the tray on the edge and carefully slid it into place.

"Don't drop it, Pius!" Henri the Parrott squawked.

The orang-utan ignored him, brought a glass over to me, which I took and then he handed the other to his master. Lifting the bottle, he stood before the Conte to show him the label before pouring a perfect measure into Gianvincenzo's glass and then into mine.

"Excellent!" Pinelli said and clapped his hands.

Pius bowed and started to retreat to the door.

Henri flapped his wings again and bobbed his head. "Idiot Pius!" he squawked.

I heard the ape make a sound so like a laugh it was almost frightening. Without breaking his step, he reached the door where Ajith stood looking on, a nervous expression still imprinted upon his features.

"Will there be anything else, sir?" the servant asked.

"Nothing for the moment, Ajith. But, if any of my guests arrive before we have finished our business here, please take them to the drawing room and allow Pius to continue with his sterling work."

Henri made a guttural sound and flew up to perch on a bookcase as Pinelli turned to me and raised his glass. He did not offer a toast, simply took a sip and made appreciative noises.

"So, what's all this about then, dear fellow?" I asked.

He took a while to speak, his eyes drawn to the glorious sight beyond the window to his left. We could both see a gondola lit up by a quartet of lamps glide through the icy, lambent water.

"I have heard that you have met the Apostolic Nuncio, Cardinal Santoro Severina."

I studied my friend's gaunt face. "I did indeed; yesterday, actually."

He sighed heavily. "He is a zealot, one of a cadre of extremists who mill around the Pope, whispering in his ear. He is very dangerous, Francesco, and I fear for our Republic."

I raised an eyebrow. "This is the second time today that someone has warned me that we are facing grave danger."

"Oh?"

"The Alchemist, Eriador. Tomasso and I visited him earlier this evening in connection with the murdered girl."

"Which murdered girl?"

I realised Pinelli had only this afternoon travelled from Padua and that the news had not yet reached there. I told him all I knew about the murder and related what the alchemist had divulged.

"I see. Well, Eriador is perhaps a little paranoid. He is deeply in thrall to the Hermetic Arts and I suspect he also samples what he sells!"

"Tomasso suggested so."

"But there is some truth in what the alchemist says. I do not believe it is, as he puts it, 'The End Times', but I think that the trial of Giordano Bruno will prove a turning point for our liberties and our independence from the Holy See."

"You don't believe the Doge is strong enough to resist Vatican pressure?"

"Quite honestly, Francesco, no, I do not. And, as our friend Eriador mentioned to you, there are many within the highest circles of power here who are, for a host of reasons, helping the Pope and his Nuncio."

"But we have our own judicial system."

"And you think that it is incorruptible?"

I sidestepped the remark with a question of my own. "You think the Pope's reach has grown long enough to force his will upon our Republic? I find that hard to believe."

"You have been away a long, long time, and only back a short while. The Church is more powerful and more extreme in protecting Doctrine than at any other time in history."

"It is under attack."

"Indeed it is, and what does a vicious animal do when it is cornered? It fights with every ounce of strength it can muster."

"I realise this," I replied. "I have not been so far from Italy that I was unaware of anything that was changing in our world, and in the time I have been back I have made efforts to catch up."

Pinelli had his hands apart, palms up. "I did not mean to . . ."

I waved it away. "What is so special about this cardinal?" I asked. "I saw him at work in the Council yesterday. He struck me as being quite typical of his kind, a shrewd manipulator, his tongue as forked as the viper he doubtless is. But what's new there?"

For the first time since Pius had left the room, Pinelli smiled. "I had forgotten what a precise judge of character you are my good fellow. Severina is, as you say, typical of his kind, but he is also powerful. He has the ear of the Pope and is Roberto Bellarmino's closest ally. But, there are two things that add fuel to the fire, if you'll ignore the horrible allusion. First, the nature of Giordano Bruno's heresy is so extreme that even some moderate theists are disinclined to protest at the Vatican's call to drag the man in chains to Rome where he will of course be incinerated. This makes his case an extraordinary one; certainly the most divisive in our history."

He paused for a moment and looked out again towards the water. "The second point is this: If the Doge submits to Rome and agrees to Bruno's extradition, it will be the start of the slide. We will be exposed, shown to be weak and pliable. This great nation of ours, possessors of the most powerful navy in Christendom, virtual emperors of far-flung lands and wealthy beyond the dreams of most mortals, shall become mere vassals of the Pope."

"Is that not an exaggeration . . . ?"

"No, it is not, Francesco." Pinelli's eyes blazed. "I feel you do not yet quite realise how much Bruno has become a symbol, a scapegoat, if you will. Pope Clement *must* have this man. Bruno has become too popular. Oh, not with the common people of course," he added quickly seeing my sceptical expression. "But with the educated, and he has gathered unto himself a substantial following in Frankfurt and Prague. His influence is growing."

"I met Bruno yesterday." I said.

Pinelli was stunned.

"You met him?"

"I visited him in his prison cell. There are some privileges associated with being a member of the Ten."

"You amaze me!"

"I wanted to learn about the man. I have read a little of his work, but I have not been able to follow his wanderings as well as you have."

"And what did you learn from him, Francesco?"

"I think he is going mad."

Pinelli raised his eyebrows. "I would not be altogether surprised. He has been kept in solitary confinement for five months now. From all I have heard, they are treating him worse than an animal prepared for the slaughter."

"That is certainly true, and I do not doubt his misfortunes weigh heavily upon his mind. But we both know he is not a truly great intellect. He is an emotional fellow, something of a dreamer with some rather exotic notions."

"But there is more to all this." Pinelli lowered his voice. "As you say, Bruno is indeed a dreamer and he is certainly a courageous soul; for all his flummery and his egomania, I like him. There is though one who will become far more important than Giordano. One who is the Christ to Bruno's John the Baptist." Pinelli shook his head. "Forgive me, my friend, my enthusiasm is running away with me. I speak of Galileo Galilei, a man I have come to know well."

"But he is a natural philosopher, not a mystic. From what I have heard, he shuns occultism, laughs at alchemists."

"You're right, Francesco, he does. But you see, natural philosophy is the real battleground now, and the way Galileo wants to present it will soon be seen as a terrible threat to conventional Church Doctrine."

"I'm confused, Gian."

He paused to gather his thoughts. "The Vatican is still obsessed with occultists and alchemists and men like Bruno who wish to alter the way the laity thinks, to change orthodoxy by attacking the institution of the Church and the Pope. Bruno shouts from the rooftops his opinions on what he perceives as the evil-doings of Clement and his cardinals. He tries to expose their debauchery, their money grabbing, their flaunting of the original principles of Christ and St' Paul. But what Galileo represents is a much greater threat.

He is a peerless genius who does not simply preach an alternate cosmology as Bruno does, he can support it with mathematical rigour, with analytical reasoning. The Church has not yet seen such a thing, and they have no idea what is about to hit them."

"And you think that if the Republic buckles and hands over our noble heretic to be burned, it will place the real genius, Galileo Galilei in grave danger?"

"That is exactly what we think."

"We?"

Pinelli closed his eyes for a moment. He looked up, and to me it seemed the weight on the man's shoulders had just doubled.

"I am sworn to secrecy," he said quietly. "But suffice it to say, I am not the only one who smells danger and wishes to save Venice."

"I'm sorry," I said gently, ". . . but I'm finding all this intrigue a little too much to handle." I suddenly felt incredibly weary again myself.

"I understand," Pinelli replied. "I have been exposed to all this for some time. I respect the fact that you are not convinced. But I hope that before too long you will begin to see my . . . our argument. In the meantime, I would just ask one favour of you."

"Of course."

"You have direct contact with Severina. Would you keep us apprised of his requests, his plans, as far as they are shared with the Ten and the Doge?"

I did not hesitate. "I will do that. In fact, I will do more. I will be listening hard to anything I overhear from my more devout colleagues concerning Bruno and pass on to you their thoughts and feelings on the matter. Let me reassure you, I have no sympathies with Rome at all, and, if you are right and our freedoms are under threat, I will move Heaven and Earth to protect us."

•

An hour after our talk I looked across the dinner table towards Gianvincenzo and found it hard to believe this was the same man who had met me that evening looking so pale and jaded. But you see, Conte Pinelli was a social animal and he came alive in the company of those he liked and admired. And tonight, in his grand palazzo, he had clustered around him some of the most exciting and intelligent people, not just native Venetians, but thinkers from all over Italy.

After the meal, we adjourned to the library. Ajith and his assistants, perhaps including the very clever Pius, had arranged a cluster of chairs facing a small dais. Rain beat against the massive window overlooking the canal. There were twelve of us in the audience, including myself and Tomasso with whom I had managed to have a quick word just before the meal. I had chastised him for attending when he should have been in bed, but he had merely laughed off the suggestion, drained his chalice and refilled it immediately.

Next to me sat a young man who introduced himself as one Hans Lippershey, a craftsman and maker of optical lenses from the Low Countries. He was, he told me, coming to the end of a year-long trip to the Italian Peninsula. He had visited Naples, Rome, Milan and Florence, but claimed that Venice was the highlight of his journey.

Directly behind me sat Paulo Sarpi dressed in his formal clerical robes. I was well-acquainted with him and liked him very much. Perhaps more than any other Venetian, this most respected philosopher, priest and political thinker was the one man who, thanks to his great learning, provided intellectual substance to support Venetian liberalism, especially over ecclesiastical matters. Needless to say, the Vatican despised him.

Galileo walked to the dais, paused for a moment behind a mahogany lectern and our chatter was quelled. Perhaps I should spare a moment to describe this noble fellow. You will have to forgive me because, although I quickly learned he was indeed a noble fellow (if from a lowly background), he did not actually offer such a wondrous initial impression. I had seen him eat over-enthusiastically at Pinelli's table and, considering he was the guest of honour invited this evening to speak on serious matters, I could not help but notice that he had consumed an inordinate quantity of strong wine.

Galileo is a hefty specimen: There, I have said it. Tall, broad-shouldered, receding orange hair, a rather ugly mole on his face; to me, his physical appearance and what I knew of his towering intellect seemed to chaff, one against the other. But then, who is to say that profound intelligence should be entwined with great beauty? For usually, it is not.

Before speaking, Galileo lowered his head very slightly as he contemplated a set of papers in front of him on the lectern.

"Gentlemen. I wish to thank you for inviting me here this evening. I know, from speaking to our esteemed host, Conte Pinelli." And he nodded towards my friend seated in a cushioned chair to the side of the dais. ". . . that you are all men of liberal mind, men of great knowledge and learning, so I have no fear of pious retribution for what I am about to expostulate."

A ripple of warm laughter spread through the gathering.

"The target of my philosophy is not the Church itself, but of course, what I have earned, and I am able to prove will be seen as dissenting from Doctrine, for the world is not as the Church would have it be.

"Some of you will have heard of my experiment atop the leaning tower in Pisa. My colleague at the University in that city, Professor Girolamo Borro is a worthy scientist, but, either through fear of Rome, or from a deep-rooted and strictly orthodox piety, he refuses to believe the evidence of his own eyes. He insists still that the great Greek philosopher Aristotle is irrefutably right about everything!"

He gazed about the room, his big dark eyes scanning our faces. He was a powerful speaker, a man with a forceful character to backup his formidable intellect. I was very impressed with the young man. "But Aristotle was wrong. In fact, I would say he was mistaken about more matters of philosophy than those about which he was right."

We all laughed again.

Galileo paused for effect. "What I have just said of course would be considered heresy, for Aristotle, as you all know, is a figure in our past whose ideas are now so intimately intertwined with the Christian faith that they may only be separated with supreme effort and with the will of the Church. Thanks to the actions of Henry in England some sixty-five years ago and the challenge of Martin Luther even longer ago, the Church is now at its most defensive. It sees itself attacked from all sides, and indeed it is. But that, my friends, is as it should be, because orthodoxy is wrong in so many ways and the Vatican is an immovable rock in an ocean of new knowledge.

"My experiments in Pisa showed that Aristotle was incorrect about one specific aspect of natural philosophy. I proved that, barring the effect of air resistance, all objects with equal mass fall at the same rate under the influence of gravity. But I now wish to proselytise far more radical notions. I believe I shall soon find *proof* to support the notion that this earth upon which we live, does not lie at the centre of the universe, but that, instead, it is merely a planet like the silver-veiled orb of Venus and the red fury of Mars. I will show that our world is nothing more than another planet circling the Sun, and that the Sun is positioned at the centre of the universe."

The room was hushed. Most of us gathered there were familiar with Nicolaus Copernicus's treatise *De revolutionibus orbium coelestium* published half a century earlier, but the ideas it encompassed had always been considered to be mere exoteric theorising, unprovable rhetoric that had been scoffed at by the Curia in Rome. Men such as him had gone around Europe pronouncing the long-dead Copernicus to have been a visionary who had offered the unalloyed truth about the universe and humanity's place in it. But Bruno himself had been perceived as an extremist, a revolutionary. The young fellow before us that night in Pinelli's home was of an entirely different breed to Bruno. Galileo was an intellectual, a mathematician, an experimenter. And now he claimed he would soon be able to *prove* Copernicus's theory to be correct. In that moment, I understood what Gianvincenzo had meant when he had compared Galileo and Bruno to Christ and John the Baptist.

I could sense a ripple of excitement pass through the gathering and Galileo was just about to continue when we all heard a crashing sound from the hall, followed by raised voices echoing beyond the library doors.

Pinelli was out of his seat. We all looked to him. "Master Galilei, gentlemen, I am terribly sorry."

Galileo seemed confused for a moment and went to say something, but Pinelli was marching towards the doors. He was already halfway there when they flew open and Ajith burst in with another, younger servant immediately behind him.

I stood up and saw Galileo stepping down carefully from the dais. Ajith took two steps into the room, came up close to his master and whispered something in his ear. I saw Pinelli's face in profile as the blood drained from his cheeks, and in the fire glow, he looked much the same as he had when I first arrived that evening; all his former bonhomie had evaporated to nothing.

He turned as the servants retreated to beyond the doors. "Gentlemen; something unexpected has happened. Could I beg your indulgence for a moment? I must attend to my servants. Please eat and drink." He waved a hand towards a table close by.

He caught my eye and I understood immediately that he wanted me to go with him. I slipped through the group as unobtrusively as I could, Tomasso following behind. We reached the doors just as Pinelli, a few seconds ahead of us, came alongside the servants standing together like statues. It was only then I noticed they were drenched through and stood in a shallow puddle on the marble floor.

"What has happened?" I asked as I approached the men.

Pinelli turned to Tomasso and me. "A man has been murdered – at the foot of the stairs outside." He led the way to the front doors. A third servant was already there and opened them. The wind blasted into the hall driving a sheet of rain before it and I felt the cold shock on my face. Ajith and one of his boys grabbed a torch each from brackets hanging either side of the doors and they stepped ahead of us into the freezing, wet night.

The moon hung behind a bank of rain clouds out of sight and even with the torches the way was dark. We took the stairs carefully. I could see a black shape on the cobbles just beyond the steps between the stairs and the waters of the Grand Canal. A path ran left and right that circled back around the palazzo and on to a lane. It was meant to be a private waterfront, but people often slipped along the path as a shortcut.

Ajith and the other torchbearer crouched each side of a man lying on his front. He was dressed entirely in black and I could see a few wisps of stringy white hair protruding from under his cap. His arms were stretched out above his head. I saw immediately that his left hand had been mutilated, the middle two fingers cut off crudely just above the knuckle.

I knelt down to the right of the body. Tomasso crouched the other side of the corpse. Together, we eased the man over. White hair plastered the dead man's face, water and blood dripped from a gapping wound across the flesh of his neck. But in spite of the horrible damage done, the identity of the man was unmistakable. It was the alchemist, Eriador.

Chapter Fourteen: In the Laboratory

I took Pinelli to one side so that we were out of earshot of the others.

"This is grave news," he said before I could utter a word.

I nodded. "It is. But Gian, will you help me get the body to my laboratory? We have to learn as much as we can about who killed poor Eriador. I don't know about you, but this is all a bit disquieting, to say the least."

Pinelli looked into my eyes. "You are convinced you may fine clues to a murder from a dead man's body?"

"I am."

"Then I shall help you."

Pinelli sent the servants off to fetch a small cart, and Tomasso, holding one of the torches, walked over to us. "What happens now?"

"I must return to my guests," Pinelli said.

"I am taking Eriador's body to my house," I said matter-of-factly. "And Tomasso, I think you should come with me."

"What? Why? I mean . . . Oh, Lord, you're not . . ."

I sighed and turned to Pinelli. "My friend, thank you for your hospitality and the chance to meet Galileo. He is everything you said he would be, and I understand your anxieties for the man's safety."

He looked solemn. "And you are right. We need to know what is behind this new atrocity." He glanced over to where Eriador lay. The servants approached pushing a wooden contraption on three wheels. It rumbled over the cobbles. One of the wheels needed lubrication and squeaked. "Please get in touch soon. I want to know what you discover; and if there is anything I can do, don't hesitate . . ." He turned and walked wearily back to the house.

The servants helped me lift Eriador onto the cart. One of the men came from the palazzo with a large square of black fabric and I helped him drape it over the dead man and tuck it under his head and feet. I then took a torch from one of the servants and the men returned to Pinelli's.

"I'm not happy about this," Tomasso said quietly.

"Well you don't have to help if you really don't want to, Tomasso. I'm sure Pinelli could get you a gondola to take you home if you prefer." I could see my friend's eyes in the flickering torch light. He looked very pale.

He shook his head resignedly. "Come on." And he picked up the left handle of the cart with one hand and held his torch aloft in the other. I saw him wince, grabbed the other handle and we pulled away, slowly at first, along the bumpy path - the rain, chill as ice, soon soaking us.

There were many people about and the taverns were full and noisy, but no one took any notice of us. In the half light we could have passed for tradesmen clattering along with a cartful of vegetables, cotton, or boxes of books for that matter. We did not exchange a word the whole way and when we finally pulled up outside my house we were both panting from our exertions; the cart and its load were heavy, the wheels old and warped.

"Feel free to go home, Tomasso," I said. "You really do look all-in."

"And who will help you get the alchemist to your chopping block, Francesco? You're housekeeper? I will help you that far, then I'll leave."

"As you wish."

I pulled my door key from my pocket and started to turn it when it opened inwards. Isabella stood there in her shift and a thick woollen robe, a torch held aloft. "Sir, I hoped it was you," she said. Then she saw Tomasso. "Lord Cicogna."

"Isabella, we have work to do. Would you be so kind as to make up a fire in the laboratory for us?"

She glanced at the cart and then at me and nodded before retreating into the house. Tom was in too much pain to help, but I just managed to lift the dead man, the cloth wrapped around him, and stagger into the house, through the living-room and down a short flight of stairs into my laboratory. I placed Eriador on the floor and cleared the table in the centre of the room before taking a deep breath, crouching down with my back straight and hauling up the dead alchemist. Isabella gave us suspicious looks as she started the fire in the grate at the far end of the room. I lit a couple more torches and placed them in brackets along the walls closest to the table.

Isabella pulled up from where she had been crouching by the kindling flames, wiped her hands on a rag beside the fireplace and took two steps towards us. I noticed her eyeing the bundle on the table.

"Thank you, Isabella," I said gently. "You may go to bed now. We will be busy all night."

My housekeeper had started to turn when Eriador's arm slipped from under the cloth covering and swung around in the torch glow a few feet from her. She saw it and screamed.

I walked around the table and went to place a hand on the woman's shoulder. She pulled back, terror and disgust in her eyes.

"Isabella," I said. "This poor man was murdered tonight. I shall examine him to find out as much as possible about who committed the crime."

The woman had a hand to her mouth and I could tell, even in the poor light that the blood had drained from her cheeks. She stifled a small squeal, swung away and left the laboratory. We could hear her climbing the stairs. I walked over to the door and closed it. "You'd better go too, Tomasso. Thank you for your help."

He stood still. "What exactly are you going to do, Francesco? I simply don't understand."

I tilted my head and regarded my friend. "You are exhausted. Just go home. I know you don't feel comfortable with this. Leave me be. I can manage."

"I want to know, Francesco," Tomasso walked over to the prone form on the table and pulled back the cloth to reveal the fresh corpse.

"You wish to help?"

Tomasso nodded. "I do. I trust you. If you believe you can learn from the dead, then that is good enough for me. It's clear this man died by a foul hand. And it is too fucking close to home if you ask me. Who might be next? We need to learn as much as we can, and you are the man to unveil secrets."

"I appreciate your faith in me." I reached up to a shelf and pulled down a small teak box, then walking to the end of the table, I opened the box to reveal my surgical instruments, a row of glistening scalpels, a small saw, scissors and a collection of spatulas. Placing this set on a side bench, I paced over to the top of the table and lowered my hands each side of Eriador's head, to position a wooden block under his neck so that his head tilted back.

"It is all a matter of empirical reasoning," I said. "In Persia I studied for many months with the great teacher Ibn-al-Aznad. He is a master of *automsia cadaverum*, the technique for learning the cause of death, especially with victims of murder. He has written of the recommended procedures to follow."

I looked up and saw that Tomasso was watching me carefully, fascination gradually overcoming his reticence.

"We begin by an examination of the exterior – clothes, skin, fingernails," I said and started to remove Eriador's garments. He was wearing an expensive fur-lined coat and under this, a woollen tunic and a pair of sturdy boots. Soon, the man's bruised and bloodied body lay naked on the table, his clothes in a neat pile on the floor.

"He has not been completely soaked through by the rain," Tomasso observed. "His undergarments are dry."

"Good point, my friend. Which means he was not lying dead outside Pinelli's home for very long. The rain has been very heavy. I estimate he could not have been killed more than ten or twenty minutes before the servants found him. I also think there was something of a struggle." I pointed to fresh abrasions and bruising around Eriador's torso. "He took a few blows to the face as well," I added and turned the man's head into the light to reveal dark flesh under his left eye and the skin of his nose split at the bridge. "Also," I said, rolling the body over and inspecting Eriador's lower back. "Little blood has collected in the tissues of the anterior which adds to the evidence that he has not been dead for long. In a corpse, blood falls under the effect of gravity."

I plucked a scalpel from my box of instruments and turned back to the corpse. Lifting the alchemist's undamaged hand, I checked his fingernails. "See here Tomasso." I showed him the dead man's fingertips.

"There is something under his nails."

"There is." I ran the blade of my scalpel under the nail and lifted the shiny tip into the glow from the nearest torch. "A small lump of bloody flesh." I said. "Eriador put up a fight."

I placed the material into a porcelain dish. "Let's take a look at his wounds."

The gash across Eriador's throat stretched almost from ear to ear. The rain had washed away much of the blood, but the wound still oozed a little even though the man's heart had stopped beating almost an hour ago. "Clearly the killer was right-handed," I said.

"How can you possibly know that?" Tomasso leaned in closer.

"See here, the flesh has been sliced at an angle."

"So?"

"Well, think on it." I shifted a few inches so that I was directly behind Eriador's head. "You slit someone's throat from behind, yes?"

"Not always."

"Very well. Eriador was attacked from behind, because, if his throat was cut face-on, the gash would look completely different. You have enough experience of these things, Tomasso. In battle, a sword wound to the throat from the front is easy to distinguish. The cut is always deeper one side than the other, deeper where the sword first penetrates the flesh." I demonstrated.

Tomasso nodded. "That is true. Go on."

This cut is at an angle of about twenty degrees and you can see here?" I moved the flap of dead tissue with the tip of a scalpel. "The incision is raised to Eriador's right side. The killer stood behind him and cut like so." I went through the motion of quickly drawing a blade across the throat, pulling up a little at the end of the sweep.

"If the murderer was left-handed, the rise in the slit would be to the left."

"Ingenious."

"Logic, Tomasso, logic. And there is more. The killer was considerably taller than the victim."

"And how the fuck do you know that?"

"Again, because of the angle," I explained. "If the killer and victim were close in height, the gash would be more horizontal, with perhaps a slight angle to it. As I said just now, this angle ..." And I opened the wound with a finger and thumb, is at least twenty degrees to the horizontal."

"Eriador was quite short."

"I would guess barely an inch over five feet. The killer is a relatively tall man because the angle is quite pronounced."

I turned to the alchemist's mutilated hand, lifting it gently and inspecting the stumps where his two middle fingers had been severed. "Amputated post-mortem."

Tomasso gave me a puzzled look.

"I noticed there was not much blood under his arms where he had lain."

"But the rain?"

"Yes, but if his fingers had been removed from his living body his shirt would have been soaked with blood and it would have collected under his hands."

"There is obviously some meaning to this," Tomasso observed, nodding towards the mutilated hand.

"Of course. It is the *Mano Cornuto*. The killer removed the alchemist's fingers to create the symbol."

"The Sign of the Horns? That would imply the killer viewed Eriador as somehow evil?"

"I'm not clear on this," I said, shaking my head. "It could mean all sorts of things. It's impossible to tell from what little we know." I bent close to inspect Eriador's wounds. "That's interesting."

"What?"

"See here, I lifted the bloodied hand so Tomasso could see the remains of the dead man's fingers clearly. "See the way the flesh is cut? The wound is at an angle, just like the slash at the alchemist's throat."

"What are you implying now my friend?"

I moved round the table, holding up Eriador's hand, the palm facing away from me. Tomasso stood beside me. "If you were to remove the fingers, you would push the hand to the ground and cut downwards, would you not?" I demonstrated the action, placing the Alchemist's palm down on the edge of the table beside him.

"I imagine so."

"Of course you would, Tomasso. You would draw the blade sideways, like so. Now, notice the stump. It tells a similar story to the neck wound."

Tomasso leaned in and I pointed a finger to the ragged edge of flesh where the digit had been amputated. "What do you notice?"

"The slice is angled upwards to the left."

"Which means the fingers were removed by a left-handed person."

"An accomplice."

"It must be so. Whoever slashed Eriador's throat did not remove the victim's fingers."

Tomasso was shaking his head slowly. "I'm not surprised some people call you a heretic. You're a fucking wizard!"

"Nonsense, Tomasso. It is simply deductive reasoning, looking at the evidence before your eyes and drawing logical conclusions that fit the observed facts."

"I get it, Francesco, but you can understand how others . . ."

"Oh yes, I do, my friend. There are few who think logically, but it is the way of the future, the way civilisation shall move forward and throw off the shackles of superstition and ignorance."

"So what now?"

"I see no reason to delve inside the man's body. He's wounds are obvious and he died very recently. I suspect there is nothing more to learn from such an exhaustive study."

"I'm very glad to hear it."

I grinned at my friend. "But our work is not yet over this evening."

"Oh?"

"I think we should return to the victim's home. Eriador was murdered and mutilated for a reason, and I fancy we may find some hints as to why in the place in which he worked, his laboratory and library."

Chapter Fifteen: Eriador's

Tomasso and I decided that we would tarry at my house until just before the dawn. We were both greatly fatigued, and so Isabella made up a bed for my friend in front of the fire in the living-room and I gave her strict instructions to rouse us no later than the fifth hour past midnight.

I fell asleep almost the moment I hit the pillow but, I was thrown immediately into a succession of troubled dreams that almost woke me. I was in this very house with my parents and my sister. It was Christmas, the winter before the plague struck the Republic, and we were all happy and light-hearted. But then, my loved ones disappeared and I was totally alone wandering through the empty rooms. The windows were boarded up. I was stumbling in the dark; a rat scurried away from me. Turning into the bedroom, it was lit by a guttering torch, but I could just make out Teresa lying naked on my bed. I crouched beside her, but as I leaned in to kiss her she had turned into a rotted corpse.

I awoke sitting up in the darkness wreathed in sweat, my heart racing, a sour taste in my mouth. Creeping through the living-room and down the stairs into my laboratory, I lit a torch and made my way to the bowl and jug of water I kept in the corner. Out of the corner of my eye I saw the dark shape of Eriador where we had left him on the table. I washed quickly, feeling the icy water invigorate me and flush away the remnants of my fraught and cloying dreams. Close to the back door stood a rolled up rush mat. I shut the door behind me and stepped out into the moonlit chill. The exit from the room led onto a tiny rectangle of grass. The dawn was at least an hour away, the sky clear, a dark velvety mauve filled with stars. I saw dense clouds arching over me. Frost sparkled in the moon's rays and I heard it crunch underfoot as I crossed the grass, arranged my meditation mat and lowered myself down. I adopted the lotus position, pinched fingers and thumbs together on my knees and let myself slide into the meditative state I had been taught by my Indian masters. Relaxing every muscle, I steadied my breathing, allowing it to become slow and shallow. Gradually, I let loose all my ties to this material existence, releasing my anxieties and my mental concerns.

I lost all sense of time and came back to the physical world to see Tomasso approaching from the doorway of my laboratory. He seemed a little surprised, unsure what to do. He knew about my habits but had never seen me meditate.

"It is quite fine, Tomasso," I said dreamily. "I am finished." I started to rise.

"You wanted us to get over to Eriador's before daylight. Isabella woke me and said you were out here. I left it as long as I could."

"That is very considerate of you." I gripped his shoulder and we walked slowly back to the door into my laboratory.

The campo had started to lighten. The temperature had fallen since last night and as we walked towards Calle del Spezier to the west of S. Maurizo I saw the first snowflake of winter fall right before my eyes. It wavered in the air and landed on the ground dissolving almost instantly. Ajith had been correct last night. By the time we had crossed Campo Sando Stefano and weaved a path to the waters of the Grand Canal, powdery flakes of snow were tumbling steadily to earth.

At the water, we found a small ferry to take us across the canal. The wind had picked up and swept the snow at us from the north. The ferry reached the far side of the Grand Canal at a quay situated along one edge of Campo d'Carita. I paid the ferryman and we stepped ashore to a silent and still square where even the pigeons slept. The wind coming off the water cast more snow at us, wetting our faces. We turned away from it and headed across the square before slipping into a sheltered alleyway to the north.

Neither of us spoke as we trudged on taking a left turn, then a sharp right, crossing a pair of short bridges and still seeing no one but hearing the first stirrings from nearby homes. This was a relatively poor neighbourhood, populated with families of workers from the markets, cleaners, apprentice butchers and bakers. I heard a baby cry, the sound of a plate being dropped, quickly followed by a loud curse.

Reaching the Church of S.Barnaba close to where we had pulled up aboard a gondola the previous evening, hazy sunlight was breaking through between the buildings to the east catching the wisps of snow twirling in the wind. We dashed across the open space and ducked into a narrow alleyway on the far side. This led straight to the front door of the deceased alchemist.

Tomasso made swift work of prising open the door. Leaning close to the wood, he slipped a small knife into the lock, twisted clockwise then in the opposite direction. My friend, it seemed, had, over the years, acquired some dubious skills.

With the door closed quickly behind us, it was black inside the house, but I remembered how Eriador had taken us to the reception room and beyond. I stumbled in the dark and felt the edge of a table a few feet to my left. Running the palm of my hand over the top of the table, I soon found a candle stick holding a slender candle, the tallow dry and clumpy about the top of the holder.

I withdrew a small tinderbox I always kept about my person and struck the flint and metal edge together to generate a spark. The charcloth inside the box lit up and I levered the contraption to the side, lighting the candle before closing the end of the tinderbox to gutter the flame.

When lit, the candle immediately gave off a strong scent of pig fat. It produced a mean glow, but with the window shutters closed and no other illumination, the room was soon relucent with a pale reddish umbra. Using the candle, I lit another and handed it to Tomasso who followed me out of the room through a narrow doorway at the far end and onto a corridor, the candle flames producing flickering shadows across the walls. We soon reached the room in which Eriador had spoken to us little more than twelve hours ago.

"Do you know how to find his laboratory, Tomasso?" I swept the light in an arc before me.

"I do. On two occasions the alchemist hosted the Hermetic group to which we were affiliated."

"Playing wizards and warlocks?"

Tomasso looked serious. "Well, if you don't want my help."

"Tom; where is your sense of humour?"

"It is still asleep," he replied, pulling a face. "Come, it is through that door and towards the back of the house."

He led the way along another narrow passageway until we reached a sturdy wooden door. It was unlocked and he eased it back. Beyond the sphere of illumination produced by our candles, a short flight of stone steps fell away into the darkness. Between us, we sparked up a row of torches along a stone wall to the right of the steps and Eriador's private laboratory stood argent in a frail, flickering light.

It was a surprisingly large room with a small door in the wall opposite the entrance which I presumed led to the rear garden of the property. To the left of this, a fireplace was set into the wall. The place stank of *sal ammoniac* such as one might smell in a fish market. Alcoves had been cut into the stone wall on the left and I could see two rows of leather-bound books. At one end of the shelf rested a human skull. On the lower shelf I saw a large jar filled with a green-hued liquid. In the weak glow from the torches, the shape of a grey, vein-laced foetus was just discernible. The area close to the fireplace was taken up with a hefty round table upon which was set a menagerie of specialised equipment. I recognised much of it; a still very similar to ones I had seen in Lebanon and used there to make the local aniseed drink, *Arak*. This was connected to an *alembic*, another piece of alchemical equipment derived from the Middle East, and used here, I suspected, to distil liquids. A pair of retorts holding round-bottomed glass flasks stood to one end of the table. I walked over to inspect them and saw a yellowy paste in the base of one; the other was empty and clean. Next to these items stood an *aludel*, for condensing vapours, a large bronze pestle and mortar, and clutched together, a collection of at least half a dozen crucibles. Two of these were charred black inside. I lifted one and wafted my hand over it to direct any vapours gently to my nose rather than sniffing directly. It possessed an intense sulphurous odour that assaulted my nostrils. Pulling back, I returned the item to the table.

Tomasso was surveying the shelves of books.

"You must have seen these before," I commented.

He gave me a puzzled look.

"When you had your gatherings here."

"Oh no. Eriador guarded his books jealously. We could never so much as touch them."

"They do look rather special." I lifted the end volume, turned back the cover and read the title: *The mirror of alchemy composed by the thrice-famous and learned fryer, Roger Bacon. Also a most excellent and learned discourse of the admirable force and efficacie of Art and Nature, written by the same Author. With certain other worthie treatises of the like argument.*

Handing the book to Tomasso, I plucked another from the second shelf. This was called, *The Aurora of the philosophers.* On the inside page was written: *By Theophrastus Paracelsus.* Chapter One was entitled: 'Concerning the Origin of the Philosopher's Stone.' The pages were marked by hand, which I assumed to be Eriador's writing. He wrote in Latin, and they were mostly remarks about what the author had reported. Eriador sometimes took issue, but mostly, he added observation. Some passages were underlined.

"So much energy, not to mention ink, expended on this stuff," I sniffed and returned the book to the shelf. Tomasso pointedly ignored me.

On a side table close to the fire stood another collection of equipment. In the centre lay a porcelain bowl about a hand's width in diameter. I lifted it up to the light and could see a pool of tiny black spheres. I knew what they were immediately, unrefined seeds of the poppy. I called Tomasso over and showed him.

"It was never exactly a very well kept secret," he commented.

"I suppose not."

I wandered over to the fireplace. A large bowl hung on a cradle directly over the middle of the grate. Under this there lay a small pile of ash and partially burned wood, and in the poor light, I almost missed the scattering of white, rough-edged rectangles.

"Tomasso? Could you bring over one of those wall torches?" I lowered my candlestick to the stone lip of the fireplace.

He crouched beside me and held the torch aloft. "What is it?"

"Paper." I sifted through the ash to pluck out the closest of the pieces.

It was almost square, about an inch to a side, the edges ragged and damaged by the fire. Rifling through the ashes with a poker drawn from a rack to one side of the fireplace, I managed to expose half a dozen other scraps. Trying not to damage them further, I placed them gently on a clear patch of table close to Eriador's instruments and vessels.

The paper was covered with writing and I managed to lay out the pieces in the correct order quickly realising I had only about two thirds of the total, the rest must have lain as ash in the grate.

"They are badly charred," Tomasso observed.

"Indeed. It is almost impossible to make out more than a few words."

"There's the number 11."

"Could be a large number though, Tom. See, the number is close to the edge, and the burn mark there could be covering up another digit."

I ran a finger across one of the fragments. "These are some sort of coded figures. They look almost like hieroglyphics. It would make sense that anything Eriador tore up and burned would have been composed in some sort of code. But there are also words of Latin . . . *resistentia nostrae*, 'our Resistance'. Eriador used the word 'Resistance' when we talked with him last night. He used it to describe those who had banded together to contest the authorities over Giordano Bruno."

"Jesus! You think the alchemist was one of them?"

"Why are you so surprised by the notion? Eriador was hardly the most conventional fellow, now was he? He would have had no love for Rome. He was clearly opposed to religious orthodoxy and the pope's political influence beyond Rome."

"True. And he would have all the appropriate connections within the Republic and beyond."

I looked up for the first time since arranging the paper fragments on the table. "Which of course casts a whole new light upon why he was murdered."

"Are you sure there is a connection, Francesco? Could it not be a coincidence?"

"It could, but there is no clear evidence to support any hypothesis yet. And indeed, the method by which poor Eriador was dispatched was all too similar to the way the prostitute, Antoinette was killed. I cannot believe that she was part of any clandestine political group!"

"But she knew Eriador."

"Yes, she did . . ."

We both heard the sound at the same time. It came from the room above, the entrance hall and reception area that led directly from the street. For a moment, I consoled myself in the belief that it was nothing more than the door to the street knocked open and shut again by the wind. But then I heard the sound of boots on a wooden floor.

"The back door," I hissed, gathering up the pieces of paper and tucking them into a pocket in his breeches. Tomasso paced over to the torches in the wall brackets and snuffed them out.

The door was locked, but Tomasso snapped the mechanism in a moment and we slipped out into the freezing air pulling the door to, leaving only a narrow gap between the edge and the frame. We heard boots on stone stairs as two men came down into Eriador's laboratory. They were dressed in black robes and moved quickly in the barren light produced by the torches they carried. Their hoods lay heavy about their heads and hung low, their faces cast in deep shadow, features completely indistinguishable. I caught a glint of steel. They were both armed, their swords unsheathed. Reaching the floor of the laboratory, they swung their torches in the air. Jagged shadows danced about the equipment. The figure closest to us stopped. I heard him sniff and then say something unintelligible to his companion.

"They know we have been here," Tomasso whispered. "Francesco, let's get the fuck out!"

"Wait."

The man who had spoken approached the newly-extinguished torches in their brackets. Even from where we crouched we could see a faint glow from the embers newly-dampened.

"Francesco!"

I lifted a hand. "Just a second."

"They're armed."

"I know that. I want to see their faces."

"God's cock, man!"

I lost sight of them for a moment and felt a tremor of fear pass through me. I started to rise and step back when a face appeared at the crack in the door no more than a few inches from me. The door flew outwards. Reacting with a speed that surprised me, I kicked the door back with all my strength, feeling it shudder. The man cried out and I did not wait a second longer. Spinning on my heel, I ran into the darkness, just glimpsing Tomasso's outline in the moonlight a few paces ahead of me. Then he was gone, and I could not understand where he had vanished to. I heard a clank of metal and a hissed curse from behind me and I knew the two men would waste no time reaching me if I tarried for even a second.

The ground was sodden and I slipped, almost falling onto my backside. Then I saw where Tomasso had gone. In the dim light, I could just make out how the ground fell away to my left. I slid down the slope, caking my hands in freezing mud and feeling it squelch down into my boots. I reached a level surface strewn with rotting leaves, and there before me, was a small, jagged opening in the garden wall.

Tomasso's head appeared at the hole. "Hurry," he snapped. "For Lord's sake, Francesco! Stop fucking dithering."

I slipped through the opening and we were on a slender laneway running beside the house. To our right lay a narrow canal, but no bridge crossed it and the path expired just before it reached the water.

"This way." Tomasso twisted on his heel and sped off, his coat flapping in the wind. The snow was heavier now and had started to settle on the cobbles, a crust of glistening white.

The two men had made it through the opening in the wall. I pushed on and caught up with Tomasso. We dashed around a bend to our left. I stole a glance behind us as we took the corner and saw our pursuers taking their bearings. They spotted me as I ducked into the alley. I ran on, feeling the sweat break out on my skin.

I was right behind Tom, so close I almost crashed into him as he pulled into a passage to our left and ran on into a tunnel little wider than my shoulder's breadth. We emerged into another lane and saw an open gate onto a small courtyard to our right. We thought as one and dived through, pulling the gate closed, crouching, holding our breath and trying to slow our racing hearts.

We heard the two men enter the tight tunnel. One of them fired an instruction, but I could not make out his words. Only one of them emerged from the exit. He ran straight past our hiding place, the sound of his boots quietening as he moved further away.

I left it a few moments before easing the gate outward, then turned left, back the way we had come. Just before I reached the mouth of the tunnel, I noticed another alleyway to our right.

"Must lead back to the campo," I said.

"Avoid open spaces," Tomasso replied.

"I'm not happy about going back through that tunnel."

He nodded and I took the lead, crouching and keeping to the shadows.

We made it to the end of the alleyway without seeing either man. I stopped at the point where the passage opened out onto the square. Tomasso positioned himself on the other side of the alleyway and we peered round the corner.

"Clear," he said.

We pulled round keeping close to the wall of the corner building and skirting along the northern side of the campo. A front door opened immediately to my right and I pulled back as an elderly man stepped out onto the cobbles. He didn't see us and walked in the opposite direction, shuffling along dragging a heavy-looking sack across the treacherous snow.

I saw the two men appear to our left and shoved Tomasso none-to-gently into the shadows of a doorway.

The hooded figures still had their swords unsheathed and were looking about warily. From their gait I could tell they were tired. They did not see

108

us and turned down the alley from which we had recently emerged. We waited several minutes to ensure they had passed further north, back towards Eriador's home, and then we dashed to the south side of the campo, dived into an alley and kept running until we reached Campo S.Maurizo.

"You get on home, Tomasso," I said as we arrived at my front door. "You look terrible!"

"I must say I have felt better," he winced and put a hand to his side.

"Be gone with you. Rest. I shall call in on you before nightfall to see how you are."

"It was fun though, wasn't it, my friend?" He laughed. "Just like old times!"

"Actually, I'm rather too old to be chased around the city by men with swords."

"Nonsense, Francesco. Where's your sense of adventure?"

I gripped his shoulder. "Watch yourself on the way home."

"Don't worry. I shall."

.

The house was empty and I immediately felt that something had changed. I could not put my finger on it. Lighting a torch, I looked around the living room and saw that everything was neat and tidy. Too tidy. Isabella was a slovenly housekeeper and I only kept her on through a sense of family duty. Something was not right here.

Isabella's apron lay on a table, her front door key rested on top. The woman could neither read nor write, but I realised immediately that it was her way of telling me she had left my employ.

I walked over and picked up the key. "I can't say I blame you, Isabella Dioli," I muttered.

Turning back to my humble living-room, I suddenly felt an overwhelming tiredness, a deep-seated weariness that I knew came from an accumulation of exertion and lack of sleep. At times like this I really felt my age and it sent a ripple of anxiety through me. I have no fear of death. I learned much on this subject from the great mystics in India with whom I talked at length, and who taught me to understand death as being part of life. Yet, at the same time, I still have no wish to die. But, that aside, I told myself, I had no time for weariness now. Two murders in as many days and quite possibly linked; and for what possible reason? Who would commit such terrible crimes? They were ritualistic murders, not simple slaughters prompted by rage or passion. They had been planned, premeditated. But why?

I poured myself a tankard of ale, walked over to the table in the centre of the room and pulled out a chair, catching sight of Isabella's apron and key and feeling a pang of ... what? Annoyance? Disappointment? Shame? It was a blend of all three. I had not made life easy for the poor woman. She was a simple soul and had obviously felt confronted, nay, offended by what she had, quite fairly perceived to be my eccentric habits. Perhaps she had even been mocked by her friends, our neighbours, egged on into walking out. But what a pity. She had been associated with the Sagredo family for a long time, and I would miss her.

Pulling myself up, I put my hand in my pocket. The paper from Eriador's laboratory crumbled to powder. Cursing, I walked over to the fire, extracted a lit piece of wood and descended the short set of stairs that led to my laboratory. The door creaked as I opened it. I ignited a pair of torches and watched the room brighten. Eriador's corpse lay stiff on the table.

I had seen many dead bodies and each had their own associated poignancy. At the Battle of Lepanto in October 1571, I had witnessed the death of many hundreds of men, Venetians and Turks. They all bled the same, all breathed their last with the same resignation. As a medic, human suffering had become part of life and I had dedicated myself to alleviating that anguish as best I could. But in this I had been soundly beaten by the plague four years after Lepanto. The Reaper had stomped all over me, crushed me into the dirt, for he had decided not to take my life but instead forced me to watch, helpless as first my parents and then my fourteen-year-old sister, Rosa had fallen under his dark persuasion.

And abroad, I had also witnessed death. I had become close friends with a Nepalese monk, a very wise man named Tenzin, which means 'Holder of Knowledge'. He died aged one hundred and twenty-one. The other monks of the monastery assured me that he was indeed this ancient. When life left him, he was laid out on a stone platform in the courtyard of the monastery and left there for three days and nights, and then his companions allowed the vultures and other animals to consume his body and return him to the cycle of nature, his flesh and his bones becoming, first food, and then excrement, to be appropriated by the earth and broken down into their fundamentals, whereupon they were re-consumed and became other living things. The monks called this *gnam sku phun gdan zhu*; or in our tongue, 'Sky Burial'.

Eriador's skin was turning grey-black and he was rigid from what the Romans long ago named *rigor mortis*. I knew from what I had learned that this phase would pass in perhaps a day, and that the alchemist's body would become pliable again.

"Who killed you, old man?" I whispered leaning over Eriador's head and surveying his mottled flesh. "And why?"

I suddenly felt terribly deflated. I knew there was nothing more I could learn from this man. I could have gone through the effort of a full post-mortem, but felt sure it would prove to be a waste of time. He had not been poisoned, there was little mystery about what had actually finished him, even if everything else about the crime remained unsolvable. I was about to find a sheet with which to cover the corpse when I was startled to see something I had missed earlier. There lay white flecks in Eriador's wispy silver hair. They were camouflaged, and indistinct.

I found some small French forceps in my medical bag and very carefully withdrew one of the white particles. Walking over to the torch in the wall bracket, I lifted the tiny object up to the light. "Well, how odd," I said aloud and lay the forceps on a side table while I rummaged around in a box close to the table. It was one of the chests Tomasso and I had started to unpack upstairs two days ago and he had pulled from it a fragile instrument which I had insisted he put back because it was precious and very delicate. I smiled to myself, remembering his puzzled expression when I had explained it was a device for seeing objects that were otherwise too small to be visible.

I found the instrument and placed it on the table while I extricated a piece of black cloth from amongst my work materials on a shelf the other side of the room. I put the cloth on the table, lifted the forceps and deposited the tiny white fleck taken from Eriador's scalp close to the centre of the fabric. I then picked up the object I had retrieved from the chest.

It was a small leather cylinder that fitted into a metal frame from which protruded three stubby supporting legs. It looked ordinary, but it was in fact a miraculous invention and a wonderful gift from Tenzin, the very same man whose sky burial I had witnessed in Nepal. He had told me his people called it a *Shenl*. It consisted of two special lenses ground to smoothness and placed inside a leather pouch. If the *Shenl* was held over an object it magnified it so that small details hardly perceptible to the unaided eye could be studied and understood. I knew this device was the only one in Europe and I guarded it jealously.

Positioning the *Shenl* over the speck of white, I turned so that I could get the torch light behind me to illuminate the tiny thing. I put my eye to the top lens and peered through the barrel, adjusting the length of the tube so as to focus the two lenses, allowing them to work together.

Nothing. Just a blur.

I went back to the alchemist's body and plucked half a dozen more white particles from his hair, returned to the table and studied them with the *Shenl*. Through the eyepiece, all I could see were indefinable white smudges, frayed and secretive. Could they simply be nothing more interesting than motes of dry skin? I mused.

Pulling back, I rubbed my eyes, then ran a hand across my forehead. That is when I felt the pain. It started in the back of my head and rushed down my neck and along my spine. I saw the table and the black cloth vibrate and become blurred. I thought I could stop my head falling forward, but it was impossible, it felt like a lead weight. The surface of the table seemed to rear up and then . . . oblivion.

Chapter Sixteen: Questions

For a few seconds after I regained consciousness I had no idea where I was or even who I was – a most disconcerting feeling. I opened my eyes and found my vision blurred. I could see a shape before me, and then I heard a voice.

"Francesco? Francesco?"

I felt my head being lifted, caught a familiar scent and then the touch of soft hands upon my face.

"Francesco. It is I, Teresa."

I went to pull up and a terrible pain shot down my spine.

"Don't try to move. What happened? I saw a figure running from the house just as I arrived in the campo. I knocked on your door. When there was no reply, I pushed on it. It was open. I knew straight away you were home, the fire was burning in the hearth. I called you, then made my way down here."

I sat up and Teresa grasped my arm as if she expected me to crumble at the attempt.

"I'm well," I said. "Did you recognise him?"

"It was no one I know."

"Describe him."

"I couldn't see much. I caught a mere glimpse and he was in the shadows. He was of average height and build and wore a plain brown tunic." She started to inspect the top of my head. I touched her fingers for a moment before she drew them away.

I stood. "Is anything missing?" I said and pulled round to check the table and the counters. I was relieved to see the *Shenl* was still there. The shelves looked to be untouched. I ran my fingertips over my crown and winced.

"You *are* hurt."

Teresa made me sit on a stool close to the stairs. She gently inspected my scalp and gauged the location of the injury by my reaction. "Stay still, Francesco. I shall prepare a salve," She stepped towards the bench below my shelf of chemicals. I watched her mix ingredients in a pestle and mortar, her strong, elegant hands working the chemicals in the stone bowl. She added water from a jug that stood to one side of the counter, stirred some more, then scraped the contents of the mortar into a smaller porcelain dish and brought it over. "May I ask why you have a cadaver in your house?"

I couldn't help a bleak laugh. "The dead man is the alchemist, Eriador."

"I heard there had been another strange murder. I didn't know he was the victim though. The poor man. How did he . . . ?"

"A slit throat, same as Antoinette. He was also disfigured."

Teresa stopped applying the paste she had concocted.

"The middle two fingers of his left hand have been removed."

She gasped and I made an involuntary noise as she touched a particularly sore part of the wound.

"Sorry." She finished, laid the bowl to one side and came round to look at Eriador's body, studying it with a professional eye. "Where is your housekeeper, Isabella?"

I let out a heavy sigh. "She has left."

"Left?"

"I don't blame the poor woman," I said. "I think there are many easier patrons – most of whom rarely keep dead bodies in the basement! Shall we go upstairs?"

She nodded and I led the way. The fire in the living-room had dwindled to little more than glowing embers. I placed a log on the remnants and it caught. Teresa was seated in the chair closest to the fireplace. I sat opposite her. "So, although it is always a pleasure, may I ask why you are here?"

"I wanted you to see this."

She handed me a rectangular package; something solid lay inside wrapped in a piece of rough cloth.

"What is it?" I unravelled the material to reveal a cheap notebook made from scraps and remnants and easy to pick up in the markets for a few soldi.

"Romia entrusted it to my keeping. It is her daughter's diary. She asked me to pass it on to you."

I raised an eyebrow.

"She understandably wants to do anything she can to help find Antoinette's killer."

"Yes."

"I've looked through it, but it is written in code," Teresa said.

I opened it gingerly. "It is, isn't it?" I glanced at a jumbled collection of words. "It will take a while to break the code and translate it."

"Of course."

I closed the book. "I need to get Pinelli's servant, Ajith to help me transport Eriador's body to a monastery or nunnery. I think whoever was here earlier will not be slow to report what he saw in my laboratory. Perhaps the good sisters of the Church of the Sacred Virgin will care for him as they did Antoinette."

"I don't think you should be doing anything, Francesco. You took a heavy blow. You must rest."

"Nonsense. I can't."

"You can, and you will. Only yesterday you were claiming I had been trained as a medic."

"Yes, Teresa, and you put me right on that matter."

"You are going to bed, Francesco. How long is it since you last slept? You look dreadful."

"Why thank you, My Lady."

"You are very welcome." She had her fingers around my upper arm and was pulling at me.

I stopped her and stood my ground. "Fifteen years ago, I would have been thrilled at the suggestion you might take me to bed."

"Oh, that's nice. But you wouldn't be now?"

"I didn't mean that!"

"What did you mean?"

"I was merely . . ."

"Francesco, it's all right; I'm teasing you. But, I'm not *taking* you to bed!" She had her hands on her hips and was barely able to disguise a smile. "I'm *putting* you to bed. There is a difference."

I suddenly felt overwhelmingly tired and knew that Teresa was right. I had barely snatched a few hours of rest during the past day and a half and so much had happened during that time that thirty-six hours had felt more like one hundred and thirty-six.

"Very well. I will lie down for five minutes," I said. "Then I must press on."

We were in my bedroom. Teresa pulled back the covers, I lowered myself gingerly to the mattress and felt the fabric coming down on me, my sore head sinking into the pillow. "Five minutes," I mumbled.

•

Teresa's diagnosis had been perfectly accurate, of course. I've heard it said that doctors make the worst patients, and I can certainly believe that to be true. When I awoke, the room was dark. Opening the shutters, I saw the stars in the blue-black firmament and could judge by the position of the moon that it was an hour after dusk; I had slept for perhaps eight hours and I felt wonderfully refreshed. I walked through to the main room and then down the steps to my laboratory. Eriador was gone. On the table lay a note. I unfolded it. It said: "Sweet dreams, I hope." I smiled to myself.

Out on the campo, I quickly found a messenger boy, gave him a note for Tomasso and headed north towards the Ghetto. Alfonzo's was quiet, the door locked. I rapped on it, but no one came to answer. A narrow alley ran along the western side, and on, past the bordello, to the water. It was a service passageway for the delivery of food and drink as well as for those patrons who did not wish to be seen entering or leaving the establishment. A high gate

115

separated the building from the alley. I tugged at a bell beside the gate and still no one came so I yanked the bell cord for longer.

After a minute of constant noise I heard a man's voice shout from the other side of the gate.

"Who the fuck is it?"

I stopped pulling on the bell. "My name is Francesco Sagredo. I would like to speak to Alfonzo."

There was no reply and for a few moments I thought the man had gone back into the bordello, but then I heard a key turning in a lock, two bolts being slid back and the gate started to move inwards. In the timid light I could see a tall, broad-shouldered young man.

"What do you need my master for?"

"You are Stefano Vanenti, yes?"

He gave me a hard look. "And I know who you are . . . The Traveller."

"May I speak with Alfonzo?"

Stefano pulled the gate inwards and I waited as he locked it again, then I followed him in through a back door that led to a storeroom, a scrappy office, and beyond that, the ballroom of the bordello.

It was a large space, the ceiling bedecked with drooping silks to give it the look of a Bedouin tent. That made me smile because on all my travels I had seen many examples of the real thing and this poor imitation did not even come close. The floor was covered with worn but colourful rugs imported from Persia. A pair of negro cleaners, who kept their eyes averted, were mopping the floor at the far end of the room. A broad staircase ascended from close to the centre of the room and curved round to a mezzanine. I counted perhaps a dozen closed doors leading off the balcony. Hearing a voice, I turned to see Alfonzo Castello.

Alfonzo the Spaniard cut an imposing figure. He was at least twice my weight, perhaps three inches taller than I, and he moved with the gait of a man who had once been very fit and athletic but had allowed his body to go to seed. He was dressed in a pair of well-tailored hose, a rather splendid shirt and jacket and a flamboyant scarf. His head was entirely bald and he had a long gold earring in his left earlobe that hung down almost to his shoulder, giving him the look of a rather well-heeled pirate. To complete the image, he wore a deep crimson silk patch over the eye that, according to Tomasso had apparently been gored by a bull some years before.

"Francesco Sagredo, I believe," he said, his voice surprisingly mellow and considered. "I have been expecting you to come a-calling, sir since I heard that you were trying to solve the mystery of poor Antoinette's murder." He extended a huge, bejewelled hand.

"Word travels fast in the Republic."

116

"I believe it has always been thus. So, what may I do for you?"

He led me to an alcove of leather chairs around a table. Stefano followed us.

"Can I offer you some refreshments, Francesco Sagredo?" Alfonzo seemed to notice his assistant for the first time. "Some wine, Stef, please."

"How many glasses?"

"Two. Could you finish up counting the takings from last night, there's a good fellow."

Stefano nodded sullenly and retreated to the bar.

"I was very fond of Antoinette," Alfonzo said. "She was a good girl, my best. But, aside from all that, I really liked her."

Stefano returned with a carafe of red wine and two glasses. Alfonzo poured.

"When did you see her last?"

"About midnight."

"That seems to be around the time everyone else I've spoken to about it saw her last, which implies she may have been snatched near here, or perhaps met her end in one of the lanes close-by."

Alfonzo looked genuinely disturbed by it all.

"I'm fond of many of my girls," he said, ". . . but Antoinette." He paused for a moment and took a deep breath. "She was special, different. For sure, the men loved her, but she was also very intelligent, very mature. I would have been proud to call her my daughter . . . but I wouldn't have wanted her within a league of here!"

"I heard her father was here two nights ago. Caused quite a commotion."

"You are well informed! Yes, the man forced his way in, and he did cause a scene; screaming her name, scaring the other girls. We chucked him out. If you ask me, I reckon you need look no further than Carlo Perugino for your killer. Maybe he lost control and beat her so badly . . ."

I kept my own council concerning the nature of the girl's wounds. I imagined there were plenty of rumours flying around anyway, but I was happy for people to think what they liked. I was only interested in empirical facts. Stefano paced over. I looked behind him and saw Tomasso standing in the doorway from the office. "It's my friend, Tomasso Cicogna," I explained as Alfonzo began to stand. "He is helping me with the . . . investigation."

"Investigation?" Stefano said with an edge of sarcasm. "Sounds very important, Traveller. And you have no less a figure than the Doge's alcoholic, whoring son to . . ."

"Stefano!" Alfonzo said. "I thought I asked you to finish with last night's takings?"

The young man gave an insouciant bow and retreated.

Tomasso shook hands with Alfonzo, saw my drink was untouched, slid it across the table in front of him and gave me a look as if to say: 'You don't want this, do you?'

"So, talk me through what happened with Carlo Perugino," I said, turning to Alfonzo.

"Antoinette had finished her shift and had come to me to be paid. There was a noise from the entrance." He nodded towards the doors. ". . . and Carlo Perugino comes in, very drunk and starts shouting for his daughter."

"I imagine you have your fair share of drunks here, do you not?" I asked.

"Indeed. But that's the first time an unhappy father has turned up! Lovers, yes, and a very displeased husband once or twice." He produced a laugh, his one good eye lighting up with mirth. "But not a father."

"So what happened then?"

"My lad, Stefano and I had to be a bit rough with him. Perugino was raving and upsetting our customers and the girls. Then Stefano took him outside and sent him packing."

"And that was the last of it? Perugino did not return?"

"No. I think he got the message."

"And did you speak to Antoinette after that?"

"Yes, in my office. I paid her."

"Any idea where she was heading? Going straight home?"

"A party apparently! I said to her ain't this place lively enough for your tastes then?"

"We would like to talk to the girls who were working here that night," I said. "Would that be possible?"

Alfonzo looked a little surprised. "Very well." He shrugged. "Most of them are here. We open the doors in an hour. So we can only spare you half an hour for all of them."

"I understand. That will be sufficient." I turned to Tomasso. "We shall divide them into two groups. You and I shall need quills and paper. Could I impose upon you, Senor Castello?"

Pulling up from the table, he walked over to his office.

"Thank you for coming, Tom," I said.

"I wouldn't miss an opportunity to see how you *investigate*. What questions do you wish me to ask the girls?"

"Just be friendly, enquire about their relationship with Antoinette. Ease into asking if they have any information that might help find the murderer."

"And why divide them up into two groups? Couldn't you interview all of them at once?"

"I want to see if there are any contradictions in their recollections."

"Ah," Tomasso said. "Clever."

"Who's clever?" said Alfonzo, returning to the table.

"My friend here," Tomasso said.

"Ah, well, from what I've heard about Lord Sagredo," Alfonzo responded. "That goes without saying!"

I talked to my group, six of Alfonzo's workers, in one of the lounges off the ballroom. It was used, I was reliably informed, for pre-arranged orgies which usually involved half a dozen men, most frequently traders passing through the Republic and perhaps ten or fifteen of the bordello's girls. The room was dimly lit with candles under red shades. Low couches had been arranged in a square. The girls smoked from a shared pipe.

"So, Francesco, you're the returning traveller," one of the woman said, smoke billowing about her face. She gave me a lascivious look that was just a little too fabricated. "You're every bit as gorgeous as they say."

Her friends giggled.

"I'm here to ask some questions about Antoinette."

It was like throwing cold water on a fire.

"What's your name?" I asked the girl who had been teasing a few seconds before.

"Josie," she said.

"Were you friendly with Antoinette Perugino?"

She produced a sullen lift of the shoulders. "Hardly knew her. She hadn't been here long."

"I liked her," said a woman to my left. I had noted how she had not partaken of the pipe.

"What's your name?"

"Lulu."

I wrote it down.

"Antoinette was a very sweet girl. But I always had the feeling that she did not belong here. She was far too good for this place."

A couple of the woman turned on Lulu, their faces flushed with anger.

"Excuse me," Josie announced. "Speak for yourself, deary!"

"She wasn't like the rest of us." Lulu went on as though her earlier remark had not been at all provocative.

"She was stuck up you mean." Josie snapped back.

I raised my hands. "Ladies. Antoinette is dead."

It did little to change the mood, but at least Josie and Lulu stopped arguing. "I've been told that she had a special customer," I said. "Do any of you know if this is true?"

The room was silent. I considered the six women. Two of them looked glassy-eyed already. Josie was drawing deeply on the pipe. The drug seemed to have little real effect upon her.

"As if any of us would tell you anything about that!" One of the women slurred.

"I understand your anxiety about such a thing, but ladies . . ."

A couple of them started to giggle again. "Ain't been called a lady for a long time," Josie declared.

"Surely you have considered that the murderer might strike again? That next time, you could be the victim?" I stared hard at Josie and then at each of the others in turn. I had imagined that taking this aggressive approach would be effective. I was though, sadly mistaken. None of them apart from Josie would even meet my eyes.

"Look," she said. "None of us knows a thing. Do we, girls?" She looked around at the others. "None of us want to get killed, but we know the risks. We live with them every day. We don't need you to point them out either, thank you very much."

"Very well," I said, feeling deflated. "Thank you for your time."

They trooped out led by Josie followed a little shakily by four of the others. The last to leave was Lulu. She stood up without a word, but as she passed me I felt her slip something into my hand. She closed the door behind her and I opened my fingers.

A scrap of paper lay in my palm. I unfolded it. It said: 'Meet me outside in ten minutes.'

Tomasso had fared equally poorly. "It was impossible to get them to talk, Francesco," he said, miserably. "They were either teasing or refusing to tell me anything useful."

"Don't feel bad about it, Tomasso. It was the same for me." I handed him the note. "One of the girls was a little bit more helpful."

"Sounds like she's looking for some private work," he said rolling his eyes.

"No, she was the only one making sense. Her name's Lulu."

"Yes, I know her," Tomasso replied.

We thanked Alfonzo for his time and left through the back before slipping along the side alley towards the south-side of the bordello. The place stank and was filthy, with rotten food, bottles and even some ripped under garments scattered about. Lulu had arrived before us. She had a shawl over a flimsy top and looked as though she might turn to ice before too long. I removed my coat and put it about her shoulders.

She looked surprised. "Thank you, sir."

"So, Lulu. In your note, you said you could help."

"Come with me." She looked from me to Tomasso: "Too many big ears around here."

She led the way along a passage to the north of the building, stopped

120

abruptly and glanced left and right along the alley. "The night of the murder," she began. "I'd finished a few minutes before Antoinette." She stared into my eyes and I could see an edge of fear there, but also a flicker of defiance, a need to unburden herself. "I was changing in a spare room. The door was ajar. I heard Antoinette across the corridor. She was talking to Stefano."

I raised an eyebrow and glanced at Tomasso. Lulu stopped and took a deep breath.

"She was asking for the poppy, but she didn't have enough money."

"Wait," Tomasso said. "Stefano is a dealer?"

Lulu gave us a surprised look. "I thought you had already worked that out."

"We hadn't," I said. "We knew Eriador produced the drug."

"Stefano worked for the Alchemist." She grimaced. "The bastard will have to find another drug maker now, won't he?"

"So Antoinette didn't have enough money?"

"No. But of course, we girls can get round those sorts of problems."

"I see. So that's what happened?"

Lulu produced a half smile. "Yes. Didn't take long!"

"Well, thank you for telling us, Lulu."

"I have to get back now," she said, handing me my coat.

"So, what relevance does that have?" Tomasso asked as we watched the girl's back retreating along the alley.

I shrugged. "Probably nothing directly, but it sheds some light on what goes on behind the scenes at Alfonzo's, does it not? I can't imagine anyone else owning up to that sort of information."

"And Lulu's right. Stefano Vanenti is a bastard," Tomasso said.

We started to walk back towards the square when, to our surprise, Lulu reappeared at the end of the alley.

"Lulu."

She had a hand up and beckoned us back a few yards. "There's something else." She paused and looked about more nervously than before. "You asked about Antoinette's fancy man."

"Yes."

"I don't know his name, but I know where they used to meet. He's rich all right. Has a place overlooking San Marco. Antoinette couldn't help herself, she was very excited about him and bragged. I think she had some very silly ideas about where it could lead."

"Do you have an address?" I asked without expecting too much.

"Not exactly, but she said it was on the top floor and had a wonderful view over San Marco towards the Molo. I suppose that narrows it down."

"It does indeed, Lulu. Thank you very much."

We gave her time to get back to the bordello alone before we emerged from the end of the passage onto the square. A couple of men were at the door to the brothel. One of them tugged on the bell.

"Come," I said to Tomasso. "Let's see if there is anything we can find out for ourselves."

The night had crept in while we were in the bordello; snowflakes were tumbling from low dark clouds. We stood outside the building and glanced back at the door and the dim glow of red light spilling from a pair of first-storey windows. I caught a glimpse of a topless woman closing a curtain.

"So, according to Alfonzo and Stefano, they kicked Carlo Perugino out about midnight. I can imagine Stefano had more than a few words with him, probably roughed him up, threatened him. It was perhaps another ten minutes before Antoinette left."

"Are you thinking Carlo could be a suspect?"

"Well, yes, of course. There are a number of suspects, are there not? Our job is to narrow that number down to one . . . or perhaps in this case, two."

"But her own father?"

"Not unheard of, to say the very least, Tom; now is it?" I held his stare for a moment. "But I don't think Carlo Perugino is a likely suspect. He had the opportunity. He was here at the right time. He even had a form of motive, did he not? Anger, shame . . . But no, I saw him at the nunnery. He was genuinely distraught over his daughter's murder."

"Just because he is genuinely grieving doesn't mean he is innocent."

"That is true."

"So what are we looking for?"

"Well, according to Alfonzo, she was heading off to a party. Let's assume for the moment that it was somewhere within the Ghetto."

"Why?" Tomasso asked as I took us away from the steps up to the bordello.

"She had a room here, remember? The place she shared with Anica? If she really was going to a party, she would probably be with others like her, young people, other prostitutes perhaps. She might not have been bothered to leave the Ghetto and then have to come back in again later."

Tomasso shrugged his shoulders.

"But anyway, we have to start somewhere."

I led the way across a square, stopped and pointed towards an alley leading away from the bordello. "That path," I said. ". . . will take us back to the gates and away from the Ghetto." I turned. "Let's go this way, it leads east and towards where Antoinette lived."

Sticking as closely as possible to the main path, I was making a valiant attempt to look everywhere at once; peering at the icy path, studying the walls to each side, the twists of the alley ahead. A patina of snow lay on the path. The alley was quiet, the way well-lit by the moon now risen above the tops of the nearest buildings and shining down directly onto the passageway.

I stopped so abruptly Tomasso almost walked into me. Ignoring his protestations, I stepped close to the left wall and stared at a patch of stone some five or six feet above the ground.

"What is it?" Tomasso said, blowing his warm breath into his cupped hands, trying to get his circulation going.

I said nothing and run my fingers along the stone, stopping just short of a faint reddish brown stain. I peered in closer. Here." I pointed to the mark on the wall. "Looks very much like blood to me."

"Shit!" Tomasso exclaimed.

I walked slowly along the lane. There were more of the same stains forming an arc stretching about ten feet or so along the wall.

"You see this?" I said. "When a person has their throat cut, blood sprays out very fast."

"I know," Tomasso remarked. "The memories of war are never far from my mind."

"Exactly." I stopped and indicated a spot on the path. "Antoinette stood here. She was attacked from behind." I grabbed Tomasso and spun him round. "The attacker was right-handed. I have ascertained that already." I ran my finger across Tom's neck. He tried to wriggle free, most put out.

"Stay still," I said impatiently and shuffled us back a foot. "Yes, just . . . here. She was about six inches shorter than you, Tom." I pulled him down the appropriate distance.

"For fuck's sake, Francesco!"

Letting him go, I stared at the ground where it joined the base of the wall. "Good Lord!"

Tomasso brushed himself down looking very displeased, but then he bent down beside me and stared. "Holy fuck! Is that a tooth?" he said.

Chapter Seventeen: Secret Liaisons

Returning home to my little house, I found the fire had burned low and the cold had taken a grip. I managed to invigorate the embers and placed some dry logs on them so that in a few minutes I had a goodly blaze going and the chill began to diminish. I found a half empty bottle of wine and a clean goblet and made myself comfortable in my favourite old chair, pulling it close to the fire. The flames licked, wood spat, and for the first time since my return, I actually felt rather contented and relaxed away from the pressures of the Council, and the constant sniping of people like Niccolo Celsi.

"So, what," I thought to myself. ". . . could be made of the information I had gathered so far?" And at once I lost that warm sense of contentment. I had precious little to go on. Indeed, all I had were unconnected facts. Two murders. Two quite different victims. They were connected via the drug trade in the Republic, but that seemed to be the sum of it. Antoinette, a prostitute, her throat cut, her body dumped in the canal. Eriador, a well-known figure, a political activist, a mystic with connections within the criminal underworld and the esoteric nether-land of the occult.

I knew from experience that the pursuit of esoteric knowledge was energetically practiced in Venice. I was aware of at least a handful of dealers in arcane literature and there would be at least another dozen or so more in the city who worked as alchemists. And my friend, Tomasso Cicogna, someone so well-connected and seemingly well-grounded in the pleasures of the physical world, had, for many years, shown an enthusiasm for the occult. I might have assumed that while I was away he had passed onto other interests, but he had as much as admitted to me that he was still fascinated with metaphysics and continued to move in what I considered to be tenebrous circles.

But, I was getting off the point. It seemed more likely that the murders were linked to the first of Eriador's preoccupations, the criminal underworld of Venice, for this was something he had in common with the first victim, Antoinette Perugino. Not only had the girl been a prostitute who rubbed shoulders, more than shoulders, with all manner of society's dregs, but she was also a drug addict. The connection between the murders had to be the poppy.

I had concluded that Antoinette's killing had been the work of two people and nothing I had learned this evening had turned my mind from that. The idea that Antoinette's father had dispatched his daughter seemed to be unlikely, and the bloodstains and the tooth did not suggest any series of events different to what I had ascertained from studying Antoinette and Eriador's wounds.

"Could the two murders have been unrelated?" I wondered aloud, staring at the fire, the fleeting colours morphing white through red and then to green. Of course the two victims were acquainted and had drugs in common, but was it possible the two of them had been killed within twenty-four hours of each other by coincidence? "No," I declared. "Not even conceivable." The wounds to the neck, I reminded myself, had been almost identical in each slaying, and then there were the mutilations; different for sure, but both ritualistic. I glanced away for a moment and caught sight of Antoinette's diary where it rested on a little table close to the couch. I had quite forgotten about it.

Sometimes, the most amateur codes are also the most time-consuming to break. Antoinette had used a well-known encryption system called the Caesar Shift Cipher. It had assumed this name because Julius Caesar had, according to legend, been the first to use it. Simplicity itself, it worked on the principle that each letter was shifted a set number of places through the alphabet.

It took me only a moment to find the shift and I could read the dead girl's words almost as though they had been written plainly. But then, without any warning, the shift changed. Instead of using a three-space difference in the letters, Antoinette adopted a six letter shift. Then, she moved on to a twelve-space code before adopting a one-space cipher. I decided against making a record of the changes or copying the entries and simply read through the diary accommodating a new shift every time it altered.

The girl's handwriting was scratchy and difficult to read, the transposed spelling, haphazard, and her use of punctuation practically non-existent, but her writing was filled with passion and dreams; not dissimilar, I surmised, to the secret diary of many a young girl.

It was also a very sad document; after all, the poor young thing who had written it was now dead, but it was also a pathetic collection, page upon page of hopes dashed and fantasies unfulfilled, all interspersed with descriptions of the mean and shabby existence Antoinette had endured during the final months of her life.

I skimmed through much of the early entries and moved rapidly ahead to recent weeks, and there, in an entry made on the First of September, a little over two months ago, appeared the earliest mention of the man fitting the description Anica and Lulu had offered.

'. . . for most of the time, he is a true gentleman,' Antoinette wrote on the Tenth September after they had met three times during the previous week. 'Tonight at No.19, he brought me a lovely necklace.'

I stopped abruptly. 'No.19'? Could that be the number of their love nest? The apartment on San Marco? I read on, fascinated, but also feeling a little guilty. I agreed with the girl's mother that if this diary could offer any clues to who killed Antoinette, then it must be read; but even so, I felt as though I were intruding, eavesdropping on the dead girl's private world.

From mid-September until the beginning of October, the diary was filled with almost nothing but complaints about Antoinette's working conditions and her growing obsession with her anonymous admirer. But then, on the Third of October, a new character appeared. Antoinette had met Eriador. She described her first experience with the poppy. Encouraged by Anica to try it, the girl had become addicted quickly and soon she was spending on the drug anything she could earn from working at the bordello. By the middle of the month, she was pawning her lover's gifts. At this time, the handwriting had become more disorganised, and in places almost indecipherable. Reality and dreams seemed often to merge on the page, and it was becoming more and more difficult to untangle the threads of what Antoinette was doing, what was actual and what was fantastical.

The twenty-eighth of October, less than two weeks ago was a terrible day for Antoinette. Her admirer dropped in at the rooms she rented in the Ghetto and had caught her smoking a poppy pipe. His fury was almost uncontainable. He beat her about the arms and legs, leaving her beautiful face untouched so as not to spoil his own carnal pleasures. He had then penetrated her anally leaving her bleeding and in agony.

Upon first reading, it seemed to me that the odd effect of this was that Antoinette wished even more fervently to make the man love her. I found this hard to imagine, but then gradually, as I read more carefully and spent time untying the linguistic knots of the girl's prose, I began to understand that I had been quite wrong. It was not love Antoinette wanted from the man. Instead, she had embarked upon a very dangerous game. She had decided to ensnare him, to transform herself from being his concubine to become his mistress. She had even dared to imagine she might lead him into marriage.

Antoinette was gold-digging to pay for her addiction. I shivered involuntarily at the thought of it. How quickly this poor child had been corrupted, how rapid had been her downfall. According to Romia, her daughter had once held down a job in a gambling house in Calle Vallaresso. That was nothing too salubrious, but it was many rungs up the ladder from where she had ended her days. She had obviously fallen in with the wrong person when she had met and started to live with Anica, and through her, she had been introduced to a drug that led to her death.

But, I asked myself: Why exactly had she died? Had she been murdered by this strange man alluded to in her diary? He was obviously cruel, but he appeared to at least feel lust for the girl. Would he have wanted to kill the object of his physical desires? Perhaps it had been a crime of passion. Could he have then cut the word 'Redemptionis' into her flesh because of the fury he felt? Had she betrayed him? Had she stolen from him? Or, had he learned that she was planning to try to exploit him?

It was all supposition, there was not a scrap of evidence to support any of these hypotheses. Yes, the man was callous, but most men were. It did not mean he was a murderer. 'And what of Eriador?' I said aloud, pulling up from my chair and walking over to the fireplace where the flames had begun to dwindle. I found two more logs, placed them carefully on the burning brands and poked at the fire. 'Could Eriador have killed the girl?' I lowered myself back in the chair, and lifted the diary. That seemed very unlikely. Why would anyone kill their golden goose? Besides, although I had only met the man very briefly just before his own murder, he did not strike me as violent.

Eventually, I reached the final page of the diary. 'The Ninth of November: Morning'. It was Antoinette's last day alive. She seemed to be in a lighter mood than she had described for at least six weeks. She conveyed the impression of being happy, confident. I cast my eyes down the page and saw why. 'He loves me,' She had written. 'He loves me. He told me, he loves me. Oh, clever girl. I am a clever girl. He will soon be mine.'

The embers had burned low again and I had lost all track of time. It was still dark beyond the shutters, but there was a pale, embryonic light that did not come from the Moon long since fallen below the horizon. I guessed that it must be no more than half an hour before the dawn. I washed, changed my clothes and set out across the campo passing women hanging out washing and scrapping snow from their door steps.

The snow that had started while I was with Tomasso at Alfonzo's had not abated one bit. Now it lay settled upon the ground, on ledges and parapets, gargoyles and statues. It suddenly struck me how it had been so long ago I had last seen snow in Venice. The winter before my exile had been a very mild one, so it must have been almost seventeen years since I had seen such a downpour here, such a deep, crisp layer shrouding everything.

There were few people about and some of the more exposed paths were already proving treacherous. San Marco lay coated with a beautiful pristine blanket of snow. I edged along the square taking a path through the colonnades before ducking down a narrow laneway skirting the north-side. This led to the entrance of a building divided into many small but comfortable abodes. Cut into the stonework to the left of the entrance were the words: 'San Marco Terrazza. 1-19'. A pair of large green double doors opened onto a grand stairway. It was very quiet. I imagined that even those who had risen early would be reluctant to leave home unless it were absolutely necessary. I crossed a wide hall and had begun to take the first steps up when I heard a voice behind me.

"May I help?"

I stopped and peered down to the hallway then slowly retraced my steps.

An old woman stood at the open door to her residence. She was holding back a very large dog who seemed desperate to escape.

"Good morning," I said and gave the woman a polite bow. She looked me up and down suspiciously and then seemed to recognise me.

"You're that . . ."

"Doctor Francesco Sagredo," I said and produced my most engaging smile.

Having confirmed her theory, the woman seemed singularly unimpressed by me. "Are you looking for someone?" she asked.

"I was due to meet the owner of No.19," I said, thinking on my feet.

"Oh? Rather early, is it not?" And she fixed me with not altogether friendly eyes, clearly waiting for me to explain some more.

"A mutual colleague told me it will soon be put up for sale. I wanted to see if I could make an offer. Now I'm back in the Republic, it would be a perfect location for me."

The woman frowned. "For sale? Surely not. This entire building has been in the hands of the Celsi family since Adamo's day."

I covered my astonishment by producing an exaggerated shiver.

"I'm not surprised you're cold, young man. Do you not own a coat?"

"You wouldn't know if Lord Celsi is home, would you?"

"I think not. He is only here once or twice a week. He uses the largest apartment; on the top floor. I assume that's the one you are talking about?"

"It is," I said distractedly, then I bowed again, turned and strode out through the doors, hearing the old crone gasp at my curtness before remonstrating with her dog.

Of course, it seemed perfectly obvious once I heard the words come from the elderly woman's lips, and I felt annoyed with myself for not having worked it out for myself. But then I calmed down a little and remembered how there were a great many wealthy men in Venice and not a few of them were 'tall and quite fair of face' as Anica had described Antoinette's admirer. 'No,' I said to myself. '. . . don't feel bad about it, Francesco. After all, you got that old prune to tell you far more than she intended, did you not? This is a real breakthrough.'

Reaching the Basilica, I turned South. Great flakes of snow peppered the view and it was not until I had reached the Molo that I could see out to the Lagoon. The grey water was swallowing the flurries wholesale.

I took the stairs up to Tomasso's rooms three at a time and stopped abruptly on the second floor landing. His front door stood ajar.

"Tomasso?" I called, immediately feeling a spasm of fear. I stepped into the wide hall and called again. "Tomasso? You here?"

Walking in, I saw my friend immediately. He was sitting, his back stiff and straight in one of his couches. He had his left arm stretched out upon his lap, his shirt sleeve rolled up. In his right hand he brandished a dagger, the blade's edge pressed hard up against the skin of his wrist.

I could smell alcohol, and as I dashed over, I noticed an empty bottle beside him and another lying in a small puddle of liquid on the floor close to his feet.

"Tom! What in God's name?" I lowered myself onto the seat beside him. His eyes were glazed over and he stared into the middle distance as though I were not there. He had obviously drunk far too much, but he seemed to be in some strange emotional state, almost a form of mental paralysis.

"Tom," I repeated softly and moved my hand slowly down to his, easing the dagger away from his arm. He did not resist. I placed the knife to one side and turned my friend towards me.

He looked straight through me. I had seen this behaviour before. Only six months ago, as I had travelled westwards returning from China to Europe, I had stayed for some time in the city of Tripoli. There, I had learned a great deal from a man called Aliba Al-Nan who called himself a 'doctor of the mind'. He refused to accept the commonly held belief that aberrant behaviour was due to demonic possession or an imbalance of humors. Instead, after a lifetime of research, he had concluded that what people considered antisocial behaviour, in all its many guises always came down to a problem seated within the brain. Just as the brain is accepted as being the controller of the body Al-Nan argued that it was also responsible for *all* behaviours, acceptable or otherwise. But, what had been most interesting about the master's work was a conviction that the brain could be altered dramatically by experience. If one were fortunate, this alteration could be a positive thing, a benevolent learning process making for a better, more grounded person; but more often, so he had learned, the brain could be damaged by terror, by extreme experiences, by the pain inflicted voluntarily or otherwise by others and by chemical means, using drugs and alcohol. I would have spent longer in Tripoli, but it had been there that I had received the imperial summons to return to Venice in order to tend to the Doge.

Slowly, Tomasso seemed to relax, to return from whatever place in which his mind had been residing. I let him calm down in his own time, fetched him some lemon water, and I watched as he slowly, silently emptied the goblet. "What happened, Tom?" I took the goblet and placed it on the floor.

He took a deep breath. "Don't want to talk about."

"I understand."

"Do you?"

I fell silent.

"I'm sorry, Francesco. I'm just . . . Oh fuck! I'm embarrassed."

I placed a hand on his shoulder. He felt bony and I had the feeling that for a good while now he had been drinking far too much and eating much too little. "How did you end up here on the couch, with a knife?"

He bit his lip, his eyes watering. "I was out last night." He raised an eyebrow as if to say: 'Well, what a surprise!' I made it home, God knows how. I have absolutely no recollection of the journey. I must have made a lot of noise for I woke the servants."

I had wondered where they were, but said nothing, just let Tomasso talk it through.

"I . . ." he paused and ran fingers over his forehead. "It's hazy. I remember shouting and ranting. Adelina and her daughter walked out. I started drinking again, threw up, drank more."

"But why were things especially bad last night?"

He was shaking his head.

"Can you remember any . . . ?"

"Fuck, Francesco!" His face seemed to physically grow, expanding with his outburst, and he shrugged my hand from his shoulder violently. "I don't fucking know!" He pulled up and immediately fell on his face. I tried to help him.

"NO!" he screamed. "Don't touch me. Fuck off! Just fuck off!"

I straightened and he slowly pulled himself to his feet.

"I thought I told you to fuck . . ." He took a swing at me, missed by a forearm's length and I caught him before he could fall again.

He was limp in my arms and I could hear him sobbing. He clutched at me and wept like a baby into my shoulder. After a short while I guided him back to the couch, helping him to lie down. I placed a cushion under his head, refreshed his goblet and insisted he drink deeply. Feeling his forehead, I checked for a fever, and without a word of protest from him, I loosened his clothes and found a fur in the bedroom which I pulled over him. Before I could speak another word, Tomasso was asleep.

The larder was well stocked, thanks of course to Adelina. While Tom slept, I made a broth from a recently-plucked chicken and a collection of winter vegetables which I'm sure my friend had no idea had even been bought for him. Then, as the food cooked in a large pot over a fire at one end of the room I sat and watched over my patient as he slept fitfully.

Tomasso proved difficult to wake, but I knew he should not sleep too long, and pushing him into eating what I had carefully prepared was like trying to force an errant child to take a remedy, but I refused to give up and he reluctantly sat up and took the bowl and spoon I had handed him.

"I'm not hungry," he protested.

"And I don't care."

After a spoonful, he gave me an approving look.

130

"Don't act so surprised!"

"It's better than that shit you forced upon me the other day," he said, eating hungrily.

"Curry? My speciality."

He pulled a face and I took the empty bowl.

"Right, up you get."

"What?"

"Up."

"Why?"

"We have work to do."

"God's blood, Francesco! The other day you tried to make me stay home, now . . ."

"You were injured. Today you're merely hung-over."

"That's right. I need to go to bed."

"No you don't."

I pulled him to his feet and he rocked on the balls of his feet for a second. I went to fetch his fur coat and he flopped back onto the couch.

"I don't want to have to get rough with you, Tomasso," I said.

"Hah! You may be bigger than me but . . ."

"But what?"

"Oh fuck it . . . nothing. Lead the way, arsehole."

Outside, the wind off the water had a nasty edge to it.

"How is it that you are always in summer clothes?" Tomasso said, shivering in his bearlike coat, his eyes puffy and squinting in the snowy brightness. "Oh, forget it . . . Eastern trickery!"

I shook my head, grinning, and before Tomasso could react, I had my arm locked about his neck and was dragging him to the municipal water pump.

"What the devil, Francesco . . . ?"

He struggled, but I was too strong for him. I had him in position with one hand, while with the other I tugged on the pump watching as freezing water soaked his head. Ignoring his protests, I made sure he received a thorough drenching, finally letting him straighten, his face burning with anger and cold as he shook himself like a great shaggy dog.

The air was blue, I can tell you! I won't repeat the names Tomasso called me. He seemed to pay no heed to passers-by as they stared at him, and I had to force myself not to laugh because that would have riled him even more.

"You need to wake up!" I hollered back just managing to look serious.

He swore some more and then seemed to be exhausted of expletives.

"You done?" I asked.

"No! You're an arse rag, you know that?"

"I've been called worse."

"Yes, I bet you have, you bastard . . ." he seethed, but the fire was going out of his protests and it was obvious that in spite of the shock and the cold, he was actually feeling better.

"It did the trick though, did it not?"

"No!" he lied and despite himself, started to grin. "You are a prize cunt." He was shaking his head.

"Charming! Come on." I put my arm about his sodden shoulder and we strode off towards the
Molo.

We found Carlo Perugino and his young assistant, Tito snowbound in a small boatshed near Spirito Santo, close to the south-eastern tip of Dorsoduro on the far side of the Grand Canal. Neither of them heard us approach as they were rubbing down the hull of Carlo's gondola with a cloth soaked in duck fat. I led the way just inside the entrance to the shed. Carlo looked up and his facial expression slipped from neutral to contempt. He returned pointedly to oiling the boat.

"Carlo Perugino," I said. "May we have a moment of your time?"

He kept rubbing the wood. "I have nothing to say to you, physick."

The boy, Tito, not daring to look up, just glanced at me askance.

"I have a few questions. I'm assuming you are keen to see your daughter's murderer caught and punished."

"And you think you can manage that, do you?" He rubbed vigorously at a particular patch of hull.

I did not reply, and after a moment, he stopped, straightened and threw down the rag. "Keep goin'," he said to Tito and walked over into the bright morning light that cut a swath across the entrance to the boatshed. Carlo spotted Tomasso and looked startled for a moment. Recognising the Doge's son, he seemed torn between deference and the desire to make a sarcastic remark. He wiped remnants of fat from his fingers with a piece of dry rag extricated from his apron. I noticed his eye was badly bruised from the way he had landed awkwardly during our scuffle in the Church of the Sacred Virgin. "You 'ave no need to make such fuckin' blunt remarks, Doctor Sagredo," he said. "I would not wish you the pain I'm feelin'."

I nodded. "You are quite right. I apologise."

He gave Tomasso a quick glance and then turned back to me. "If I knew anything I would 'ave told you straight away, don't you think?"

"Are you aware there has been a second murder?"

He looked genuinely stunned. "Another . . . ?" He couldn't bring himself to say the word 'prostitute'.

"A quite different victim," Tomasso said. "An alchemist called Eriador."

Perugino seemed confused. "How do you know there's any connection?"

"We don't for sure," I said. "But there are certain things the two deaths have in common and Eriador and Antoinette were acquainted."

Perugino dipped down his head to stare at the flagstones between us. "I heard rumours that my daughter had started to use the poppy." He looked up, and for the first time, I noticed just how ill the man appeared. It was quite obvious he had not slept for the past two days.

"Signor Perugino, do you know anything about the last few weeks of your daughter's life? I know you and she were estranged. I . . ."

"I was ashamed, weren't I?" Perugino stated blandly. "There. I ain't afraid to admit it. Why should I be? I can't lie. I still love my daughter and I pray for 'er, but she had disgraced me. Surely, you understand that, don't you?"

"When was the last time you spoke to her?"

"I ain't stopped thinking about that. The Twelfth of October. She'd taken up with that Anica creature. I visited her at the rat-hole she called an apartment; living with the Jews. I'd gone there to try to get her to come 'ome. Her mother and I were still together then. But it went bad."

I could see in the man's face that he was ashamed of himself as well as his dead daughter. Clearly, he had been rough with the girl.

"Do you know anything about the relationships Antoinette had outside work?"

Perugino screwed up his eyes and shook his head. "I ain't sure what you . . ?"

"She apparently had some special client, a wealthy admirer," Tomasso said.

"No. No, I . . ." Perugino suddenly seemed to run out of steam. He took a couple of steps backwards and slumped onto a large stone block close to the door into his boatshed. "I know nothin' about that."

Tomasso and I walked around the headland of Dorsoduro, the wind gusting fiercely.

"Perugino is still the one with the most obvious motive for killing both his daughter and Eriador," Tomasso said.

"Because the alchemist had turned the girl into an addict? The final straw for a father already ashamed that his daughter was a prostitute?"

"Well, yes."

"But Eriador wasn't her main supplier, Stefano Vanenti was. Surely, *he* would have been the second victim if the gondolier had killed Antoinette? And what about Anica? He clearly blames her for introducing Antoinette to the drug."

As we turned northwest away from the snow-obscured view over to the Molo and the Riva Degli, the wind started to propel us onward and we turned towards the southern bank of the Grand Canal hoping to find a hardy boatman or gondolier looking for custom.

"Besides," I added. "Perugino does not fit the physical characteristics of the killer."

"Based upon your ideas about the wounds?"

"I can tell by your tone you are not convinced. But the evidence does not lie."

Tomasso had his hands up. "I'm not doubting you. I bow to the superior knowledge of the master."

"Oh shut up, Tomasso!" I said. "Sarcasm does not become you."

An hour later I was being led by a liveried butler through the grand double doors onto the Sala Grimani, part of the Doge Cicogna's private chambers. Tomasso had gone home, frozen through to the bone, he claimed, and very sniffy about the fact that I seemed quiet warm enough in my favourite tunic bought almost a decade earlier in an Indian bazaar.

The Doge was seated in a high-backed heavily embroidered chair. Assistants stood to each side. As I bowed before him and kissed his ring of state, Cicogna dismissed the men, leaving us alone in his drawing-room.

My Doge," I said. "Thank you for seeing me at such short notice."

"I am always here for you, Francesco, dear boy. You should know that." He appeared tired with dark rings under his eyes.

"My Lord, you look weary."

He produced a half-smile. "Indeed I am. More tired than I have been for a long time." He rubbed his eyes with gnarled fingers. "It is this situation with Giordano Bruno."

I suddenly realised how that drama had slipped my mind during the past twenty-four hours. "You are being hounded by His Holiness?"

"Jeremiad would be a more accurate word. I'm finding myself growing steadily angrier by the day. And I know that in the game of diplomacy that is never a good thing."

"I take it the sub-committee you convened with Arturi, Deivo, Celsi and Mendoso to try to reach a collective approach to the Bruno problem has not yet advanced matters much?"

He produced a cynical laugh. "I'm afraid our single meeting so far achieved nothing other than to further fray nerves and raise hackles."

There was a tap at the door and an official entered. "Lord Doge," he said. "His Eminence Cardinal Severina awaits you in the Sala del Collegio."

Cicogna turned to me and rolled his eyes. "Come, walk with me, Francesco."

We emerged onto a wide, high-ceilinged hall and followed the official towards the stairs. Cicogna was using a cane and walking with exaggerated slowness; none-too-keen to meet Severina, I guessed.

"So what has been happening?" the Doge asked. "I have of course heard about the second murder. A mystic of some shade, yes?"

"A well-known alchemist, My Lord; one, Eriador. He was also a drug-maker and opium dealer."

"Another slaying. I'm at a loss how to end this scourge." He turned to me and it seemed he slowed even further. "And I hear you believe there is a connection between the two crimes."

"Yes, I do. The two victims suffered almost identical fates, slashed throats. Eriador was also marked ritualistically."

"Yes, I have not been spared the details. Repulsive. So, what can I do for you?"

I paused to gather my thoughts and then decided the best approach to getting what I needed would be to tell the old man what I suspected and what I felt ought to be my next step. "Lord Doge, I am little closer to finding the murderer, and I fear we may have to be patient, that it will take time. The killer is devious and has so far left little evidence of his presence at the murder scenes, let alone who he might be or why he is killing these particular people. I have determined that the girl, Antoinette was a customer of Eriador's. I have learned that her father was near the scene at the time of her death and that he was recently estranged from his family, but I do not think he is a likely suspect." I took a deep breath. "And I have just this morning discovered that there may be a link between the murdered girl and someone close to you."

"What!" The Doge stopped. Our escort of guards clanked to a halt several paces behind us. A few steps ahead, the official had also paused in mid-stride.

"What do you mean?" Cicogna asked.

"Lord Doge, I don't wish to . . ." I looked around at the men behind and in front.

"Come," Pasquale said and indicated that we move across the corridor out of earshot. We stopped at the edge of the hall close to a mural I vaguely recognised. I took a step closer to the old man and leaned in towards his ear. "Lord Celsi was engaged in an affair with Antoinette Perugino."

Cicogna closed his eyes for a second and let out a heavy sigh. "I see."

"I realise it is . . ."

"What do you want to do?" He fixed me with a dark expression, and I suddenly felt an irrational stab of guilt that I had just piled more trouble upon the man's already overloaded plate.

"He has not committed any crime," I said. "At least none that we are yet aware of."

"But?"

"But I would like to question him . . . in the strictest confidence, of course."

135

The Doge was nodding thoughtfully. "Yes, I can see the sense in that."

"However, I think if I asked him any leading questions he would simply refuse to answer them."

"Yes, he would. So . . ." The Doge rubbed his forehead again. "I will have to order him to speak to you and to answer truthfully whatever you need to ask him."

I said nothing, just studied the old man's lined, careworn face as he considered the ramifications. "You are absolutely sure about this, Francesco?"

"I am sure they were having a relationship. I know almost nothing more about it."

"Which is of course why you have to question the man. Very well. I shall speak to him immediately after my discussion with the cardinal is over. I shall then send you a private message with a meeting time and place acceptable to Lord Celsi."

•

After leaving the palace, I walked the short distance to Tomasso's apartment. I was about to start on the staircase when I saw coming down the final few steps, the servant girl, the rather frail and timid creature who had been so horrified by my friend's condition the morning Antoinette had been dragged from the Lagoon. She made to slip past me, eyes down to the floor. I stopped her, taking her arm gently and she shrunk back.

"I didn't mean to scare you."

She looked like a frightened fawn.

"I had assumed that you and your mother had left Lord Cicogna's employ."

"Oh no, sir." She looked shocked. "We were just scared."

"Yes," I said kindly. "I can understand that. So, is your master home?" I asked.

"He is asleep, My Lord," the girl said. "And he asked that he not be disturbed."

"Ah," I said. "That's good to hear. He should get as much rest as possible."

The girl said nothing, just kept her eyes down. I got the feeling she was itching to get away.

"Off to the market?" I asked pleasantly.

She merely gave a tiny nod and trotted off and out onto Riva Degli Schiavoni.

I caught a gondola at the water's edge opposite Tomasso's apartment and directed the gondolier to take me along the Grand Canal to a house I had not visited for more than fifteen years, Palazzo Duolo, a home I had once frequented.

136

Palazzo Duolo lay on the western side of the Grand Canal just as the first curve of the waterway swept past the northern limits of Dorsoduro. It had been in the Alleganza family for almost three centuries, and after Teresa's parents, Marco and Silvia Alleganza had died during the mid-1570s, the twelve-bedroomed palace had passed on to their only child.

An elderly servant opened the front door, saw me, and his face lit up. "Lord Sagredo!" he exclaimed. "This is indeed a great pleasure."

I stared back at him and he shook his head slowly. "You do not recognise me, do you, sir?"

"Erm . . ."

"It has been a long time, My Lord, and perhaps I might not have known you immediately except for the fact that your name is now famed throughout our Republic. It is Papi. I have grown old."

"Papi!"

He beamed, his wrinkled cheeks pulling up, his eyes sparkling.

"It is wonderful to see you." I added quickly. "Of course I remember you . . . and we have all grown older, my dear man." I surprised the servant by taking his hand in mine and then patting him on the shoulder as he turned to lead me into the hall.

And with that first step, the growing trickle of memory I had been resisting for the past few days, erupted into a flood of long-since forgotten images.

Teresa emerged from a room across the hall. A young man walked confidently beside her. She saw me and broke into a smile. "Francesco. This is a lovely surprise." She walked over with the boy. I took Teresa's hand and kissed the back of it lightly. "This is my son, Piero," she said.

The boy stepped forward and shook my hand with a firm grip. He looked me straight in the eye. "Lord Sagredo," he said. "I am delighted to meet you." He was tall and broad-shouldered, looking more mature than his years. He had a fine face, high cheekbones and his mother's tender, almond-shaped eyes.

"Piero," I said. "Your mother speaks highly of you."

I glanced at Teresa and she put an arm about the boy's shoulders. "You'd better get along, young man, or you'll be late for your archery lesson." She turned to the servant. "Papi, can you flag down a gondola, please?" The old man turned slowly towards the front door.

"Is this a bad time?" I asked.

"No, not at all," Teresa said.

Piero gave me a small bow. "I hope that next time we shall have the opportunity to speak at length, sir," he said. "I have a great desire to know about your travels."

"I hope so too, Piero," I said and watched the lad stride across the marble floor to where Papi stood in the light cascading into the hall from outside.

"A fine boy," I said.

"He is."

"I never met your late husband, but Piero looks very much like you, Teresa. Which must be a good thing however handsome the Marquis may have been."

She tilted her head. "I had quite forgotten about your silver tongue!" She looped her hand through my arm and led me into the drawing-room. "So, what brings you here, Francesco?"

I gazed around, letting the memories come. The palazzo had not changed at all. "I was just passing," I replied with a sly smile, and she laughed.

We sat in an arrangement of couches that looked out to a courtyard. Papi returned and Teresa asked him to bring us some lemon juice.

"How is your head?" she asked.

I put my hand to my crown involuntarily. "I had quite forgotten about it."

"And the investigation?"

"Not progressing as fast as I would have hoped," I said. "But then again, this is my first, so I'm travelling blind. How quickly is an investigation such as this supposed to proceed?" I shrugged. "The ladies at Alfonzo's were not that helpful," I added, deciding to keep well away from anything I had learned about Niccolo Celsi. "But we have at least narrowed down the time of Antoinette's murder."

"And the alchemist?"

"There are but a few clues, and nothing that tells me anything conclusive."

Papi arrived with a silver tray, a very old jug containing the lemon water, and two goblets. He placed them on a table in front of us, poured the drinks and retreated without a word.

"I've actually come to ask a favour."

Teresa looked at me over the rim of the goblet, and for an instant it was exactly as though we were youngsters again. I could almost believe that the past fifteen years had not slipped away. I could imagine that in a nearby room her parents were talking or playing cards; that if I were to move forward my hand, I could take Teresa's, and that I might even steal a kiss.

"It's Tomasso," I said, deliberately breaking the spell.

She looked instantly concerned. "I have heard the stories that he is not in the best way."

"Did you see him much, while . . . I remember the three of us were pretty thick, were we not?"

A smile flickered then died on her lips. "We were, Francesco. That was a special time. But no, I have hardly seen Tomasso since returning to the Republic. We no longer move in the same circles, and from what I have heard, he has made a conscious effort to reject his past and to shun those he once knew."

"I have seen him and we are rebuilding bridges," I said. "He has been helping me."

"That is good news." She smiled. "I am very glad to hear it. You two were the very closest of friends."

I sipped at the lemon juice and looked out to the courtyard. "I am very worried about him," I said. "He is quite ill."

"What malady ails him, Francesco?"

"I do not believe it is a physical disease, although he drinks far too much and he seems to sleep only rarely. His symptoms are those of a disturbed mind. A complaint that, to most physicks, does not really exist of course: Unless such an affliction is attributed to demons."

"Nonsense, of course."

"Indeed. Nevertheless, the sickness is very real and I fear that he has slipped into such bad ways that he can no longer pull himself together without a lot of help." I paused for a moment, not knowing whether I should add any more detail. "I'm afraid he might take his own life."

Teresa brought a palm to her mouth. "Heavens!"

We had all been brought up as faithful Catholics, for whom suicide was a terrible sin. And no matter how far our reason and experience had taken us from the religion of our forebears, and in my case that was indeed a very long way, some ideologies were so ingrained that at times those indoctrinations were hard to view logically or dispassionately. I remembered how in our youth Teresa had been as much a rationalist as I, and I suspected that, like me, maturity and a growing weariness with the world had done nothing but calcify that rationalism, but fear and insecurity can run very deep in us all.

"Which is why I need to beg a favour," I said. "Could I ask you to keep an eye on Tomasso?"

She looked puzzled.

"I am trying to involve him in my investigation as much as possible, but I cannot always be with him. There may be times I need to go away for a short time, or I might become preoccupied, my energies spread too thinly."

Teresa did not hesitate. "Of course," she said. "I'm not sure I could be much help, but I promise to do my best."

"I think you would be a wonderful help," I said. "And it is good of you. I realise how your life has become complicated."

"Don't be silly, Francesco. It is not complicated, really. Please don't tell me you have forgotten that I can be quite determined and hard-headed if I want to be. Lord Celsi does not own me. I intimated as much to you before, did I not?"

"You did. And I have not forgotten."

"Good," she said and reached out to lightly touch my hand.

Chapter Eighteen: More Questions

The meeting with Celsi took place the next morning. I received a brief message from the Doge to say that it had been arranged for eleven in Lord Celsi's office in the palace.

As I walked across San Marco, a leather bag across my shoulder, I followed a winding path where the snow had been shovelled haphazardly into unruly piles, I thought about how the choice of venue was quite an obvious one. Niccolo would want the meeting on home turf but not at his palazzo, for the last person he would wish to be aware of the interview was his controlling mother, Violetta. By arranging for us to talk at the palace it was also a power-play on Celsi's part, allowing him to show off his important position within the Venetian government and to offer him the chance to wrong-foot me from the start.

And if I were to be honest, I was indeed intimidated by Niccolo, but only because of the one obvious piece of history we shared. I certainly did not envy his wealth nor his power in the Republic. I thanked my lucky stars that I had not be damned with a mother like Violetta and I was also quite aware the man had been endowed with no special intellectual ability. He was not liked, and probably had few, if any, real friends. No, in actuality, there was really only one thing he had over me, and that was Teresa Damas. I was of course happy in the knowledge that Teresa did not love Lord Celsi and probably never would, but he had succeeded in getting me exiled just as I had been on the point of proposing to her, and now *he* was to marry her. And I shall not even attempt to deny it; I did still love Teresa. My feelings for her had not dulled during the time I had been banished. But, long before my unexpected return to Venice I had realised that our time had passed. Although I loved her, I had gone through too much to ever conceive of a domesticated life with Teresa as my wife, even if such a thing were the remotest bit possible. I had been forced to throw off both the shackles and the delights of my previous life. I had been forced to learn the hard way to fend for myself, to rely upon no other soul for anything, to be completely self-contained. Those imperatives had become an indelible part of me.

Celsi's office was as big as I had expected it to be, and it was decorated in predictably vulgar style. Although members of the Council of Ten served for just a single year, Celsi was the Doge's second-in-command, chief advisor and Head of the Small Council. Because of this, he had been granted a lifetime position within the government. This was quite unique in Venetian politics, and those who were not allies of the Celsis believed it to be transparently unconstitutional. But somehow, the Celsi family had managed, over two decades, inch-by-inch and through passing into law one decree after another, to manipulate the constitution so that Niccolo Celsi's power was bolstered immeasurably. By the time the family's opponents had realised what was happening, it was too late, the man had consolidated an enviable and singular position.

I was shown in by a silent assistant, a short, slightly-built young man who never once made eye contact with me nor with his master and who pulled shut the doors behind me as he retreated back to the hall.

Celsi family portraits hung around the room, including on the wall behind the desk, a vast painting of Adamo. The desk was a monstrosity of overly ornate mahogany with ivory and gold inlay. It was obviously intended to intimidate any visitor, but as I set eyes upon it, I smiled inwardly because, for me, it actually produced the reverse effect; it made Celsi look smaller than he really was.

He did not stand as I approached, and with the air of a man who was preoccupied with far more important matters than anything I might be there to trouble him with, he merely nodded towards a chair. With tiresome affectation he spent what I estimated to be three minutes reading a single sheet of paper on the desk in front of him before slowly lifting his head to meet my calm gaze. I slipped the bag from my shoulder and began to disgorge its contents, a wooden writing box, which I opened upon my lap.

"I believe you wish to ask me some questions related to the unfortunate recent deaths," he said in a voice completely devoid of expression. "What is that thing for?"

I looked down at the box and continued unpacking a quill, a pot of ink and a sheet of paper. "It's a writing box."

"I can see that."

"I wish to take notes." And before he could object, I dived in. "Yes, I do wish to ask you some questions, Lord Celsi, and thank you for agreeing to see me. I realise you must be a very busy man," I managed this with no trace of irony or sarcasm.

He gave a curt nod, eying my writing materials, but deciding not to object to them.

"Did you know either victim?" I asked.

"Hah! Correct me if I'm wrong, Sagredo, but wasn't the woman a prostitute and the other an alchemist?"

"That's correct."

"Well then, why on God's good earth do you think I would have crossed paths with either of them?"

"Do your family own property overlooking San Marco?"

He screwed up his eyes and tilted his head as though I had asked something that was not immediately comprehensible. "We own a lot of property."

"San Marco Terrazza?"

He covered his surprise well; the politician and the deceiver in him had gained plenty of experience, I surmised.

"I can't quite understand what point you are trying to make, Sagredo."

"Lord Celsi. We are speaking here in private and I realise you could have refused to see me, even if it had displeased the Doge. I can only assume you agreed to speak to me because it would look better than refusing."

He had a hand up. "Stop, Sagredo." He produced a nasty grin. "I have nothing to hide. I have no fear of 'how something may look'. And actually, I take offence at the suggestion."

"In that case, this discussion is going to be painfully drawn out."

His face fell. "Not if I simply ask you to leave."

The room was silent. It was situated deep in the heart of the Doge's palace, on the second floor. No sounds intruded from beyond the building. We stared at each other, neither of us wanting to blink first. I let the moment stretch on for a while, then said: "You may wish to throw me out after you hear what I'm about to say, but I can assure you, Lord Celsi that to do so would be a grave mistake. No one but the Doge shares the information I shall impart, but unless we can discuss it like adults, many, many others shall soon learn what I have discovered."

Celsi folded his arms. An interesting reaction, I thought. Aliba Al-Nan, whom I mentioned earlier, had illuminated for me what he called 'Involuntary Expressions of the Body'. He had spent years studying the subject. Without being at all consciously aware of what it is we are doing, we all give away our moods and our thoughts outwardly by the way we carry ourselves. Celsi's folded arms, I understood, meant he was putting up a defensive barrier between us. He had something to hide of course, but he was unable to admit to it; so, without being cogniscent of the fact, he was saying: 'Back off . . . I will guard myself against you'.

"Do your worst, Sagredo," Lord Celsi said, the nasty smile returning.

"You were having a secret, sexual liaison with the dead prostitute, Antoinette Perugino. This had been going on for perhaps two months. One of the venues for your assignations was No.19, San Marco Terrezza. Another, less frequent meeting place, was the woman's apartment in the Ghetto."

Celsi was a professional, I have to admit that. But then, I reasoned, if he could not lie convincingly, could not disguise well, could not cover his true feelings, could not bluff and pretend, what was he actually good for? These abilities were a crucial part of his armoury. They were skills honed by years of

142

practice and backed up with the confidence that vast wealth and enormous power provided.

"Sounds to me like you've been sampling some of the commodities the dead alchemist sold. Yes," he added. "You are not the only one who has done his research. I know Eriador supplied refined poppy to addicts."

"Will you either deny what I have said or admit to it?"

"Have you never fucked a prostitute, Sagredo?"

"That is not the issue. Can you please answer my question?"

He leaned an elbow on his desk and pulled at his lips with his left hand. "I knew the girl," he said. "But I did not engage in frequent liaisons with her. We met a couple of times outside the bordello. She was good . . . very good."

I scratched at the paper laid out on the top of my writing box. "And were you at the bordello the night of the ninth?"

"Oh! So, you do consider me a suspect!"

"Have I said I did not?"

For the first time, his composure slipped. The shiny confidence of his demeanour, intact since my arrival, had cracked a little, and a deep-rooted fury had peeked through. But only for a moment. My former instructor, Aliba Al-Nan would have learned far more than I might from Celsi's fleeting mood shifts, but I gleaned enough from them to realise that he was actually more anxious about the events of recent days than I had previously imagined.

"I was not at the bordello. A fact easily verified by Alfonzo Castello. I assume if you have not done so already, you will be questioning him."

"Could you talk me through that evening, Lord Celsi? I'm sure you would like me to cross you off the list of suspects as quickly as possible and if you have a clear alibi our conversation will not take long to complete."

He sighed heavily. "We had a little dinner party at home."

"Could you tell me who attended?"

"Of course. Guest of honour was His Eminence Cardinal Severina who came with his amanuensis."

"That is Father Berlinghiero Gessi, is it not?"

"Correct. A couple from Milan, Guiro and Stephanie Pastolo. My mother and sister. Oh, and of course, my betrothed, Teresa Damas and her son, Piero.

"I see," I said carefully, writing diligently without emotion. "And at what time did the guests leave?"

"Let me see. Father Gessi left first about nine o'clock, claiming he had some work to catch up on."

"You sound sceptical."

Celsi brought his hands together on the desk in front of him, intertwining his fingers. "No, it's just that the man was uncomfortable from the moment he arrived. He is quite the bore, to be honest. He wanted to leave as soon as manners permitted."

"Who next?"

"That would be the Lady Teresa and her son, at about . . . Oh, ten o'clock. The Milanese couple left soon after. Guiro Pastolo was horrendously drunk."

"So, the cardinal stayed for a time?"

"Yes. He is an old friend of the family. We had a lot to catch up on. My sister, Sofia retired to bed at the time the Pastolos departed, and the three of us, my mother, His Eminence and I stayed up for a while."

I noted it all down. "When did Cardinal Severina leave?"

"I really couldn't say. I lost track of time."

"When did you retire . . . and your mother?"

He was shaking his head. "I do not keep a tally of every moment, Sagredo!"

"It would be helpful if you could try to remember."

"I'm sure it would, but . . ." His voice trailed off and I let the silence hang there between us. He had nothing further to add on the subject.

"The next evening, the tenth, Lord Celsi. Could you please tell me what you did?"

"This would be in reference to the second murder, the alchemist?"

I nodded.

"I was here, working late."

"And I imagine this could be verified by your assistant?" I flicked a look back towards the door.

"Probably not. My staff left at seven. Luca, the young man who showed you in, stayed behind, but was gone by eight." He waved a hand towards a large clock in an ornate case to one side of his desk. "As you see, I have a reliable timepiece to hand here, so, while I'm at work at least, I'm aware of the hour."

"And when did you leave here?"

"Just after nine o'clock."

"And you returned directly home to Palazzo Arragio?"

"No. I spoke to the Doge in his private chambers."

I raised an eyebrow and stared at Celsi, my quill poised above the paper. "May I ask what that was in connection with?"

"Of course you may ask, Sagredo, but I shan't tell you. It was secret state business." He had a hand up. "And before you say anything else; it's a matter outside the remit of The Ten."

"I know the Doge also possesses a few timepieces," I said. "So what time did that meeting end?"

"It was over within half an hour."

"And you?"

"I returned straight home. My mother was already in bed, as was my sister. I was seen by at least three of our servants, one of whom poured me wine, the other prepared my bed."

"Did you know Eriador, the Alchemist?"

"I told you . . ."

"Yes, Lord Celsi, but you also told me you did not know Antoinette Perugino."

"I met the man a handful of times. He rented one of my properties."

"Of course," I replied with a small sigh.

Celsi's nasty grin returned and he pulled up from his desk. "I think you must agree, Sagredo, that I have been more than cooperative." He puffed out his chest. "Now, I must catch up with some urgent work. You do understand?"

He rang a hand bell, and almost immediately, the doors to his office opened and the diminutive young assistant, Luca appeared. I packed up my writing equipment and returned it to the bag. Celsi did not offer his hand, of course, which was a relief, a I simply gave him a brief nod and turned to walk over to the waiting servant. Two feet from the young man, I let slip the strap of my bag, and it dropped to the marble floor with a clunk.

Luca, the well-trained servant, immediately ducked down to pick up the bag, and I noted how he grabbed it instinctively with his left hand.

Chapter Nineteen: Master and Servant

The Vatican Embassy, Venice.

They walked through the chilly garden of the embassy, the Apostolic Nuncio and the wealthy nobleman. Cardinal Severina wore a full-length fur coat over his ecclesiastical robes. Niccolo Celsi had donned a beaver fur that reached his ankles, along with a matching round-domed hat. The snow had dwindled here, but frost glazed rose bushes otherwise stripped bare and sorry-looking.

"You seem preoccupied, Niccolo. What troubles you?"

"Nothing really. I've just had a rather galling conversation with Francesco Sagredo."

"Oh?"

"He's been appointed by the Doge to investigate the murders."

"The girl and the elderly occultist? Yes, I have heard. But why did he come to trouble you?"

Celsi shrugged. "I have no idea. All I know is that the man is utterly insufferable."

"You thought you were rid of him for good," the cardinal said unnecessary and with a little too much cheer for Celsi's taste. "Well, perhaps after we have sorted out Bruno, we should turn our attention to Doctor Sagredo." He paused for a beat. "And on that topic . . . What news do you have for me?"

Celsi sighed. "I believe I can get a majority in the Council and have the man extradited, but it will be close."

Severina shook his head and stopped to bend towards a clutch of small white flowers in a low-hanging basket. He brought his face up close to the blooms and inhaled. "Ah . . . quite divine. *Campanula isophylla,*" he said, pulling back and turning to Celsi. "'Star of Bethlehem'. Quite appropriate for the Vatican Consulate, don't you think?" He produced an uncharacteristically genuine smile.

"Yes," Celsi responded, quite uninterested.

"You know, I find your system of government so quaint." Severina's smile had vanished so quickly it was as though it had never actually been. "You all have an equal vote over major decisions of government. It's . . . it's . . . *utterly charming.*"

Celsi felt his hackles rise. It had been a maddening morning already. First, he had been practically forced by the Doge to face a veritable inquisition from a man he loathed, now he was being mocked by this foreigner over the

146

customs of his country. But he managed to contain himself. In his mental ranking of imperatives, money always came first, second and third. "We pride ourselves on our democracy, Your Eminence."

"Oh I'm sure you do!"

"Cardinal, I'm not quite sure why you are speaking this way. I thought the news I have just given would be considered a sign of real progress."

Severina said nothing, paying more attention to the flowers than to his guest.

Celsi produced a small cough. "If I may, Your Eminence, I would like to draw your attention to the fact that the latest payment is not yet in my Medici bank account. I'm sure it's merely an oversight." Celsi waved a hand between them as if to partially dismiss the matter. They had begun to walk again and reached a crossing of gravel paths. Severina steered them left towards a stone fountain.

"It is not an oversight, Lord Celsi. His Holiness is not satisfied with the pace at which you have been working on this matter. We need results . . . fast. And we need them first, you see, before any more Papal money changes hands. You must ensure that your little Council does indeed vote to send Bruno to Rome and then you, Niccolo, shall receive the rest of the money."

"That is not what we agreed."

Severina shrugged. "Take the matter up with His Holiness."

Celsi stopped walking.

"In that case." The nobleman strutted up to the cardinal. "You shall no longer have my support."

Severina tilted back his head, exhaling through his nose, haughtily, and gave Celsi a patronising look. That finally ignited Niccolo's wroth. "Quite who the fuck do you think you are dealing with, Severina?"

"Ooooh!"

Celsi did not flinch. "You can 'oooh' as much as you like *Your Eminence*. You are a guest in my home state. You should remember that. I have extended you every courtesy, but you seem unable to reciprocate."

"You are a good Catholic, are you not, *Lord* Celsi?"

"And, what is that supposed to mean?"

"I would have thought it a simple enough question."

"Of course I consider myself a devout member of the faith."

"Do you now? Yet, you address a cardinal, a man close to the Pope, with expletives?"

"I am not subservient to *you*, Cardinal Severina."

"Perhaps not, but you are a servant of my master, Pope Clement VIII, are you not?"

"As are you."

"That is not the issue. You are a servant of His Holiness, yes?"

"In a manner of speaking," Celsi snapped.

"In a manner of speaking? An interesting turn of phase." Severina's eyes narrowed, and for a second, Celsi was almost unnerved. "So, you admit you are a heretic, Conte? A heretic no better than Giordano Bruno? Perhaps you too should be taken to Rome to meet my master? Would you like that?"

"I did not imply any such thing . . ."

"Oh, but you did, Conte. You did. You said: 'In a manner of speaking'. What does that mean precisely, my friend?"

"Cardinal, you do not impress me with the tricks you use on pious fools. You won't succeed in twisting my words and turning them against me. I'm not one of your worshipful peasants. And I am not your fucking friend."

Severina took a step back and made to resume the walk, but Celsi stood firm and the cardinal paused. "You have almost overstepped the limits of my patience, Niccolo. But I am willing to let that pass." He turned from the flowers and the shrubs, and even managed a benign expression. "You are wrong though. I am *your* friend; perhaps your only friend." He placed a hand on Niccolo's shoulder, making Celsi flinch involuntarily. "Conte Celsi . . . Niccolo." The Nuncio's expression was now a fraction too friendly, benignancy had slipped into a terrifying parody of itself. "I have the ear of the Pope. I am the gateway to salvation or . . . Well, I think you know how extensive are my powers, how . . . persuasive I can be . . ."

Celsi felt a tremor pass through him and only his long experience in dealing with powerful men gave him the strength to meet the cardinal's eyes.

"You *do* understand me, Niccolo?"

For all his urbanity, his wealth, his power, Niccolo Celsi was still, submerged deep within his psyche, a good Catholic, and Cardinal Severina, he knew, was far, far closer to God than he; and before the Lord, all other power was immolated.

"Good. Very good." And Cardinal Santoro Severina, Chief Advisor to His Holiness Pope Clement VIII and Holy Apostolic Nuncio to the Vatican turned and continued his walk between the lines of frosted winter flowers, enjoying their fragrance.

Chapter Twenty: Visiting the Magus

I returned home directly from Celsi's office feeling encouraged. I knew I had gathered some useful information and felt surprised that Niccolo was actually as forthcoming as he had been. And then there were those final moments in his office. The fact that Celsi's servant, whose full name I learned from the doorman was Luca Lamon, was short and left handed did not mean much, of course; it could certainly not be construed as evidence to implicate him or his master, but it was at the very least, intriguing.

I knew Celsi to be a ruthless operator and he was familiar with both victims - and I was sure he had not told me everything he knew about Eriador – but most importantly, he did have the motive to kill Antoinette Perugino. If he had learned that she was gold-digging, it would have been understandably unnerving for him. And who could say what his real relationship had been with Eriador?

To add further suspicion, Celsi could not adequately explain his whereabouts at the time of the two murders. On each occasion he could have slipped out of Palazzo Arragio and killed his victims; Antoinette was murdered some time after midnight, whilst Eriador was slain not long before he was found, around ten-thirty-five. In each case, Celsi could have committed the crimes before slinking back to his rooms without being seen. If I was correct in my conclusion that two men had been involved each time, one taller than the other, and that the smaller man was left-handed, Celsi could have met his accomplice at a pre-arranged location before travelling on to the murder scene.

But, I wondered as I walked south-westward towards home, if Celsi had murdered the girl and the alchemist, why use an accomplice? That fact did not ring true with the man's character. He was very much a lone wolf. For sure, he was hen-pecked and dominated still by his mother, just as I remember him being when we were young men, but he was at the very least a cunning, calculating and very successful businessman who operated according to his own agenda. He was not the type to rely upon anyone's help. He might have considered hiring an assassin, but here, within our small Republic, that would have been an extremely dangerous path to follow. No, someone like Celsi would consider it far better to take care of such business himself. Actions so dangerous and delicate required subtlety and secrecy from an accomplice, and Lord Niccolo Celsi was the least trusting of men.

Time was pressing. I had decided earlier as I had waited to see Celsi that I would step out of the claustrophobia of Venice for a while and follow up on something that had been playing on my mind since I had first spotted the white particles in Eriador's hair a day and a night ago.

I reached home at one hour past noon and quickly packed a bag, pocketed some money, carefully secured the *Shenl*, my prized optical instrument in its box, and added it to my luggage. I then scribbled two brief notes, tucked them into separate envelopes and headed towards the Grand Canal. En route to the water, I flagged down a messenger boy and gave him the two envelopes, directing the lad to take one to Lord Pinelli at his palazzo and the other to Teresa at Palazzo Duolo. The first note informed my friend that I was making a brief trip to Padua and hoped he could meet me the next morning for breakfast at our favourite inn, The Pilgrim, close to the Rialto. In the second message, I asked Teresa to look in upon Tomasso for me that afternoon and to tell him I would like to buy him breakfast at The Pilgrim the following morning. I had also told Teresa that I was heading for Padua but that I did not plan to stay there overnight. A boat then took me to the mainland and the Allegro Stables.

Padua, lies ten leagues to the south-west of the Republic and it is under the purview of the Doge and the Venetian government. I knew the city well, and so the journey from the Molo to the Portello in Padua was a familiar one.

The wealthy of Venice and Padua usually travelled aboard a local curio called the Burchiello, a splendid barge that wended its sedate and famously luxurious way along the Brenta Canal, allowing passengers to wine and dine in comfort and to take in the splendid homes of rich Venetian merchants lining the banks of the waterway. On the one occasion Galileo and I had met at Pinelli's two days earlier, the scientist had described the experience to me. He had been awestruck, and had joked that it could become something he might all-too-easily grow accustomed to if only his salary at the University of Padua were ten times its actuality.

I had no time for such things, which is why I disembarked the gondola at the Allegro Stables where I procured a healthy-looking and bright-eyed chestnut mare named Sirocco: I hoped she would live up to her name.

The road from Venice to Padua had, I noticed, become neglected in the time I had been away. I surmised this was probably due to the Burchiello and because the rich citizens who would have been the ones to persuade the government to pay for the maintenance of the highway rarely had need for it, so it had been ignored. It ran approximately parallel with the Brenta, passing through the tiny hamlets of Priggo and Nira before turning a few hundred yards inland and skirting Fiefso. Just beyond the edge of this small town, I crossed the canal at the Star Bridge and rode on at a goodly pace.

Two hours after picking up Sirocco, I reached the city wall and led my ride to the nearest stable. I gave the ostler an extra few soldi and insisted he accord the horse star treatment including a double serving of oats and hay.

I have a fondness for Padua that many might consider disproportionate to its place in the world, especially as it sits so close to La Serenissima. But I had spent five very happy years at the School of Medicine at the University and those times have stayed with me. According to some locals, Padua was actually the first city to be founded in the whole of Italy and they can back up the claim with no less an authority than Virgil who wrote in the *Aeneid* that the place had been established by a Trojan prince called Antenor almost twelve-hundred years before the birth of Christ.

I walked the short distance to the university. It had been established in the thirteen century, and if we discount a small collection of other establishments including of course the esteemed seats of learning at Oxford and Cambridge in England, it was one of the earliest established places of higher education in the world. I was proud to have my name linked to such alumni as Nicolaus Copernicus, Andreas Versalius, an anatomist whose work had been an enormous influence upon my own medical progress, and Sir Francis Walsingham, the recently-deceased Principal Secretary and famed Spymaster for Queen Elizabeth.

I passed under the arched entrance to the main building and was told by the porter that Professor Galileo was teaching in Room 6. He started to direct me, but I cut him short with a 'thank you'.

Easing open the door to the lecture room, I slipped inside as quietly as I could. The class was well-attended and I was obliged to stand at the back as there were no available spaces for me on the benches.

Galileo Galilei stood at a dark wooden lectern. He looked rather shabby, and I was struck by just how much of an effort he had made when attending Pinelli's gathering, for the gown in which he was now attired was ill-fitting and looked as though it had never been washed. To top it off, he wore a ragged hat, beneath which his ginger locks spilled in unruly fashion. But none of this mattered because he commanded the room like no other lecturer I had ever experienced. It has to be said that many of my masters here had been as dull as dishwater, but a few had kept alive within them the spark of intellectual curiosity and had been able to convey it well to their charges. Galileo though, was truly exceptional. And as I settled against the back wall and listened to what he was teaching I realised that his power to enchant was not all about the delivery; what he was saying seemed to me to lie at the extreme edge of accepted scientific thought.

Galileo was lecturing on the same subject as his discourse at Pinelli's home, but he was more focussed upon one of his great scientific antecedents, Nicolaus

151

Copernicus, who, as I mentioned just now, had been a student here almost a century ago before returning to Poland where he had lived out the rest of his days and had written his famous book, *De revolutionibus orbium coelestium*. Of course, two nights ago, Galileo may have been about to go onto a closer analysis of Copernicus's ideas, but his talk had been cut short dramatically by the discovery of Eriador's fresh corpse, after which the gathering had dispersed with a promise from Lord Pinelli that he would reschedule the talk.

I remember Galileo's words as clearly as though it were yesterday that I last heard them. And for the first time, I was able to grasp what it was that Copernicus had offered the world, the radical depth of his extraordinary thinking.

"De revolutionibus," Galileo said ". . . is a treatise divided into six books. And in those six books, collectively numbering no more than two hundred pages, by the way, the man radically altered human thought. Really . . . nothing less can be said of it!" He leaned forward on the lectern and surveyed the room, daring his flock to dissent.

"In Book One he gives us an overview of the heliocentric theory, the notion that the Earth upon which we stand here today, passes around the Sun, not the reverse of this, as previously believed. The Heavens, he said, is spherical. So too is the Earth, as are the celestial bodies, and these proceed around the Sun in circular paths. But even this is not all of it." He paused and took a breath. "In the other five books, Master Copernicus offers the beginnings of a *proof* to support this model."

I remember at that point a hand shot up amongst the group of students. A brave lad, I thought. But then I realised what an exceptional dynamic existed between lecturer and student, and why. As stunning as the thought may have been, Galileo Galilei, was at the time just twenty-eight and not much older than some of the students he was teaching.

"What possible proof could there be, Professor?" the young man asked.

Galileo eyed the boy. "Edward Cooper, is it not?"

The student nodded.

"Well Edward, a reasonable question, and one I was on the very brink of answering anyway."

A peel of laughter rose from the gathering. I remember smiling too.

"He used mathematics, and with mathematics he was very cleverly able to predict how the stars should look from the Earth if his theory were correct. And this is the crucial piece of the puzzle," Galileo went on excitedly. "He also gathered facts from observations of the real thing." He pointed a finger to the grey plaster ceiling. ". . . the Heavens, the celestial spheres, the stars. He actually made very few observations himself, that was not where the man's strength lay; instead, he was provided with observational evidence by at least three astronomers scattered about Europe, including invaluable information from a man named Berhard Walther in Nuremburg, who had spent many years observing the planet Mercury."

I recall that at this point a tolling bell sounded beyond the quad. I knew what it meant of course; I had heard it a thousands times. Galileo nodded to his audience and said something like. "I will see you all tomorrow, I hope. We shall then continue with this extraordinary story."

The room emptied quickly and I watched as the eager faces passed me, young boys not so different to the way I had been almost a quarter of a century past. Galileo had not noticed me at the back, standing in the shadows. But then he looked up from his papers to see me approaching along the gangway to the side of the semi-circular benches.

"Doctor Sagredo!" he said, his deep resonant voice warm and welcoming. "What an unexpected sight!"

He stepped down from the lectern and we shook hands.

"What brings you here?"

"It's a bit of a long story,"

"Well in that case, you must follow me. I know a very hospitable tavern a stone's throw from here. That was my last lecture of the day, so I owe myself a drink!"

I knew the tavern well. The Goblet was as welcoming as it had been over twenty years ago when I had frequented it. We found a quiet alcove - it was still early for the majority of the tavern's regular clientele - and I thanked the scientist as he passed me a small watered down ale and he tucked into a tankard of the full-strength variety.

"So explain all, Francesco," he said, smacking his lips appreciatively.

I lifted my bag to the table between us and removed the *Shenl*, positioning it equidistance between us.

"May I?" He drew the device towards him and began to study it. I watched him, fascinated by the way he seemed to instinctively grasp its function. He found the eyepiece and peered through it, considered the bottom lens and the shape of the tube then looked up at me, marvel in his eyes. "I've contemplated such a thing as a theoretical possibility," he said shaking his head in wonder. "But never have I dreamed it would be possible to actually . . . it works, I take it?"

"Yes, it does."

"Where did you acquire such a thing?"

"I was given it by a very wise man in Nepal. It is called a *Shenl*."

"*Shenl*," Galileo repeated, and then, to my surprise he plucked a long ginger hair from his whiskers. "Is this correct?" he said, fixing the hair into place beneath the bottom lens. He then peered through the eyepiece. "It is blurred

153

... How do I adjust it?"

I pointed to a small dial to the right of the central column of the *Shenl*.

"Ah, of course." He made the necessary adjustment and let out a gasp. "The Blessed Virgin!" he exclaimed. "Francesco, this is . . ."

I sat back and watched, enjoying Galileo's enthusiasm. He was one of only a handful of people I had met since leaving Nepal who really appreciated what I was showing him.

"What is its maximum magnification?"

"I estimate that it can enlarge about ten-fold."

He looked up. "I'm very grateful you decided to visit me, my friend. But, why did you travel all this way?"

"I've come to beg a favour."

He gulped at his beer and eyed me over the rim of the tankard. "Is it connected with the incident in Venice two nights past?"

"You are an astute fellow," I said genuinely impressed. "It is indeed. As you probably learned from the other guests at Lord Pinelli's on Thursday evening, I have been asked to investigate the murder of a young woman, a prostitute called Antoinette Perugino who was killed the night before Pinelli's dinner."

"Yes, I heard it mentioned."

"The alchemist, Eriador whose body was found outside our friend's palazzo, died under similar circumstances."

"I saw his slit throat, Francesco."

"And the disfigurement?"

Galileo nodded grimly. "Just after you and Tomasso Cicogna took Eriador's body away, I was also made aware of the similarities shared with the murder of the girl."

"I have been granted tacit permission by the Doge to use my medical knowledge to see what could possibly be unearthed to help me catch the perpetrator."

He nodded and stared into my eyes. It was clear he understood perfectly what that meant and seemed to accept it quite readily. To be honest, I would have expected nothing less from a man with such a flexible and razor-sharp intelligence.

"I found some strange white particles in Eriador's hair," I said. "The problem is, the *Shenl*," and I nodded towards the device on the table. ". . . is not powerful enough to make out any clear details, and I'm convinced that there is something important about these white flecks."

"I see. But, I still don't quite understand why you are telling me this."

"I was hoping you might know how the *Shenl* could be improved upon, to make it more powerful, to increase the magnification."

He looked genuinely startled, but then straightened his back and appraised me with a confident air. "I would relish the chance to try, Francesco. This is a wonderful opportunity. I am grateful."

"Time is of the essence," I cautioned.

"Yes, yes, of course it is. The murderer has killed twice and is still at large."

"Do you think you might improve the power of the device?"

"I cannot guarantee it my friend," Galileo said. "But let me put it this way . . . I've never been one to turn down a challenge!"

I stayed for a second drink and we chatted about life in Padua. I could not resist a little reminiscing about my time at the university, and Galileo listened with good humour. Then it was time for me to be on my way. I had considered staying overnight and leaving for home early the next morning but decided I would rather sleep in my own bed. Galileo's last words to me as we shook hands outside the tavern were: "Take care on the road. These days it is infamous for cutpurses and bandits."

Sirocco was well rested and we made good speed back to the bridge. I rode through a quiet and blacked-out village, the waning moon offering but an exiguous light. Turning east at the crossroads, I had started on to the dark road towards Fiefso when the horse reared up and made an awful screech as she staggered to one side and fell, throwing me from the saddle.

I was lucky; I landed in some bushes and was saved by mere inches from slamming my head against a rock. Shaken, I quickly pulled myself up and saw Sirocco springing to her feet just as a sound from behind distracted me. I turned quickly and saw a man leap from a rock, a cudgel raised above his head. I dodged his blow and spun round to land a kick in the small of his back. He crashed to the ground heavily.

I did not hear the second nor the third man in time. One was at my back, a strong arm about my neck, the other flew round in front of me brandishing a knife. I used the weight of the man behind me and pushed back, lifted both legs and slammed my boots into the knifeman's face. Then, yanking the man behind me over my head, I sent him crashing, face first, to the stony path. I didn't wait a second but dashed over to the man with the knife, pulled it from his loose grip and twice landed my boot in his face. Spinning round, I just managed to block the first man who had come at me with the club. He caught me a glancing blow to my left shoulder but lost balance over my extended foot, fell badly and smacked his head on a boulder.

I picked up the club and threw it into the bushes. All three men were out cold. I dragged them to one side of the path and stripped them of weapons, finding another cheap knife and a cosh. Panting from the exertion, I pulled up and stepped back onto the path ready to lead Sirocco away only to find she had bolted.

155

I cursed the empty air and perched on a rock to try to work out what to do next. The horse had my bag attached to her saddle. I was penniless. Without hesitation, I rifled through the pockets of the cutpurses. I reasoned that they owed me, not only for my money and my expensive leather bag, but I would also have to recompense Sirocco's owner. Leaving the felons to what I hoped were extremely unpleasant dreams and a good amount poorer, I trudged on foot to Fiefso in search of an inn for the night, berating myself for deciding against staying over in Padua.

Chapter Twenty-one: Rialto

Next morning, soon after sunrise, I was back in Venice and had arrived at The Pilgrim Inn where I sat watching the water of the Grand Canal and the fresh morning light glistening upon the white stone of the new Rialto Bridge. Considering the experiences of the previous night, I felt surprisingly invigorated. I had found very pleasant lodgings in Fiefso. Paying a fair price for a horse to take me back to the Allegro Stables, I had set off a good while before the dawn, preparing, on the way, my explanation for the loss of Sirocco, the horse I had hired. I was delighted to learn that the mare had found her way back, riderless but none the worse for wear. From the stables, I found a gondola, and had time to bathe and change at home before heading off to meet my friends.

I was lost in reverie and did not hear Pinelli's voice calling me as he approached my table on the balcony. I felt his hand on my shoulder, making me start, and turning, I saw him and his man servant, Ajith.

"Good morning," Pinelli said. Ajith gave me a bow and pulled a chair back for his master. He did not sit until Pinelli nodded to a chair next to me.

"You look very relaxed, my friend," the nobleman said and caught the eye of a young serving maid. "Do you want anything, Francesco?" he asked.

"I am content with my lemon water, thank you."

Pinelli ordered a light breakfast for himself, and Ajith said he was happy just to sit and enjoy the view.

"It is wonderful, is it not?" I said. "I missed the whole thing with the Rialto. It was the improbably named Antonio da Ponte who designed and built it; am I right?"

"You are, Francesco. And you were lucky to be away when it was under construction. It caused no end of problems on the canal."

"But it looks very fine," I replied. "A bit better than the wooden one that was there for goodness knows how long. And there had been talk of a permanent bridge for centuries."

Pinelli rolled his eyes.

Tomasso appeared at the door to the balcony. He ordered something from another serving girl and strode over to us, his hand extended. After the greetings, he pulled up a chair.

"How are you today?" I asked.

"Starving, but apart from that . . ."

"A good sign," I said with a laugh.

"So, Francesco, Tomasso, how is your investigation going?" Pinelli asked.

"It's not my investigation," Tomasso said. "This man is the genius. What did you call yourself the other day, Francesco?"

"A detective."

"A good name," Pinelli said. "That makes you the Venetian Detective," he added with a laugh.

I brought Pinelli and Ajith up to date. The elder man raised an eyebrow at the news, all of which had occurred in such a short space of time; talking to the brothel owner, interviewing Celsi and the dead girl's father and learning of the relationship between Niccolo and the girl. He looked consternated as I described being attacked in my own home, and again on the road from Padua. He seemed to be fascinated with the idea of the *Shenl* and nodded appreciatively as I told him about seeing Galileo and asking for his help. Throughout, Ajith maintained a singular expression, one of calm interest.

"Well you make me feel quite the laggard," Pinelli said. "You have lived a hundred days in two!"

"You should have taken me with you to Padua," Tomasso said, looking genuinely affronted. "I keep telling you, you need a bodyguard!"

The food arrived for Pinelli and Tomasso. The elder man ate slowly, while Tom hoed into a heaped plate of pasta. I talked a little about my suspicions, but then finished on a low note with the confession that I had gained very little insight into what was going on, except the conclusion that the two murders had to be in some way related.

"On what evidence have you reached this conclusion?" Pinelli asked.

"The wounds on Antoinette's neck are almost identical to those on Eriador's, each were made by someone wielding a short blade and drawing it with very similar angles and direction. But, most significant to me is the fact that, in each case, the killer seems to be making a very clear statement. With the girl, we have the word inscribed into the sorry flesh of her forehead. With Eriador, there are the two missing fingers creating the *Mano Cornuto*, the Sign of the Horns."

"Yes," Pinelli said, placing his knife on his plate. We should talk about that."

I gave him a quizzical look and he held out a hand to indicate that Ajith had something to say on the matter. The servant cleared his throat. "Sirs." He looked from me to Tomasso. "I have what I think might be some valuable information in connection with your . . . investigation."

I had known Ajith a long time. He was, I reckoned, about fifty years old and had been Pinelli's servant for many more years than the two decades I had known the nobleman. He was no more than five feet in height, his head entirely bald, his big brown eyes conveying a keen intelligence. He was almost obsessively loyal to his master, and would, I am sure, have readily died for him if the job had called for it. Long ago, he had risen to the position of head of the palazzo staff, and he ran Pinelli's homes with skill and efficiency. He remained though, an enigma. I remember Pinelli telling me that he had met the teenage Ajith while on his travels back in the late '50s, when Pinelli himself was in his early twenties. He had rescued the boy from unimaginable poverty, taken him under his wing and taught him to read and write Latin. Ajith had, for the past thirty-four years, sent a large portion of his salary to his extended family in the Punjab.

"Yesterday," Ajith began. ". . . one of my staff, a young boy named Cesare Torricello who had been one of the two servants to find Eriador's dead body close to the palazzo, came to see me. He was very agitated and seemed to be torn over whether he should or should not talk to me, for he harboured what he believed to be a terrible secret."

Ajith's Latin was flawless. I said nothing, waiting for him to continue as Tomasso munched away.

"He is a good lad, a little over-anxious, but his heart is, I believe pure and I would trust him in preference to many others. Cesare eventually plucked up enough courage to come out with his secret. He said that Bertino Magallore, the other young man who had been with him two nights ago when they found the alchemist, had been boasting that he would very soon be leaving our household and that he planned to set up his own business far from the Republic. Cesare had laughed at him, which had the effect of emboldening Bertino, and with his machismo fired up, he had told Cesare he had acquired a valuable ring which he would soon sell for a large sum. When the boy pressed him, Bertino had gone on to say that he had taken the ring from one of the severed fingers of the dead occultist. He had spotted it close to the body, and in the faint light, had managed to slip it off and into his pocket. When Cesare challenged Bertino and said he did not believe him, the puffed-up youth showed him the ring hidden in his room."

I shook my head slowly and made a quiet exclamation. "Did you check the boy's story?"

"Yes sir, I did." He lifted his hand to the table between us and opened out his fingers to reveal a beautiful but overly-large gold and emerald ring which I recalled noticing when I had visited Eriador at his home the day he was murdered. "It was just where Cesare said it would be."

"God's teeth!" Tomasso exclaimed through a mouthful of food.

I picked up the ring from Ajith's palm. "And the boy? Bertino?"

"Vanished," Pinelli said.

I looked at the impressive, if rather vulgar ring, turning it over and holding it up to the light. In the bright sunshine, the green glinted on my tunic and across my hand. It was of very good quality and to my untrained eye it appeared to be of German workmanship. I remembered Tomasso telling me that the alchemist had attended the Court of the Emperor Rudolf in Prague and imagined that Eriador had perhaps come by the ring in the Emperor's service, or during a trip to another part of the Holy Roman Empire.

"I've had a little more time than you to think on this, Francesco," Pinelli said. "And Ajith and I have been discussing the possibility that Bertino could have been concealing an even greater crime."

"You're suggesting he may have killed Eriador for the ring?" I replied without taking my eyes from the jewel.

"Well, yes."

"I assume you questioned Cesare further?" I looked from Pinelli to Ajith.

"Yes, sir," the servant replied. "The lad was with me in Bertino's cubicle when I retrieved this." Ajith nodded towards the ring. "I asked him to run through the events the night the alchemist was killed. That is what has prompted Lord Pinelli to make his assertion."

"Go on."

"Cesare said that he and Bertino had been awaiting the arrival of the alchemist."

"I had sent them out there," Pinelli explained. "If you remember, it was a foul night, freezing and foggy. Eriador had said he would not miss the evening for the world and had been extremely keen to hear young Galileo speak."

"According to Cesare, the boys had stood close to the house, stomping their feet and moaning about the perishing cold," Ajith said. "But then, Bertino had said that he needed to piss. Cesare had said they could not go back inside, so Bertino had dashed off to find somewhere to relieve himself. Cesare said that his companion was away for longer than he had expected, for perhaps several minutes."

"It's a little convenient, isn't it, Ajith?" Tomasso said, placing down his spoon and wiping his mouth with a cloth napkin.

"Would a few minutes be enough to bump into Eriador in the fog, overpower him, slit his throat, amputate a couple of fingers and steal his ring?" I said.

"Our suggestion," Pinelli replied, extending a hand to include his servant. "Is not that it had been planned in any way. How could it have been? Bertino Magallore would have had no idea he would be given the job of waiting outside the palazzo at just the right time. Indeed, I don't think he would have known the alchemist by sight, although Eriador has visited my home before. No, it must have been an opportunistic attack."

"It is possible, I suppose." I shrugged and placed the ring on the table. "How did Bertino himself claim to have pocketed the ring? How did he have the chance with Cesare around?"

"In his version of the story, he came across the ring not when he went to pass water but immediately after they had found the dead man; he spotted his chance and took it."

"What did he mean by that?"

"Bertino had sent Cesare to run back to the palazzo to sound the alarm. This left him alone with the dead alchemist. He claimed he found the severed fingers, stole the ring and tossed the digits into the canal."

"So then, he did have an opportunity without needing to kill Eriador himself." Tomasso said.

"I struggle to give the benefit of the doubt to anyone who could steal a ring from a dead man's severed finger," Pinelli insisted, looking from Tom to me with a pained expression. "Such a person, in my view, would surely be capable of anything, including murder."

I gave my friend a doubting look. "As I say, Gian, it is possible, but I have to say that I always insist upon applying Occam's razor."

"As do I, Francesco."

"I know you do. But let me ask you this: Why were two fingers amputated from Eriador's hand?"

"Perhaps he wore more than one ring on that hand." Pinelli stated.

"I do not recall that to be the case. But then I only met him briefly. He was a rather flamboyant man, not shy about showing off his wealth." I turned to Tomasso. "Tom? You knew him best of all of us. Did he wear more than one ring on his left hand?"

"Now you're asking!" he said and gulped at his drink. "I can't say for sure."

"If he did have two rings next to each other, Bertino would have surely taken both," Ajith added. "Am I right, my Lords?"

"You are, Ajith," I said. "So, why did he cut off two fingers?"

"I can only assume it was a mistake, a botched job," Pinelli said. "The whole thing must have been done hastily. As you said yourself, Francesco, if the boy did indeed murder the man he must have acted with great speed and circumspection."

We fell silent for a few moments. I finished my drink and placed the tankard down. "I'm annoyed with myself for forgetting about Eriador's fingers," I said. "A stupid mistake."

"I think we were all a little shocked at the time," Tomasso said.

"Perhaps. Have you tried to find this Bertino Magallore?" I asked Pinelli.

"I have written to his parents. He comes from Florence."

"What do you know of his personal life? Anything? Did he have close friends, or a girl perhaps?"

"I did question Cesare about that," Ajith said. "But he knows almost

161

nothing about his colleague. We have forty-three staff, Lord Sagredo, and Cesare has only been with us a few months. He did say though that Bertino was not much liked by the others in Lord Pinelli's employ, that he was a bully and a bit too full of himself."

"Has he worked for you a long time, Gian?"

"A year, perhaps a little longer."

"Yes, my Lord, he came to us in June '91, some sixteen months ago," Ajith said.

"Has he been in trouble before now?" Tom asked.

"No, sir," Ajith replied.

"Very well." I lifted the ring again. "Let me think on it. May I look after this?"

Pinelli nodded. "Of course. It is of little use to us. Is there anything more we can do?"

"Finding Bertino Magallore would be helpful.

Tomasso and I made our farewells to Pinelli and Ajith and we walked out through the main doors to the tavern.

"How are you really feeling today, Tom?" I asked.

He tilted his head slightly. "You're worrying too much, Francesco. I'm fine. I am; really. I just had a bad turn. It's over now."

"I must say you look well rested."

"I am," he said. "And full." He patted his stomach. "Now I plan to let my hair down."

"Oh?"

"A party at the house of Mario Turroro that will go through the day and the night, perhaps even late into tomorrow."

"Turroro, the art collector?"

"The same. He has a special houseguest, a promising young artist from Milan called Caravaggio. He's here for the winter, and doubtless you have heard how Turroro likes a party."

"I wasn't sure he would still be alive," I replied with a grim look. "He was renowned for his . . . hospitality fifteen years ago."

"Indeed, but he is very much alive, I'm pleased to say. Mind you, I think the fat old bastard is deeply in love with this Caravaggio boy!"

"Nice!" I commented. "Well, don't enjoy yourself too much, Tomasso. Although I must say your constitution amazes me!"

"You're welcome to join me. You could keep an eye on your patient!"

"I might take you up on that later," I waved him goodbye before walking along the edge of the canal.

The sunshine was more intense now, a rich lemon glow dappling the water

162

and the paths, but it carried very little warmth with it and the ice on the paths and on the lintels remained untroubled. I wove a course away from the water as the path came to a dead-end, passed a busy market and then headed back towards the Grand Canal and the Rialto Bridge.

I could not understand what the sound meant at first, nor from where it was emanating, but as I walked on, it grew louder and somehow clearer. It was the sound of shouting, hollering, and immediately I felt alert, primed for imminent danger. Rounding a corner, I almost collided with a small knot of men as they lost their footing and stumbled backwards towards me. Just in time, I managed to sidestep them and slipped to my left to crouch behind a stone plinth with a view onto an open square close to the end of the bridge.

There were at least a hundred people gathered there, but they made the noise of a thousand, I am sure. A couple of the men were holding up canvas signs, but I could not discern what they had written upon them. But then, I saw a rag effigy bobbing around in the midst of the throng. The man holding the life-sized doll clambered up onto a stand or some sort of platform hidden by the crowd. As he turned I saw that the effigy was tied to a makeshift stake fashioned from a log, and about its neck hung a frayed cloth bearing the words: BURN THE HERETIC. It was only then that I managed to distinguish words chanted by the people pressing together in a frenzy. They were yelling: 'Death to Bruno. Death to Bruno.'

And suddenly, I was almost surrounded. As I had watched, horrified, the mass of people had moved and now they were all around the stone plinth. I realised I had better move fast or be crushed. But then, a piercing scream cut through the chanting and the shouting. I saw a flash of colour. The crowd opened up like a ham under the chopper and half a dozen palace guards strode along the path, swords sweeping before them sending the protesters running. Two more guards made straight for the leader of the demonstration, the man with the effigy. I could see him now, a priest, his face contorted, sweat streaming down his cheeks in spite of the bitter cold. One of the guards went to grab the cleric and a shout of fury went up from the protestors. A group of ten or so men, many of them waving clubs dashed up to the guards who were trying to pull down the Bruno doll.

I felt a hand grip my arm and I was spun round, almost losing my balance. "This is about to turn very nasty," I heard a voice shout in my ear. I stumbled to my left, felt the hand slip from my arm and a large man knock against me as he was almost pushed to the floor, face first. I managed to grab him and pull him to his feet as together we barged our way into an opening in the throng and slipped down a narrow alley, tumbling into a doorway, the crowd rampaging past the end of the laneway, their animal noise diminishing as they scattered.

I drew breath and bent forward, my hands to my knees. Then straightening, I saw the man with whom I had escaped. It was Titus Rinilto, the creator of *The Republic*. "Ah! My favourite writer," I said and sighed.

He gave me a sheepish look. "You didn't like what I wrote?"

"No," I said. "I did not."

"Well will you honour me with a proper interview, Lord Sagredo?"

"And why would I do that?"

"To get the story straight from the horse's mouth. I had only rumour and third-hand stories to go on."

"I don't think so."

He nodded. "I understand your annoyance."

"Do you?"

"Yes, I do, and I apologise. I'm trying to create something new here. Forgive me, but I'm still feeling my way along."

I considered him for a few moments. He wore an earnest expression, his features suggested honesty, and from what I understood of these things, I had the impression from the way he carried himself and the way he held my gaze that he was actually a decent young man.

"If it's of any interest," Titus Rinilto added. "I think in exchange I could pass on some information that might help you find the man who killed Antoinette Perugino and Eriador, the Alchemist."

•

Titus's printing shop was housed in a small warehouse off Via Pisato near the northern perimeter of the city a few hundred yards from the eastern border of the Ghetto. It composed of two rooms, one, a storage area for reams of paper with an access hatch from the canal used for deliveries. The other space was the printing shop itself housing the press and all the other paraphernalia needed for the production of Rinilto's newssheet. We came in through the front directly off the narrow path running beside the canal.

The place was abuzz with activity and Titus very proudly showed me how everything worked. I had seen printing presses before; they were hard to avoid with over a thousand printers working in this city. Venice had long-since established itself as the printing capital of the world; but I had never been at such close quarters to a working operation with the staff actively producing something as revolutionary as a newssheet for public consumption.

Titus led me across the room. There were four men working there and he had a quick word of encouragement for each of them, stopping to give advice or to answer a question. One man was preparing the ink in a worn metal tank in the far corner, another was arranging the wooden letter blocks in what Titus told me was a frame called a *forme*. This, he explained, would be placed on a flat stone called a *coffin*. A third man was carefully pouring ink into a set of pads filled with sheep's wool, and when he was satisfied the pads were ready, he turned his attention to positioning a sheet of paper between two wooden structures that held it in place.

"We've arrived just as they are printing a new edition of the sheet you read," Titus explained. "It seems we sold out really quickly."

We watched as the screw at the top of the press was spun round using what Titus called a *Devil's Tail*. This was a metal bar that ran through the handle to allow some torque and to lower the press itself onto the pinned-down sheet. Then the motion of the *Devil's Tail* was reversed, the screw lifted, the sheet was taken out and handed to Titus to check.

"Julius," the printer said to the youngest of the team busily stirring the ink in the canister. "Could you please bring us some ale?"

I followed Titus over to a corner of the room where he had a small desk. He found a chair close-by and brought it over. I sat as he lowered himself slowly into his own seat, his eyes intent with concentration as he checked the text from the Press.

"Just a moment please, Lord Sagredo," he said and walked over to the man setting the letter blocks. I could see him tapping the newssheet and the workman nodded. Titus left it with the men at the press and headed back towards me.

"Just a couple of minor errors," he said. Julius appeared with two tankards and Titus made room on the edge of his cluttered desk so the boy could place them down.

"Cheers," Titus said knocking my drink with his. He took a healthy gulp before resting the tankard in his lap.

"How many do you print?" I asked.

"We started printing five hundred each week, but that's stepped up since October. We have managed to find an opening in Padua and I've been talking to my backers about going further afield. This latest edition has sold almost one thousand."

"Impressive," I said.

Titus drank some more and said. "Now, Lord Sagredo, as I was saying outside near the Rialto; would you honour me with an interview?"

"I will," I said, ". . . on two conditions. "First, I would like you to tell me what it is you think will help with my investigation into the two murders."

He nodded.

"And the other is that you stop calling me Lord Sagredo. As I keep telling everyone, I'm not a nobleman, just a mere doctor. My name is Doctor Sagredo, or just plain Francesco."

He laughed and stretched out a hand. "It's a deal." Then he added: "You do though seem to have a problem accepting your new-found celebrity."

"Perhaps I do. It is a shock for me to be back here. I have thought about that quite a bit."

"Seems like a perfect segue into your remarkable story," Titus said with a cocky grin.

"Very well. I shall go first, but your information had better be good!"

"Oh, it is Lord . . . Doctor Sagredo."

And so I told the man about my adventures. Not everything of course; in fact I found myself falling into a form of reportage I had used many times over the years as I had travelled from one place to the next. With each new audience, the tale had become that much more elaborate as I wandered first east as far as I could go, and then back west, ending up precisely where I had begun, in this Most Serene Republic, the place of my birth forty-three years ago.

By the time I had finished, Titus's workers had packed up and gone and the light in the warehouse was turning russet with the rays of the setting sun filtering through the grimy windows. Titus had interrupted my flow on only a couple of occasions to clarify something, and had made copious notes as I took him from Venice to the Middle East, through India and China, and then on, to the return journey. I had barely touched my drink, and when I had finished my story I quenched my dry throat with a half pint.

"Truly remarkable, Doctor Sagredo! A unique journey."

"Not really. Marco Polo and his father and uncle followed a similar route long ago."

"But not alone, sir. And not enforced, a punishment for trumped-up charges. Have you considered writing a book? I would happily print it for you."

I laughed. "Perhaps, one day, when I'm old and I have nothing else with which to fill my time adequately. Which brings us to your side of the bargain, my friend."

He stood up. "We must have a top-up first." Clutching the tankards in his hands, he wandered over to a barrel that had been raised on a makeshift stand. In a few moments, he was back again and clanking my drink with his. Then, from his pocket he pulled out a long, small-barrelled pipe and began to pack it with tobacco. "You don't mind, do you?" Titus asked.

I shook my head and watched him fill the barrel and then light it using a tinderbox that had lain under some papers on the desk. The rich aroma of the tobacco made me miss the days when I smoked, before the events of the story I had just related to Titus had transpired.

166

"You'll appreciate that I get a lot of people coming to me with their tales. Women who want to expose their cheating or abusive husbands, businessmen wishing to tell incriminating stories about their rivals. I have learned to take almost all these in my stride. I verify them when I can, and if two sources match up, I decide whether or not to write something about it. The vast majority of the time, these reports prove to be exaggeration, anecdotal or fabrications of the spiteful, half-truths that cannot be justifiably reported. But, yesterday I was visited by a man who told me that he had seen Antoinette Perugino the night she was killed. He did not want money and he seemed genuine. What I mean is, he did not appear to have a hidden agenda, and for reasons I cannot go into, he was, I believe, trustworthy."

"He saw her in the bordello?"

"Outside of it. He said he had been passing across the far side of the campo from Alfonzo's. He saw the girl emerge from the building, and as she turned at the bottom of the steps, she was accosted by two men."

I felt a twinge of excitement in the pit of my stomach. "Did this person see their faces? Give a description?"

Titus drew on his pipe and exhaled a plume of grey smoke that hung about his face for a moment before it dissipated into the room. "He said one man was tall, cloaked and carried a cane. The other was a stocky fellow who had the look of a workman or labourer about him; fierce and pugnacious. He claimed that he caught a glimpse of the tall man. He was reluctant to tell me who it was because the mysterious figure was a well-known, wealthy and influential member of the government, and he feared for his safety if the fellow were to be exposed for reporting what he had witnessed. It took a great deal of reassurance before his tongue was loosened some more."

I waited, searching Titus's face as he puffed again on the pipe before lowering it to his lap. "The tall man outside Alfonzo's was Niccolo Celsi," he said.

A large part of me had known what he had been about to say, but even so, it sent a shiver down my spine. "What exactly did he see?" I asked.

"He said Antoinette came out of the bordello. She looked like she was about to head towards the north of the campo when Celsi appeared. They exchanged a few words. Antoinette appeared to know him well. The witness couldn't make out more than a few things the girl said, and nothing from Celsi, who for most of the time had his back to my informant. But something unpleasant must have been said because apparently Celsi raised his cane. He was about to strike the prostitute when the second fellow I mentioned, the stocky one, appeared out of the dark and raced across the cobblestones shouting at them. The girl screamed, but then slunk away as the men started fighting. My witness said he saw Antoinette Perugino run across the campo and disappear into an alley."

"Then what?"

"He didn't wait It's a rough neighbourhood and he had only been out because he couldn't sleep, and had wandered towards Alfonzo's without realising it. He went straight home."

"And he wouldn't give you his name?"

"He did, but I can't be sure it is real or a cover."

"Can you describe him? Tell me the name he gave?"

Titus was shaking his head, the pipe smoke churning about his hair and his neck. "I cannot. It is completely against my professional code."

I felt the impulse to make a sarcastic response, but thought it would achieve nothing and upset the man who might still prove to be a useful ally. "Very well," I said. "I appreciate you passing on this information and I trust you will come to me if this witness returns or if you hear anything more about either murder?"

He nodded.

"And I take it you will not report this or tell anyone else?'

"Not for the moment," Titus said.

"For the moment?"

"Well, so far it is just the word of one person. As I said, it is an unverified story. It could be a hoax. But, if a second person independently confirms that Lord Celsi was outside Alfonzo's that night. Well, then it's different."

"Another rule from your professional code?"

"Yes," Titus said, his gaze steady as he drew hungrily on his pipe.

•

The only light in the lane beyond Titus's printing shop came from a few stray moonbeams reflected off the canal. I walked the half-mile or so through the stillness towards the Rialto and the scene of this afternoon's riot.

Approaching the end of the bridge, I found more people, revellers out for the evening and tradespeople packing up. There was little sign of the trouble that had exploded here just a few hours before, save for some splinters of wood from the banners, and rather disturbingly, a small brown stain, little more than a crystalline remnant of blood spilled. And for what reason had the violence erupted? I mused as I tarried near the scene of the conflict. Did the public really feel that strongly about Giordano Bruno? I wagered to myself that many of the common folk in Venice barely even knew of the man's existence, and certainly none of the details of why he was here in the first place - what his so-called crimes were, the nature of the heresies of which he had been accused. No, I realised, this must have been a fabrication, a manufactured demonstration. Those forces railed against the excommunicant, people employed by the Pope, Cardinal Severina and the Celsis, they would have been paid a handful of coins to start a riot.

I headed south-east, past the old church of S.Bartolomeo, and turned, a few yards on, into Calle Galeazza S. Marco, a quiet side street, leaving behind the sounds of the evening crowds and those headed to and fro across Ponte di Rialto. I had walked barely ten feet into the lane when I was brought up abruptly as I stared, confused, into the sparsely-lit night. Six, perhaps seven figures rushed straight towards me, bounding, gambolling along the path. One seemed to have fire coming from his fingertips, another was spinning a plate atop a slender stick, two others, racing forward at incredible speed suddenly ascended the walls several feet either side of the lane before landing back onto *terra firma*, whereupon they executed perfect somersaults. The man with the glowing in his hands I now realised was actually juggling a set of wands all lit up with red and orange prancing flames.

I was so startled I could not move, and within seconds they were upon me rushing by my ears laughing and whooping. They wore the most incredible costumes, pantaloons of bright lemons and limes and strawberry stripes, feathered hats and delicate, pom-pomed slippers. And as I came out of my stupor, I realised that all but two of them were already past me running onto the campo at my back carrying with them the scent of the burning twirling sticks and animal sweat. I drew breath for what felt like the first time in several minutes and accepted meekly a flyer thrust into my hand as the remaining two figures dressed as harlequins skipped past.

I read the leaflet. It said:

Renowned thespian, the great Franco Andreini, shall appear in the role of Lord Castorin Oli Vero Giamotti's acclaimed play: Love and Honour with the Florentine Players.
For One Night Only at Palazzo Cavalini.
Thursday, 18th November, Sunset.

I smiled to myself. On my most recent voyage, heading home from the Levant, I had shared a tiny cabin with a young man who told me he was an actor with a group he referred to as *Commedia dell'arte*. To him, Franco Andreini was nothing less than a deity; the most famous actor in the world, he had told me. I had never heard of the man until then, but I had not been in Europe for almost a decade and a half and had left Venice when the renowned thespian was prepubescent, I supposed. I folded the leaflet and put it in my pocket, making a mental note that I must attend on Thursday evening.

I had crossed San Marco and emerged onto Calle Vallaresso when I suddenly realised how hungry I was. I had not eaten since leaving the stables when I had bought a piece of bread and cheese at the dock before boarding the ferry to head back to the city. I was trying to decide whether to dine out at one of the many fine and reasonably-priced taverns and eateries near my house, or to cook something at home. Perhaps after a good meal, I thought, I might even accept Tomasso's invitation to join him at Turroro's party.

I emerged onto Campo S.Maurizo, and as I crossed the cobbles, I caught sight of a huddled figure in my doorway. I slowed, all senses heightened, ready for any trouble. But then, as I drew nearer, I saw that the person was a young woman shivering in a shawl pulled tight over a dirty, mud-coloured ankle-length dress. She saw me and stepped forward, her face filled with a blend of anxiety and pain. Her teeth were chattering.

"Lord Sagredo?" she asked in a frail voice, and I realised just how young and slender the poor girl was, she could not have been more than twelve-years-old. Her face was bone thin, her eyes black and huge against her pastry, spotty flesh. Her mouth was small, teeth filthy and chipped.

"What is it?" I said. "What brings you here?"

She could barely speak for shivering.

"Come inside." I said. "You'll freeze to death."

"No . . . no, sir. I will be all right. I've been sent for you, My Lord."

I surveyed her face and yanked off my jacket, slipping it about her shoulders. She looked startled for a moment.

"It's your friend," she managed to say. ". . . the Doge's son, Tomasso Cicogna. He's very ill. He has collapsed and was calling for you. My master, Lord Turroro dispatched me straight away. Can you come? I was told to tell you it is very serious."

I felt a tremor of shock run along my spine and shivered involuntarily. I gripped the girl's shoulders. "Your master's home? It is Palazzo Londisi on the Grand Canal close to the Church of S. Moise, yes?"

She nodded. I turned and ran, leaving the girl without another word.

"Your jacket, My Lord," she called, but I barely heard her as I dove into the nearest lane off to my left.

For some strange reason, I have a particularly vivid memory of the journey from Campo S. Maurizio to Lord Mario Turroro's home. At the reckless speed at which I ran, it was a journey of perhaps three minutes, but as is sometimes the way with these things, it felt as though time had slowed, the sand tumbling as a trickle through the pinched hourglass. Buildings flashed past me in a blur. Twice I slipped and almost fell, but somehow I managed to stay on my feet. I received strange stares from the people out and about, but cared nothing for them. All I could think of was my friend, my feckless, crazed friend who

I loved so much, a man now set, it seemed, upon an uncompromising path to self-destruction. I could only pray to a God I did not believe existed that I could get to Tom quickly enough and that I would be able to help him.

A towpath ran between the water and a set of wide steps that opened out onto a marble pavement cutting through floral gardens dusted with frost and the remnants of snow. I tore along it, barely catching my breath and came to a vestibule where two liveried guards stood before the huge double doors to the palazzo. From inside, I could hear raucous sounds, women shrieking with laughter, a bellow of a male voice. And there was music, a strange, and to my ears, cacophonous barrage of noise, angular and atonal.

The guards stopped me in my tracks.

"I am Doctor Francesco Sagredo," I shouted. "Lord Turroro asked me to come. One of the guests is sick."

"Wait here." The guard on the left shouted back.

"It's an emergency."

The man ignored me, turned and entered the hall, the volume tripling to an ear-shattering shrillness. I made to step forward and the other guard drew his sword. I stopped, breathing deeply, calming myself. I would be no good to Tomasso if I were dead.

The first guard reappeared and ushered me in. "Lord Cicogna is on the ground floor, the back room."

I swept between the two men and found myself in a brightly-illuminated hall. It seemed like hundreds of candles had been lit; the place glowed, but the soot from the burning wicks had produced a haze and a strangely sombre aura; not at all, I supposed, the effect that had been intended.

I took my bearings. Before me a vast curving staircase swept away to the first floor. It followed a shallow arc hugging a set of massive candelabra suspended from the high ceiling. I could see people on the stairs, standing, sitting, lying. A woman was bent over the bannisters, staring down at me. Her breasts were out of her bodice and she was being fucked vigorously from behind. Her mouth was open and I supposed she was crying out, but the sound was completely swamped by the noise all around.

The music I had heard was coming from a large ballroom to my right. I could see a group of string players performing like demons, their movements furious and crazed, and the sound they made . . . well, I've told you about that already. I sped on beside the stairs into a massive room lying at the heart of the ground floor. There were perhaps a hundred people gathered there in small groups, drinking, smoking pipes, their talk and their laughter coalesced, increment by increment to produce what I can only describe as a collective braying.

I pushed through the revellers and reached the far side of the room.

Small chambers led off a wide corridor. I peered into the first. A man I half recognised stood in the candlelight. It was Turroro himself, obese and hairy. He was posing naked on a circular plinth that turned slowly. Next to him, and moving on the stand, was a very pretty young man. He was crouching down and running paint from a brush along the art collector's small erect shaft. Perhaps a dozen people stood around the slowly turning platform, watching, amused.

I swung back to the corridor and sped into the second, smaller room. The air heaved with the stink of opium. Two young girls lay semi-conscious on the floor, a pipe between them; and there, in the far right corner I caught a glimpse of Tomasso lying on his back on a broad sofa.

I ran over, jumping over the women and almost crashed into the sofa before leaning over my friend's prone form. He was bare-chested, his long, black hair plastered to his face. A line of vomit ran across his neck and down his side. His mouth was gaping open and he looked as white as a gutted and boned pike. I could not see his chest moving.

"Tomasso . . . what have you done?" I hissed and put my ear to his breast. Nothing. I seized his left wrist and felt for a pulse. It was incredibly faint. I checked his airways; then, using a technique I had learned in India, I pinched his nose and breathed air into his mouth. Leaning down, I pumped his chest with both hands, counted to three and breathed into his mouth again before returning to pump his torso once more. Putting my ear to his chest, I tried to detect a heartbeat, but there was nothing.

Chapter Twenty-two: Close to the Edge

I pulled myself up and leaned forward to breathe into Tomasso's mouth again and pumped his chest a second time. A spasm passed through him and he gasped. I quickly rolled him onto his side and he vomited profusely, his body convulsing, a dreadful grinding sound coming from his throat. He fell off the sofa on to the floor and I picked him up, checked his airways then listened again to his heartbeat before positioning him onto his left side, his knees pulled up, his head tilted back slightly.

"Is that lemon water?" I yelled towards the two women close by and pointed to a bottle on a table near where they lay together. One of them turned dreamy eyes towards me and they both giggled and went back to the pipe. I picked up the drink and took a sip. It was strong spirit.

I was not sure what to do. I was fearful of leaving Tomasso even for a few seconds, scared that he may choke on his own vomit while I was gone; but then I had a piece of luck, I saw a servant pass by the doorway carrying a tray of drinks and caught his eye. Beckoning him over, he seemed undecided as to what he should do, but I hollered so loudly he deposited the tray on a table just inside the room and ran over to me.

"I need you and one of your colleagues to do me a service. It is a matter of life or death."

He looked at me goggle-eyed and I withdrew two silver coins from my pocket.

"Forget the tray." I pointed to where it rested on the table. "You will have no trouble from your master. I shall smooth over any problems. This is the Doge's son, Tomasso Cicogna." I nodded towards Tom's prone form on the couch. "And unless you help me, he will die."

The young servant listened intently, hanging on my every word. "I need you to find a bier and another servant to help transport my friend. Give him one of these coins for his service. After we get Lord Cicogna to my house you must make all haste to the home of Lady Teresa Damas." I gave the boy directions how quickest to reach Palazzo Duolo. "You must then escort the Lady Teresa to my house without a moment's delay. She knows where I live. I will then reward you and your colleague with another silver coin each. Do you understand?"

He nodded.

"Then go. Go now! Every second counts."

The boy did his job well, I'll give him that. Within two minutes, I had

Tomasso on a stretcher and a half an hour later, he was in the spare bedroom of my house, conscious at last. Teresa came through the front door with the young servant from Turroro's palazzo. I paid the boys as promised, and after they had left I explained to Teresa what had happened.

"You think it was too much opium?" she asked looking down at Tom's face. He was staring up at us in a delirium. I suspect he had no idea at all where he was.

"I would say it is a combination of things - opium, strong alcohol, perhaps other substances."

"Well, whatever help I can offer, Francesco . . ." I walked towards the door. "Please watch him while I fetch some powders from my laboratory."

It took me only a few minutes to gather everything together and Tomasso's condition seemed unchanged in that time. Teresa had managed to get him to drink some fresh lemon water. I laid out the materials on a cabinet close to the bed.

"What are you thinking of using?" Teresa asked.

"My first thought was to give him an emetic, make him throw up what he has imbibed, but it's too late for that. I think the only thing we can do is try to counteract the effects of the poisons."

"I know of nothing that reverses the effects of the poppy, except time, perhaps."

"There is a blend I learned of in India where opium is widely used," I said. "I have a jar of it here." I lifted a glass container holding a pale green powder. "It is called *Nanriat*. It has to be administered with the utmost care as it is at least as dangerous as opium itself. Too little will have insufficient effect, too much will still Tom's heart."

Teresa felt Tomasso's forehead. "He is feverish, Francesco. I'll find some chilled water."

"There is a well in the garden. You may even need to break the ice - should be chill enough!"

I dissolved a level spoonful of the powder in a goblet of lemon water and stirred it. I then poured the solution through a muslin cloth into a smaller cup. I had just finished when Teresa returned with a small pail of water.

"Here," I said, finding an old tunic in a drawer of the cabinet. I tossed it over and she ripped a couple of strips from it, dunked one in the pail and placed the cold cloth on Tomasso's forehead. He did not flinch.

With the *Nanriat* solution filtered and purified by two more pourings through fresh muslin, between us, Teresa and I lifted Tomasso's head and I poured a spoonful of the solution into his mouth, forcing him to swallow it before the gag reflex undid the effort. We then settled him back on a pair of large pillows in case he should vomit again. He was moaning and mumbling

174

incoherently, slipping in and out of consciousness.

"What now?" Teresa asked.

"There is really nothing more I can do, My Lady. We just have to hope the curative does its job. The alcohol, will not help, but he has been vomiting copiously, so I hope much of that has been expelled."

Four times during the next twelve hours, Tomasso regained consciousness only to pass out again, but each time this happened he was awake for longer and seemed more lucid, and gradually his temperature lowered to little above normal. I administered a second and then a third dose of *Nanriat*, and with each application he seemed to improve. Teresa and I took turns watching over him while the other slept in my room.

I shall not bore you with the details of the two days that followed, except to relate two important events. The first occurred early on the morning after the drama began, and before either Teresa or I had rested. There came a gentle knock at the door. I opened it to find, Teresa's son Piero, the bright orange of morning sunshine glowing all around him as he stood on the doorstep. Next to him was Papi, the Damas family servant.

"Come in, Piero, Papi," I said and shook their hands. "You must be frozen."

Hearing us, Teresa appeared at the door to the bedroom in which Tomasso lay.

"How is Lord Cicogna, mother?" Piero asked after kissing her on the cheek.

She turned to me. "Best ask Franc . . . Lord Sagredo."

"I am hopeful the worst is over," I replied. "Your mother has been a wonderful help, I could not have coped alone."

"Oh nonsense!" Teresa said, rolling her eyes at her son.

"Well, it's good to hear your friend shall hopefully recover. I thought I would offer my services. Lord Sagredo, I understand your house-maid has left. Papi here can collect groceries or any other things you may need. I too could run errands."

"That is extremely kind of you . . . both," I began. "I hope Lord Cicogna is on the mend," I said to Piero. "But he was as close to death as anyone could be, so I am still very worried for him. He is still fluctuating between times of awareness and long stretches of semi-consciousness. I need either myself or your very knowledgeable mother here to stay with him at all times, so another pair of hands would be most welcome."

"And you fair well, my son?" Teresa asked.

Piero laughed. "Oh mother! I'm starving and lonely and know not what to do!"

Teresa punched her son's shoulder playfully and we all laughed. From the spare room came a scream. Teresa and I ran in, leaving behind Piero and Papi.

Tom was sitting up in the bed, a crazed expression possessing his features.

175

He looked straight at me. "Francesco! Oh, thank God!" he said with surprising coherence. "The Turk. They are tricking us, my friend. If we sail on, we shall be ambushed."

I reached the bed and lowered Tom back to the pillows, but he forced himself upright with surprising strength. His face froze and he gripped his stomach. "I am stabbed!" he yelled. "Look, the blood, Francesco. The BLOOD." He was ripping away his nightshirt and glaring down fiercely at his naked torso.

"Tom, Tom. You are dreaming. Listen to me, Tom."

He screamed again.

"Tom. It is a phantasm, a fantasy of your mind. It is not real."

"Not real? NOT REAL. Are you mad? Agh! The pain! Francesco . . . the blood. Oh my fucking Christ, stop the blood. Please . . . stop the blood!" He fell back against the pillows, unconscious.

Tomasso slept for many hours after that. Papi brought food from the market and cooked for us while Piero entertained himself with my small library of books. Then we all ate and Teresa went for some much needed rest in my room. Papi returned to the family home. I saw him off at the door and slipped a couple of coins into his hand.

"No, My Lord, please," he responded, holding out the coins and pushing them back towards me."

"Papi, I insist. You are not my man servant."

"But really, sir . . ."

"Oh hush." I smiled and nudged him out onto the campo, closing the door on his protestations,

I sat beside Tom's bed while Piero seated himself in a chair next to me. We shared a wonderful few hours. I learned much about his upbringing in France and about his father, the Marquis Louis Damas, who, as Teresa had told me, had been a good man and a decent father, whom the boy missed. But he was also delighted to now be living in Venice, the home of his ancestors, and he had made many friends here. The boy was fascinated by my past and so I answered his questions with genuine delight. He was a very bright boy with a quick mind; so like his mother, I remember thinking.

The second incident occurred the following day, and was most unexpected. Teresa and I were seated either side of the bed, Piero had returned to Palazzo Duolo, Tom was awake and Teresa was encouraging him to eat some broth, the first food in which he had partaken in at least two days. It began again with a tap at the door and when I opened it this time I was startled to see my former servant, Isabella standing shivering on the stoop wrapped in a shawl about her head and shoulders, her face tinged blue with the cold.

"Isabella!"

She gave me a contrite look. "I'm so sorry, My Lord."

"For goodness sake, woman, come in," I said rather roughly, making her sit in the chair nearest the crackling fire while I found a woollen blanket in an oak chest. I opened out the blanket and insisted she wrap it about her half-frozen legs. I was stunned to see a tear run down each cheek.

"My Lord, you are a saintly man."

I shook my head and pulled a face. "Rubbish, Isabella."

"Most masters would have horse whipped such an errant servant as I."

"Well, I don't have one to hand, my dear woman. Now, tell me, what brings you here?"

She looked at her lap unable to articulate her thoughts for a few moments. Then she said: "Master, I left because of all the strangeness . . . that dead man . . ." She began to sob again. "I do not pretend to understand much of what you do and say, My Lord. I'm a simple, unlettered woman. But I do know you, and I also knew your beloved parents and your sister." She crossed herself. "God rest their souls. And I know that the things people say about you are lies. I do not believe you to be a heretic or a man of evil intent. But I was shocked and mightily afraid, Lord Sagredo."

"I understand, Isabella. I never intended for you to know about my work or see such things as you did the night poor Eriador was murdered."

"But there are evil people in the world," Isabella said. "And often they come in fair guises, people who profess to be Christianly and yet they have hearts as black as soot."

I gave her a puzzled look.

"I do not know how they could possibly have known of my departing, but the day after I left here, I was visited by a woman called Agata Mantini who is a servant of the Celsis, the Lady Violetta's maid. She offered me money to tell her everything I knew about the goings on in this house and especially in your private room downstairs."

"What did you say to this Agata?"

"I refused to speak of anything private of course, My Lord." Isabella looked a little affronted.

I smiled. "I would never doubt it, my good woman."

"But then she offered to pay me to return here to spy on you and report what I see. She offered me a large amount of money."

"And again, you said you would not."

Isabella nodded.

"You are a good and loyal friend. I'm grateful to you for coming to see me and for telling me this. You were careful not to be followed here, or to be seen?"

"As far as I know, Lord Sagredo. But, sir, I am sorely afraid."

I gave her another quizzical look.

"Agata Mantini is a very suitable lady's maid for her mistress. She has a wicked eye and is a very cold fish. I have met many unpleasant people, and I sense that she is a genuinely evil woman."

"They say that when it comes to people, likenesses attract."

Isabella's expression was grave. "When I refused her, she was not best pleased, although she disguised it well, as those types of people seem to do so well. She said that she would leave me to think on it, but that if I refused to help the Celsi family I would not do well from the decision. She did not say it in so many words, but she made it very clear that her mistress would ensure no one in the Republic would employ me and I would die in penury."

"Well then, there's no question about it, we must fulfil the wishes of this lovely lady, and through her, satisfy the equally charming Lady Celsi."

"But Lord . . ."

"Think upon it, Isabella. We have been handed a very useful opportunity, have we not? You must put on a great show. Pretend you have decided that you shall do the Celsis' bidding. Return to work here, and then we can pass on to that darling family whatever nonsense we wish!"

It took her a moment; but then Isabella understood. She shook her head and allowed a slight creasing of the lips that was almost a smile. "It would be fair justice, would it not, My Lord?"

"It would, Isabella, and besides, you have been sorely missed around here."

"I am sorry for leaving, sir."

I told her about Tomasso and took her through to the spare bedroom. Teresa had been reading, but pulled up from the chair as my returned servant entered the room with me. Tom was asleep.

"Lady Damas," Isabella seemed only mildly surprised.

"You may not know this, Isabella," I said. "But the Lady Damas is a knowledgeable physick, who, but for the silly conventions and rules of our society, would have been accepted as a practicing medic many years ago."

Teresa gave me an embarrassed smile. "He's exaggerating, Isabella."

"Well, young Lord Cicogna looks as though he is not as sick as I was led to believe."

"You had heard about it?" I asked, startled.

"Gossip travels like the wind through Venice," Isabella said. "And like all gossip and scandal, it becomes more bloated with each fresh telling. The word was that the Doge's son would not live."

"Well, as you can see; he is alive and I expect him to be out of bed and on his feet later today."

And so, he did. By noon, Tomasso was well enough to leave his bed and to sit by the fire in the living-room. He recounted to Teresa and I what he could remember of the night at Turruro's palazzo, but it came as a painful memory. I was quite insistent that he go through it in detail and to dredge up every scrap he could recollect. I explained that it would be far healthier to get it all out like a physical poison, to not leave the vitriolic memories to fester; for I knew that Tomasso's problems of the mind had come from doing just that before. And, from the things he had said during his times of delirium, I was beginning to formulate a theory that I hoped would get to the root of the affliction.

A short while later, Teresa packed her things ready to return home. Tomasso was effusive in his thanks and it was wonderful to see the warmth and love between the two people who meant the most to me in this world. I escorted Teresa to the front door where a servant was waiting to take her luggage. He headed off to the canal to hail a gondola.

"I cannot thank you enough, My Lady," I said. "Tomasso owes his life as much to you as to me. I always thought you beautiful, and I knew you to be the cleverest woman in Venice, but you have grown fairer with age, and wiser."

I was gratified to see her blush. "Francesco!"

I put a finger to her lips. "Make haste, or your servant will leave alone on the gondola."

She laughed. I lifted her hand and kissed it and she turned away.

By the following day, Tomasso was well enough to join me on a short walk. He was wrapped up against the bitter wind and he had to be particularly careful on the icy stones of the pathways and campos. He was eating well and had desired nothing stronger to drink than weak ale. We talked about many things: How odd it was that gossip about him had not reached his father, the Doge; but then we concluded that our leader was a cloistered man and that he was probably used to hearing grotesquely inflated rumours about his son. Tomasso mooted the suggestion that if Pasquale had indeed heard about what he euphemistically referred to as 'the incident' at Turroro's, and that he was being cared for by me, then he would know he was in the best possible hands, and that if he were to recover at all, it would be thanks to me.

On the second day, wandering the pathways and passages, wending our way to the Grand Canal running grey under a cloudy snow-laden sky I broached the subject of his mental condition and edged carefully into talking about the things he had said when he was feverish and still suffering from the effects of the opiates and alcohol.

He seemed quite happy to listen as I suggested that he was suffering from horrific memories of the Battle of Lepanto that had lodged deep in his mind and would not fade like many other memories do. In fact, I proposed that those memories had become exaggerated and allowed to grow distorted and fouler than the reality.

"But, why would that lead me to opium and excess?" he asked. "And why only during the past year or so, when Lepanto was over twenty years ago?"

"You never told me why you and your father no longer speak. Could there be something there? How long ago was your falling out?"

"It is not that, Francesco. We have not shared a civil word for more than a decade."

I looked aghast. "This feud has been going on for ten years?" I shook my head. "It must stem from something pretty serious."

"It does."

"But you don't want to talk about it?"

"Not really, but I shall, if you wish. It has nothing to do with my recent . . . difficulties."

"No, probably not," I said. "Don't feel obliged."

"It is a simple story. I fell in love with a woman, Daniella, and I wished to marry her. My father forbade it."

"Forbade it? You were already in your thirties!"

"He was close to gaining the leadership. He had already been passed over twice, and Doge Nicolò da Ponte was almost ninety. The woman I loved was married to my father's closest ally, Neri de Melo, a man who could make or destroy my father's political career. I was told I would be disinherited if I persisted with the relationship."

"What did you do?"

"I was willing to give up the money, of course. But it made no difference. Neri de Melo learned his wife was having an affair, but he did not know that I was her lover. He tried to force her to confess. When she refused, he lost his reason and stabbed her to death."

"Tom . . . that's . . ." I fell silent, unable to find appropriate words. Eventually I said: "I assume de Melo was executed."

"Yes. But I cared not. It could not bring back Daniella and it did nothing to assuage the fury I felt towards my father."

We fell silent for long moments after that and walked along a narrow path beside a tiny canal almost frozen over. "It must pain you to talk of it," I said eventually. "And I think you are right, it probably has little to do with your current emotional problems, my friend. But Tom, I cannot pretend to know all the answers. A part of me wishes I could have spent six months or a year longer with Aliba Al-Nan in Tripoli before my return to the Republic. He is a truly great and knowledgeable man and would have many answers for us, but from what little I learned, I believe that you do these things to try to obliterate the memories. Further than this perhaps, there is a part of you that wishes you were dead so that you would no longer have to face bad memories.

"Then I have no hope, Francesco. I will either continue with my excesses and one day go beyond even your help, or else I shall kill myself in despair, taking a knife to a vein or placing a rope about my neck."

I fell silent for a while, not entirely sure how to respond, but then I said: "I believe there is a solution, but I am not skilled enough to apply the techniques. However, my friend Aliba Al-Nan would know what to do. He has cured many people with similar ailments of the mind and other varieties of brain sickness. You would not believe how many ways the brain can become diseased. I would go so far as to say that it is the seat of many of the worst afflictions, and the most difficult to mend. With your permission, I would like to write to Al-Nan to ask for his advice. You would have to allow me to describe the symptoms and the background to those. I shall not mention your true name, of course. He may be able to instruct me. I might even be able to persuade him to visit us here in Venice."

"I would be very grateful, Francesco. And of course I would not mind you describing what has been happening to me."

We had reached the front door to my house, Isabella opened it and prepared us a broth. We sat by the fire, eating hungrily.

"I must say, Tom, you have recovered with remarkable speed."

"I do feel so much better. That's one in the fucking eye for the naysayers and the rumour mongers, is it not?" he laughed.

Looking down at the floor beside his chair, he noticed a piece of paper and picked it up, read it and showed it to me. "What's this?"

It was the flier I had been given four days ago by the performers advertising Franco Andreini's appearance with the Florentine Players in *Love and Honour* at Palazzo Cavalini. I told him about the surreal experience on Calle Galeazza S. Marco when I had been handed the leaflet.

"Fuck, Francesco! Franco Andreini! Why didn't you tell me?"

"Well, you haven't exactly been in any fit state ..."

"Shit! It's tonight!"

I glanced at the leaflet again. "So it is."

"We must go."

"Tom, I think that would be foolhardy."

"Horse shit, Francesco," Tomasso said.

I had to laugh. It was so nice to hear again his habitual foul-mouthed way of speaking. "But ..."

"But nothing. I want people to see me there. I shall wear my finest and I shall be the life and soul of the gathering, without having to drink strong alcohol or poison myself in other ways. That will fuck the rumours!"

"Very well," I said, shaking my head. "God, it's good to have you back, Tom."

Chapter Twenty-three: Silenced

I had better explain a little about the theatrical performance Tomasso insisted we attend.

Writing this account as I am in 1611, some nineteen years after the events, such occasions as the appearance of Franco Andreini in a play in our city serves to remind me just how much has changed in the intervening years. Back in 1592, there were no theatres in Venice. Indeed, there were only two in the entire world and they were both in London, The Theatre and The Curtain. Plays were performed at these venues at least twice weekly and attended by all sorts of people from the poor to the landed gentry of Elizabeth's England, and it was through these establishments and the attention they drew that Andreini had gained his fame and reputation as the finest thespian of his generation.

We Venetians were very slow to catch on. Plays were certainly known about in Venice and respected, but theatre was a pleasure enjoyed solely by the wealthy and educated, and performances were held only in the ballrooms of grand palaces owned by the richest patrons who realised the social kudos of laying on such entertainments, especially with such a famous actor as Franco Andreini to boast about. And the reason jesters and minstrels had been running all over town advertising it? Pure vanity. Like the Celsis, the Cavalini family were new to money and it showed in their lavish lifestyle, the decor they chose for their ridiculously ostentatious home, and the manner in which they revelled in having powerbrokers and the famous as their guests. They had gone to great expense in turning the grand ballroom of the palace into an auditorium with a large, curtained stage constructed at one end, and fitted out with splendid backdrops of landscapes and other settings that were raised and lowered at appropriate points using specially commissioned mechanisms. The seating was arranged in a sweeping arc about the stage and had the capacity for almost one hundred. At least a dozen stagehands had been hired and a further dozen servants took coats and found seats for the audience.

Glancing round, I saw that the cream of Venetian society were in attendance. Veronica Franco, the most famous high society courtesan in Venice was seated with an elderly gentleman whom I did not recognise. She was fanning her face and looking expectant. In the same row, close to the centre of the arrangement of chairs sat Lord Mario Turroro, the art dealer at whose palazzo Tomasso had so nearly died. Beside him was a beautiful young man wearing the most exquisite gold embroidered jacket and purple hose. His face was so perfectly symmetrical he barely looked human, a perception only exaggerated by his dark almond shaped eyes and long lashes.

Tomasso nudged me. "The pretty boy? That's Caravaggio."

I nodded and the curtain across the stage began to lift.

I had been rather too preoccupied of late to enquire about the performance, but as soon as Tomasso learned of the show, he had operated with remarkable stealth acquiring for us two seats close to the front. When we arrived and were met by the hosts Secco and Lena Cavalini, they could not have been more thrilled to have the son of the Doge and the 'mysterious, returned traveller' at their expensive gathering.

I knew very little about theatre, but it was clear immediately why Franco Andreini had so captivated the culturally aware of the age. He was a tall, slender man whose looks were indistinct because he was adorned with layers of heavy makeup and wore different wigs for specific scenes: but actually, none of this mattered, his fame came from his ability to command attention; it was difficult to take ones eyes off him. He was a mesmerising human being, and although this was the first time I had seen him perform, I knew almost immediately and quite instinctively that no matter what role Andreini were to play, he would always engender this reaction. He was a natural mimic, a consummate weaver of mysterious webs of attraction and seduction.

To be honest, the play itself did little to move me. I felt that it was not particularly well written and the performances of some of the other actors were not especially inspiring. The first half of the play passed very quickly, the curtain fell and the audience burst into applause. Lord Secco Cavalini then stood and announced that refreshments were to be served at the back of the ballroom, that everyone was welcome to eat, drink and make merry. The second half of the play would begin in twenty minutes.

Tomasso was on top form, just as he had promised. He was dressed in his finest clothes and he had a natural eye for sartorial elegance. He had lost some weight from about his face, and when it came to putting on a show that all was well with him, he was almost as fine an actor as Andreini.

We pulled round the end of our row of chairs and that is when I saw them; Niccolo Celsi and Teresa, arm-in-arm gliding towards the back of the room where the finest wines and petit fours awaited. They mixed with ease; men stopping Celsi for a few words and a shake of the hand and many of the ladies engaged the Lady Teresa in what I assumed to be small talk. Tomasso and I arrived at a long table heaped with food and drinks and we each accepted glasses of wine from a servant. I turned and caught Celsi's eye and then Teresa saw Tom and me.

"Inevitable really," Tomasso whispered.

I expected Lord Celsi to pretend I was not there, but of course he was far too much of an egotist for that. He had the woman I loved, his betrothed on his arm, and I was there without female company. He came striding over with a horrified-looking Teresa in tow.

"Cicogna, Sagredo, what an unexpected pleasure. I didn't know you were acquainted with the Cavalini family." He looked around spotting Secco to whom he gave a nod.

"I know the family, Lord Celsi," Tomasso said. "And of course, *everyone* knows Francesco. Secco wanted him here almost as much as he needed Franco Andreini."

Teresa could not hold back a smile, which Niccolo failed to notice; he simply gave Tom a frosty look. A pair of women approached. It took me a moment to recognise the younger of the two as being Sofia Celsi. I did not know the other woman. She was an archetypal elderly dowager, who wore too much white carbonate of lead around her eyes and caked-on rouges on her cheeks. Her rather old-fashioned dress was far too revealing, putting on display rather moley and wrinkled breasts.

"Lord Sagredo," Sofia Celsi exclaimed. "I'm so thrilled to . . ."

"Sofia!" Niccolo snapped. She rolled her eyes at her elder brother but refrained from a retort.

"I am Lady Flora Defino," the old woman said, her hand extended. "My daughter is Lena, Secco Cavalini's wife."

I bowed and took the elderly lady's blue-veined hand. "It is a pleasure."

Lady Defino turned to Tomasso. "And you must be Lord Cicogna," she said. "You have your father's nose."

"Oh goodness! I hope not . . . he needs it!"

Teresa and Sofia both burst into a laugh and I smiled at Niccolo's expressionless wafer-thin tolerance; the elderly lady simply looked confused. Then she said: "I hear you have been very ill, sir."

The atmosphere changed immediately, but Tom did not flinch. "Yes, indeed, Lady Defino. But I had my great friend, Lord Sagredo, a medic *nonpareil* caring for me, and so I was in very good hands."

The Lady Defino produced a small nod and was about to speak when Sofia Celsi cut across her and turned to me. "And I hear," she said. "That the Lady Teresa made a very helpful assistant for you as you both nursed your friend back to health at Chez Sagredo."

The emotional charge that passed between the six of us was almost palpable. All Celsi's bravura evaporated and at that moment I realised that he was actually the only one of us who had no idea Teresa had been helping me with Tomasso. With an almost imperceptible twist of his hand Celsi shifted to his right and Teresa's fingers slipped from the nook of his elbow. I could see the man struggling, his mind a chiaroscuro battlefield of emotion. He was trying desperately to disguise his fury in such a public place, yet in spite of his best efforts, jealousy and loathing were beginning to overwhelm social decorum. But the outburst never came; instead what could have turned into a very unpleasant scene was averted by something far more dramatic than anything Sofia Celsi's words might have precipitated. A terrible scream reverberated around the vast, high-ceilinged room.

All other sounds were immediately silenced; all the chatter, the clinking of cutlery on plates and the voices of servants, quelled. A second scream, even more piercing than the first come from behind the stage. It sent a chill down my spine. Not hesitating, I grabbed Tomasso by the arm and found a way through the party in as genteel a manner as I could manage. But I had heard that sort of scream before, and it was not the sound made by anyone pretending fear, it was absolutely genuine, a cry from deep in the gut.

I reached the arrangement of chairs and ran towards the stage, pulled back a curtain and found myself in complete darkness at the entrance to a passage that led to the backstage area. Light came in as Tomasso caught up with me and dashed aside the curtain. I saw another closed drape no more than three paces ahead and charged towards it, pulled away the fabric and emerged onto a corridor brightly illuminated by twinned rows of candles in holders along the walls. A woman was kneeling with her back to the left wall, hands over her mouth, vomit running between her fingers, her eyes averted from the sight in front of her. A small group of cast members stood clutched together at the far end of the corridor. None of them moved, nor did they make a sound.

On his back close to the far wall lay a man in a deep puddle of blood, the liquid moving still, spreading outwards from his body; a shirt stained crimson clung, wet, to his torso. His face was covered with blood. There was a crude jagged gash in his throat, half his windpipe had been torn from his neck and now stood obscenely erect at one end of the wound. His mouth gaped and the opening looked larger than it should have been. On his chest lay a red object, which from where Tomasso and I stood, was completely unidentifiable. A wide streak of blood stretched across the floor, from the body to the wall.

"Could one of you gentlemen please come and assist this young lady?" I called to the group at the end of the corridor, and after a moment, a short, barrel-chested fellow I recognised from the first half of the play stepped forward. Keeping his eyes averted from the corpse, he walked over quickly to the girl. I strode towards the body, Tomasso a pace behind me.

The dead man was Franco Andreini. He had been murdered in similar fashion to the way Antoinette and Eriador had been dispatched, but it was only as I crouched down beside the body, just managing to avoid kneeling in the blood, that I realised that Andreini's mouth had been brutally gashed open at each corner and was filled with congealing blood. The object on his chest was his tongue.

I went down on one knee beside the fresh corpse and looked at the man's front. He was drenched in blood, but I could just make out a few flecks of white. I found a handkerchief in the pocket of my tunic and placed a couple of the motes on it. Then I checked the actor's hair. I found a few more particles there, just as I had with Eriador. I added these to the small collection, folded the kerchief and put it back into my pocket. A sound came from the far end of the corridor where Tomasso and I had entered. Secco Cavalini stood close to the curtain, his eyes like black dishes.

"Tom," I said. "Could you please gather all the cast members in a room close to here and get a couple of the owner's servants to watch over them? We'll need to talk to them."

I pulled up and walked over to Cavalini. "Sir," I said. "The dead man is Franco Andreini."

He looked utterly confused and swung round to his left as others came along the passage behind him.

"Could you keep them back, please?" I said.

It took the man a moment to snap out of his daze, but then he commanded the group of new arrivals to return to the main ballroom. "This is . . . this . . ." he began, turning back to me. He could barely string two words together. Taking a deep breath, he managed to say: "This is so terrible."

"Lord Cavalini. I have been appointed by the Doge to investigate the two mysterious murders in the city during this past week. It appears we now have a third. Here, tonight, I am representing Doge Cicogna directly, and with respect, I must therefore insist you comply with my every instruction over this tragedy." I was crossing the Rubicon and was quite aware of it. This series of killings had gone too far already. I could no longer play such a passive role.

"Yes," Cavalini said. "Yes, of course, Lord Sagredo. I completely agree. What would you like me to do?"

"Could you please try to entertain your guests? Make up a story. Tell them that Andreini has fallen violently ill or been injured. If you could placate them; and please take no objections from people like Lord Celsi. I'm sure you realise we have to get to the bottom of this, and we do not want to cause any embarrassment for you and your family." He understood the implication immediately. "Please use your staff to stop anyone leaving your home, and I do not want anyone venturing back here. Is that clear?"

Tomasso approached along the corridor with a young man, whose face in the candlelight possessed a greenish tinge. I could see tear stains traversing his cheeks. Behind him walked the woman who had been on her knees across the passage when Tomasso and I first came into the corridor. Cavalini slipped away, pulling the curtain closed behind him.

"This is Paolo Lamborgio." Tomasso flicked his head towards the fellow. "He is Franco Andreini's assistant and appears to be the last one to have seen the man alive. The lady is Angelina Gena. She found the corpse."

"Can you talk me through how you found Senor Andreini?" I asked the girl as gently as I could.

She was finding it as difficult to speak as had Cavalini, and all four of us were painfully aware that the mutilated dead body of the world's most famous actor and a friend to these two was lying in a pool of his own blood just a few feet away.

'He was just as he is now, sir," the girl replied shakily. "I came around the corner." She indicated towards where Tomasso had led the pair a few moments earlier. "At first I couldn't understand what it was I was seeing, but as I got closer I . . ." She started to sob and brought a hand to her mouth.

"Take your time, Angelina."

"I saw that it was Franco, and that's when I screamed."

"And you did not touch anything?"

She looked horrified. "No, Sir!"

"You did not see a weapon? Nothing is now missing?"

"No. I simply fell to my knees. I was so shocked."

"Of course." I turned to Tom. "Lord Cicogna, could you please take Angelina back to the others while I speak with Senor Lamborgio?"

I watched Tom lead the girl away with an arm about her shoulder. She had her head down the whole way back to the doorway at the end of the corridor. "You are the deceased's personal assistant?" I asked Paolo Lamborgio.

"Yes, sir. I have worked for my master for three years."

"And aside from his killer, you appear to be the last person to have seen Franco Andreini alive."

He nodded. "I was with him no more than three minutes before Angelina . . ."

"And where was this?"

"In his private dressing-room. My master is always provided with the finest . . ."

"Yes, yes, I can imagine," I replied. "And the rest of the cast?"

"There are two rooms over there." He flicked a glance towards the end of the corridor. "One for the female members of the cast and the other for the men."

I pointed to a door close to the young man. "And I'm assuming this leads to FrancoAndreini's dressing-room?"

"Well, yes, it does, sir." He looked surprised.

I had noticed the door off the corridor between where we now stood and where the corpse lay when Tom and I first burst through from the curtained passage. A streak of blood ran along the floor from the door to the body.

"Lead the way, please," I said.

It was a small but luxuriously-appointed room with a large chandelier of at least twenty candles hanging low from the ceiling. A cerise chaise longue stood against one wall, and across the room from this was a large dressing-table topped with an oval mirror. A second, full-length rectangular mirror stood in the corner, a rack of costumes on hangers took up the far wall. It would have made a pretty sight except for the streaks of blood up the walls, over the furniture and across a thick pile white carpet, the last of which was also smeared with a wide trail of blood created when the body was dragged from the room into the corridor. Paolo Lamborgio emitted an effeminate little squeal as he took in the vista of tarnished glamour.

I searched the room, but found no sign of a murder weapon. Signalling Lamborgio to close the door and stand back, I crouched beside the swath of blood that stretched across the carpet from close to the dressing table to the door. There was a single boot print in the wet.

"Paolo, could you please fetch me a piece of plain white linen at least so big." I indicated with my hands.

"Linen, sir?"

"Yes, that's what I asked for. If that is not freely available, a similar sized piece of white cotton would suffice. You may have to speak to Lord Cavalini. Tell him I sent you."

Alone in the room, a deep melancholy descended with a suddenness that surprised me. I pride myself in being a rational man, and indeed, I had lived by an empiricist code since I first studied medicine, but I still remember the distinct impact on my emotions that evening. I could feel the presence of malice that maintained itself in that room even though its source was by now probably far away from the palazzo.

Having thought on this for many years, I know that the sensation was purely phantasmagorical, a construct of the shock I felt but was unable to show to anyone. I do not believe in the concept of evil. I believe there are men, and some rare women, who suffer a mental disturbance, a damage to the brain which causes them to express twisted feelings towards their fellow humans. Some of these very sick people discard the notion that life has any value: to them, a person is nothing more than fodder, nourishment for their brain's sickness. And yet I cannot deny the relief I felt when the door opened and Lamborgio poked his head around the edge.

"Don't step onto the bloodstain, please." I said quickly, pointing towards the carpet. Lamborgio handed me a rectangular piece of white fabric.

"Excellent," I said and lay it carefully on the carpet over the boot print in the still-damp blood strain. I then quickly looked around for a suitable object to place on the material and spotted a book on the dressing-table. I glanced at the spine. It was a recently published edition of Christopher Marlow's *Tamburlaine*. I placed it very carefully on top of the cloth and pressed down as evenly as I could. Removing the book and the cloth, I held up the piece of linen and could see a reasonable reproduction of the boot print.

There came a tap at the door and Tomasso appeared. "Trouble, Francesco," he said. I lay the fabric flat on the floor near the dresser and paced over.

Walking into the corridor, I saw Niccolo Celsi, his expression unreadable, nerves twitching along the line of his left jaw. Beside him stood Secco Cavalini. "Quite who do you think you are, Sagredo?"

I tilted my head to one side and gave him my best quizzical look even though I knew exactly what troubled him.

"I am the most senior member of the Venetian government here," Celsi steamed on. What makes you think you can order around Lord Cavalini and impose sanctions on the movements of his most distinguished guests?"

"I think Lord Sagredo's suggestions are perfectly fair, Lord Celsi," Cavalini said.

Celsi ignored his host. "You have no authority here." He fixed me with his hardest look.

"Well, that is actually incorrect," I replied. "I have authority given to me directly by the Doge; your master and mine."

"What are you talking about?"

"The Doge has asked me personally to investigate the two murders that have disturbed the city. This latest atrocity is clearly related."

"How do you know that? And besides, I do not believe His Serene Highness has given you any such powers," he said pointedly.

"Oh, he has," said Tomasso. "My father has given my friend unconditional authority to solve these murders."

Celsi looked at Tomasso as though he were a dead rat his pet cat had brought in. "And you would know, would you Cicogna? I don't imagine you have so much as spoken to your esteemed father in at least a year. Besides, from what I can gather, you are a hopeless drunk and drug addict. Why should I or anyone else on this good earth take any notice of your opinions?"

I expected Tomasso to lose control and burst into a fit of violence directed at Celsi. Such a fulmination would have been long overdue. But I was relieved that he did no such thing. He simply smiled and said: "I think that seeing as this is Lord Cavalini's home and we are his guests, he should be the one who either gives Lord Sagredo permission to do what he has been asked to do by our worshipful leader, or he objects and offers reasons for that decision. What do you say, Secco?"

Lord Cavalini did not hesitate: "I appreciate your concerns, Lord Celsi," he said calmly. "But I would like Lord Sagredo to be afforded every respect and to let him at least try to discover who is behind this atrocity." He glanced involuntarily at Andreini's corpse.

"I see," Celsi gave Cavalini an almost imperceptible bow; the very least that good manners required of him. "I shall respect your decision." He glowered at me, undiluted loathing in his eyes, turned and strode towards the curtained passageway leading back to the auditorium.

"Thank you, Lord Cavalini," I said. "I appreciate your support and will endeavour to be discreet and to work as speedily as I can." He turned and I watched as he disappeared behind the heavy curtain. "Look at this, Tom."

"What?"

I pointed to the floor. As well as the streak of Andreini's blood, there were small variegated patches of red on the stones. They ran in a broad curve from the door to the late actor's dressing-room along the corridor to the corpse. A second set trailed back towards us and away to a door a few yards along the passage. I took a closer look. The first two or three looked like partial footprints, but from then on they diminished in size and detail. I followed the trail up to the door. It was unlocked. Beyond, lay another passage that led on to a door to the outside. I could see the patches of red had faded to nothing before they reached the exterior of the building.

We walked back and stood outside the dressing-room. "The killer stepped in the blood staining the carpet in there," I told Tomasso, indicating Andreini's room. "I've made an impression of the boot mark. These patches are where he ran from the room and carried the blood with him as he dragged the body to its position over there." I pointed towards the prone form. "Clearly, he then ran back this way with blood on his boots and escaped through that door to the outside. He either had no idea he had made that mistake or was in too much of a hurry to do anything about it."

"Not much help unless we can match the imprint exactly to a suspect's boots though is it, Francesco?"

"No, and it is not clear proof even then, but every little piece of information helps."

We found two servants and pressed them into requisitioning a cart. The similarity to events at Lord Pinelli's was sobering, and I suddenly felt extraordinarily depressed as it brought home to me just how little I had achieved in a week.

"Tomasso," I said taking my friend aside as the servants returned with a makeshift bier. "I need you to supervise getting Andreini's body to my laboratory as inconspicuously as possible. These two servants will assist you." I pointed to the pair of young liveried men standing close to the entrance to

190

the curtained passageway. "I will help you get the corpse onto the carrier and you must leave the building though the back entrance. Secco Cavalini has organised one of his own boats and a crew to get you over the canal."

He nodded gravely.

"Here is my key. Once you arrive at Campo S. Maurizo go into the laboratory through the back from the rear garden so as to not disturb Isabella. I do not want her knowing anything about this. Make sure the door from the room into the living area is locked, then retreat through the back and return here."

He sighed heavily.

"Is that something you can do?"

"Yes, of course, Francesco. What the fuck do you take me for? I'm just finding the whole affair awfully mournful. This madness has to end."

"I agree." I placed a hand on his shoulder. "We will win, my friend."

I helped them with the body and escorted Tomasso and the servants through the back to where the boat was waiting.

Returning to the corridor, I observed that the blood around Andreini's body was congealing. In the dressing-room the blood-imprinted cloth had dried. I rolled it into a cylinder and tucked it into an inside pocket of my jacket. I was about to leave, glancing around the room one last time, when I noticed something incongruous. I walked over to the strip of blood running across the white carpet. Close to the end of the blood pattern, nearest to the dressing-table was another, much smaller red stain. "How did I miss that?" I said aloud. But then I understood. Five minutes earlier, in the candlelight, the two stains had been almost indistinguishable, but now it was clear they had been produced by very different liquids; the larger patch had darkened, but the smaller one had not.

I dipped a fingertip into the still wet smaller mark and smelt it. It was red wine. I stood up and looked around the dressing-table searching for a bottle, but there was none to be seen. Scouring the other surfaces and the floor close to the chaise there was no sign of a wine goblet or bottle. Leaving the room, I almost crashed into Secco Cavalini. "Pardon me, Lord Cavalini," I said. Then I saw his anguished face.

"My guests are very unhappy. Word has got around that some great tragedy has occurred. I really don't know what to do, Lord Sagredo."

"We cannot keep the pretence going any longer. I expect you would like the guests out of your home as soon as possible and this mess cleared up." I tilted my head towards the gore and blood on the floor. "I believe there is nothing more that can be ascertained from the remnants. I will speak to the gathering, but would you be able to furnish me with a full list of everyone who attended the play?"

He sighed. "Of course."

I followed him along the curtained passageway and into the ballroom. The atmosphere was not as bad as I had imagined it would be. A few groups seemed to be quite relaxed, drinking and talking, but there was a distinct susurration of disquiet.

"Ladies and gentleman," Cavalini said and tapped a fork on a crystal champagne glass. The chatter ceased. "Lord Sagredo would like to make an announcement."

"I'm afraid something terrible has happened," I began. "Franco Andreini has been murdered."

At least twenty of the gathering gasped almost simultaneously, and then a couple of the ladies broke down in tears. A few, those in whom Celsi must have confided, did not seem to be quite so shocked by the disclosure. I noticed Niccolo close to the back studying me intently, his arms folded across his chest, Teresa stood a little way to his left.

"But how? How could such a thing happen? Here?" an elderly man close to the front of the gathering blurted out. "It's an outrage."

I recognised him as Antonio Gammanti, a senior statesman from Pasquale Cicogna's generation, who had long-since retired from politics. "I cannot go into great detail about anything, sir" I said. "But it seems very clear that the murderer is the same person who killed the two victims last week."

There was another collective intake of breath.

"Now, I'm sure you all wish to return to your homes, but I would like to request that each of you try to recall where you were just before we all heard the screams. If you could spare the time to write down your memories when you reach home that may prove very helpful to me in my investigation. If you can recall seeing or hearing anything strange or unusual as we began the interval in the play, then that would be especially useful."

I could see that Celsi was itching to make some snide comment but was restraining himself.

"Thank you ladies and gentlemen," I concluded and walked back to the curtained passage and the corridor beyond. My next task was to talk to the performers who had been kept under guard in a side room.

"Why have we been held here like this?" demanded a slender fellow with straggly blond hair and beard and wearing an over-ornate army officer's uniform. From the programme I recalled his name as Dominico Fortunio; he had played a character called General Il Fanto.

I walked to the centre of the room in which the actors had been kept since Andreini's body was found. There were nine members of the company who had supported Andreini; three women, including Angelina Gena, who had alerted us all with her screams; and six men. Paolo Lamborgio was also there. I could smell strong alcohol and saw that there was an ale keg in the corner; most of the cast held wooden tankards in their hands.

"I apologise," I began, looking from Fortunio to the others. "But it was a necessity."

A woman standing just behind Fortunio stepped forward. "Why?" she snapped. "Why was it a *necessity*?"

"Because I need to know if any of you saw anything strange that might help me discover the identity of your friend's murderer." I paused for a moment and looked around at each of their faces. "My name is Francesco Sagredo. I have been asked by the Doge personally to investigate a series of murders that have shaken us here in Venice during the past eight days." None of them spoke, only a few of the performers could look me in the eye. "There are certain aspects to Franco Andreini's murder that are similar to the killings from a week ago which suggest strongly that whoever killed your fellow performer also killed the first two victims, a prostitute Antoinette Perugino and an alchemist named Eriador."

"I've heard about the murders," Fortunio offered. He looked about him and several of the cast nodded in affirmation. "But none of us were in Venice a week ago. We have several hundred witnesses who will attest to the fact that we were performing in Verona. We only arrived here yesterday even though our visit was advertised by Venetian harlequins employed by Lord Cavalini."

I raised my hands again. "I realise this, good sir. I was not suggesting any of you were involved in the terrible death of Franco Andreini. I merely wish to ask you some questions about where you were when Angelina here found the body and whether you might have seen anything unusual or strange when you last saw Andreini alive."

A young woman seated at the back of the small room stood up. "I saw a man," she said. "Only a glimpse. That is all."

"Please go on, young lady. Sorry, what's your name?"

"Dea. Dea Giottinelli."

"Where were you?"

"I was in a backroom close to the door out to the rear courtyard."

"You reach that area from the door further along the corridor from Senor Andreini's dressing-room?" I said. It was where I had been with Tomasso a little earlier.

"Yes sir. I was sorting out some props and heading back to the corridor. I planned to go through the curtained passage and then on to the stage to arrange things."

"Could you describe the man?"

"Sadly, not well, sir. I saw him only fleetingly as he disappeared through the door."

"Tell me precisely what you recall, Dea."

"He was a small man, no taller than I, and but slightly built. He was dressed in black. But . . . well, that is all I can say."

"His hair? Footwear? Was he carrying anything?"

"He wore a hat, or at least his head was partially covered, Lord Sagredo. I cannot say what shoes he had on his feet, if any, and no, I saw nothing he might have been carrying. I'm sorry."

"What happened next?"

"I was a little preoccupied and thought nothing more about it. I assumed the man was one of the staff or someone associated with the Cavalini family. I walked out onto the corridor just as Angelina screamed. Then I saw . . . Franco."

"What you have remembered is very helpful." I paused for a moment to gather my thoughts. "Did anyone hear anything strange? Did any of you hear Senor Andreini cry out?"

One of the women gasped and stifled a small sob.

"The last time I saw Franco," said Dominico Fortunio. He belched loudly. ". . . was as we left the stage to the applause of the audience. He went straight to his room. I followed Umberto, here." He nudged a younger man beside him, "To get a tankard of ale. Lord Cavalini supplied food and beverages for us, nothing so fine as the fare out there." He flicked his eyes towards the ballroom. "But it serves." He gave me a sour look and took another swig of his ale.

I glanced round the room. "So, Senor Lamborgio," I said, seeing Andreini's personal assistant in a chair to my left. "You were the last to see your master alive. Tell me what happened as the curtain fell."

"I was at the side of the stage as the cast exited stage left and I escorted Franco to his private room. I told him I would fetch some food and wine. He seemed a little disgruntled and snapped that he was not hungry; he just wanted water and perhaps a little fruit."

"You then left to get these things?"

"Yes, but I was delayed. The palazzo caterers were preoccupied with the guests and had nothing ready. I had to go on a search of the kitchens for some grapes and some dates, an orange or two along with some fresh lemon water or weak ale. I was just leaving when I heard Angelina's screams."

"Where are the kitchens?"

He pointed in the opposite direction to the dressing-room.

"And you had gone there directly from Andreini's room?"

"Yes."

"And, Angelina? Why were you in the corridor so that you were first to

194

find your colleague's body?"

"I'd been next door in the ladies dressing-room," she replied nervously. "I had changed into this." She glanced down at what she was wearing; a men's tights and fur-trimmed tunic. I was returning to the passage beside the stage. I like to sit for a while alone during the interval because mine are the first lines of dialogue in the second part of this play and I always feel a little anxious about them. I stepped out of the ladies dressing-room, turned into the corridor and . . ."

"So, Lord Sagredo," Dominico Fortunio said with an air of self-confidence. "What does all this suggest to you? Why would anyone want to kill Franco Andreini?"

"Perhaps you can shed some light on that for me," I replied.

"What do you mean?"

"Was the man liked? Do you know anyone who may have held a grudge against him?"

"I'm not sure I like what you're implying."

"I'm not implying anything, Senor Fortunio. But you all knew him well, I assume. You have been on the road together . . . how long?"

"Six months," Angelina offered. "Most of us are from Florence. We came together to rehearse in May, performed locally at first then set off to the southern regions in June. We only returned north in October. And yes, we all know one another very well. Franco put on airs and graces, there is no denying that, but it was only with patrons, the wealthy who employed our company. Never with us."

"Franco knew his value," Fortunio said. "He pissed off a lot of the people who saw themselves as socially superior, but he was more famous than them and better loved. He was never big-headed with us. He was the manager of the company too and he looked after all of us." He turned to the others and they all nodded in agreement. Angelina crossed herself and a tear drained from the corner of each eye.

"I'm sorry if what I'm about to say comes across as insensitive, but I need to ask some difficult questions." The room was very quiet, everyone still, looking towards me. "As far as you are aware, did Franco Andreini use opium?"

For a moment, no one reacted, but then Fortunio broke into a grin. "We are performers." He said. "By our very nature we are not average, conventional people." He looked around at his colleagues and a couple of them looked away but he got a few sly smiles. "I cannot speak for Franco because I never saw him use the pipe. But perhaps he did. And like all of us, he drank a lot."

"And," I said. "An even more sensitive question . . . the man's sexuality?"

Again, none of the actors seemed too disturbed and I quickly accepted this. I was not, after all asking such questions of a group of old maids like Lady

Defino and her ilk. This time it was Dea Giottinelli who replied. "It was no secret, Franco preferred the company of men." She caught Lamborgio's eye. He looked down.

"Well," I said after a few silent seconds. "Thank you for your cooperation. I'm sorry to admit this, but, I still have very little idea about the perpetrator of these murders. However, I am sure that your friend was killed by the same person who murdered Antoinette and the alchemist." And even as I spoke, some vague idea of a motive at least, was starting to present itself to me.

Returning to the corridor, I saw a man walking towards me. It took me a few moments to recognise the young painter, Caravaggio. He was staring at the smeared blood across the floor. It seemed no one had yet ordered the servants to clean it up.

"A fabulous colour, is it not?" the young man said nodding towards the crimson streaks.

"'Fabulous' is one possible word to describe it."

He leaned forward, his hand out before him. "You are Lord Sagredo. I am . . .'

"Caravaggio.'

"Oh Lordy, my fame precedes me.'

"It would seem so. You have slipped away from Lord Turroro," I observed.

He smiled. "I saw you at Palazzo Londisi. You were very impressive."

I looked at him seriously. My friend almost died."

"Yes, he was rather overdoing it."

I appraised the young man and thought how strange that such a beautiful creature who was also immensely talented could be so vacuous. And a thought struck me. "Would you be able to do me a small favour?" I asked.

"Well, that depends what it might be," Caravaggio replied archly.

I ignored his flirtatious manner. "A young lady, one of the actors in the performance, caught a glimpse of one of the men who I believe could have been involved in Andreini's murder. If she were to speak with you would you do me the great honour of sketching the man from her description?"

He looked startled for a moment, then broke into a smile. "What a curious fellow you are, Lord Sagredo. And what would be in it for me?"

I must have pulled an odd expression because the youth suddenly burst into a high-pitched laugh. "Oh, just look at you, sir, so serious. I am joking with you!"

I forced a smile. "So?"

"I would be delighted to help," Caravaggio said.

Chapter Twenty-four: Autopsy

Tomasso had followed my instructions to the letter. We spoke briefly upon his return and he insisted he should be off to his own place, claiming understandably, that after being so ill he had no stomach for watching me work on Andreini's body.

I entered my house through the backdoor to the laboratory, and using my tinderbox, I lit up two torches on the wall at the far end before standing back to survey the actor Franco Andreini's mutilated body where it lay on the table occupied a few days earlier by the alchemist, Eriador. It was an almost surreal sight, for although I was not impressed by celebrity in any form, if a few days before, someone had told me that in a short time the most respected thespian in the world would be lying dead in my laboratory, I would have been rather disbelieving.

The room was so cold I could see my own breath. I walked over to the fireplace and quickly started a fire with some dry wood and a little kindling. Once it had caught I placed a log on the yellow flames. I then lit a candle which I placed at the end of the table before picking up the actor's tongue and holding it in the corona. The flesh was black and stiff. It was clear from the crudity of the surgery that it had been removed quickly. Laying the tongue on a counter to my left, I turned back to the cadaver and carefully removed Andreini's clothes. They too were now stiff with dried blood and not the easiest garments to pull over the victim's arms and legs. Taking my handkerchief from my pocket, I tipped onto the counter top the white flecks I had removed from the body at the Cavalini's palazzo. In the light from the candle I could see they were almost identical to the ones I had discovered in this very room on Eriador the Alchemist's body.

There came a quiet tap at the door leading from my laboratory to the courtyard, and although it was a gentle knocking, it startled me. I picked up the candle and walked to the back of the room.

"Who is it?"

"It is I, Teresa."

I unlocked the door, and there she stood in the icy cold, the still black night punctured by specks of light spread out behind her. "Teresa. Come in," I said and took her arm, quickly closing the door. "What are you doing here?"

She saw Andreini's corpse. "I assumed you would get the body here somehow. Poor man, and such a great talent. It's senseless."

"I'm rather hoping it isn't actually. It is obviously a murder connected to the previous two and it has to have some sort of weird meaning." I saw her face in the candlelight and noticed a small cut under her left eye. Drawing her close to one of the brighter torches, I gave her a hard stare and did not need to ask.

"It is nothing, Francesco." she said very calmly. "He has a temper and sometimes he lashes out."

"Because of you being here to help with Tomasso?"

She shrugged.

"Can you remind me again why it is you stay with him?" I was angry, and only just able to control myself. "You have private wealth. You do not need his support."

"Francesco, please."

"I just need to know, Teresa. I don't understand."

She looked down at the dark floor. "It is a matter of respectability. Surely you have not forgotten such things in all those years away from our way of life here? I'm too young to be a noble widow and unless I remarry, there shall always be evil men out there trying to prey on me; at least until Piero comes of age."

"And you do not think that Celsi is preying on you?"

"He is head of one of the richest families in Italy, Francesco. That is not very plausible."

"I did not mean it so much in a fiscal sense, Teresa. He knows you are vulnerable, only recently widowed. He has always lusted after you."

"Perhaps he loves me."

I could not help showing my surprise. "If he loved you he would not harm you. He would cherish you and protect you. He should worship the ground you walk upon."

Teresa tilted her head in that old familiar way I loved so much. "You are a romantic, my darling, Francesco. You always have been." And quite unexpectedly, she kissed me on the cheek.

"Now, enough of this. Down to business. Tell me everything you have deduced about this terrible crime." She glanced over at the wretched form of the dead actor.

"It was the most audacious murder of the three," I began. "In a palazzo packed with people. The killer could not have had more than two minutes to dispatch Andreini, disfigure him and place him in the corridor for all to see."

"And the tongue? Another ritualistic signifier?"

"I'm sure of it. I was about to start an autopsy." We paced over to the table. "It is clear he died from this wound." I pointed to Andreini's lacerated neck. "The same as Antoinette and Eriador. Teresa? Could you please hold the candle close to the throat for a moment?" I made a close study of the wound, probing my fingers around the loose blood-drained flaps of flesh. "Yes, as I would have expected," I said.

"What, Francesco?"

"The killer was right handed. The same as the man who slew Eriador and Antoinette. See the wound in the throat?" I explained about the angle of the fatal cut as I had described it to Tomasso a few days earlier. "The killer then very hurriedly enlarged the victim's mouth and slashed away at the back of the tongue with a very sharp blade. It was all rather clumsy as you can see from the stump of the removed tongue and also from the fact that the murderer severed Andreini's windpipe and pulled it out through the wounds in his neck. It was all rushed and brutal." I checked these mutilations closely. "Aha!"

"What?"

"These slashes to the windpipe, the savage cutting after the murderous stroke were carried out with the left hand. See here?" I pointed to the way the flesh had been split open from strokes that rose and dropped to the left of the gash. "Whoever did this." I pointed to the wounds, ". . . would have slashed and ripped from the front. Like so." I demonstrated with an imaginary knife in my left hand.

"Yes," Teresa said considering the injuries. The blade ended up on the left, hence the upward or downward turn on that side. But, my God . . . the brutality! It is almost as though the poor man were attacked by a wild animal."

I explained my theory that two people were behind the murders. "I did not do an autopsy on Eriador," I said. There seemed little point as it was clear how he was killed. With Antoinette I did not have the opportunity, but perhaps there is something of value to be learned from a dissection of this corpse. I watched many procedures in Arab countries and again in China where court doctors studied the corpses of executed prisoners immediately after death." I lifted a razor sharp blade from a small packet I had laid out beside Andreini's body. "The standard practice is to first cut open the chest. A great surgeon in China, Yung Ho referred to it as a Y-section. We begin at one shoulder, immediately below the clavicle." I brought the knife down to the dead man's bruised skin at his left shoulder. ". . . and cut diagonally to a point here." I stopped just above the sternum. "We then repeat from the other shoulder." I duplicated the action meeting at the same point above the breast bone. I then switched blades to a longer, heavier implement. "Finally, we draw a line down to beyond the navel. Like so."

There was no blood, just a trickle of orange ooze from the wound. I placed both hands on Andreini's torso. "We may now open the flesh." I made a few more slices and soon had the man's rib cage exposed. Lifting a small saw from the packet of instruments, I set to work, cutting through the cartilage where the bones connected to the sternum. After cleaving three of the ribs each side

199

of the central part of the sternum, I reached in and pulled the entire rib cage apart.

The process was incredibly violent, but Teresa did not flinch. Instead, fascinated, she watched my every move. With the ribs pulled apart, we could see in the light from the torches the red and grey sheath over the organs. I then sliced this away to expose them.

"The next step would be to make a close inspection of each of the organs before moving on to the head, remove the top of the skull and study the condition of the brain; but I think that would be a waste of time. Let us take a closer look at the heart and the structures up to the mouth. Just a little closer with the candle please, Teresa." I pulled aside flesh and reached in to the region above the heart leading up to the actor's throat. Finding the rest of his windpipe, I loosened it from the membranes and cartilage that held it in place. Next, using a third and smaller blade from my collection, I made a careful incision in the windpipe, bringing the knife down the length of the tube to where it branched in two.

"What's that?" Teresa said and gently moved my left hand aside.

We could both see a white rectangle.

"If I keep the windpipe open can you reach it with your spare hand?" I asked Teresa.

Very steadily, very professionally, she transferred the candle to her left hand and reached into the mess of Andreini's neck to pluck out the object.

"Over here," I said walking to a counter directly beneath the wall torches.

Teresa lowered the candle holder to the bench and lifted the object very carefully. It was a folded piece of paper. I opened it out and in the light from the torches we could both see a single smudged word: 'silere'.

I straightened. "Latin again."

"'Silence'," Teresa said.

"Yes, as cryptic as 'Redemptionis' or the horned hand of Eriador's mutilation."

I lowered my head again. "And look at this." There were pink-red stains on the paper.

"Blood, obviously."

"I don't think so," I replied and pulled back from the pool of light. "Too pale." I touched the paper. "Too watery."

"Well it could be blood mixed with saliva, could it not?"

I shook my head. "It's wine. Red wine. And that would make some sort of warped sense."

Teresa straightened and leaned back on the counter. "You're speaking in riddles, Francesco."

"I'm sorry," I began. "I found red wine stains on the carpet of Andreini's dressing-room; very close to the huge blood streaks."

"Well he had a bottle of wine, on his dressing-table, perhaps? It could have been easily knocked over when he was attacked. These stains could be wine that was in his mouth or which somehow got into his windpipe when he was viciously assaulted. Doesn't that make sense?"

I stared into her dark eyes. "It certainly would, except that Andreini's personal assistant, Paolo Lamborgio told me specifically that his master did not want wine, just water and a little fruit."

"Could the wine have been in the room already?"

"That is also a possibility, but I'm beginning to wonder about something else."

I started to turn back to Andreini's body when the back door flew open. Three men burst into the laboratory, the man at the front had his sword drawn and was striding purposefully towards Teresa and I. The other two soldiers were unsheathing their weapons.

"Stop!" A voice boomed from the doorway. The men halted immediately. The leader of the three slowly lowered his weapon. The voice was Niccolo Celsi's. "Caught in the very act of heresy," he proclaimed, looking along the room towards the table where the remains of the dead thespian lay. "Take him." Celsi snapped at the guards.

Teresa marched towards Lord Celsi, but one of the men grabbed her arm roughly.

"Leave her be," I shouted.

Celsi grinned. "How touching."

The guard with the sword had the blade at my neck, the remaining soldier grabbed my left arm and yanked it behind my back as I was marched towards the door.

"This is a very bad idea, Celsi," I spat out the words as I reached him near the opening onto the courtyard. "The Doge will be after your blood before the dawn breaks."

Celsi shook his head slowly. "I don't think so, Sagredo. His Serene Majesty has been called away on very important business at short notice. I am now Acting Head of State."

Chapter Twenty-five: Imprisoned

Out in the courtyard one of the men bound my wrists behind my back. I saw no point in resisting, at least as long as Teresa remained untouched. Celsi was not though the sort of man to hit a woman in public and he certainly would not want to give me the slightest impression that he was disturbed by the presence of his betrothed in my laboratory.

"Please Niccolo, will you stop this nonsense," Teresa implored as they joined us in the courtyard. There was a faint silver glow on the horizon which meant the dawn was perhaps an hour away.

"This is not your business, my dear."

"It is the business of every right-thinking person," Teresa implored. "Doctor Sagredo is doing nothing wrong. He is merely trying to ascertain facts to find the killer in our midst."

"Heresy is heresy, My Lady, and the orders for this man's arrest have come from the Pope himself."

"The Pope?" I said. "So we Venetians are no longer a free people?"

Celsi ignored the comment. "Take him away," he commanded.

"Where to, Niccolo?" Teresa asked. "What in the name of the Lord are you doing?"

"Sagredo will be held in the prisons of His Most Serene Majesty. When the Doge returns, the heretic will be put on trial."

"This is madness!" Teresa snapped.

"Take Lady Damas to her home," Celsi instructed two of the guards. "Ensure she remains there under house arrest."

I was shoved into the laneway beside my house where two more palace guards were waiting. I heard Teresa calling after Celsi, but he acted as though she were not there. She was whisked away across the campo and I was escorted by Lord Celsi and his men in the opposite direction, towards the closest canal. There, a boat awaited us. I said nothing the entire journey from the tributary and on to the Grand Canal where we turned northeast towards the Molo. We passed over the smooth water, unseen in the crisp, cold pre-dawn, before gliding north along the waterway to the prisons.

Those who do not know Lord Niccolo Celsi well might assume that he would have placed me in one of the larger, less repulsive cells, that he would have done the decent and honourable thing, to treat a fellow gentleman of rank with respect; but anyone familiar with the man, whether his friend or his foe, would have known what I too expected. I was placed in the very worst part of the prisons, a short distance from Giordano Bruno.

Once in the cell, I remained calm, steadied my breathing and spent a long time in meditation. The blackness was total and very few sounds reached me save the occasional scurrying of rats or a scream of existential anguish from a nearby cell. The place stank of mould and shit and decay.

The training I had received in Nepal and through long years of practice had never proven more valuable. Although I was able to assuage my fears, ignore my thirst and the airless heat, I soon completely lost track of time. So, it may have been an hour, a day or a week after my confinement that I heard a new sound and opened my eyes to see a dim glimmer illuminating the grill in the upper part of the door. Then came the sound of jangling keys, a clearing of a throat, and I could just make out the bulk of the jailor, Marcel Fabone before catching the reek of his spirit-heavy breath. He held open the door, handed a torch to another man and wedged the door open before placing a wooden stool on the stone floor. He then retreated into the corridor. The man holding the torch crouched as he came in, and in the meagre light, I could see that it was Niccolo Celsi. I watched silently as he flicked back his cloak and settled himself onto the stool.

"You look disappointingly well," he said, his black eyes twinkling.

"One makes one's own Heaven, one's own Hell."

"How very profound. It was an oversight not having you clamped in irons. I shall have to make arrangements."

"Lord Celsi, are you here for a reason, or simply to gloat?"

"Well, it would have been easy just to come for the entertainment value, but no, I have news. His Serene Majesty, Doge Cicogna will be away a little longer than originally planned. He is caught up in formal talks with the Habsburg Emperor, Rudolf, in Trieste. In the meantime, I have been granted temporary, but complete executive power."

"You must be very pleased with yourself, Niccolo." I deliberately used the familiar to irritate him. "This is the second time you have had me imprisoned on trumped up charges of heresy."

He smiled. "Yes, and of course, that means this time the judiciary will not be quite so lenient as it was before."

"I hope the Lady Teresa is unharmed."

"Ha! Of course she is. But what if she were not? What could you do about it, Sagredo?"

"If you harm her, when I am freed, which I most certainly shall be upon the Doge's return, I will ensure that you are punished appropriately."

Celsi beamed. "Sagredo, you will not be freed, and so, that eventuality is not even worth discussing. Lady Teresa is under house arrest and her part in your heresy will be investigated, respectfully, of course, as befits her social rank. The same cannot be said of you, because ... well, you have no social rank now. You have been dismissed from The Ten by my orders and arrangements are underway for your torture."

None of this surprised me in the slightest. I had had plenty of time between cleansing meditations and yogic exercise to consider what it was that Celsi would do with me next. In clandestine ways, he could do what he wanted; he could let his imagination run riot in dark tunnels and behind the locked doors of rooms equipped with a fire and suitable implements. But, he would have to act quickly. He could not keep the Doge away on some fanciful mission for long. I could even now picture Pasquale Cicogna sitting in a luxuriously appointed set of rooms awaiting the arrival of Emperor Rudolf, who in fact knew nothing of any formal meeting. At some point, the Doge would realise he had been duped or lose patience and Celsi would cleverly explain it all away as a misunderstanding which he would support with forged diplomatic papers and royal letters.

"I trust you are being well looked after?" he mocked.

"Niccolo," I said very calmly. At that moment, for all his mendacity and egotism, I felt genuinely sorry for him. "If you are winning the fabricated conflict that lies between us and has weathered well the years, why demean yourself with such silliness?" He remained calm. He was a man experienced in politics and verbal jousting. "It does you no honour."

"And who are you to speak of honour, Sagredo? You, a so-called doctor, an occultist and a heretic, an exile, disgraced but dragged back here at the whim of a senile and self-adoring Doge?"

"You know none of this has anything to do with heresy, nothing to do with politics or rank," I replied. "It is all about a misguided idea of power."

He looked at me genuinely puzzled.

"Perhaps you do not realise why you act the way you do, but I would find that surprising; you are a very intelligent man, Niccolo."

"Stop calling me that!" he snapped. "To you I am Lord Celsi, or Most Serene Acting-Doge."

"But I called you Niccolo when we played in the streets together thirty-five years ago."

"I find it remarkable that you can be so light-hearted at a time like this. I give you credit for that, heretic."

"Of course you would go as far as to call me that. I favour the familiar and you counter with the most negative epithets. But, let's not slip back into ridiculous banter. As I said, you *may* not know what motivates you, but I suspect you are actually quite aware of your drives. You want to destroy me now, just as you tried to destroy me once before simply because you want to possess the Lady Teresa."

"And of course you know all about that. The man who has been back in the Republic for little more than a week. The man who knows almost nothing about Teresa's life since his ignoble exile."

"We have talked."

For the first time his cool detachment began to slip. There is a sea creature found in warmer climes about which most people in Italy, would have no knowledge. It is called a shark and I once saw this creature caught by fishermen in Goa. It is a ferocious beast and according to the locals in the fish market, a perpetually hungry one. But aside from its impressive, inward-facing double row of dagger-sharp teeth, for me, its most striking feature had been its eyes. Lidless, and so I was told, never closed, they were like holes poked by fingers through a layer of snow to jet black soil. They expressed no emotion at all. Indeed, they were quite incapable of such an act, and although I knew Niccolo Celsi was all too capable of feeling and expressing emotion, in the dim flickering light of the torch, his eyes looked very much like a shark's.

"She is beyond your reach, heretic," he said and took a deep breath. "Even if you were not imprisoned here at my pleasure, she is far too good for you, and always has been."

I shrugged. "Your thoughts are of course your own, Niccolo. But whatever the emotions that connect the three of us, one thing is quite certain. Lady Damas is a women of honour. If she has committed herself to be your betrothed, she would never do a thing to threaten that nor bring the vaguest semblance of dishonour to you or your family."

"Oh, so you are speaking for Teresa now, are you? You foolish man. I know Teresa does not love me, the same as I'm sure she never loved her late husband, Louis Damas; but although she may once have had feelings for you, she now sees you as the misanthropic failure you are. You have been back in this city one week and you have already stirred up discontent and find yourself in the dungeons of the Doge. As I said, you are a foolish man and Teresa no longer loves you. We too have talked."

And that actually was the moment I felt most sorry for Niccolo Celsi. It was the moment I realised just how frail his life was. Oh, of course, there was I in a stinking cell, left to starve or die from dehydration, my life stripped from me once again; I had no hope of ever being with the woman I knew I still loved more than anything or anyone in this world, and there was Celsi, all-powerful and with my very life in the palm of his hand. But it came down to this: Niccolo's soul was as flimsy as a sheet of linen, yet heavy beyond imagining. I could sense his self-doubt and guilt. I had known him as a boy, and understood that beneath it all this man before me was really little different to my friend from the cobbled alleyways. In spite of myself, I could not conceal these thoughts. "Oh, Niccolo," I said gently, sympathetically.

And that was when I unwittingly stabbed at his Achilles Heel. Even in the Spartan light, I could see the blood drain from his face, those shark eyes conveying nothing. He simply rose from the stool and lashed out his fist, catching my jaw. "I shall instruct your torturer, a man skilled in these things, to hold back nothing," he hissed. "I shall instruct him to keep you for as long as possible balanced agonisingly at the point where life ends and death begins."

·

And so it was back to darkness and the knowledge that the Doge was far from the Republic, that Celsi, who believed he was in position of unimpeachable power, was in fact in thrall to Rome, and the certainty that I would soon face extreme torture; something my enemies would have to get on with at the earliest opportunity so they could get rid of my body and invent a plausible explanation for my most unfortunate death before Doge Cicogna's return.

Celsi kept to his word and soon after he left, he gave orders for my feet to be shackled. And again came the loss of senses, save that of smell and the ability to taste the foulness of my parched mouth. It was back to confusion, of not knowing whether it was night or day. I was fed a few scraps and given water at sporadic intervals. Once more though, I was saved by my training. I breathed, I meditated and I allowed the passage of dream worlds through my mind; images that kept me from despair and held the fears at bay, things people believed to be demons and devils, but are merely the manifestation of one's natural fear of darkness and the terror of knowing that pain and slow death await.

An immeasurable time later, the spirit odour of Marcel Forbone's alcoholic's breath reached my nostrils, this was followed by the sound of keys knocking, one against the other, a key being turned in the lock. This I thought, was the beginning of the next stage of my journey and I mentally braced myself as best I could, for I knew that I would need all my skills and strength to face the horrors of what Lord Celsi and his masters were prescribing for me.

It was as before. Forbone handed the visitor a torch and I saw a figure bent low. A stool was put into place and a tall, broad-shouldered man sat. Forbone closed the door and I saw the light beyond the grill fade as the jailor retreated along the narrow corridor. The seated newcomer leaned forward, his face just visible in the glow of the torch. I was shocked to see that it was Piero, Lady Teresa's son. "Good Lord!" I exclaimed. "Piero. How? Why?"

He looked grim. "Lord Sagredo, I'm sure you were not expecting me."

"How did you get in here?"

"It is well known, sir that Marcel Forbone is just about the most corruptible man in the Republic. He has a great thirst to satisfy! Even so, I have but a short time."

"So why are you here? Your mother has not been hurt, I hope." I was unable to keep the fear from my voice.

"My mother is fine, sir . . . considering."

"Considering?"

"She is under house arrest, and the mood in the city suddenly has a wild edge to it. We are afraid her confinement might be only the start. That contemptible individual, Lord Celsi is behaving unpredictably and strutting around like a peacock that has drunk a barrel of ale. He visits our home and is rude and threatening, only to return a few hours later or the next day offering charm and words of reassurance and reconciliation."

"What date is it, Piero?"

"The 22nd, My Lord."

"So, I have been here three days."

"Yes and this is the first chance I've had to slip past the guards at home. I have some things for you which I managed to smuggle past that fat oaf, Forbone." He flicked a glance towards the corridor and handed me a bottle of ale and some lemon water along with a packet of food wrapped in cloth.

"What you've done is very brave, Piero. Celsi will have no love for you, my boy. You are not his son."

I could see in the faint illumination that Piero was putting on a brave face and suppressing his fears. "Now that you are away from home for a while, may I call upon more of your help, Piero?"

He held my eyes with a steady gaze. "Anything, My Lord."

"But please take great care."

"I shall, sir."

"I believe that Celsi and those with whom he is conspiring have passed on lies to my friends. If they knew I had been imprisoned, Tomasso Cicogna and Lord Pinelli would have been here by now, so I imagine they have been told that I have been called away on some unexpected business. Could you try to get word to them that I am here?"

"Of course," Piero said. "But I must make haste. If my absence is noted, I fear my mother shall be blamed."

"Indeed. That is the last thing I want to happen." I gave the boy the addresses.

"I also have a message from my mother," Piero said. "She asked me to tell you that she is doing everything she can to have you released, but her powers are very limited."

"Of course they are," I replied. She is in trouble herself. Please thank her for me but remind her to look after herself and you before worrying about my fate." I gave him my most encouraging smile. "You are a good boy, Piero."

"Thanks you, sir, but I'm hardly a boy. I turned fifteen over a month ago."

I laughed and reached forward to grip his shoulder. "You are a good man!"

The door opened and we could see the voluminous form of Marcel Forbone standing in the anaemic light. "Time's up," he said in a monotone.

I patted Piero on the back and watched him disappear into darkness as the door was closed. Returning to a half lotus position on the hard stone floor, but impeded by the chains and ankle braces, I tried to quell my fears, but there was something that Piero had said that kept prodding at my efforts to slow my heartbeat and to clear my mind of disturbance. It was like an itch that could not be scratched because as soon as I thought I might recall what it was that he had said, the precise wording would dissolve and I lost the thread. I could not retrace or retrieve the moment the remark had been made, but I knew with all my intellect that it was something very important.

Chapter Twenty-six: The Celsis

"I assume you have completed arrangements for the imprisonment of Lady Teresa Damas?" Violetta lounged back in a damask covered chaise longue and sipped at her wine. She and her son, Niccolo were in the drawing-room of the Palazzo Arragio.

"It has been a trying day, mother. Must we discuss this now?"

Violetta placed her glass on an occasional table and scrutinised her son. "That would imply that you have not."

Niccolo took a deep breath. His mind was racing. He had been up since before the dawn shouldering the burdens of government, acting the patient diplomat with Severina and his entourage and trying to slow Father Gessi's enthusiasm to use the infrequently employed torture chamber in a room on the lowest level of the prison, close to Sagredo's cell. He had though acceded to the wishes of the cardinal and his poodle Gessi to arrest a man named Marco Guito, a bookseller who was suspected of selling occult tomes. Gessi wanted the man as a guinea pig for the new set of implements of torture that had been specially forged by a local blacksmith. Now he wanted to relax, not to have to face his own Inquisition.

"Mother, could you please let me deal with these matters in my own way?"

"So, you will not have the Damas woman imprisoned?"

"God's teeth, Mother!"

Violetta was startled. "I beg your pardon?"

"You heard me. I will deal with this situation alone. I do not want, nor do I need your interference."

"Oh, please don't tell me you love the woman still! Not after the way she has behaved." Violetta stood up and started towards Niccolo.

"Sit down, Mother."

She kept coming. He stood. She had never seen Niccolo so fierce.

"Sit down!" he commanded. Violetta stopped mid-stride, gave her son a look of utter contempt, but backed down, returning to the sofa.

"My feelings for the Lady Teresa are my business and none of your concern."

Violetta simply stared at her eldest. The blood had ebbed from her face but it barely showed thanks to the heavy white ceruse she wore. She plucked up her wine glass and drained it. "You foolish boy!"

"Oh for the sake of Christ! Desist, Mother or you shall make me angry."

"Hah! I would like to see you get angry with me, you young pup. In the eyes of society you may be deemed the head of this family, but you and I both know that I am the mistress of all we survey, so please save me your childishness. When is the women to be imprisoned?"

"She shall not be." Niccolo's face was rigid. He had never stood up to his mother, not once. But they had never before had any reason to argue. They were both covetous, cruel and self-obsessed, but they had always been on the same side over everything that had mattered, and the family had always come first. But now Niccolo could no longer hide from himself his feelings for Teresa. He did love her. He had always loved her. Violetta had believed that the marriage plans had been purely Machiavellian, arranged entirely for commercial gain. She had no notion that Niccolo even had the capacity to love.

"I think Cardinal Severina will have something to say about that."

"Do you now, Mother? You presume to know the man's mind?

Violetta looked at him askance. "What has got into you, my son? You sound possessed by a demon."

"Stop being so melodramatic," Niccolo responded. Now that he had broken an unspoken taboo, he was feeling confident. His exhaustion had abated and he was energised. "I shall handle Severina."

Violetta laughed. It was a nasty, grating sound and totally devoid of humour. It came from somewhere high up in her throat.

"You find it funny?"

"You cannot tell Cardinal Severina what to do, Niccolo. Surely you know that?"

"You are forgetting that I have a number of cards up my sleeve. I could recall the Doge at a moment's notice and destroy the Papal Nuncio's grand plans to dispatch Sagredo and Bruno. And, it is also a matter of Severina owing me a favour. I ensnared Sagredo for him. The cardinal allowing Teresa her freedom is merely a matter of *quid pro quo.*"

"And you think you may strike bargains with a man as powerful as the Pope's right-hand man?"

"Yes, I do, mother. I am Acting Doge. While Pasquale Cicogna is away, I rule the Republic. I have at my disposal a well-armed palace guard, a powerful army, the largest navy in the world, and many friends in very high places."

This time Violetta could find nothing to say. She was stunned into silence, not understanding how her son had gained quite such confidence so very suddenly. Before she could formulate a response, Niccolo stood. "Now, if you'll excuse me, I have much to attend to." And with that he walked out, leaving the old woman too taken aback to be angry. She was not the type of woman to burst into a rage; she would employ her fury later, at the most apposite moment.

•

Niccolo Celsi did not go directly to his study as his departing words had implied to Violetta. Instead, he climbed to the third floor of the Palazzo Arragio and took the narrow spiral staircase to the roof where his dove aviary had been constructed under the eaves.

He felt surprisingly calm. It had always been him and his mother against the world, and although he had just told her he had friends in high places, they both knew that those people were not really friends; they were a collection of sycophants, manipulators and users, people who smiled and struck deals and traded favours for their own ends, simply because the Celsi family was so rich and powerful.

But something had snapped inside Niccolo's mind. He had come to an important realisation. He had pretended that he was only interested in Teresa because of her estate and the kudos her beauty would give him. In that way he had behaved much like the 'friends' he had just contemplated. And perhaps he had also been lying to his mother, pretending that he viewed his betrothal to Teresa Damas as leading to a marriage of convenience. Maybe, he now realised, he had done this simply to allay the jealousy it would ignite in the old woman if he were to claim genuine love for Teresa. But now he no longer cared. Soon, he would dispose of Sagredo once and for all, and then he would have Teresa freed and exonerated. She would still express little fondness for him, of that he had no doubt, but he believed that she would grow to appreciate his many qualities as they spent more time together after the wedding. Perhaps, he mused, it was the threat of Sagredo that had awoken in him feelings of love for Teresa, feelings he had long suppressed. With Francesco out of the way permanently, there would be a real chance for him to nurture a relationship with the woman he loved and she would gradually learn the error of her ways and realise she had been a fool ever to have cared for such a man as Sagredo.

He opened the cage and took out his two favourites, letting them cling to fingers of his right hand. He gave them some seed and stroked their feathers. There were times, he mused, when he really believed these birds were his only true friends. They loved him unconditionally. Even his own mother did not offer that, and after tonight their relationship would never again be the same. The perpetually obedient son had stood up to her, and far worse than the principle of disobedience itself was the fact that he had challenged her over a woman, one whom she despised.

The birds cooed and Celsi rewarded them with some more seed which they pecked from his free palm. Then he gave each of them a gentle kiss on the head and placed them carefully back into their cage. "First light tomorrow, my friends, you shall soar above this city; and so shall I," he said.

211

Chapter Twenty-seven: The Chamber

They came when I was least prepared, as I awoke from troubled and confused dreams. There were three of them, two men I had never seen before, with Marcel Forbone in tow. One of the men tied my hands with rope and I was dragged roughly into the corridor, the torch shoved close to my face, its glare making my eyes sting. I took deep breaths and slowed my racing heart. The men said nothing. One shoved me hard, causing me to trip. I landed heavily on my left shoulder, sending a ripple of pain down my arm and my spine. The guards tugged me to my feet, hustling me onwards.

We remained on the same floor, the lowest level of the dungeons, turned a corner to the right and passed a row of cells. I heard a low trembling sound and recognised it immediately; it was the moan of men in pain, chained behind locked doors, shivering, feverish in damp cave-like rooms; rooms fetid and dark with low ceilings; rooms that held a thousand sorry stories. I could smell the piss and shit and tried to submerge it all, blot it out. We stopped at a heavy oak door strapped top and bottom with iron. It opened inwards and I was pushed hard from behind again. This time I just managed to keep my balance as I stumbled forward. The door was slammed shut and the guards stood motionless a few inches inside the room watching everything in absolute silence.

The chamber was wreathed in a red blush. I saw a fire and a row of metal objects, instruments of torture lying on the floor, a poker and a pair of pincers, their tips in the flames. Beside these had been placed a short paddle with a rectangular end the size of a man's hand.

Although torture was practiced on those convicted of the most heinous crimes, it remained a rare thing in the Republic, and during his entire reign, Doge Cicogna had not once sanctioned such punishments. Consequently, this room had fallen into desuetude. As I surveyed the chamber I saw more of the torturer's implements. On one wall hung chains and clamps, and in the corner, a strappado had been constructed, a pulley system hanging from the ceiling and used to suspend victims by the wrists as they were winched up with weights attached to their ankles. Pushed up close to the far wall stood a rack. Upon it lay a man, naked but for a loincloth, his hands and feet had been attached to ropes at each end of the contraption. He had weeping burns across his torso and along his arms and legs. A young man in a leather apron stood close to the prisoner's head. Next to him was a large wooden wheel through which passed the ropes tied to the victim's wrists.

Out of the shadows stepped a small man in a cleric's habit, a brown robe with a belt of hemp loose about his waist. I recognised him as one of the two priests who, a week earlier, at my first meeting as a member of The Ten had attended the Council with Cardinal Severina. He stood close to me, deliberately intruding into my personal space. His breath was sweet; his black eyes seemed to be absorbing every detail of my face as though I were a painting or a sculpture.

"I am Father Berlinghiero Gessi, First Assistant to Cardinal Santora Severina, Apostolic Nuncio to his Holiness, Pope Clement VIII. I have been given special dispensation to subject you to torture in order to extract a confession of heresy from you."

"How do you expect me to respond to that, Father Gessi? Is it meant to impress me?"

He gave me a blank look. He understood what I had said, but behaved as though I had been speaking to him in some obscure foreign tongue.

"Now you may notice," he went on, ". . . that this room." And he swept a hand around to encompass the space. ". . . has been refurbished at short notice. I understand that it is another of your whimsical Venetian customs that torture is rarely used; and it is reported that the Doge has not once given permission to employ any of the methods I have here at my disposal tonight." He produced a shrill little laugh. "So quaint. But never mind. As you can see, we are now fully prepared."

I glanced at the man on the rack.

"Ah yes . . . him. That is Senor Marco Guito. He was arrested this afternoon on charges of selling heretical books. He is my experimental subject . . . to test this equipment. You'll understand we need to ensure everything functions efficiently. You know how this works, don't you? Johannes over here turns the wheel, the ropes tighten, stretching legs and arms. The first to give are the muscles, then the ligaments and finally the tendons. Each step becomes exquisitely more painful. If we go too far, the prisoner's limbs will end up as floppy strings of meat. He will not be able to stand, his arms will hang, useless by his sides . . . for ever."

Gessi nodded to Johannes. He rotated the wheel a quarter circle and the prisoner screamed.

"Ah! There go the muscles of the calves, I believe. Merely, an early stage, as you would doubtless know, Doctor Sagredo. I am told it is as nothing compared with the renting of the ligaments. That's *very* nasty." He walked over to the wheel at the end of the rack and leaned in, stopping an inch from Marco Guito's face. Straightening, he added: "And I won't even start to describe how it feels to have the tendons ripped from one's bones!"

The prisoner was shaking, wreathed in sweat. "But, I have already confessed," he groaned, his voice catching and breaking with the terror he felt.

"Oh, I know, Marco. And that's very good of you," Gessi said, taking two paces back towards me. "But, I need to know how well this machine works. You see, I have a few warm-up procedures for our noble traveller here, but I will need to rack him after those. I would like him to see that the machine is well oiled and efficient after it has been so neglected."

"I confess. I confess," Guito screamed. "Oh my sweet God in Heaven; please, father, please release me. I confess."

Gessi gave a signal to Johannes and the man dutifully turned the wheel again causing the prisoner to screech in agony. A low guttural sound emerged from the back of his throat. The priest turned to me slowly, fixing me with eyes that no longer seemed human. I couldn't help noticing a slight tenting of the robe about his groin.

He looked back towards the rack. Johannes had let go of the wheel and was leaning in towards Guito's wrecked body. The bookseller had fallen very quiet. Gessi ran back and yanked his assistant upright then bent in towards Guito's chest. After a moment, he pulled up, his face like a bleached skull. "Fuck!" he yelled. "Fuck! You killed him, you idiot! You turned it too far . . ."

"Father, I . . ." Johannes protested.

"Shut the fuck up!" Gessi kicked the rack and spat in the dead man's face.

I sensed the guards behind me moving, shuffling with unease. Standing absolutely still, I followed the priest with my eyes.

"Prepare the instruments," Gessi snapped to his assistant.

Johannes leapt to it. Close to the rack facing the fire, a wooden bench was fixed to the floor with metal bolts. I could see thick leather straps at each side and around the front legs. Father Gessi stepped out of view, and from behind, shoved me to the stone floor. I heard the cartilage of my nose shatter and the shock of pain streamed under my eyes and through my head. He grabbed me one side, Johannes the other and together they dragged me to the bench. I felt dazed as the young man in the leather apron cut the rope about my wrists with a single slice of a blade. He then tied the leather straps, first about my hands, then around my feet. My head was pounding and my vision blurred from the fall, but I could see Gessi's face as he came up close to mine, his sickly sweet breath blended with the smell of my own blood. I could taste the blood as it flowed into my throat and down to my lips. The priest ripped open my soiled and ragged shirt exposing my chest.

"I find it hard to believe you have your ambassador to the Republic, His Excellency Buto Testa's permission to do this."

"Lord Testa does what the Nuncio tells him to do; so fret not." Gessi paused for a moment, bringing his hands together in front of him and interlocking his stubby little fingers. "You cannot begin to imagine how much I'm enjoying

214

this, Sagredo. I hate heretics, hate them. So what do you have to tell me, *Doctor?*"

"Would it make the slightest difference what I said?"

"I wonder if you will be so free with your thinking in a moment when I place a burning rod against your face, or bring it slowly to your eye as Johannes here holds your head in his very firm grip?"

"It did not stop you torturing the bookseller, Senor Guito, did it? He had already confessed. But you just wanted your pleasure."

Gessi produced a strange chortle. "That was different. I really did want to test the equipment, hence my anger when the frail old fool died before I had barely started on the truly amusing stuff. You though, Sagredo, are different. You must not die here, for if you were to, then I would be in terrible trouble. No, I have plenty of time to administer exquisite pain. I've heard you are a resilient fellow and strong, so you may tolerate a great deal, you may at some point slip into unconsciousness. That though will not present a problem, so we will not be too perturbed." He winked at Johannes. "We will keep reviving you."

I showed no reaction. "I told you, Father Gessi. I have nothing to confess. I am not a heretic. But, if you want to call me one and accuse me of that crime, you may. It makes no difference to me."

"I may? Oh, how kind." He laughed. "You people always amuse me. You resist and resist as if you're spitting in my eye, as though I *want* you to submit. But you see, I actually don't; well not quickly anyway. Where's the fun in that? I have a powerful disposition. Some may consider it an unusual one. I enjoy seeing people like you suffer." He straightened and turned to his assistant. "The pincers."

Johannes walked to the fire and crouched down to where the row of metal implements lay, their ends glowing red in the flames. He pulled on heavy leather gloves and grabbed a pair of long-handled pincers, plucking them from the fire and walking back towards me. He stopped a couple of paces from the chair awaiting orders.

"I'm still more than happy to proceed, Francesco Sagredo," Gessi said very quietly. "In fact, I would still prefer you to refuse to talk because I know I shall win. I know I shall *make* you speak. The longer this goes on, the worse it will be for you and the better it will be for me!"

"But, Father, what sense is there in what you say?" I stated. "I told you. If you wish to name me a heretic, then do so. I care not. And, even if I declare to you and this young man and to the guards that I am a heretic, you shall still burn me and take me as close to death as you dare. You will ruin my body and be able to report back to your master, Cardinal Severina and his master, Pope Clement, that I confessed."

"I wish to hear you confess it, Sagredo. I wish you to admit that what you have done is evil, against God's law, against Nature."

"But, I have told you that you may think whatever you like. Carry with you this description of me. Label me and I shall not mind. Mock me and I shall laugh along with the joke. I do not care. I have no respect for you and your masters and your rules and your twisted views."

"Oh, what an amusing time we shall have then," Gessi exclaimed and rubbed his hands together. "I shall take such pleasure in making you beg for mercy. I can scarcely wait to see your blistered and bubbling flesh as the poker and the pinchers scythe their way through to your bones and melt your eyes and your genitals. You will smell like a pig on a spit. Have you smelled burning human flesh? It is like nectar." He smacked his lips. "Then we shall move you on to the rack."

Yanking up the sleeve of my stinking and ripped tunic, he exposed my arm. "We shall begin gently, Johannes," he said, turning to his assistant. "Pinch the flesh of Doctor Sagredo's left arm midway between his wrist and his elbow; just around here . . ."

Chapter Twenty-eight: Resistance

The jailor, Marcel Forbone had turned away at the door to the torture chamber as the guards shoved Doctor Francesco Sagredo into the room and slammed shut the door. He took the stairs with a heavy heart. He liked the man some called The Traveller and thought him a noble fellow, in an entirely different league to most of the politicians and wealthy men of the Republic by whom he was viewed as little more than a slave. Doctor Sagredo had always treated him with respect, thanked him for delivering a bowl of water or a crust of bread and never spoke down to him. And now that same man was to be tortured by one of the vilest Forbone had ever met, that worm, Father Gessi, arse-licker to the equally repulsive Cardinal Severina.

Forbone, took the turn between the lowest level and the next and saw a flash of movement so incredibly fast that he barely registered it. Next came an excruciating pain in the side of his face that seemed to shake his brain inside his skull. He toppled backwards, his torch sending fragmented silhouettes across the walls as it fell with him. He tumbled down the stone stairs and came to rest headfirst on the cobbles, dying almost instantly.

The man who had hit the jailor was dressed in black, his mouth and nose covered with a scarf. He pulled back from the edge of the step and managed to keep his balance before descending the stairs to where Forbone lay. He rifled through the dead man's pockets and found his bunch of keys, straightened, grabbed the torch that lay a few feet from Forbone's head and beckoned to three men standing in the shadows at the top of the stairs. Each of them was dressed in a dark tunic and hose; black masks covered their faces. One of the men held aloft a torch, and stealthily, they descended in single file. "Come on," the first man hissed. "Can't waste a single second."

They reached the lowest level, the air damp and hot. The leader held up his right hand and they all stopped to listen. The only sound was the low moaning and sobs of the punished. The leader pressed on, the lit brand in his left hand offering a shifting puddle of mean light. He moved with purpose, knowing exactly where he was headed as the others followed, keeping close with just the occasional glance backward along the corridor. He slowed and drew to a halt. The others came up behind him, panting. "This is it." He put a finger to his lips and stepped up to a door. A narrow grill was positioned at head height.

"Giordano," he called quietly, his mouth pressed up against the metal of the grill. "Giordano."

There was no response. The leader turned to his nearest companion. "Hold this, Eduardo." Handing him the torch and clutching the bunch of keys in the pool of light, he began sifting through them. He knew the type of key he was looking for but there were at least half a dozen of them. The locks to the cells did not have unique keys, but six variants covered randomly the fifty-six cells in the dungeon. It was a question of finding which one of them worked for the lock of Giordano Bruno's cell door.

He slipped a key into the slot and attempted to turn it. It would not budge. He chose the next one, eased it into the lock and tried to twist it anticlockwise, then clockwise but again failed to move the key even fractionally. "Fuck!" he exclaimed, then leaned in to the grill again. "Giordano!"

He heard a shuffling sound and the clanking of metal.

"Who speaks?" came Bruno's bruised voice.

"Friends, here to help you." As he spoke, the man lifted the bunch of keys to the light and selected a third one, slipped it into the opening of the lock, turned it anticlockwise and it gave, shifting a full turn. "Christ! At last," he exclaimed. "Wait here," he said to his three companions. Taking back the torch, he opened the cell door.

At first, he could not see Giordano Bruno, but then a slight figure swayed into the light and stopped: the prisoner's left ankle was chained to the floor. "Shit!" the man said, turned back to retrieve the bunch of keys from the lock and returned to the cell.

"What are you doing here? Who are you?" Bruno asked, his voice little more than a croak.

"We are getting you out of this place."

"How, how can you do this?"

The man pulled back his hood and lowered his scarf.

"Who . . . ?" Bruno exclaimed.

"I am Tomasso Cicogna."

"What! How? What is this?"

"The Resistance, Giordano. We are the Resistance. You heard of us when you were in Prague, yes?" He crouched to study the locked chain.

"The Resistance?" Bruno looked confused, his eyes wandering around the dark walls. "Yes, yes. I know that name, and I know Cicogna. The Doge . . ."

"I am his son, Giordano."

"Yes, yes, of course. And I knew of your role, son of the Doge," Bruno replied. "But I never believed . . ."

"Enough talk," Tomasso said. "We need to get this off you." He lifted the chain and slowly pulled up making sure not to bang his head on the ceiling. Stepping back, he called to the man closest to the door. "Eduardo, hold the torch, will you? He handed it over and started to search again through the collection of keys.

218

"It is a bronze key," Bruno muttered. "Smaller than some of the . . ."

"This one?" Tomasso held up a key the colour of dull and tarnished gold about half the size of the others.

"Yes, I believe it is." He nodded vigorously, almost childlike.

Tomasso found the cuff about the prisoner's narrow ankle. Bruno's flesh was black with bruising and chaffing, streaks of dark dried blood ran to the sole of his filthy bare foot. Tomasso turned the key in the lock and the cuff clicked open. He lifted it away and helped Bruno to his feet. The man could barely stand and had to be supported under each shoulder as Tomasso and one of his men guided him out and into the passage.

"Proper introductions can wait. My friends here are Eduardo, Nofri and Dido." He pointed to the men brusquely. "Let's go."

Dido relieved Tomasso of his burden and with Nofri coming up the rear, Tomasso led the way back along the corridor. They took a right and reached the foot of the stairs up to the next level. To their left stood a heavy wooden door strapped with iron bands. Without breaking step, Tomasso turned to the others, his torch held above his head. It was the first proper view he had of Bruno and he was shocked to see the state of the man. He looked like a starved rabbit held up on its hind legs. His face was a mass of hair, matted and filthy; his eyes looked huge and filled with fear and confusion. He was mumbling. It sounded like a prayer, but it was impossible to know for sure.

All of them heard the scream. Bruno barely reacted, continuing to mutter garbled words, but Tomasso and his three companions stopped. The cry had come from a door to their right. Tomasso closed his eyes for a second and took two deep breaths.

"Let's go!" Dido spat, his jawline rigid in the torch light.

Tomasso simply stared back at his companion. A second, louder scream came from behind the door. None of them moved.

"What . . . ?" Eduardo exclaimed. Bruno continued to mumble.

"I can't just walk away." Tomasso said.

"Are you mad?" Eduardo's face was wet.

A third horrible yelp came from the room.

"Eduardo. You stay here with Bruno." Dido, Nofri? Will you help me?"

They appraised each other, turned back to Tomasso and nodded. He drew his sword. Eduardo and Dido lowered Giordano to the floor with his back against the wall and Nofri handed Eduardo his torch. "I shall turn the handle," Tomasso said."We must rely on the fact that the torturer would have no reason to lock himself in."

"There will be more than one of them," Nofri whispered.

"At least two. That is the law."Tomasso leaned forward and slowly, carefully turned the handle. He looked up to Dido and Nofri, saw their swords at the

219

ready and whispered: "One, two . . ." On 'three', he rammed the door inwards with all his might and charged into the room, Nofri and Dido close behind.

The chamber was brightly lit by the red glow of the fire in the far wall. It took each of them less than a second to take in the scene and to spring into action. The two guards by the door were no match for the three men. Dido sliced open the throat of the guard to his left and watched the man fall forwards, a look of incomprehension receding to agony as he clutched at his neck. Nofri imbedded his sword into the other guard's side an inch below his breast plate, thrusting so hard it passed right through the man, exiting close to his spine. He sank as though he were a puppet whose strings had been snipped.

Tomasso had run straight to the centre of the room. Francesco was bound to a chair facing the fire. Leaning close to him was a short, solidly-build priest. His face was pale, teeth bared, a demented look on his face. He held a poker, its tip glowing a vibrant crimson, just a few inches from Francesco's face. Beside the priest stood a younger, much taller man in a leather apron. The vile smell of burned flesh hung heavy in the air.

Tomasso swung his sword at the priest. Father Berlinghiero Gessi looked up just in time to see him swoop down and with surprising agility, he threw himself backwards avoiding the weapon, the poker clattering across the floor. The young man, Johannes tried to move away, but tripped backwards, landing heavily against the rack bearing Marco Guito's abused body.

Before Johannes could pull himself up, Tomasso was on him. His sword passed through his torso, and a great stream of blood poured from a gash in the leather apron. Tomasso span round to face Gessi. The priest was grovelling on his knees, his face blank and albumen white with terror, his hands clasped before him.

"Please, sir," Gessi yelled above the screams and moans of the dying around him. "I am a priest, Father Berlinghiero Gessi, assistant to Cardinal Severina. I am simply following orders. Please, show mercy. Think of your immortal soul."

"Hah!" Tomasso took a step forward and turned to Francesco as Dido and Nofri reached the fireplace. "My God! What have these bastards done to you?" He quickly cut the ropes binding his friend's arms, noting the burns on his wrists and upper arm on his left side. Francesco was speechless with shock and pain. "Nofri, Dido. This is my dear friend, Francesco Sagredo."

Dido turned back to the priest as Gessi made a strange sound in the back of his throat.

"We should behead the priest," Tomasso said.

Francesco grabbed his friend's arm and managed to shake his head. "No . .." he croaked.

"Nofri, Dido, take Francesco. Get outside. I will deal with the priest."

The two men lifted Francesco carefully from the chair. He cried out in pain as one of the men caught his burned arm.

"I'm sorry, Lord Sagredo."

"Tom." Francesco's voice was stronger now. "Do not kill him."

Tomasso simply jerked his head towards his men. Supporting Francesco under each shoulder, they encouraged him to walk towards the door where the guards lay twitching in spreading puddles of blood.

The priest watched the men retreat and then turned to Tomasso. "You are the Doge's son," he said.

Tomasso sheathed his sword and picked up the poker Gessi had used. Stepping towards the priest, he held the glowing tip an inch from the priest's sweating face, slowly twisting the steel in the air, teasingly. The priest followed Tomasso's every movement.

"My friend asked me not to kill you. Perhaps he too was thinking of my soul. I do not believe in souls. I do not believe in your God. But I do believe in the Devil. He is in each of us, in some of us more than others; and in you Father Berlinghiero Gessi, he is strong. So, consequently, I have no fear for that which you manage to convince others with soft minds to believe. I may just kill you. Or maybe I shall just burn you." He moved the poker closer to Gessi's face, making the priest cry out in panic.

Eduardo appeared in the doorway to the torture chamber "Tomasso. We *must* go. Come . . . Now!"

Tomasso did not look away from, the priest. "I must hurry. I shall not harm you, priest, for I have a strong feeling that you and I shall meet again, and then I shall have no restraints. I shall kill you without a second thought." Still holding the poker, he pulled up, turned towards the door and heard a gurgling laugh from behind him.

"Doge's baby boy!" Gessi hissed, pulling himself to his feet, a half-crazed smirk distorting his sweat-lathered face.

Tomasso whirled round, swinging the glowing poker through the air and slapping it hard onto the left side of Gessi's face, bearing down with all his strength, pushing the man to his knees. The stench of burning flesh wafted from the floor as the priest fell onto his back, screeching, his hand shooting up to his bubbling, grey flesh.

Chapter Twenty-nine: The Pyre

The practice of torture is a singularly vile and cowardly thing. Indeed, I do believe it to be *the* most vile and cowardly thing any human being can inflict upon their fellow man or woman; and I feel this way not simply because I have been the victim of such nefariousness and pusillanimity, but because I know it is a reflection of the torturer's basest instincts - to hurt, to maim, and sometimes to kill through the application of carefully orchestrated and premeditated pain; all while the victim is completely defenceless, unable to put up any sort of fight. Often, people who have experienced terrible things possess an involuntary ability to obliterate the memory of them, and indeed, I too have done this with many of my life's misfortunes, but this did not happen in the wake of the horrors I lived through at the hands of Father Berlinghiero Gessi. Seated here as I am now, nearly two decades after the events, I can remember almost every detail; even if, so very often, I wish I might not.

We stumbled up the stairs beyond the chamber, the air so filled with shouts and screams we knew that at any moment someone must come to investigate; Forbone's assistant perhaps or a troop of palace guards. I was half-dragged along a corridor, and then we were out in the freezing cold. The change shocked me. My body must have been so shaken, for normally I could cope quite well with extremes of heat and cold, but it was also the fact my shirt was ripped open and I was barefoot that the November night produced such a dramatic effect.

Yet I could hardly complain. After the momentary shock, I relished the scent of freedom, the wind through my hair and my beard, and above us, the gorgeous velvet sky. We ran on. I had managed to keep my limbs toned and supple thanks to my yogic exercises and careful attention to the breathing techniques I had been taught, but it took all of my resilience to quell the pain in my left arm and side where the pincers were employed and my skin and the flesh beneath had been split and run through with fire.

We reached the water, but I had no idea where we were. It was very dark and there were few sounds save for water lapping on stone and the occasional screech of a gull. I counted the shapes around me in the shadows. There was the unmistakable form of Tomasso, but I had no idea who the other four people were. I could tell one of them was injured or unsteady and was being helped along. We stopped at the end of a stone promontory. Then I discerned the shape of a boat, a man holding a lantern, the flame behind the glass flickering as he moved to the stern. Tomasso's face reared up in front of me.

"My dear friend are you managing?"

I nodded. "I cannot thank you enough, Tom."

"Sssh!" he said. "We can pat each other on the back later. Right now we have to keep moving."

"What exactly is going on? Who are . . ."

The man in the boat leaned forward, the lantern casting a subtle light across our party. That was when I caught sight of Giordano Bruno. "My God!" I said rather loudly.

"Francesco, keep your fucking voice down!" Tomasso hissed.

"I'm sorry. I . . ."

"Come," he said kindly. "Let us get away into the Lagoon and perhaps I can explain." Two of his associates guided Bruno onto the small skiff and then Tom and another of his companions assisted me onto the vessel. The man with the lantern, a squat fellow with cropped hair and a neatly trimmed beard, held the light aloft so we could see a couple of benches. We sat as he retreated to the rear to take up the rudder and the sail ropes. Tomasso found a cloak and pulled it about my shoulders. I could see the shapes of the others in front of us, felt the sail close by billow as it was brought round by the boatman to catch the breeze, and we moved away from the pier.

Tomasso offered me a bottle of strong spirit. I shook my head. "Water if you have any, Tom."

He rummaged in his bag, found a jar of lemon water, and I drank from it greedily. "Do you have any cloth in there?

He gave me a confused look and searched in the dim glow from the lantern. "Just this." He lifted a scarf.

"Perfect." I said. "May I have the bottle of spirit again?"

He handed it to me. I lifted the cloak from about my shoulders and poured the alcohol over my burns. The pain tore through me but I breathed it out, keeping control of my senses, then bound the scarf about my wounds. "Reduces the risk of infection," I explained.

"Infection?"

"Some other time, my friend. Now, please, tell me what is going on?"

"Well, you're the luckiest man in the world, Francesco. Three days ago I was sent a message to say you would be in Verona for at least a week. We were here solely to rescue Bruno."

"But Piero Damas? He visited me and was sent to warn you and Gianvincenzo that I was imprisoned."

"I've been lying low in Padua for two days in preparation for tonight, and Pinelli has been in his palazzo there. What the hell happened?"

"The Doge was tricked into travelling to Trieste for a meeting with the Emperor Rudolf. It was set up by Celsi and Severina, to get your father out the way. Celsi is Acting Doge. He had me imprisoned and has placed Teresa under house arrest."

"Fuck, Francesco!"

"What's the plan for Giordano? And why you? How are you involved?"

"Do you remember the afternoon we visited Eriador . . . he mentioned the Resistance?"

"Of course."

"Well, I am a key member, as was the alchemist. Pinelli is our leader. That's why I was in Padua with my three companions." He indicated towards the cloaked figures who had snatched Bruno and saved me from Gessi. We were making final preparations there. We have been active for two years, but only after Bruno was arrested back in May did we turn our attention to thwarting the Vatican's attempts to get the Giordano to Rome."

"I see. So when Eriador was murdered you must have believed it was related to your cause."

"Part of me did, but we discussed it . . ."

"We?" I interrupted.

"The Resistance. I went over it with Pinelli and Paolo."

"Paolo?"

"Paolo Sarpi."

"Good Christ!"

"You were away abroad a good while." Tom patted me on the shoulder.

"Who else?"

That's it. A small, tight-knit company. It was created by Pinelli. Ajith helps and knows some things. Sarpi is integral, but as you might imagine, he has to behave with extreme circumspection. My friends here: Eduardo Samposo was a Major in the Paduan army, Dido Forsi and Nofri Amolino are sons of Venetian nobility, whose families know nothing about their clandestine activities."

"I should imagine not!" I exclaimed. "Homer Amolino is a friend of the Celsis."

"Yes, and there is no love lost between Nofri's father and his son!"

We were far out into the Lagoon now and the only light came from the stars and the boatman's lantern. "Where are we headed?"

"Mestre. There is a secluded inlet off the main waterway. We have arranged for a vessel to meet us there to pick up Bruno. He'll be taken along the coast to Portegrandi and then overland out of Italy and hopefully onwards to a safe haven in Prussia."

"You realise he's half-mad, don't you, Tom?"

"Pinelli said you thought that was so. He is definitely in a daze. We may only hope that freedom, the chance to breathe fresh air and to eat and sleep well will aid his recovery. No one could blame him for seeming crazed after being held in that place for months."

"Believe me, I can vouch for the truth of that. It took all of my training and practice of yoga, meditation and breathing techniques to survive mentally, even for a few days. I do not think he has undergone torture, at least not the physical variety, but he is half-starved and probably suffering many afflictions from the damp and cramped conditions."

In a short while, I could make out some definition on the horizon and the boat came close to shore. Reeds and rocks dotted the water; but I could make out little more in the darkness and simply had to trust in the boatman's skill to guide us to our destination.

We passed along a short narrow stretch of water and then into a broader waterway walled on each side. Beyond the low stone banks the darkness was broken only by a smattering of stars. We pulled up to a narrow, deserted quay made from rough stone. It looked very old and had clearly fallen into disuse. The boatman jumped ashore and tied a rope to a thick stumpy rusted post and we all clambered ashore. "As agreed," he said. "I shall wait a few leagues along the coast for one hour before returning."

Tomasso shook his hand and re-joined the group as the boatman made ready his vessel again. We stood huddled together, the wind picking up and the chill growing with it. The skiff slid away towards the starry horizon.

"The galley is due one hour before midnight," Tomasso said and looked up at the sky. "I think we shall not have long to wait. There is no shelter. I suggest we sit and hope our friends have not been delayed."

I felt remarkably relaxed. It is hard to convey the sensation of sudden freedom after a captivity such as I had experienced and the terror of being powerless and at the mercy of a madman intent upon inflicting as much pain as possible. It was not simply an emotional release; it was a physical joy. I felt every muscle in my body slip off the bonds of tension, and the knot of fear in my guts untangle itself. I breathed in, taking the cold salty air deep into my lungs.

Dido was on watch and the first to spot the faint outline of a sail approaching through the night, blotting out the stars. "It's here," he said and pointed along the shore.

I pulled up with the others, but Giordano lay supine, covered in a blanket. We stepped a few yards closer to the edge of the quay, the breeze whipping up the water. The vessel drew close and we watched as the mainsail was lowered. A man jumped ashore and roped the ship to the same post our man had used. I hung back and Tomasso led the others to greet their friends.

I tightened the cloak about me, looked up and saw half a dozen palace guards leap from the ship, swords raised. They charged at us along the stone pier. Tomasso did not have time to unsheathe his weapon. Two of the guards grabbed him, tackled him to the ground, and rolled him on to his stomach to tie his wrists behind him. The remaining four guards rushed the others. Dido was too slow to level his weapon before the lead soldier was on him burying his sword into the young man's chest. Eduardo and Nofri had a better chance. Eduardo attacked the next guard, while Nofri held off the remaining two. Slicing the arm of one, Nofri adjusted his balance and was about to swing his weapon in a deadly arc to behead the injured man, when the other soldier slid sideways with astonishing agility and slipped his blade into the pit of Nofri's arm. It emerged from his shoulder and pierced his neck.

The three troops then turned on Eduardo. All I could do was watch powerless as they cut down the young man. I scrambled over to Giordano who was sitting up staring at the scene, bewildered and panting for air. I crouched beside him and saw Tomasso struggling to pull himself up, but one of the palace guards had him pinned to the ground with a knee in the small of his back.

Two men emerged from the small ship. At first, I could not see their faces. The one in front moved with the confidence of a man well used to the water and wearing a cloak over hose, boots and a thick tunic. I recognised his gait almost immediately. The figure behind was less certain of his footing and held up his robes as a sailor helped him onto land. Two more soldiers stepped onto the quay, each with a sword in one hand, a fiercely burning torch in the other. As they came closer, I could see them more clearly. Between the two troops walked Niccolo Celsi and Cardinal Severina.

"Pull him to his feet," Celsi snapped as they reached Tomasso. "You only remain alive because of who your father is," he sneered. "But that will not always save you, Cicogna." Two of the guards pushed Tomasso along, the point of a sword at his back. Celsi and Severina walked on towards Bruno and me. Dido was in his death throes. "Finish him off," the Cardinal told a guard to his left. The man stepped forward obediently and beheaded the youth. They then walked past the fresh corpses of Eduardo Samposo and Nofri Amolino.

The group reached the Nolan and me. I pulled Bruno to his feet, but he was still a little unsteady, so I got him to lean on my shoulder. Two of the guards stood with their swords at our necks.

"Look at the pair of you," Severina said and sighed heavily. "Filthy wretches. On the outside you look precisely as you are on the inside; disgusting, repulsive trash. Heretic scum. And for all your fine words and your so-called learned opinions, you are both powerless; entirely at my mercy." He smiled. "And I have no mercy!"

There came a sound from the ship and four more men appeared. They were dragging two bulging sacks and a pair of wooden poles some eight or nine feet

226

in length. The group reached us. "Set up over there," Severina instructed. "The ground should be soft enough. Hurry up about it."

"It's clear of course what happens next, is it not?" Severina chuckled. "You, Doge's son, shall watch your best friend, Sagredo, and the arch-heretic Bruno burn. You shall smell the flesh as it melts from their bones; their skin and muscle shall dissolve in the flames; their hair will crackle and fly like dandelion seeds in the breeze."

"You shall not . . ."

"Shut up, Doge's brat." The Cardinal turned to a guard. "Gag the idiot."

I turned my attention to Celsi who had been standing silently, his hands clasped in front of him. "Lord Celsi, you know this is not lawful. Do you not fear the Doge's wrath when he returns?"

Severina raised a hand. "There are greater laws than . . ."

"I was not addressing you," I said very calmly.

Niccolo looked a little stunned and just glared at me. Severina realised he had his mouth open and closed it slowly. "Your sword," he said to the nearest soldier. The man handed it over. His Eminence took two steps forward and smashed the hilt into my temple, sending a shock of pain across my head and down my face. I stumbled backwards, landing heavily on the ground. A guard yanked me up. I stared at Severina, showing no emotion and heard Tomasso protesting under his gag, trying in vain to struggled free from his captors.

Twenty feet away, a group of troops had been busy. The stakes had been pounded into the soft earth. Cardinal Severina nodded to his men. They grabbed Bruno and forced us to walk towards the stakes. Giordano stumbled twice and each time he was pulled roughly to his feet and dragged onward. I made to shake off my guards, but they just gripped me harder, a third soldier walked a couple of feet behind me, his sword poised carefully in the middle of my spine.

They shackled Giordano first, using a chain about his ankles and another longer one to twice circumvent his chest and loop about his wrists before being wound about the stake. I was next. They used the same technique and I watched them pile logs from the sacks about the base of first Bruno's stake and then mine. Between the logs, the soldiers squeezed handfuls of dry moss and hemp and small twigs.

Bruno looked towards me and at last there seemed to be a flicker of comprehension in his face and I saw a line of tears roll down his cheeks, drip from his unruly beard and land on the wood all about him up to his hips. Then I caught sight of Tomasso a few yards away. He was still struggling to break free. Severina stopped beside him and ruffled his hair as though he were a child. "Save your energy, Doge's son. Your friends are beyond your help. He turned to the soldiers bearing the torches, and nodded. They walked slowly towards Giordano Bruno and me, crouched and let the flames flicker over the kindling, setting it alight.

"Be brave, my friend," I said to Bruno, my voice little more than a croak. "It shall soon be over."

Chapter Thirty: Ashes

Crackling. The sound of branches crumbling into shrunken grey embers. And then the smell of burning wood, damp wood that burns slowly. I vomited, but brought up nothing but bile as the first tendrils of heat rose from the piled faggots. I felt a growing hysteria, a terror I could not control. Beneath the bonds, under the chains, I was shaking, every muscle twitching, every nerve alert, waiting, waiting for the first stab of pain, the start of the ordeal. My eyes were blurred with tears and wetness lay on my cheeks. I dry retched. And then, shapes, a flash of colour. I thought a branch had caught alight and was racing upward to lick my flesh. A face appeared close to me and I felt myself being unbound and dragged brutishly from the burning logs, the stake still caught to my back. Two men wearing leather gloves grabbed me, ripping me away from the fire while another soldier scattered the burning wood with rough wary kicks.

All was a blur. I felt the men yank the wooden pile from my back and I was dragged across the ground, the heat receding quickly. The tail of my shirt had caught alight and a piercing pain stabbed my side. One of the men saw it and slapped the fire with his free hand. I was away from the stake and the chains and the men let me go. I lay flat on my back on the chill, wet soil. It felt like a God-given balm. I drew into my lungs air that smelled of brine, its tang, a perfume. I pulled up and rubbed at my eyes, but for a few seconds it made things worse, dust and soot half-blinded me. I found the sleeve of my ripped and burned shirt and enough saliva to wet it and clean away the mess.

What lay before me brought to mind paintings by the artist Hieronymus Bosch from the Low Countries, a vision of how a corner of Hell might be arranged. Dying fires were spread around as branches scattered from the stakes continued to burn and fume. They lit up the mournful night with reds and licks of orange. I saw Bruno gasping and struggling, his hair smouldering as men pulled him across the ground and poured water over him. Two large ships had joined Celsi's galley. Men were fighting, swords flashing crimson in the flame's light. Just a few yards in front of me, Tomasso dashed into the fray, a sword in his hand. He brought it down on one of Celsi's men, cleaving his head almost in two. As Tom span on his heel, I saw his face speckled with blood and grey matter, his eyes wild.

It took only a few minutes for the new arrivals to gain control. I gazed around and caught a glimpse of two figures slipping away from the firelight and into the darkness. I could not see their faces, but from the way they moved and the flow of fabric about the slightly shorter of the two they were marked out as Niccolo Celsi and Cardinal Severina.

I pulled myself up to my knees and tried to make sense of the madness all about me. A group of men in chainmail were grouped close to one of the galleys. They moved forward slowly, and in their midst I could see the Doge's litter, borne by four liveried servants. Tomasso stood down as the last of Celsi's men lay dying. I tried to get to my feet. Tom saw me and started to run across the ash-strewn ground. I watched him come close, feeling my legs give way as though they had been rendered boneless. Losing consciousness, I crumpled to the dirt.

•

There were consequences of course. How could there not be? But only Doge Pasquale Cicogna could determine the ramifications of what had happened during the past few days. Later, I learned that Bruno had been bound, escorted to the Doge's vessel and returned to goal; the dead had been carried away, while I was taken aboard the returned skiff with Tomasso and cared for by a medic who had been travelling with Pasquale. We all then returned to the Republic. The next morning, I received a letter to inform me that my presence as a key witness would be required at a private royal inquiry to be held at the palace three days hence.

I had suffered no permanent damage. From the pyre, a few singed hairs and relatively inconsequential injuries, and from Gessi's attentions some more serious burns. Nevertheless, Teresa and Isabella fussed around me, forcing me to eat far too much and to rest by the roaring fire in the main room. But there was no denying Teresa's great skills. She used a balm of her own concocting to treat my burns and expertly bound my wounds and salved the chaffing on my ankle caused by the manacle Celsi had ordered for me.

The second evening after the terrible events in Mestre, an exhausted Isabella had retired early and Teresa stayed up with me. Piero was due a little later to escort her back to the Palazzo Duolo.

"Your wounds are healing, Francesco," Teresa said sitting beside me close to the fire. "They will take perhaps two or three weeks to be completely mended, as you well know. But what of your other wounds? The emotional anguish you must have suffered? Are you able to talk about these things?"

"I learned long ago that it is always best to be open about terrible experiences. Indeed, I have learned from men I respect greatly that it is a bad thing to bottle up trauma and fears. But, really, Teresa, I am fine."

She gave me a doubting look.

"I will confess that as I was chained to the stake and the brands were lit, I was more terrified than I had ever been in my life. I've sometimes wondered what death by fire would be like."

"And being imprisoned?"

"I am fortunate to have learned ways to deal with such punishments, but it certainly was not easy to bear, Teresa. My heart goes out to Bruno or anyone incarcerated in that dreadful place. But, you know, I have heard that the prisons of the Doge are much less terrible than some. It is said that the cells beneath Castel Sant'Angelo in Rome offer a waking nightmare for those unfortunate enough to be taken there. Indeed, I have been told that most die in captivity before ever coming to trial."

"Yes, I too have heard such things. And the vile treatment by the cardinal's man, Gessi?"

"Well, as much as it is difficult to feel sympathy for the creature, I imagine he is in great trouble now. He will be hated by his master for failing with me, and shall be subjected to the full force of His Serene Majesty's wroth."

"And all of this caused by Niccolo."

I just stared at her. I had no need to criticise the man, Teresa knew the things he had done during recent days.

"You say nothing of him, Francesco."

"What is there to say? You must know him well. You have always known what sort of man he is."

"Yes," she said. "But he has surprised even me these past few days."

"That's what power does. Niccolo Celsi's megalomania has always been counterbalanced by the influence and strength of the Doge and his close allies. Severina has tipped that balance, and through trickery, your betrothed had the freedom to do what he wished."

"Betrothed!" Teresa exclaimed. "Why use that word, Francesco? It sounds like you are spitting it at me!" She had reddened and I could see anger in her beautiful dark eyes.

I was a little taken aback. "That was not my intention, My Lady," I replied. "But surely you have always known the nature of the man? You could accept his cruelty just so long as he employed it against others and not you."

Teresa looked shocked. "You have a short memory," she said quietly. "Remember he beat me after the play at the home of the Cavalinis."

"Yes, Teresa, and I asked you then why you stayed with him."

"What wife is not beaten by her husband?"

"If you were my wife, I would show you only love. Nothing you could do would provoke me to lay a hand on you."

She was readying to say something, but stopped, closed her eyes for a second and exhaled. "I'm sorry, Francesco. I don't know what to say."

"There's no need."

"But there is. After all you've gone through, you should not have to put up with my harridan outburst!"

There was a quiet tap at the door. I got up from my chair, but Teresa pulled up faster and gave me a look as if to say: You sit there, Francesco or I'll beat you about the head in spite of your injuries. I let her answer the door and lowered myself, wincing, to my seat. I heard Piero's voice before I saw him, and stood, ignoring Teresa's protestations. The young man walked in with his usual confident stride. There was a sprinkling of snow on his hat and the shoulders of his coat. He removed the hat and produced a broad smile. It was then, as the light from the fire fell on his face, glancing it from the side that I remembered what it was that Piero had said in the cell, words that had clung to me throughout my recent ordeal. At that moment, my world shifted on its axis. I stood rigid, unable to speak. Teresa touched my arm and it brought me back to the moment. Still speechless, I looked at her and saw her lips move. "Francesco? Are you unwell?"

I did not reply, just looked at her, then at Piero and let myself be led like a child back to the chair near the fire. I sat and stared into the middle distance.

"Francesco?"

Teresa and Piero both looked down at me, concerned.

"Could I speak with you, a moment?" I finally managed to say.

She gave me a puzzled look.

"Alone?" I glanced at Piero. "My laboratory door is open, Piero. Would you mind?"

He nodded, still a little confused and walked off towards the stairs down to the basement.

"Please, sit," I said to Teresa after we heard the door close behind the boy. I looked at her earnest face, the flames dancing in her dark eyes.

"What is it, Francesco?"

"I don't know why I did not understand before. I can only put it down to facing one crisis after another since my return, but it is obvious now. Why did you not tell me that Piero is my son?"

I expected Teresa to be startled, but she was not. It was as though she had been expecting this at any moment, and perhaps she had; she had always been far more perceptive than I. She looked down at her hands, fingers interwoven on her lap. "I'm proud to say he is our son, Francesco. Piero is a child born out of love. But, dear Francesco, we were not fated to raise him together, were we?"

I shook my head slowly. "You would have been three months pregnant when I was exiled."

"I was beginning to show. I told my mother. You will remember my parents were very tolerant, forward-thinking people."

232

I nodded. "I remember them with great fondness. They arranged the marriage to Louis Damas?"

"Yes. My husband knew I was pregnant before the marriage was agreed. A large dowry was involved."

"And then you moved straight to Paris, so that no one might suspect."

"Yes."

"Did you ever love, Monsieur Damas?"

"As I've said before, he was a good man and cared for me and for Piero. He never once used against me the fact that he was not Piero's natural father; but no, Francesco, I did not love Louis." She glanced towards the stairs down to my laboratory. "I do not want Piero to know . . . not now."

"Is that fair on the boy?"

"Now is not the right time, Francesco. He is already in turmoil thanks to recent events. He detests Niccolo and has always been against the marriage. It would be one more huge burden to place on his young shoulders."

"But, he is fifteen."

"It is not something I wish to discuss," Teresa said forcefully. "No one must know, not now."

I fell silent, thoughts racing each other through my mind. I was also in turmoil, I considered; home for little more than a fortnight and my life had been upended, the past re-written, the future a blur of uncertainty. "So what do you plan to do?" I asked.

"About what?"

"Your future."

"I do not know, is the honest answer."

I looked at her, sighing deeply. "Please tell me you will have nothing more to do with that man."

Teresa looked down again.

"Oh, Teresa, this is madness!"

"It is easy for you to say, Francesco. You have been out of my life for so, so long. And I know that you had to write us off."

"How did you . . . ?"

"Tomasso told me you had said as much to him. And, it is understandable. Of course you did. I had to do the same thing. And although Tomasso likes to be sanctimonious about it, he did it too. We've all done it. How could we not? None of us could have believed we would see you again."

"But Celsi? After all he has done to you and Piero!"

"I understand what a sour taste that must leave in your mouth. But as I have said, I have to think of Piero . . . and myself. For all his dreadful faults, Lord Celsi offers security, respectability. I do not know what else to do."

"He also offers physical abuse, violence . . ." I let the words hang. A large part of me wanted to attempt to end the matter with a word. At least that, perhaps naively is what I thought I could do; that Teresa would want to start over where we had left off, but another part shut down such thoughts with a roughness that held my tongue. I knew exactly what Teresa was saying. Could she assume I would be staying in the Republic? What were *my* intentions?

And as though she had read my mind, she said: "What of you, Francesco? Let me turn things around. What do *you* plan to do?"

And for a second, I could not answer. I gathered my thoughts. "This will always be my home," I said lamely. "And to be honest, I have had enough of travelling to last several lifetimes. But this is not the Venice I left fifteen years ago, and no one I knew then is the same now."

"And neither are you, my darling Francesco."

"I know, Teresa, I know." I closed my eyes for a moment. When I opened them Teresa was pulling up from the chair and pacing towards the stairs down to my laboratory. I suddenly felt very old and very tired and swallowed hard to rid myself of the lump in my throat.

•

It was late, but I could not sleep. I needed to speak to Tomasso. I had not left the house since I had been brought here by the Doge's personal guard. Stepping out onto the campo, I almost collided with a young messenger. He was about to slip a note under my door.

"Who sent you?" I asked opening the envelope.

"The artist, Caravaggio," the boy explained as I read. The message said simply: 'My dear Sagredo, Come as soon as you are able, I have completed the likeness you requested. C.'

"Did he look like he would soon be retiring to bed?" I asked.

"I could not really say, sir. I was called into his studio at the Palazzo Londisi. He seemed very industrious."

"Good," I said and gave the boy a coin before closing my door and heading off.

The city was quiet, frosty-cold, the paths slippery, the cloud low and heavy with snow. I walked slowly. I was tempted to take a boat, but needed the air and the exercise. My legs felt stiff, but once I had walked a hundred yards past the campo and onto the main thoroughfare east towards San Marco, the cobwebs began to fray. I breathed in deeply.

What I had said to Teresa about the mental trauma of torture and imprisonment, the horrors of the pyre, they had only been partially true. I was indeed grateful for the lessons I had learned from the yogi, Master Tenzin, and never more thankful that I had continued to practice the techniques ingrained into my mind during my stay in Nepal, but I had glossed over any talk of it and I had changed the subject as quickly as I could. I knew I had not fooled Teresa for a second; nor could I fool myself.

During moments such as these, the night enveloping me, not another soul around, the cry of gulls, the bite of the wind in my face, I could recall what had happened and felt an almost uncontrollable feeling of panic and fear. I knew it was irrational and I did my best to clamp the feeling, stem it at the source, but the cause had been such powerful evil, and death had been so close, it took all of my self-control to rein in my emotions. I knew from what my friend Aliba Al-Nan had taught me in Tripoli that to suppress the pain was not healthy, but I had a job to do. There was no time now for self-absorption; that would come later. Perhaps, I mused, Tomasso and I would be treated by Aliba Al-Nan at the same time.

I walked along a narrow path close to the Grand Canal, reached a tributary, turned north-east and heard a commotion at the canal bank of a tiny waterway off to my right. It took me a moment to realise what was happening. A couple were trying to remove themselves from a gondola that had stopped at a set of steps. They were complaining loudly to the gondolier. I was going to walk on, but ten yards from the bank I recognised Carlo Perugino. He was swaying at the back of his gondola, clearly inebriated. The irate customers clambered ashore and the man turned on him, yelling and gesticulating wildly. Perugino scowled back and started to pull his pole from the water. I guessed what he was going to do with it. The man understood too and backed off, bundling his partner along the path.

"Perugino," I called.

He looked up trying to focus, saw me and shook his head. He had drawn up his pole, but just as he was about to lay it inside the boat, it slipped from his fingers and landed flat no the water. I took the steps down to the water's edge and managed to get a grip on the pole. "Come ashore," I said and held it out for him. He gave me a look of disgust, trotted the length of the gondola and hopped expertly onto the steps.

"Impressive," I said.

"Pff!" He stepped onto the path. "What do you want? You followin' me?"

"Just passing. But I have been thinking about you."

"I'm touched," he slurred. "But if you don't mind, I 'ave customers."

"Indeed, you do, Carlo, very happy ones!"

"Fuck you!" He had the pole and was lowering it back into the gondola.

"Why didn't you report the encounter with Niccolo Celsi outside Alfonzo's?"

He was startled, but in spite of the state he was in, he recovered quickly and shrugged. "What good would it 'ave done, eh? Wouldn't 'ave brought me little girl back."

"It might have helped my investigation."

"Investigation, my arse!" He looked me up and down. "And how's that goin'?"

"You don't care that Celsi might have been involved in your daughter's murder?"

"Course I do." He gave me a fierce look. "But you really think anyone would've listened to me? I'm a nobody, aren't I? My girl, she was an 'hore, another nobody. And Lord Celsi and his kind? . . . Hah!"

I looked at the man and felt a surge of sympathy. He was right of course, who would have listened?

The Palazzo Londisi was lit up, the shutters open in spite of the cold drafts that must have come through the glass where it fitted the mullions. 'There seems to be one long party going on in this house,' I said under my breath.

I was met at the door by a rotund servant in black livery. He bowed as I introduced myself. "Caravaggio has been housed in a small outbuilding in the grounds, sir," the man said and waved towards the doors. I followed him into the hall. I could hear a viola da gamba playing plaintively, the sound drifting down the grand staircase from an upstairs room. Two voices were just discernible both male, then came the sound of a woman's giggle.

The servant led me through the hall to the collection of connected rooms I had been in so recently when I had been alerted to Tomasso's over indulgence. The man pushed back a pair of French doors. These opened out onto a patio illuminated by torches that gave off a pungent aroma. I detected sandalwood, violet and patchouli. We crossed a lawn via a curved line of marble slabs, and ahead I could see a neat little pavilion. Designed along the lines of a Turkish garden house, it immediately reminded me of he sort of buildings common in Constantinople. The inside was brightly lit, a lemon glow spilling out at the edges of blinds pulled down over large windows. We arrived at the door and the servant gave it a brusque rap with the knuckles of his right hand while turning the handle with his left.

"Hugo . . . I have told you Lord knows how many . . ." Caravaggio was at an easel, a paintbrush in his hand, another clasped between his teeth. He tugged the latter from his mouth. "Sagredo. How excellent!" Then he turned back to the servant and flapped his free hand at him. "Go, go . . ." As Hugo passed me he rolled his eyes and I could not help smiling.

"Come in, come in," Caravaggio said, throwing the brushes onto a wooden tray under the easel and stepping towards me. I put out my hand to shake his, but he gripped me by the upper arms and before I realised it, he was planting kisses on my cheeks.

"Er . . . you sent a message," I said.

The artist was beaming. "I just love your seriousness, Francesco. You don't mind me calling you . . . ?"

"No," I said.

"So, as I said in my note, I have the piece for you. The girl you foisted upon me, though!" He shook his head and checked his nails, plucking a filament of paint from under a cuticle.

"Dea Giottinelli?"

"Yes, Darling Dea. She could not make up her mind. One moment the man she saw was about five foot tall, the next he was five foot six inches. He began with dark hair and ended up a strawberry blond for Goodness sake!"

"She did say she caught only a glimpse."

"Anyway," Caravaggio said and flounced towards the back of the studio. "I think I managed to scrape something together from the girl's *observations*."

We reached a small table containing a scattering of sketches made in charcoal and beside this stood another easel containing a canvas covered with a cloth. I expected him to pick up one of the drawings, but instead, with great ceremony, he dashed aside the drape over the painting and stepped back.

It was a wonderful piece of work, a panorama of the Cavalini's palazzo as seen from a gondola positioned directly in front of the main doors and close up to the bank of the Grand Canal. In the doorway stood many of the guests from the night of the 18th, including Tomasso and myself. Towards the right edge and far from the principal action, I could see a hooded figure fleeing the palazzo. He wore a black robe and had a white rope belt about his waist. And that was all that could be discerned, the figure was small and inconsequential, almost an afterthought.

My heart sank, but to disguise my disappointment I stared hard at the painting without comment for perhaps twenty seconds before turning to the young painter. "This is quite wonderful," I said. "Thank you."

It took me almost an hour to prise myself away from Caravaggio's studio, and then only after fielding innumerable questions about his work. He was excited about the new detection technique I had opened his mind and at no point did I have the heart to explain that for all its beauty and the skill with which it had been created, his work was completely useless to me.

A flock of pigeons flew up from the shadows as I crossed San Marco. In front of me the great arches of the cathedral entrance loomed out of a mist that had rolled in. The front of the Doge's palace stood enveloped in brumous grey, just the triangular frieze above the great Byzantine windows on the upper floor remained visible against the dense and dark low cloud. The fog was heavier close to the Lagoon and along Riva Degli Schiavoni. Indeed, by the time I reached Tomasso's place it was so thick I was almost nose to nose with the two palace guards at the front door before I saw them.

"Stop. State your business."

"I am Francesco Sagredo."

They both recognised me. "Sir, Lord Cicogna is under house arrest."

I felt a stab of shock but said nothing to let it show. It made sense, I quickly reasoned. "So, that means he cannot leave his house, but not that I am forbidden to enter."

"Could you tell us the reason for your visit . . . at this hour?"

"No I could not," I snapped. "My friend is a nocturnal creature." I stepped back to glance up, and sure enough there were two candles just visible at the window on the second floor. "He is awake and there are matters we need to discuss."

The two men regarded each other.

"We're talking about the son of the Doge, for Heaven's sake," I said uncompromisingly.

"But, sir . . ."

"Very well. I shall have to call on the Doge himself, rouse him from his bed."

I knew that I was not capable of such a thing, but there were few in Venice who did not know me and most had heard stories of my closeness to the Doge and his family. The men stepped aside and a moment later I was in the hallway heading for the stairs.

I tapped quietly at Tomasso's front door just in case I had been wrong, but a few moments later I heard him approach.

"Francesco," he said, standing there fully clothed except for his bare feet. "Are you sure you should be out?"

"Who's the doctor here?" I laughed. And then a thought dawned on me. "Oh, I'm sorry, do you have company?"

"No, unfortunately!" he laughed and waved me in. "I was just burning the midnight oil."

"It passed midnight a good two hours ago, my friend," I said as he led me to a roaring fire. The warmth was welcoming after being out in the still, freezing night, and I was reminded again of how my body had been weakened by my ordeal, for normally I would have barely noticed such a thing.

"You look pale, Francesco. Are you really recovered? You took something of a battering, there can be no denying that."

"Teresa has been by my bedside."

"Oh, indeed; she is a fine medic." He winked.

I gave him a sour look and shook my head. "Yes, she is, Tom, and that is all!"

He glanced at me sceptically. I noticed a candle on his desk close to the window. There were books and manuscripts piled either side of a sheath of papers, a quill and ink well next to them. "You've been working on something?" I asked.

"Writing a detailed account of events," Tomasso said. "My father has called a private inquiry for tomorrow . . . this morning, three hours after sunrise."

"I know," I replied. "I have been called to attend. Do you know what it involves?"

"No more than you," Tom replied. " But I wish to be as prepared as well as I possibly can be."

"Especially now the existence of the Resistance has been exposed."

"Well actually, my father and the government know almost nothing about that . . . and I intend to keep it that way. Officially, we were rescuing you. Releasing Bruno was an afterthought."

"And you think you can keep up that pretence, Tomasso?"

He ignored the question. "A drink? Beer?"

"Please," I said and eased myself into one of Tomasso's sofas. He left the room for the tiny scullery.

"Are you alone or have the servants long since gone to bed?" I asked as he handed me the drink.

"They have vanished into thin air." He shrugged. "First hint of trouble and that was that . . ."

"To be fair though, Tom, the poor things have had to contend with quite a bit."

He produced a thin smile. "Yes, you're right, they have. And I think that having palace guards posted outside the front door was the final straw."

"I was surprised by them myself."

"My father insists they are there for my own protection and that he has put me under house arrest for political reasons."

"Makes sense."

He looked at me askance. "My fucking father does everything for *political reasons*. And one of those is to keep me out of things while he machinates. He is a canny old man."

"We both might be grateful for that before tomorrow is over."

He nodded. "We shall see. So why are you out so late?"

I shrugged. "I was not able to sleep and then . . ." I told him about the visit to Caravaggio.

"Fuck me!" he exclaimed and laughed uproariously.

"Tomasso, you seem different," I said gently after he had calmed down.

239

"I feel different, Francesco, very different actually. I've long had a sense of purpose as a player in the Resistance, but before three nights ago it was all talk, all theory. I'm convinced the frustration and the need for absolute covertness, even excluding you from the secret, were adding to my strained nerves. I feel liberated."

"And not anxious?"

"Of course I'm fucking anxious! I'm not naive, especially not now, after the mission failed. Bruno is back in chains in the palace dungeons and three of our members have been killed."

"And Pinelli and Sarpi?"

"Their involvement will never be revealed."

"So are you ready to tell me more about the Resistance now?"

He gave me a hard look. "Are you sure you want to be privy to such dangerous knowledge?"

"I think I have enough dangerous knowledge up here." I tapped my head. ". . . to last many lifetimes."

"I'm not jesting, Francesco."

"Nor am I."

"Very well, what do you want to know?"

"Why would you, Pinelli and Sarpi, amongst others, risk your lives for Giordano Bruno?"

"Well, for starters, he is in the firing line, the vanguard, if you like."

"Yes," I said. "Gianvincenzo told me this before Galileo's talk at the palazzo the night Eriador was murdered. He described Bruno as John the Baptist to Galileo being Christ."

"A fair description," Tomasso replied and drew on his beer. "But it goes deeper than that. The Resistance would be viewed by the Vatican as the Antichrist."

I raised an eyebrow. "Isn't that a little melodramatic?"

"No. We want to see radical change within the Church. It has become a corrupt, perverted mockery of what it should be."

"Nothing new there, Tom. A century ago the Borgia pope and his grotesque family were not exactly pure of heart, were they now?"

"No, they most certainly were not, but in those times a group such as the Resistance could never have stood a chance. Now though precedents have been set. Martin Luther, King Henry of England. The Church is no longer an unassailable fortress."

"So you are inclined towards the new religion, Lutherism . . . Calvinism."

"Fuck, no; those hold little appeal. They are as bad as the old faith, and well . . . they are plain dull, Francesco."

"A strange word to use."

"Not really. The alternative we conceive of is the occult."

"Alchemy and spooky magic?" I gave him a smile, but he was having none of it.

"God's arse, Francesco, don't fucking mock." Tomasso's face was hard, anger in his eyes.

I put my hands up. "Sorry, but you know how I feel . . ."

"Yes, you have made that abundantly clear. But respect the opinions of others: You're a clever man, but you're not the fucking oracle of all knowledge."

I was a little taken aback. I knew that Tomasso had always been interested in arcane studies, but only in a loose sense . . . or so I had always thought. It seemed yet another thing had change while I was away from the Republic.

"I never claimed to be . . ."

He waved away the comment. "You always used to say that alchemists were little more than drug addicts. That they fooled themselves into believing they had discovered 'universal truths' and great 'mystical secrets' because they had sampled too many of their own hallucinogenic concoctions."

"I remember," I said stiffly.

"Well, perhaps there have been some . . . maybe many who fit that description, but there are also true mystics, men of great wisdom who are making real progress in our understanding of the Hermetic world, men who believe there are alternatives to orthodox religion."

"I realise that, Tom," I said defensively. "I experienced alternatives while I was on my travels and you know I have very little patience with traditional Christianity. I agree with you when you say the Church is corrupt and no better than many temporal institutions, but . . ."

"But you cannot accept the notion of a spirituality separate from the Church?"

"No, no, Tomasso. You are wrong. I do try to follow a secular spirituality. I studied a doctrine called Buddhism for a long time in Nepal."

"I've heard of it of course . . . I did not know."

"But it is a different thought system to what you are talking about - entirely different."

"Well, perhaps it is, Francesco and I would like to know all about it, but this is not the time. You wanted to know about the Resistance."

"Yes, I do, but something I do not understand is how Galileo fits in. He is, after all an empirical thinker. His ideas are grounded in experiment and mathematics not the principles of magic. Pinelli confirmed this when I talked to him about it."

"It is true. Galileo is certainly no occultist. Indeed, you and he probably have more in common than do you and I. But the Resistance is not a disciplinarian philosophy, each of us holds different views on many things. At one end of the spectrum is Galileo's science, at the other there lie the beliefs held by men like our dead friend, Eriador. But we all see Galileo as key to reforming the Church, changing it into a more open proposition. We know that the battle against the strict traditionalists, men like Pope Clement and that fucker, Severina will be long and brutal, and that it shall not come even close to ending in our lifetimes, but science will be at the forefront, so will the Hermetic tradition, pure Reason and a Humanism that is still young in form but will evolve and grow quickly once we eradicate the dogma of the Vatican."

"Bold words," I said.

"Perhaps, Francesco, but they are sincere and backed up with a determination that would surprise you."

"I don't think it would, Tom." I gripped his shoulder. "I know you . . . and Gianvincenzo Pinelli too well to question that."

He yawned.

"You were not injured in Mestre," I said, ". . . but you look completely exhausted, Tom. Stress and emotional strain may be every bit as damaging as physical injuries. I should leave you to sleep."

"Stay Francesco. It is cold outside and we can have another beer at least, catch a few hours sleep and then make our way to my father's Inquiry together."

"That's kind of you," I said. "And very tempting, but I would like to bathe before the inquiry, and I will be expected to wear my finery, for although Celsi told me I had been removed from The Ten, I have a strong feeling the changes made during his brief moment in the sun shall no longer apply!"

Chapter Thirty-One: A Royal Summons

The meeting took place in the Sala della Quarantia Civil Vecchia, a room usually reserved for the appeal court. It was a small room leading off the Liagò on the first floor of the Doge's Palace. Tomasso and I had been escorted to an anteroom close by and then directed by two palace guards along the Liagò, and into the chamber. We were the last to arrive and as we entered, the soldiers closed the door and took up their stations in the other corridor.

A large table took up most of the room. At its head sat the Doge. A small desk stood just behind him and a scribe was seated there with a quill in readiness. At the other end of the table was Councillor Pagolo Abate, the government's chief advocate and the state's leading expert in Constitutional Law. Seated next to each other on the far side of the table from the entrance were Lord Celsi, Cardinal Severina, and the Vatican Ambassador to Venice, His Excellency Buto Testa. It was the first time I had met the ambassador. He was an athletic-looking man, whom I immediately had pegged as an ex-military man. He was dressed in a suit of fine black satin, his hair wavy and a not unattractive blend of sandy brown and grey. He had a narrow face and emerald eyes. As befitted his rank, Celsi was nearest Pasquale Cicogna, Testa next to him, Severina at the end of the row. The Doge indicated we should sit directly opposite the three men.

"Thank you for attending this Inquiry," Cicogna said looking around the table at each of us. "I think we all know each other here." He indicated with a wizened hand towards Abate. "And this of course, is Ser Pagolo Abate, our chief advocate." The man gave the gathering the briefest of nods and sat very still, his hands on the table either side of a pile of papers.

"We are here to investigate the events which occurred between the 19th and the 23rd day of this month, during which time I was unexpectedly called away on government business. I would like to begin by summarising the key elements of what it is I have called you here to discuss; matters based upon extensive questioning of witnesses, councillors and those gathered around this table." He again waved a hand to encompass the six of us.

"On the evening of the 18th I received an urgent message from Emperor Rudolf requesting I meet him at Trieste. His court was on progress and was in Graz only twenty leagues north of Trieste. He wrote that he needed to discuss a pressing military matter important to both nations, and that if we could meet halfway it would be to everyone's advantage.

"I replied that I would meet him and we left early on the 19th, reaching

243

Trieste late on the 20th. However, once there, we found no sign of the Emperor nor anyone linked to the court of the Holy Roman Empire. Messages were sent to Graz and by late on 21st we learned that, although Rudolf was indeed staying in Graz, no message had been sent to me. It was all a hoax.

"We left at first light and had almost reached home, just two leagues from Mestre, when my galley was met by a Venetian naval vessel. Aboard was one of my junior ministers who informed us of events that had transpired in the Republic during my absence. His report concluded with news that the palace dungeons had been breached and prisoners freed, including, he said, the heretic, Giordano Bruno. A skiff with the prisoners aboard had been spotted leaving from the northern waterfront. To add to the intrigue, my minister reported that Lord Celsi had ordered a company of palace guards to head towards Mestre aboard a galley made ready to sail from Cannaregi.

"We immediately changed course to intercept the vessels, and well . . . I think all of us here know what transpired in Mestre, do we not?" He gazed first at Tomasso and me then at the cardinal, Celsi and Ambassador Testa. The Doge then placed his hands in his lap as passive and as still as a statue. He looked down for a moment then raised his head to scrutinise the Papal Nuncio. "Cardinal Severina, would you please tell the gathering what you may know of these events."

Severina adopted a benign look of subtle confusion. "I'm rather at a loss as to why I have been called to this inquiry, at all, Lord Doge."

"You were there in Mestre."

"Yes, indeed I was . . . doing God's work."

I heard Tomasso make a scoffing sound. Severina ignored him. The Doge said nothing, just held the Nuncio's gaze with stone-hard patience.

"During your absence, Lord Celsi was Acting-Doge. His spies learned of the breakout from your prisons, Your Serenity. I was notified because reports claimed one of the escapees was the arch heretic, Bruno himself. I travelled aboard the galley from Cannaregi. We intercepted the party of rebels, for that is the only way to describe them." And he flicked Tomasso and myself a sour look. "They were making ready Bruno's transportation beyond Venetian territory and to freedom, far from the Mother Church. I could not allow that to happen. I was guided by God."

Tomasso couldn't help himself; he laughed cynically and loudly. His father gave him an angry look and to my surprise, Tom actually appeared contrite for once.

"You find something amusing, Tomasso Cicogna?" Severina asked.

"Your Eminence, please continue. Your fictions aremost entertaining."

"I have nothing more to add at this juncture," the cardinal said, quietly. "God's will guided me, as it does at all times. It was the decision of His

Serenity to intervene."

The comment was heavy with meaning of course. Fascinated, I maintained eye contact with Severina for a few moments considering the man and how he really did seem to believe he was answerable only to his God and the divine mouthpiece, Pope Clement.

"Your Excellency," the Doge said, turning his attention to the ambassador for the Vatican. "Do you have anything to say on this matter?"

"Your Serene Majesty, I can only support what the Nuncio has said. He was guided by God to take action.'

"Did he seek your approval first?"

"No, Lord Doge. But, he had no need to."

"Your Eminence." Cicogna turned back to Severina. "It is just possible, at a stretch, to see why you might think you could take it upon yourself to have Bruno executed; but how do you explain the fact that you also had our honourable Councillor, Francesco Sagredo chained to a stake and that it was only by virtue of the fact that my galley reached Mestre with such speed that he and Giordano Bruno's lives were saved?"

"Francesco Sagredo is a heretic," Severina replied dispassionately, his features arranged to suggest calm benevolence.

"That is quite unproven," the Doge snapped. "It is purely the malicious claim of Lord Celsi here, who has long harboured feelings of personal resentment towards my councillor. Was Francesco Sagredo tried and found guilty in an authorised court during my brief absence?"

Severina refused to answer.

"No, he was not. So, on what basis did you think you could have him burned at the stake, Your Eminence?"

Severina turned to Celsi. "The Acting Doge sanctioned it."

I watched the Doge. He was as calm as Severina. He took a deep breath. "So, let us turn to you Lord Celsi. Could you perhaps explain to me how you justified your actions?"

Niccolo was about to reply when they all heard a commotion coming from just beyond the doors to the chamber. It was a woman's voice, shrill and loud. I glanced at Celsi and saw the colour drain from his face.

"You *shall* allow me into the meeting." We all heard her. "I hope you know who I am ... and if you do, you know I could have your head on a spike as soon as look at you."

The lawyer, Pagolo Abate was rising from his chair. "Your Serenity, I think that is ..."

"I know who it is," Cicogna responded wearily and turned to Niccolo. "You look embarrassed Lord Celsi."

Niccolo rose quickly. "Lord Doge, I am sorry ..."

"Sort it out," the Doge hissed.

Celsi paced around the table, reached the door and pulled it inwards. A guard almost fell into the room, just managing to maintain his balance. Niccolo stepped back and seemed unable to react as his mother, Violetta stormed in. One of the guards made to grab the old woman's arm, but one look from Niccolo stopped him in mid-movement.

"I demand to be party to this meeting," Violetta said, her voice now disarmingly subdued.

"You demand, Lady Celsi?" the Doge said. I could tell he was struggling to maintain his decorum.

"Yes, Pasquale Cicogna, I demand. Don't you forget who I am, and who you are."

"I have not forgotten, Violetta Celsi. I am His Most Serene Doge, ruler of the Venetian Republic. You are a private citizen who has managed to . . . How *has* this . . . woman reached this chamber?" Cicogna turned first to the guards, then to Abate.

No one could answer. Then Niccolo broke the quiet. "Mother. Could you please leave us to discuss . . ."

"I have things to say that should have been said a very long time ago," Violetta declared.

"Guards," the Doge barked. "Remove *Lady* Celsi."

"Do that and I will destroy your government." She looked directly into the eyes of the Doge. "For the word of God is on my side, and it would be just and right. 'May the Lord judge between you and me, and may the Lord avenge me on you'."

"You are coming close to treason," Cicogna answered.

"Mother!" Niccolo yelled.

Violetta ignored her son and seemed quite unmoved by the Doge's threats. Instead, she gave him a look of breath-taking arrogance. It was easy to see how she had threatened her way into the very heart of the palace. A combination of her fame as the wealthiest and most powerful woman in the Republic and her indomitable self-confidence could break many a man.

"You know I could destroy your reign. My family control more then seventy percent of all trade through our nation. We could bring Venetian commerce to its knees."

"And damage yourselves into the bargain?" Cicogna hit back. "Something of a pyrrhic victory!"

"If the stakes are high enough . . . And I would also add that His Holiness the Pope officially sanctioned our actions while you were . . . abroad. And that includes the arrest of Sagredo. Pope Clement is aware of his . . ." And she stabbed a finger towards me. ". . . heresies."

246

For Cicogna, it was the final straw. "Guards, arrest this woman and take her to the dungeons," he bellowed.

"No!" Niccolo Celsi stepped threateningly close to the Doge. "My Lord Cicogna." The man's voice was suddenly very calm. "Your Serenity, please. Could we all try to calm down?"

I stood. "Lord Doge," I said, then paused to glance at each of the faces in the room. Tomasso was wearing a smirk and appeared far too comfortable with the ructions. "Might I suggest an adjournment?"

The Doge considered me, his face showing the terrible strain he was under. "An adjournment?"

"Yes. If Lord Abate was willing to wait here with Lord and Lady Celsi, His Eminence Cardinal Severina, and His Excellency, the Ambassador," I replied. "There is something I would like to suggest to you . . . in private."

"A fine cabal!" Violetta hissed. "The Cicogna family and their dearest friend, the Heretic Traveller."

The Doge gave the woman a withering look. It did nothing, she merely responded with a sickly smile.

"I was going to suggest my son stay with you here," Pasquale countered. He turned to Tom.

He shrugged. "I care not," he said coldly. "Just so long as the guards remain. I do not wish to be left alone in a room with this bunch of criminals."

·

There was a small office off the Liagò. The Doge and I walked along the wide corridor in silence, thoughts churning around in my mind. We were boxed in by four guards and escorted across the marble floor. A bell tolled midday as we sat in a pair of chairs in front of a lively fire.

"So, your thoughts, Francesco?" Pasquale Cicogna said, clasping his gnarled hands together and looking at me earnestly.

"Clearly this is a very dangerous situation, Lord Doge."

"Indeed, it is. And that obnoxious woman . . . how dare she?"

"She is the real power behind the Celsi family."

"Yes, of course she is, always has been, even when Adamo was alive. He was actually a reasonable enough man. We were business rivals but we respected each other, and if we were not exactly friends, we were always civil towards each other. Violetta is simply evil . . . and uncouth!"

I nodded. "But of course, as you well know, she can cause immeasurable harm. The best weapon you have is that any damage she does cause would, as you pointed out, also hurt her family."

247

"There is also the fact that I have the support of the people and the military as well as our allies abroad."

"True, My Lord, but we both know how people can turn if their livelihoods come under threat."

We fell silent, each of us staring into the flames. "So, what do you suggest, Francesco?"

"You must strike a deal."

He kept staring at the flames. "Using the recent … events to shape some sort of compromise between what I would like to do to Lord Celsi and Severina and what they might find acceptable?" he said. "If I had my way, the Nuncio would be packed off to Rome this very day, Celsi would be flung into jail and put on trial for murder, and Severina's flunky, Father Gessi tried for attempted murder. But that would simply strengthen the alliance between Severina and the Celsis, and the Pope would come down heavily in support of his Man and his friends, including Ambassador Testa, who, we must remember, simply stood by passively and let it all happen. As it is, Clement is itching to cause me pain."

"I think these should be the terms," I said. "One: Severina and his retinue will be allowed to stay for seven days, then they must return to the Vatican. Two: During those seven days, a judgment must be made over Bruno, the prisoner must be given a hearing and his fate decided by the end of it."

"That may prove to be difficult, logistically."

"I think it has to be done if nothing else but to act as a sweetener for Severina and his master. It is why he has been here this past two weeks, is it not? I had heard that the legislature had been pontificating on the matter, Lord Doge. Bruno has been in jail since May. He is half-dead. I don't need to tell you that if he were to die in a Venetian jail, there would be awful consequences from several directions simultaneously."

Pasquale stared into my eyes. "I agree. I will force it through. Go on."

"The Celsis should be fined a sum you think appropriate and the money given to the families of Dido Forsi, Eduardo Samposo and Nofri Amolino, killed three nights ago."

"As much as the idea pleases me, that will cause trouble, Francesco. Celsi will claim that the men who were with my son committed a capital crime and deserve what they got. And what am I to do about Tomasso?"

"He must be freed from house arrest and all charges dropped."

The Doge shook his head. "It seems very obviously skewed in our favour. But actually, I am in no mood to appease that family." He produced a sly smile. "The Celsis will claim Tomasso committed a serious crime, perhaps even treason, but with this." He reached into the pocket of his robe and removed a sheaf of papers. "I have clear evidence that Niccolo Celsi led me to Trieste under false pretences and has himself committed treason."

"What is this evidence, My Lord Doge?"

"It arrived an hour before the meeting. Sworn testimony from three senior council members stating that they were coerced into faking letters that took me from the Republic last week."

"Who . . . ?"

"My son, Francesco. Tomasso acquired this information." He waved the papers in front of me. "He had this document brought to me here by messenger."

"So that is what he was writing last night."

"What was that?"

"Nothing, My Lord. Just that your son is as slippery as an eel."

Cicogna looked confused.

"Well, that document," I went on. ". . . tips the balance of power in our favour. You would agree, would you not, that for all the Celsis' influence and wealth they are behoven to Severina. The cardinal's sole interest is Bruno. He cares not about the Celsis feud with you, My Lord. Nor is he really that interested in me. He hates me, yes, but all his talk of the Pope considering me a heretic is simply hot air. Clement probably does not even know I exist. The bait of promising a final decision on the matter of Bruno will be like catnip to the Nuncio. He will force the Celsis to agree to the terms."

The Doge smiled. "There is a very pleasing symmetry in the fact that this uses the very alliance between Severina and the Celsi family against them both. It is ingenious, Francesco. I knew I was right to bring you into government."

"This sort of scheming does not come naturally to me, Lord Doge. In fact, to be honest, I find it all rather distasteful, but perhaps during my travels I've picked up a lesson nor two in political manoeuvring."

"It would certainly seem so! Very well, let us go over this with Abate and get a couple of scribes on to it right away."

An hour later, the Doge, Pagolo Abate and I returned to the Sala della Quarantia Civil Vecchia. A fine lunch had been arranged on the table but only a little of it had been eaten. As we entered, Niccolo was chomping on a chicken leg and I noticed a half empty carafe of red wine close to his goblet. There was no sign of Tomasso.

"Where is my son?" the Doge asked.

"I'm here, sir."

We turned to see Tom at the door. "Just went to stretch my legs," he said and found his seat, picked at a bowl of grapes and munched noisily. "What now?" he said with his mouth full.

I took my seat, Abate headed for the end of the table, a scroll in his hand,

and the Doge stood behind his chair, leaning forward, his hands grasping its cushioned back.

"If I had known you were going to take an age I would not have stayed," Severina said acerbically, his mood clearly unsettled by being made to kick his heels for over an hour. "I am a very busy man."

"I apologise for keeping you all waiting," Cicogna replied magnanimously. He waved towards the food. "I trust the cuisine helped."

Niccolo exhaled noisy through his nose. "So, what is it we have been waiting for precisely, Lord Doge?"

Cicogna nodded towards Abate and the lawyer stood. "We have drawn up an agreement we hope you will all accept as a fair settlement over recent unfortunate events. We would like to have the episode closed and put behind us." He leaned forward and handed out four copies of the deal the scribes had written up, one each for Severina, Niccolo Celsi, Testa and Tomasso. Violetta stood beside her son and was obliged to lean in to read the document.

For several minutes as the gathering read, the silence in the room was almost overpowering. And then it was broken; by Violetta Celsi. She screamed. It startled all of us, even, I believe, her son. Lost for words, I looked at the woman. She was making the strangest sound I think I have ever heard. It was a combination of furious squealing and mirthless, spine-tingling laughter. I studied Niccolo who had been distracted from reading momentarily, but had quickly returned to glance at the paper as though he had experienced this most peculiar behaviour before. The ambassador had jolted at Violetta's eruption; but Severina, engrossed in the document, showed no reaction at all. Tom put down his copy and gave me a look that said he thought his father and I were almost as insane as Lady Celsi.

Then the woman startled us all anew. She jumped to her feet, knocking her chair backwards, sending it clattering across the stone floor. "This . . . this is an outrage!" she screamed, barely able to get the words out.

Niccolo finished reading the scroll at the same moment as the Nuncio. Celsi was, I could tell, a little drunk. The cardinal's face seemed almost lifeless, as devoid of expression as a carnivale mask. Only his eyes displayed a spark of life and I could see there a hint of surprise . . . and satisfaction.

"This is completely unacceptable," Lord Celsi declared. "My Lord Doge, what do you take us for?"

Violetta was walking around the table towards His Serene Majesty. I could sense the guards at the door behind me bridle and I saw the Doge flick them a glance, warning them to hold back.

The old woman reached the end of the table and stopped. Even she was not bold enough, nor crazy enough, to try stepping any closer to Cicogna. He merely eyed her with a superior air. "You are not happy?" he asked without a trace of irony.

"Not happy! Not happy!"

"Mother . . ." Niccolo began. Violetta snapped her head round towards her son and his words died mid-sentence.

"Lord Celsi," the Doge said, looking past Violetta as though she were not there. "You say the terms are completely unacceptable. Could you please elaborate?"

"A fine? Your son exonerated?" He stood. "Tomasso Cicogna has committed treason. He should be put on trial. He . . ." And he pointed a shaky finger towards me, " . . . is a heretic. I caught him in the very act of dissecting a corpse. I have witnesses to prove it. I'm sorry." And he glanced at his mother's ashen face. "Lord Doge, I will not conscion more talk on this subject."

"Lord Celsi." It was Severina. "Could we please discuss this maturely?"

Niccolo whirled on him. I could not tell whether it was the alcohol that had strengthened my old foe's backbone or the fact that he could not bear to lose face in front of his mother, but he had the bit between his teeth. "Cardinal, I can see why you would see this worthless piece of paper," and he waved the freshly written document in the air before him. ". . . as agreeable. But it is an insult to my family. We will never agree to these terms."

"Are you sure about that?" The Doge asked calmly. He looked from Niccolo to his mother and produced the sheaf of papers I had seen earlier. "I have here sworn affidavits from high-ranking government officials that you, Lord Celsi, instigated a plot to have me sent on a fool's errand to Trieste; a treasonous act, but one of which this document." He nodded towards the papers drawn up by Abate and his scribes, ". . . absolves you."

Violetta snorted loudly, her conniptious face screwed up, her fury undiminished. "Lies! There is nothing to *absolve*! You are trying to trick us into believing that it was not your own incompetence and the stupidity of your ministers that led you to leave the Republic in my son's very capable hands. While you were away he served the state admirably. He caught a murderer and a heretic." She glowered at Tom and I. "You heard my son, false Doge . . . you have insulted our family. That is a very serious mistake."

"I urge you to sign the agreement," the Doge said.

"Urge us?" Niccolo retorted. "With respect, Lord Doge, I urge you to completely rewrite the terms, have your son and *him* imprisoned and all mention of fines and compensation written out."

"Lord Celsi . . . please!" Severina tried again, his voice like a razor blade through butter.

"And that is your final word?" Pasquale said.

"Are you deaf you old fool?" Violetta began. The Doge nodded towards the guards. They stepped aside, opened the doors, and two dozen fully armed soldiers stomped into the room and to take up positions around the chamber, six to a side.

"I think you should sign it," Doge Cicogna said.

Chapter Thirty-Two: Father and Son

"I'm very impressed, father," Tomasso said. "Witnessing the look on their faces is something I shall always treasure." Then he suddenly seemed to realise to whom he was speaking and looked down at his boots.

We were seated in the Doge's apartment, just the three of us, father, son and me. Doge Cicogna looked exhausted, but then he always did these days and I was reminded of the fact that he was very old. He was clutching the signed documents that legally bound each of the parties to the terms foisted upon the Celsis. He looked at me and sighed heavily then, staring at the top of his son's head, he said. "Are you able to explain what happened three nights ago, Tomasso?"

Tom looked up and fixed his father with a black look, his former levity gone. "What do you mean?"

"What were you and your colleagues trying to do? What have you got to do with Giordano Bruno? It has taken all of my power and energy to stop Celsi's lawyer friends in the government from having you bound over for questioning. If it were not for the fact that we could drive a wedge between Severina and the Celsis today, I may not have been able to save you from arrest, and a trial."

"Not without that shit Celsi being up there with me on charges of treason," Tomasso spat.

"I agree, my son. But the fact that Celsi might have been found guilty, as well as you, would not have provided much compensation for the tragedy of losing you."

Tomasso did not change his expression, but simply exhaled noisily through his nostrils. "I care about Bruno because I think he has been unfairly imprisoned."

"He is considered a heretic of the first order by the Head of the Church, Pope Clement."

"And I disagree with him. Clement and his henchmen, Roberto Bellarmino and Santoro Severina see heretics everywhere. You know that."

The Doge sighed again. "But risking your life? Risking being caught and put on trial for treason?"

Tomasso shrugged. I feel strongly about it."

"Well, I am setting Giordano Bruno's hearing for two days hence, the 28th. During the past few months the judiciary has heard both sides of the argument. The prosecution nuncio, Ser Laurentio Priuli will be allowed a summing up and Bruno will be permitted a final statement, but a judgement will be made by the end of the day." He paused for a moment. "I have heard rumours of an anti-establishment, anti-Catholic group calling itself the Resistance," Pasquale stated. He looked from Tomasso to me and back to his son. "Its members apparently believe the Church must be radically reformed, that the Pope himself is a figure of evil. In short, they are as heretical as Giordano Bruno. Do you know anything about them?"

"I have heard of them, Lord Doge," Tomasso replied coldly. "But what you have described is the limit of my knowledge about them."

The Doge turned to me. "During the course of your investigation into the recent murders has the name the Resistance come up, Francesco?"

"I paused for a moment a little surprised by the question. "Yes," I said and felt Tomasso's eyes bore into me. "The alchemist, Eriador mentioned something about a radical political movement when I interviewed him shortly before his death on the tenth day of this month, Lord Doge."

"And do you think there is any connection between the series of murders and this nefarious group?"

"I'm not sure what you mean."

"Naturally, I have no clear theory," Cicogna began. I feel content to leave that up to you. It's just that on the one hand we have the misfortune of having Bruno imprisoned here in the Republic, and on the other, we have the tribulation of being host to a series of gruesome murders. Before May this year when Bruno was arrested, we had seen the occasional murder, almost always a crime of passion or as the result of some petty feud between neighbours, but nothing so . . . devilish as the slayings we have witnessed. Indeed, I have never seen nor heard of anything like the three murders that have followed so closely on each other's heels. You said right from the beginning that the murder of Antoinette Perugino was somehow ritualistic."

"So?" said Tomasso.

"So," The Doge put out his left hand, palm up. ". . . ritualistic murders." And then he extended his right hand. "A bunch of heretics, who, according to rumour at least, are steeped in the occult."

"Where does your Intelligence on this Resistance come from?" Tomasso asked.

"How do you think the government knows of any sedition or risk from any group? Naturally, I have informants, spies. It would be naive to think any nation could do without an Intelligence network in this age, would it not, son?"

We fell quiet for a moment. I noticed the ticking of a pair of clocks, one on the Doge's desk close by, the other on a mantelpiece. I could not help but note that they both seemed to be running fast and to the same degree; by my estimate about twenty minutes.

"Anyway," the Doge said, snapping us from our reverie. "I think we can agree on one thing at least. What happened earlier in Sala della Quarantia Civil Vecchia must be considered something of a triumph, but, we must not let it go to our heads. Francesco, I think we have damaged the Celsis, but a vicious animal is most dangerous when it is wounded. Niccolo has his own reasons for wishing you ill; and you, Tomasso." He turned to his son. ". . . were already on that family's hate list if for no other reason than the fact that you are a Cicogna."

"I know that."

"You must both be extra vigilant."

"And you don't think we know that too?"

I glared at Tomasso and his jawline tightened, his lips pursed to paleness. But his barbs seemed to have no effect upon the old man. "Francesco, I realise you are doing everything you can to solve these terrible murders, but I just want to reiterate that we must . . . we must have a perpetrator in the cells, or dead, soon. I am growing increasingly aware of fear spreading through the populace."

"I understand, My Doge."

"The murderer seems to be killing indiscriminately: a prostitute, an alchemist drug dealer and a visiting actor. It is understandable that mothers are fearing for their children, husbands worry for the safety of their wives. The next victim could be anyone."

"I sincerely hope there will not be another victim," I said.

"Have you any theories? Any instinctive feelings?"

"I am developing a theory, but it is not yet clear enough to explain."

The Doge nodded. "I believe you will find this killer. I also want you to drop all inhibitions now. I give you free rein to use whatever methods you wish. I have no plans to leave the Republic in the near future." His lips curled in a half-grin. "And I truly believe that Celsi will not openly impede you in your work. There will be no more raids on your laboratory."

"No, that shit will simply stab us in the back if he gets a chance," Tomasso said.

"Yes, he will," Doge Cicogna replied. "So, we must take great care to watch each other's backs. In that way he may not get a chance."

The Doge rose to indicate that the meeting was concluded.

"Sir," I said. "Your clocks."

Puzzled, the old man looked around at the two timepieces.

"I couldn't help noticing that they are both running at least twenty minutes fast."

The Doge grinned. "Ah, Francesco, you must put that down to the foibles of an old man. I have them kept like that deliberately to help me arrive at meetings on time!"

·

It struck me just how long we had been in the palace when Tomasso and I emerged onto San Marco and the sun was but an hour from setting, our steamy breath billowing around us.

"My father opens his mouth and shit comes out," Tomasso hissed, pulling a hood over his head and clapping together his gloved hands.

"Always *contra mundum*, Tom."

"No, only when it comes to my father."

"You're very hard on the old man."

"You think so?" Tom pulled a face. "I find it hard to breathe the same air as the old goat."

"And you certainly don't disguise the fact, Tom."

"Why should I?" He stopped and gave me an uncompromising look. "I will never forgive him; you have to accept that."

I shrugged. "It's not my feud. I just find it uncomfortable being caught in the middle."

Tomasso snorted and we walked on. We had turned north and realised simultaneously that Niccolo and Violetta Celsi were walking no more than a dozen paces ahead of us. I was about to say something to Tomasso and turn in a different direction when a dark figure flashed into my field of vision. It was a short man, his face obscured by a hood. As he rushed towards the Celsis, he raised a knife through the air and swung it round. I yelled, Celsi turned just in time and caught the man's arm.

"You killed my baby girl," the man howled and his hood fell back. It was Carlo Perugino.

Violetta screamed, and with amazing agility for her age, she dived at the attacker. Niccolo staggered backward, tripping over his own feet, Perugino going down with him. Tomasso and I dashed forward, and a few yards to our right, a pair of palace guards sprang into action.

Tomasso reached the fray first and yanked his right arm around Carlo's neck. Violetta was beside him, clawing at the man's face making him scream in shock and pain. His knife fell clanging across the cobbles and Niccolo landed a heavy punch in the man's face.

"My darling," Violetta said, helping her son to his feet. "Are you . . . ?"

"I'm quite unharmed, mother."

"Perugino," I said turning to where he stood gripped firmly at each arm by the guards.

He gave me a look of contempt.

"Who is this creature?" Violetta screeched. She was out of breath, her face drained pale.

"It is Carlo Perugino," I said. "The father of Antoinette Perugino, the young woman killed in the Ghetto."

"The whore?" Violetta flicked Perugino a spiteful look. "Take him to the cells," she said imperiously.

Perugino seemed to have passed into a daze, his face completely devoid of expression as though in his own mind he were already dead. I watched as he was dragged away. A small crowd had gathered, but then two more soldiers arrived and waved away the curious. I heard a few disgruntled moans, but the guards had their swords drawn and no one wanted to make trouble unnecessarily.

Niccolo was looking a little shaken, the shoulder of his coat was ripped and a smear of wet dirt ran along one sleeve, flecks of sludge pot-marked his face. "I owe you my gratitude," he said to Tom and I. His mother glared at him and gave us a vicious look. "A second later and . . ."

"Come, we are late," Violetta snapped and spun on her heel. Niccolo turned with her and we watched their backs as they crossed the square and soon disappeared from view.

"Well, that was interesting!" Tomasso said with a grin.

Chapter Thirty-three: Servant to Servant

Adamo Celsi's tomb in the family crypt under the Palazzo Arragio was every bit as ornate and ostentatious as one would expect. Constructed from the finest black marble quarried from Pietrasanta in the Tuscan foothills of the Apuan Alps, where a century earlier Michelangelo had personally supervised the obtaining of the stone he had used, it was a perfect Celsi statement. Atop the tomb was a lid of solid gold, and sculptures of angels each hand-carved in gold and placed on the tomb five years after Adamo's death, added to its gaudy splendour. The whole grandiose artifice was said to have cost no less than eight-thousand ducats.

Across the tomb lay Violetta, her body trembling from the cold and the pent up frustration she felt. "Those devils humiliated us today, my darling," she said, her voice breaking with emotion. "If you had been there you would have destroyed them, strimmed them, my love. But then, if Lord God had not, in his infinite wisdom, needed you in Heaven, you would have been Doge long ago and the Cicognas would be nothing . . . Nothing." She began to sob. "Oh, Adamo, why did the Lord call you to Him so soon? I know I have asked you before, begged you to answer; but you have never told me your purpose in Paradise." She wiped her face and forced back the tears. "I know you must be important to Him, and that gives me succour, but only just enough to carry on, dear husband, just enough to give me the strength I need to watch over our beloved children. But oh, Adamo, for you to have been there today. If only. I tried, I tried so hard to support Niccolo, but we were tricked, caught between the wishes of the false Doge and the ambitions of that bastard, Severina. But we shall have our revenge. Yes, you know that, don't you, Adamo? We will never be humiliated again. I must make sure of that. Did the Lord not say: 'Vengeance is Mine, and retribution. In due time their foot will slip; For the day of their calamity is near, And the impending things are hastening upon them.' That shall be the least of it, Adamo, my love, the least of it."

She began to sob again, and this time her pain and bitterness welled up inside and she cried so that the tears ran down her face and onto the polished gold. Her body racked with her weeping, she was shaking her head, and as the wetness dried on her hollow wrinkled cheek, and chilled, she shivered so much her back arced and her bony shoulders knocked against the top of the tomb.

Pulling up, she grabbed a shawl she had deposited on the floor, wrapped it about herself, leaned forward to the freezing surface of Adamo Celsi's tomb and kissed the gold. Straightening, she took the steps up from the crypt slowly, every inch of her body aching, every corpuscle every nook and corner of her mind throbbing with hate and dreams of vengeance that would manifest as waking nightmares for her enemies.

At the top of the stairs, the sky was striated, purple, blue and orange. She looked up and almost walked into her lady's maid, Agata Mantini. "Goodness! You startled me, Agata," Violetta Celsi exclaimed, bringing a hand up to the shawl about her scrawny throat. "What are you doing here?"

"I have made the enquiries you wished of me, My Lady."

"About my son?"

The servant nodded.

"And?"

"He was indeed seeing the murdered girl. They used to meet at Alfonzo, the Spaniard's"

Violetta hissed. "It confirms my suspicions, Agata, and it was further confirmed only an hour ago in San Marco."

The young woman gave her mistress a questioning look.

"It matters not," Violetta said and waved a hand between them dismissively. "The whore worked at the Spaniard's bordello, didn't she?" Violetta was talking to herself, but Agata nodded anyway.

"They also met regularly at an apartment on San Marco," the servant said.

Violetta eyed the woman through narrowed eyes. "San Marco Terrazza? Yes, that would make perfect sense." She gazed at the servant, her mind working so that she barely focussed on her face. "Well, thank you, Agata. You may go."

The servant stood still.

"What is it, girl?"

"A messenger called earlier."

"From whom?"

"Francesco Sagredo's servant, Isabella Dioli. Remember, I approached her for information?"

"Yes, you did mention it. You failed to persuade her, did you not?"

Agata Mantini bristled a little but quickly suppressed any emotions she felt. "She has been taken back by Lord Sagredo . . . would you believe that!"

"Yes, I can believe it, Agata. I've never met anyone so Holier than Thou as *Doctor* Sagredo. He's *not* a lord, girl. Some might question whether he is even a real medic. So, what of this Isabella woman?"

"She has agreed to spy for us after all."

"I see. And the messenger?"

"He said Isabella Dioli wished to see me today, around sunset. She has some information she thought might be useful."

"And you send back a reply?"

"I told the boy that would be fine."

"Good. Let me know when she is here." Violetta said, her features slipping again into the far-away expression she had exhibited only a few moments earlier. It was the look of an evil woman plotting evil things.

•

Isabella had always enjoyed shopping at the old market. She had gone there when her children were young, before the plague years, before her babies had been taken from her and the disease had left her widowed. Rather than it reminding her painfully of her terrible loss, it invigorated her, took her back to a time when she was young and the sun seemed warmer on her face, the future unimagined.

It was freezing cold, but she was wrapped up against it. She knew many of the market stallholders and they always gave her good deals and the best produce they had; and it was relatively quiet, most people were already at home, cooking.

Fifteen minutes after arriving, her basket was filled with fresh vegetables and resting on top was her best purchase of the trip, a punnet of Tuscan olives preserved in vinegar. They would make for a wonderful addition to the winter vegetable pie she was planning to cook that evening.

The shopping done, Isabella walked the short distance to the Palazzo Arragio where she had arranged to meet the Celsi servant, Agata Mantini. She rang the bell of the servant's entrance at the rear of the palazzo. Agata met her there and led the way to the palace kitchens where she had a little room off the main area. The cook and her assistant took no notice and busied themselves with dinner for Violetta, Niccolo and Sofia.

"You've done well at the market, I see," Agata said eyeing the groceries. "Those olives look delicious."

"Yes," Isabella said stiffly.

"So, you said there was some news."

Isabella made a good performance of looking torn as though she were struggling inside, tormented by treachery. She peered over her shoulder nervously, but the cooks were preoccupied and could not hear the conversation anyway.

"I did as you asked," Isabella said. "I listened in to conversations and followed my master's comings and goings. He has been out all day."

"I have heard about the drama at the Doge's Palace."

Isabella had not, and gave the woman a querying look.

"It matters not," Agata said impatiently.

"I haven't heard my master talk much about yours, but he has been mightily aggrieved for being held in the cells."

Agata gave Isabella a crooked smile and shook her head slowly. He must have nine lives that Sagredo."

"I did though overhear one thing. He was on the sofa by the fire yesterday and writing something out on pieces of paper and talking to himself. He said something like: 'Celsi must have killed her in a fit of passion. The other murders were carried out by someone else . . . that must be the way things went."

Agata shook her head again. "Come, Isabella, let us take a walk in the vegetable garden. I might have some basil for you to add to your basket." Isabella appeared a little surprised but rose from her seat obediently. "We can talk some more out here, as I pick the herbs."

The two women passed through the kitchen, the cooks ignoring them, and out onto the frost-covered garden.

"Did he say anything else?"

"He was writing on these little bits of paper. I would not know what they said."

Agata gave her a condescending look. She had been taught a little how to read and write, and because of this and the fact that her employers were amongst the wealthiest families in Italy, she considered herself a superior example of her class. "No, of course you would not, my dear," she said patronisingly. "But did he say any more?"

Isabella paused making a show of thinking it through. She had had the measure of Agata Mantini the moment she first met her over a week ago and was rather enjoying herself. "Yes, I remember now. He said: Niccolo had the motive, he had the opportunity and he is the sort of man who would kill out of fury."

"Any more?"

"He used a word I did not understand." Isabella looked at the frozen ground as though she were struggling to remember. "He said: Niccolo Celsi has a vol . . . volatile mind. He could do such a thing."

Agata had no idea what the word 'volatile' meant either. But she memorised it so she could use it when reporting back to her mistress, then nodded sagely as though it all made perfect sense and said: "That's good, Isabella, very good. Let us return to the warm."

"The basil?" Isabella said.

"Oh yes." Agata produced an awkward smile, squatted and plucked up a handful of green leaves, the invigorating scent of crushed stems reaching Isabella's nostrils. They turned back towards the door into the kitchen, and on

261

the stoop, Agata made a noisy performance of stamping her feet to remove the ice and flecks of hard mud from her shoes before indicating that Isabella should do the same. Then she opened the door and led the way back to the little room off the kitchen. There, Agata placed the basil on top of the olives and the other produce, picked up the basket and handed it to Isabella. "There we are," she said, reaching into her apron to remove a couple of soldi which she handed to Isabella. "Let me know straight away if you overhear anything else or if you see anything odd." She turned and led the way back through the kitchen into the courtyard and out through the servant's gate.

Chapter Thirty-Four: Olives

"So what exactly *are* you doing, Francesco?" Tomasso asked.

"Just a moment," I replied. "All shall be revealed." I had four sheets of paper upon which I had written blocks of text, some in large font. I was attaching these to a softwood board on the floor using rabbit skin glue which I had prepared the day before. We were seated cross-legged on the floor of the living-room.

"What does it say?" Tomasso went on.

"God! You're like a small, child," I exclaimed and straightened the final piece of paper. The four sheets were joined almost seamlessly and covered completely the softwood board. In total it was about two foot to a side. Across the top in large capital letters were three names : 'ANTOINETTE PERUGINO', 'ERIADOR' and 'FRANCO ANDREINI'. Below each was a block of smaller writing running down the page.

At the bottom of the board were other names 'NICCOLO CELSI', 'CARLO PERUGINO' and 'ALFONZO CASTELLO'. Below these were three more: 'LUCA LAMON', 'TITO BRAGLI' and 'STEFANO VANENTI'. Between these sets of names in the centre of the board, I had written, 'MEANS', 'MOTIVE' and 'OPPORTUNITY'.

Before applying the paper, I had set up an easel a little way from the couch. I now placed the board on the easel, adjusting it so that it settled level on the wooden ledge and rested back squarely on the vertical support. On the couch I placed a small box of pins and some lengths of fine string.

"Right, what's this all about?" Tomasso said, waving at the board.

I gave him a few moments to study the board before I started to explain. "It's what I call a thought chart."

"Looks confusing."

"No it's all perfectly logical. Let me explain." I stood close to the board and Tomasso sat on the couch beside the items I had placed there. "At the top we have the names of the three victims. At the bottom, the prime suspects. I've written what we know about each of these people." I pointed to the columns of text. "In the centre are the three aspects of any crime: 'Means, 'Motive' and Opportunity'.

"Wait," Tomasso said. "What does that mean exactly?"

"Imagine for a moment, a man has been cuckolded by his wife and stabs her with a knife while she is asleep and no one else is in the house."

"Very well."

"In that scenario, the means was the knife used by the murderer, the motive was the jealousy caused by the perfidious wife, and the opportunity? That was the fact they were alone and she was asleep.

"I see."

"Now the first thing this board does is it allows me to lay out my thoughts and what I know and what I suspect about each of these individuals."

"Yes, I can see that." Tomasso nodded at the board and the blocks of writing.

"So, let's review things. First, consider the victims. Antoinette Perugino: What we definitely know about her – she was a prostitute who worked at Alfonzo's." I leaned over to the couch and plucked up a handful of pins and two pieces of string. I then attached one end of each length close to Antoinette's name, pulled them down to Alfonzo Castello and Stefano Valenti and stuck them there. "She was having an affair with Niccolo Celsi." I used another three pins and two lengths of string to connect Antoinette with Celsi and to his assistant, Luca Lamon. "She was sharing an apartment with another prostitute, Anica Rosen. They were both users of the poppy and that was supplied to them by Eriador, via Alfonso's assistant, Stefano Valenti." I ran a string from Antoinette to Eriador and on to Valenti.

"Now, Eriador: He knew Antoinette, but only vaguely. He was also loosely associated with Celsi because the alchemist rented a property from him. But other than these flimsy connections we know no other links. Eriador was a member of your Resistance, anti-establishment, anti-Catholic. He once worked at the Court of Emperor Rudolf in Prague."

"He was also a prominent drug dealer, Francesco. He did not just supply Stefano Valenti and the whores at the brothel."

"Quite," I said. "So, he would almost certainly have had business dealings with the Celsis. The fact they trade in the poppy is not exactly a secret."

Tomasso was nodding. "But of course, they cover their tracks expertly and there is no proof."

"All right, so this last is really speculation, but you would not get good odds if you gambled against the fact that Eriador had, at some point, worked with the Celsis or their minions." I paused for breath. "So, what else do we know of the man? You knew him far better than I."

"I told you just before he was killed. I was being honest then when I said I did not know him well. He served at the Imperial court during the mid-'80s and first arrived in Venice just over five years ago. But then he left again in 1589. He apparently travelled first to Helmstedt and then the following year to Frankfurt. He met Bruno there, became a disciple and returned to the Republic about eighteen months ago, early '91."

"About nine months before Bruno first started instructing Mocenigo?"

"Yes," Tomasso said. "Bruno spent a while in Padua and then came back to the vile bastard Mocenigo's palazzo in March this year. As you know, he was arrested in May. And what of the ring Ajith discovered stolen by the servant, Bertino Magallore? You weren't very convinced by the possibility he could have killed Eriador."

"No, and I'm even less inclined to believe it now. But it has made me wonder if the alchemist wasn't killed for something else he possessed."

"Meaning?"

"Some knowledge, some information, perhaps. I wonder if your friend Eriador is not the key to this entire mystery."

"Well, if he is, I reckon whatever it was he knew, he took with him to the grave."

I sighed. "Right, let's consider Franco Andreini. When it comes to him, the connections with every other name on this board are even more flimsy."

"Fuck, we know almost nothing about him!"

"What we do know is that his arrival in the city was known about well in advance; but there is no tangible connection between him and Eriador or Antoinette. Equally, I can see no relationship between Andreini and the suspects down here." I tapped the bottom of the board. "Andreini's colleagues implied that he may have used the poppy. They certainly were not shocked at me asking about it. But there is no proof, and even if there were, the link with either Eriador, who purified the stuff, or the go-between, Stefano Valenti, is tenuous."

"Franco Andreini and the troupe were in Venice less than twenty-four hours before the performance. That may have been enough time to connect with the drug network here – underlings of the Celsis perhaps, or that Valenti shit."

"That's correct. The other thing we know about the actor is that he was a sodomite."

"You didn't tell me that, Francesco."

"To be honest, it slipped my mind. Remember, after you left with Andreini's body that night I barely saw you until you rescued me from Gessi. Besides, I'm still not sure if either of these things have any relevance to the investigation."

"And I assume no one who attended the play has offered up any information?"

"No, nothing from that quarter. I asked the audience specifically, but either no one saw anything incriminating . . . '

"Or else they feel it's beneath them to get involved!"

"Possibly."

"So, the names at the bottom," Tomasso said. "Your suspects. What do we know about them?"

"Well," I began and tapped Celsi and his assistant's names at the bottom left. "Celsi was having an affair with Antoinette and was seen close to the scene of the crime just before the woman was killed. He also knew Eriador. Additionally, his assistant, Luca Lamon is small and left handed."

"And that fits with what you determined about the wounds to the neck in each murder. Celsi is tall, he could have killed the victims and the mutilations might then have been carried out by the assistant because whoever mutilated Eriador was left-handed."

"Yes, which is where this middle section comes in: 'MEANS', 'MOTIVE' and 'OPPORTUNITY'." With pins and string, I linked Celsi and Lamon to Antoinette via all three words. "Celsi had the motive – his relationship with the girl: it was either a crime of passion, or he could have killed her to shut her up. He had the opportunity - he was close-by, and he had the means – a knife is not hard to find. There is also the fact that his assistant is left-handed and could be involved in the crimes." I then linked string between the names and Eriador. "The same applies here. Celsi had plausible motives to murder the alchemist."

"Not because he knew Eriador was a member of the Resistance?"

"No, it's much more likely to be a drug connection. It could even be because the alchemist supplied Antoinette with the poppy, and that infuriated Celsi. Again, he had the opportunity. He cannot really account for where he was at the time of Eriador's slaying. We only have the word of his servants as an alibi and they could be bought off easily. Remember I asked your father about his clocks?"

"Yes, what was that for?"

"Well when I interviewed Celsi, he made a big issue of the fact that he knew the time he left the Doge's office the night Eriador died. But he probably has no idea your father keeps the clocks running twenty minutes fast."

"So, he would have left the palace earlier than it seemed and that would have given him more time to be in the right place at the right time to murder the alchemist. Clever of you."

"It makes it easier to argue for his opportunity and the means has never presented itself as a problem. His assistant could have carried out the mutilations."

We heard some sounds at the front door and it opened inwards. Isabella was standing on the stoop holding a basket filled with fruit and vegetables. Tomasso jumped up and paced over. "Here, Isabella," he said. "Let me help." She gave him a grateful look and I watched as Tom lowered the basket next to the water pail.

"I found some wonderful bargains, sir . . . Francesco." Isabella said.

"Excellent."

She looked at the board blankly.

"Don't mind us," I said.

"I visited the Celsis servant."

"You did?"

"I passed on the message we discussed."

"Good."

"And she seemed pretty convinced?"

"Yes, even gave me some basil from the Celsis' garden."

"It's a clever idea to be a double agent," Tomasso commented.

Isabella looked at him a little startled.

"We have no secrets, Isabella, don't worry," I said, and Tom gave her a cheeky grin.

"Well just so long as you remain tight-lipped, Lord Cicogna."

We turned back to the board and Isabella busied herself with the market produce.

"So, what about Celsi being behind Andreini's murder?" Tomasso said as we refocused our attention. "It doesn't work, does it?"

"No, Tom, it definitely does not. There is no possibility Niccolo Celsi could have murdered the actor, no opportunity, and probably no motive."

"But he and his assistant, this Lamon, may have killed Antoinette and Eriador?"

"Only if Andreini's murder is unconnected with the first two; which strikes me as unlikely."

"So, Carlo Perugino and the kid, Tito?"

"Perugino had plenty of motive and the opportunity to kill Eriador. He may have had reasons to murder his own daughter – shame, fury; but Andreini? Why would he do that? And the boy Titus is right-handed. I made a note of that when we visited them at Perugino's boat house."

"Anyway, Francesco, it strikes me that these killings have been committed by someone rather clever, evil and twisted certainly, but clever. I don't think Carlo Perugino has the intelligence to carry out these three murders and leave such few traces."

"I agree."

"Which leaves us with Alfonzo and his ape."

"Means is again no problem, but what about opportunity?" I stated. "I think it would have been noticed if both Alfonzo and Stefano slipped out of the bordello, and the same goes for the second murder – that was at a busy time of the evening for them. And motive? Well, they both knew Antoinette of course and Stefano certainly knew Eriador, so it could have been a business matter gone wrong. But as far as we know, there is absolutely nothing to link either man with Franco Andreini. To top it off, neither Alfonzo nor Stefano are left-handed."

"So . . . and I don't mean to be rude, but all this cleverness." And Tomasso nodded towards the board. ". . . leads us precisely nowhere."

"Well, that's not entirely true," I replied. Eliminating suspects is an important part of the process, and this board serves to clarify a few things about the crimes . . ."

We both span round at a horrible sound from where Isabella had been washing and chopping the vegetables. The poor woman was grasping her neck, a ghastly, contorted look on her face. I saw her sway and dashed over in time to catch her as her legs gave way. A terrible grating sound came from her throat and her eyes were bulging. She was trying to say something and pointing to the olives where they lay still in their punnet. There were four olive seeds on the counter.

Tomasso was beside me and looked at the olives. "Fuck, Francesco. They've poisoned her!"

"Here, take her shoulder." Together we helped the stricken woman to the couch and laid her down. "Keep her head back, make sure her airways remain open." I ran back to the counter and picked up the punnet to sniff at the olives. I smelled almonds and knew immediately what the poison was.

"Tom, help me sit Isabella up." We eased he into a seated position. "Could you fetch that bowl over, please?"

Before Tom could get back, Isabella had vomited copiously, her body shaking, stomach heaving. Then Tom was there with the bowl. "Look after her," I said. "I can produce an antidote."

I ran for the stairs to my laboratory, and in a moment, I was rifling through the jars and boxes of herbs and powders on the shelves. From upstairs came the sound of Isabella retching and Tom's soothing words. I quickly found my pestle and mortar, ground together half a dozen ingredients, ladled some water from a bucket into the mortar, ground some more, then filtered the concoction through a square of linen into a receptacle. I repeated the filtration until the filtrate was a clear green solution and poured this into a small ampule.

Isabella was clutching her stomach and leaning over the bowl.

"She's stopped bringing anything up," Tom said.

"Good. Hopefully she has expelled most of the poison."

I gently lifted Isabella's head. She was groaning. I caught a few words. "I'm . . . so, sorry."

"Don't be silly." I made her drink the draught I had prepared. She gagged on it and I held her head back so that the antidote reached her stomach. "Lie her down again," Tom. We have to make sure she keeps it down. That's it, head back," I said to Isabella reassuringly. "You're going to be all right. I know it's difficult, but try to stay calm. You've been poisoned, but I have administered

268

an antidote. You're going to be fine, believe me, Isabella."

She stared up at me, terror in her eyes and tried to speak. "Sssh," I said and put a finger to her lips. "Just lie still." I turned to Tom and said quietly. "Thankfully, they used a solution, and a weak one at that, and she only ate a few or else I would have been powerless to save her."

"Obviously meant for you."

I nodded grimly. "Yes, and I feel terrible putting Isabella in danger."

"Don't blame yourself, Francesco."

I exhaled through my nose and noticed my fists were clenched.

"Are there no limits to the evil of that repulsive old bitch, Violetta fucking Celsi?" Tom spat.

Chapter Thirty-five: Reluctance

The next morning, I checked on Isabella. She had slept well and seemed quite recovered, if a little pale. She had been very lucky. I knew arsenic to be a deadly poison, but she had only consumed a small dose and I had given her an effective antidote which I had learned about in China. I insisted she stay in bed for the day and assured her nothing needed to be done about the house.

Tom had stayed over and was asleep on the couch close to the fire. I took myself off to meditate for half an hour in the garden, then, returning to the main room, I called to Tomasso, but he ignored me. I tried to shake him awake, but he simply complained bitterly and turned away pulling the blanket over his head. There came a knock at the door. I answered it and saw a young man in palace livery. He was well wrapped up against the cold with a scarf and hat, and in a mittened hand he held out an envelope. Thanking the boy, I found him a couple of soldi and took the letter into the house, opening it as I went.

"Christ, Francesco, your house is fucking cold!" Tomasso exclaimed sitting up and rubbing his eyes. Then he saw the letter in my hands. "Good news or ill?"

I finished reading before looking up. "Good. I said. Your father has made arrangements for me to question Cardinal Severina."

"Christ!" Tomasso exclaimed. "The old bastard's some use after all."

"I must ready myself for the first job of the day, and it's one I'm not looking forward to."

"Oh?"

"A second interview with Celsi."

"You'll need an assistant." Tomasso grinned.

I looked at him sceptically.

"What?"

"Nothing," I said after a moment. "At least freshen up first."

My second meeting with Niccolo Celsi had been arranged immediately after the confrontation at the Doge's palace the day before. Obviously, he was not keen on the idea at the time and he would be no more keen now. As Tom and I had discussed, Celsi could not possibly be the murderer of all three victims, but he did have the means, the opportunity and possibly the motives to kill Antoinette and Eriador. I felt increasingly sure that all three murders had been committed by the same person or persons, but, I needed to clear up one remaining aspect of what happened the night Antoinette Perugino died.

The interview was again scheduled for Lord Celsi's office. We were met at the door and escorted through a succession of passageways by Niccolo's personal assistant, Luca Lamon who showed us to a pair of chairs close to the fireplace the other side of the room from the councillor's desk. "Lord Celsi will be here in just a moment," Lamon said and retreated, closing the doors behind him.

Tomasso sat in one of the chairs and I paced in front of the fire, glancing at the items on the mantelpiece; a jewelled box, a gold candleholder and unused beeswax candle, a rather gaudy gold and onyx bowl holding some lavender. Above the fireplace hung a painting of a stern-looking woman in formal dress, her silver hair pulled back and netted in black mesh. I guessed it was either Adamo's or Violetta's mother. I turned as the door opened and Celsi strode in. He looked up only briefly, barely meeting my eyes and indicated I should sit. Then he saw Tomasso.

"Oh, you're here too."

"It's wonderful to see you too, Niccolo," Tom responded.

"I was told the meeting would be between just myself and Doctor Sagredo."

"As you know, Lord Cicogna is assisting me in the investigation," I said.

Celsi shrugged. "Very well, sit. I'll stand here by the fire . . . If that meets with your approval. No writing boxes today, Sagredo?"

I sat in the spare chair and leaned forward, my elbows on my knees. "I just have a few simple questions."

"Well, thank the Lord for small mercies."

I felt a knot of anger in my guts. I was quite sure that Niccolo had had nothing to do with what had happened to Isabella and was indeed probably quite unaware of any intrigue involving my servant, but there was no getting away from the fact that only a few days ago this man had tried to have me killed and he had physically abused Teresa as well as forcing her to be placed under house arrest. This though was not the time to bring up such matters, and besides, I reasoned, I had no clear proof at all that it had been Violetta Celsi who had attempted to poison me and made my servant grievously ill. "I'm really most interested in the night Antoinette Perugino died," I said.

"Oh, that old chestnut, Sagredo. I thought we had gone through all of this two weeks ago."

"We did, and on that occasion you told me you had dined with a group of visitors to the Palazzo Arragio including Cardinal Severina. You told me that after your guests left, you and your mother retired. But that was a lie wasn't it?"

Celsi held my gaze with his dark eyes and pursed his lips. "You are calling me a liar?"

"Yes," I said matter-of-factly. "New evidence has come to light, placing you outside Alfonzo's close to midnight on the ninth."

He raised an eyebrow. "New evidence? Tell me about that."

"I cannot reveal my source, but according to a reliable witness," I replied. ". . . you assaulted Antoinette and was about to beat her with a stick when her father, Carlo Perugino intervened."

I have to hand it to Celsi, he was very cool and calm; or at least he made a convincing act of it. He gave Tomasso an icy look then held me with a steely gaze. "Very well. Yes, I was there and I did confront Antoinette. Her father was very drunk and there was something of an altercation."

"Give me your version, please." I glanced over to Tomasso. He was sitting, right ankle rested on his left knee, staring at Celsi intently.

Celsi took a deep breath and seemed to be gathering his thoughts. "As you say, it was around midnight. Antoinette emerged from Alfonzo's. I had only just reached there in time. We exchanged words. I was angry. Then, out of nowhere, this horrible little man appeared. I say little. He was short, but strong and muscular. I had never seen him before. I of course know his name now – as you say, it was that vile peasant, Carlo Perugino - the man who attacked me in San Marco. "We struggled for a bit. As I said, he is much shorter than me, but powerfully built and quite strong. I eventually managed to subdue the fellow with a good whack across the head with my mace walking cane. By the time I had unmanned him I realised that Antoinette had used the distraction to slip away unnoticed."

"What did you do then?" It was Tomasso.

Celsi looked at him showing no expression. "I did not waste time trying to find the woman. She could have run anywhere. As you know, that part of the Ghetto is a labyrinth."

It seemed reasonable enough to me. I glanced at Tomasso again, but he was concentrating on Celsi's face. "And can you tell me why you were there in the first place, Lord Celsi?" I said. "What did you say to Antoinette?"

For the first time, he looked uncomfortable, and peered down at his boots for a few moments. "I would rather not talk about this, but I know that I am obliged to, for if I refuse, you will go running to the Doge and tell him I'm not cooperating, and to be honest, I've had enough humiliation at your hands recently, Sagredo."

"And I have had quiet enough actually physical pain at your ordering," I snapped back with an aggression that surprised me. Then Celsi did something quite unexpected; he nodded. "Perhaps that is a fair retort." he said.

"Oh . . . you're so full of shit, Celsi!" Tomasso said quietly.

I leaned over and placed a hand on my friend's arm. "Tom."

He gave me a black look and I could see the fury in his eyes. He sighed and let it go.

"So, Lord Celsi. Why were you there?"

"I had given Antoinette some baubles during the time I was seeing her. I

272

had made her a special gift of a necklace. It was relatively valuable. The night before Antoinette was murdered . . ."

"The eighth." Tomasso said.

Celsi thought for a moment then nodded. "Yes, the 8th. I had been at Alfonzo's and a pawnbroker, a Jew, named Slovo . . . I don't know his first name, approached me to tell me that he had some information about Antoinette that might be valuable. I took his meaning immediately of course. He is a horrible little arse-licker and I don't take kindly to being blackmailed."

"So you told him to fuck off," Tomasso said.

"No, Cicogna. I did not tell him to fuck off. Perhaps I was in a relaxed mood. I gave him a few coins and he told me his dirty little secret: that he had paid Antoinette for a necklace that very afternoon. He had seen us together and suspected it had been a gift from me as the piece was finely made and worth more than Antoinette could earn in a year. I asked him to return the necklace and said I would pay him handsomely for it. I then left early without seeing Antoinette. In fact, I did not see her again until the following evening when I confronted her. I paid Slovo too much for it, two lire. It was indeed the necklace I had given the woman. I think you can understand why I was angry. She would have used the money to pay for the poppy."

"So, you actually got the money back anyway, Celsi!" Tomasso mocked. "She bought the drug from Eriador who paid a cut to his boss – you!"

To give him credit, Celsi ignored the comment and turned to me evenly. "There, now you have it. I was made a fool of by a hooker." He saw I was about to say something, but added. "Not enough to kill the girl, Sagredo. I am actually rather saddened that such a beautiful creature could meet such an . . . unpleasant end."

"Oh, said with feeling, Niccolo," Tom retorted and started to slowly clap his hands.

"All right," I quickly interjected. "That's really all I wanted to know. Thank you for the time."

"What a shit!" Tomasso exclaimed, as we took the steps down from the main doors of the palace after leaving Celsi's office.

"Yes, he is. But, can I just say Tom that you're not behaving very professionally."

"What?"

"I'm trying to coax information from people like Celsi and it requires subtlety. There's nothing to be gained from aggression."

"Oh come on, Francesco! The bastard said it himself . . . he has to answer your questions."

"Yes, but in my experience, it's more effective to wheedle out what you want to know than attacking it head on."

Tomasso fell quiet and a few minutes passed with an uncomfortable silence between us. We wound our way north, heading towards the Rialto. Then Tomasso said: "You are right, Francesco. I apologise. I'm not sure how you keep your cool with such a repulsive animal as Niccolo Celsi. You're a better man than I."

"Nonsense," I said.

"So where now?"

"The second unpleasant job of the day," I replied. "But first, we both need some refreshments. I'm thirsty and hungry. Lord Celsi may have been forced to cooperative, but he had no imperative to treat us with any hospitality."

"And he certainly didn't do that, did he?" Tomasso laughed.

•

The second meeting was with Titus Rinilto, the man who published *The Republic* newssheet. Tom and I had eaten some pastries and downed several cups of strong coffee to invigorate us, and just before ten o'clock, we reached Via Pisato.

I had read the first instalment of Rinilto's interview with me that had been published while I was recovering from my experience in the Doge's dungeons and thought it measured and sensible. It had revived my respect for the young man after his first piece about me, and I now felt bad about what I had to do this morning.

Tom and I paced along the narrow path beside the canal and reached the door to the warehouse. We could hear a raft of noises coming from inside and so I was not too surprised when no one came to answer the door. Turning the handle, I realised it was unlocked. The place was even busier than the last time I was here, with men at the press, preparing chemicals and transporting paper from one part of the building to another. For a few moments, I could not see Titus himself, but then he emerged from behind the press where he had been oiling the mechanism that allowed the press itself to be lowered to the *coffin* where the paper was placed. He was wearing an apron over his clothes and had oil smears on his cheeks. He saw us, grinned and paced over.

"Lord Sagredo. This is a pleasure." He recognised Tom immediately. "Lord Cicogna." He bowed politely.

"I've read your paper," Tomasso said. "I enjoy it. It's a bold idea. Well done."

Titus glowed with pride. "Thank you. We work hard and we make some mistakes." He gave me a rueful look.

"You redeemed yourself, my friend," I said. "The first part of the interview you produced was very well made."

He nodded. "So, what may I do for you?"

"Could we sit somewhere quiet, Titus? It's a rather delicate matter."

"Oh? Sounds ominous." He called over a young apprentice. "Three beers please, Gino." He look to us for approval, and we nodded.

"Make mine a watered down one, please," I said to the boy. "Busy afternoon ahead."

Titus led us over to his desk a little out of the way from the working men and found a second chair for us before pulling himself around the other side of the desk and shifting aside piles of paper. He had just finished when young Gino appeared with the drinks. Titus found his pipe, packed it with tobacco and ran a flame from his tinderbox over the top of the bowl. "So, a delicate matter you said."

"I'm here about the man who came forward to report seeing Niccolo Celsi outside Alfonzo's the night Antoinette was killed," I began.

"Yes, what of him?"

"You said you could not divulge his identity."

"Well, no, I can't."

"You said it was against your ethical code."

"You have to understand, Lord Sagredo. If people cannot trust me to be circumspect when they ask for my silence concerning their identity, no one will come to me with information, and information is my business . . . quite literally." He looked from me to Tomasso and back again.

"Yes," I replied. "But obviously, sometimes those people who come to you with information want to keep their identity a secret for their own, perhaps nefarious reasons. Would that be correct?"

"Well, yes. I suppose so." Titus took a pull on his beer and smacked his lips.

"And on occasion, would there not be a greater moral imperative for you to reveal the identity of an informant than to keep it secret?"

"I'm sorry, I don't really follow."

I paused for a moment and Tomasso interjected. "What our friend is saying in his typically roundabout fashion, Titus, is that we are investigating a series of terrible murders and your information might be vital. You are obligated to tell us anything you know that we believe could be important in helping us catch the killer."

Titus eyed me.

"That's a fair summing up," I said, frowning.

"But, I told you last time we met, sir; I can't do that if it means betraying someone's trust."

I glanced at my untouched beer and ran a hand over my forehead. I suddenly felt weary. "Titus, we have just come from Lord Celsi's office. We talked to

275

him about the events outside Alfonzo's immediately before the slaying of Antoinette Perugino. He verified what your contact told you. This murder was the first of three and we have still not had a breakthrough in the investigation. Any scrap of information is of great importance. As Lord Cicogna has said, you are obligated . . ."

Titus had a hand up. "I'm not obligated to do anything, Francesco." He drew on his pipe and I suddenly felt a surge of anger, but managed to keep it bottled. "In that case, Titus," I said. "I'm sorry, but we have no other choice but to take you into custody on the orders of the Doge." Strictly speaking, I was bluffing, Pasquale had given me no formal permission to do such a thing, but I recalled the Doge's exact words to me when Tomasso and I had talked with him yesterday after the extraordinary meeting with the Celsis and Severina: 'I also want you to drop all inhibitions now. I give you free rein to use whatever methods you wish.'

There was a momentary silence and then Titus laughed. "You're joking, of course."

"No, I'm not. Unfortunately, I'm being deadly serious."

Titus's fair skin turned so pale, his cheeks were almost blue. "But . . ."

"But nothing," I pressed on. "I like you Titus, however, this is a very serious matter."

"I don't doubt that it is, Lord Sagredo." He cast a nervous look at Tomasso. "Lord Cicogna . . . But you are placing me in an impossible position."

"Not really," Tom replied. "It's not impossible at all. If you think your professional code is more important than stopping a crazed killer who has already taken three innocent lives in the most grotesque manner imaginable, then don't tell us the identity of your informant and you shall be arrested and imprisoned at my father's pleasure. If you think catching this madman is the number one priority and you value your freedom, for God's sake give us his fucking name."

Titus studied Tomasso's face, then looked into my eyes. I felt a pang of guilt, but only for a second; the vision of three mutilated corpses swam before me and I could never before have felt so certain that the ends justified the means.

Rinilto removed the pipe from between his lips and let out a heavy sigh. "I can see you are serious about this."

"Don't doubt it." I said firmly. "The last thing I wanted to do was to threaten you with charges of obstructing the Law, or perhaps even treason, but I will do it if I have to, Titus."

I think it was the word 'treason' that did it. The man seemed to fold in upon himself like a punctured balloon. He placed his pipe on the desk. I noticed the glow of burning had expired from neglect. Placing his palms on the desk,

276

he lifted his gaze to us. There was no trace of malice there. Instead, he looked disappointed, and that actually stung for a second.

"My informant's name is Father Beringhiero Gessi," he said.

•

The Vatican Embassy, a palazzo dating from the 12th century, stood on Calle Frezzaria. It was set back from the thoroughfare and we entered via a courtyard behind a high wall. A man dressed in a fine silk tunic, his long hair tied back to show off his high cheekbones escorted us to Cardinal Severina's suite of rooms on the first floor towards the rear of the building. We were shown into a large, square office, a cheerful room painted in a very pale lemon and freshened further by the afternoon sun streaming through tall windows. In front of the windows stood a large, very old desk, and seated with his back to the light was the Nuncio, Santoro Severina himself. He rose wordlessly as we entered and came round the desk indicating two seats before retreating to his own. The well-dressed man left and the three of us were alone.

"It is good of you to grant us an audience, Your Eminence." I said.

He did not reply, just inclined his head at a slight angle for a moment. He looked very relaxed and although he wore his official robe, his head was uncovered to reveal very short, entirely white hair. As had been his habit when I had first seen him in the Sala del Consiglio dei Dieci, the Council Chamber of the Ten, he was holding a large crucifix where it hung to his waist on a gold chain. I was though surprised to find him alone without even an amanuensis and I could only conclude that it was a move made in order to send a clear signal to us. 'You do not worry me,' was the message.

"I have to confess to being a little puzzled," Severina said. "What possible insights into your investigation could I offer?"

"My main focus is the murder of the prostitute, Antoinette Perugino."

"A most unfortunate thing," Severina said, a look of genuine sadness playing across his handsome features. "And only a day after I arrived here in the Most Serene Republic."

"We," and I waved an inclusive hand towards Tomasso, ". . . are trying to piece together the timing of the tragedy. We understand from Lord Celsi that you were at the Palazzo Arragio that evening."

"Indeed I was, along with my assistant, Father Beringhiero Gessi. You know him of course."

I completely ignored the implication behind Severina's last remark, but I sensed Tomasso tense a little. "According to Lord Celsi, Father Gessi left early and you stayed with the hosts for a while after the other guests had left."

"That is correct. The family and I share a long association. I knew Adamo and Violetta when I was a young priest."

"Do you recall when you left the Celsis' home?"

"I'm not exactly sure. I believe it was about an hour before midnight. Yes, that would be correct as I reached here about fifteen minutes after eleven."

"Unfortunately, when I questioned Lord Celsi two weeks ago, he was unable to put a time to it. Do you know of any way this time might be verified, Your Eminence?"

"Are you questioning my honesty, Doctor Sagredo?" Severina said very evenly, staring straight into my eyes. "I don't mean to make what must be a very difficult job for you any more troublesome, but I am a man of the cloth, a close advisor to His Holiness."

Tomasso snorted.

Severina turned his head very slowly taking his intense gaze from me and fixing his cold green eyes on Tom. "Has some dust reached your nose, Lord Cicogna?"

"Must have done, Your Eminence. One finds dirt in the most unlikely places."

Severina produced a smile that did not shift above his lips.

"You are right that this job is a difficult one, Cardinal Severina," I said. "And I have had to ask some people some difficult questions. I am not doubting you. I just need clarity and accuracy, and when at all possible, statements have to be corroborated by impartial witnesses."

He nodded sagely. "I understand. Well, there are perhaps three or four servants here at the embassy who could confirm that I arrived back around about the time I gave you."

"Servants may be malleable folk," Tomasso commented.

"So, let me make sure I understand that comment, Lord Cicogna. You are saying that I am lying and covering up the facts by paying off servants to verify what I claim to be true. Is that correct?"

"Succinctly put . . . Severina."

"Cardinal Severina, or Your Eminence."

For the first time, I caught a flash of anger in Severina's eyes, and although I was not happy with Tomasso's heavy-handedness, I was delighted that he had opened a chink in the man's armour.

"Pompous cunt," Tomasso said and held the Cardinal's stare unflinchingly.

Severina was too strong a character to be drawn in. He turned to me, the anger still there but carefully controlled. "Would the word of the Ambassador serve as sufficiently trustworthy, Doctor Sagredo?"

"If he is willing to spare his time. I would be happy to hear what he has to say, cardinal."

Severina rang a bell positioned close to his hand. Almost immediately, the office door opened and the assistant who had brought us in appeared. He hurried over to the desk.

"These gentlemen would like a word with the Ambassador. Could you see if he is free to speak and invite him here at his earliest convenience?"

While we are waiting," I said. "Could you tell me where you were at about two hours before midnight on the tenth of this month? The night after Antoinette's murder."

"The time Eriador the Alchemist met his end, I take it?" the cardinal said.

"Yes."

"That is very easy. I was here in the embassy all evening and retired early, about nine o'clock. I did some administrative work at this desk."

"Alone?" Tomasso interceded.

"Alone," Severina replied without taking his eyes off me. "I then went to my bedroom." He inclined his head slightly towards a door to his left. I was asleep by ten thirty."

There came a tap at the door and it opened. Tom and I turned together and saw Ambassador Buto Testa striding in. We stood, but Severina stayed seated.

"Excellency," I said. "I am sorry to disturb you. I hope we have not interrupted anything important."

"I am between appointments, Doctor." He looked at Severina. "Your Eminence asked for me to call by."

"Yes, thank you, Excellency. These gentlemen are here to ask me about my movements when the recent terrible murders occurred." He produced a faint smile, not much more of a wrinkling of the skin each side of his lips.

Testa raised his eyebrows and frowned at me. "You do not trust the word . . ."

"We've already been through this," Tomasso snapped.

Severina had raised his right hand. "It is quite all right, Excellency. I am happy to discuss the matter."

"And what do you want from me?" Still frowning, Ambassador Testa looked from me to Tom.

"His Eminence has said that after dining with the Celsis on the night of the 9th November, he arrived back here a little after eleven."

"Some time around fifteen minutes after eleven," Severina said.

"That would be correct," the Ambassador replied.

"And how can you be so sure almost three weeks after the event?" Tomasso asked. "You must possess a remarkably good memory."

"As a matter of fact, Lord Cicogna, I do have an excellent memory. But I remember it in particular because I had been in a late meeting with an envoy from Verona. I had just said my farewells to him and he had left via the main gate as His Eminence arrived. I recall glancing at the clock just as the envoy was departing my office. It was twelve minutes past eleven. The meeting had been incredibly tedious and gone on far too late. I felt most relieved to see the man go and for His Eminence to arrive. We then shared a few words, did we not, Cardinal?"

"We did indeed, Eminence. I remember telling you I had tried coffee for the first time."

"That's right."

I took a deep breath. "I'm very grateful, Ambassador Testa," I said and gave the man a small bow. "Your remarks have been most helpful."

"I'm glad to be of service." He nodded curtly to Tom, produced a rather ostentatious bow for Severina and left. It was very quiet in the room as the door closed.

"Thank you for helping us today, Cardinal," I said.

He rose indicating the audience was over. Tom and I remained seated. "I would like to interview Father Gessi." I said.

"You can make an appointment."

"No, I want to see him right away."

I had surprised the man, but he barely let it show.

"How is Beringhiero? His face has started to heal, I hope?" Tomasso said.

Severina registered no interest in the remark. "May I ask why, Sagredo?"

"We wish to question him about the night of the ninth. Does that surprise you, Your Eminence?"

"No . . . no, I suppose not. Very well. Could I ask you to please wait in the embassy reception. I will get one of my assistants to find Father Gessi." He came round the desk and we followed him to the door. He ordered a servant to find the priest and we headed to the reception.

"Tom," I placed a hand on my friend's shoulder. "I think I should speak to Gessi alone."

"What? Why? How can you after what he . . . ?"

"I have an urgent task for you elsewhere."

He gave me a suspicious look. "It's because I spoke my mind again, isn't it?"

"Well, there is that. But, no, really, I need you to call on Teresa. If she is free I would like you to go to my home with her so that she may check on my servant. I told Isabella I would be back this afternoon to see if she was recovering well, but things have dragged on. I didn't expect to have to see our friend Father Gessi with such urgency."

"Very well."

"Could you also ask Teresa to stay for dinner, and bring her up to date with everything we have learned this past two days? Can you stay for dinner too? I hope to be home by six o'clock. I shall cook."

He gave me a wary look. "You're cooking? I think I may have a prior . . ."

"Be off with you," I said with a smile. Then I heard a sound behind me, turned, saw Father Beringhiero Gessi, and my smile vanished.

•

We were shown to a quiet, windowless room off the reception. It was warm from a roaring fire in the hearth and we sat on a pair of stalls, a small table between us, a candelabra with a dozen lit candles overhead. A guard stood out of earshot at the door.

Father Gessi's face had been quite ruined by Tomasso. A huge burn stretched from beside his left eye down to his mouth. It was suppurative, weeping and red raw. The rest of his skin had a grey hue about it and the flesh around the eye close to the start of the burn was puffy and bruised.

"Thank you for seeing me, Father Gessi," I said. "I realise you must be in great pain."

He lifted his head and held my gaze for the first time. "It is nothing compared to the agony you shall soon feel, Sagredo, both in this life and the one beyond."

I ignored the comment. "I have orders from the Doge to question anyone I deem fit. If they refuse to answer, they will be arrested. I think you know how things are in the Doge's prison."

"Will you have me tortured, heretic?"

"You know more than anyone that in this Most Serene Republic we are very rarely reduced to such barbaric practices, Father Gessi."

He produced a cynical laugh and then winced in pain. "What questions do you have for me? I know nothing of the crimes you are apparently investigating."

"I have to disagree with you there."

"Explain, if you must. I'm tired. Can we get this over with?"

I crossed my legs and cupped my hands in my lap. "I have it on good authority that you were very close to where the prostitute, Antoinette Perugino was murdered not long before the crime was committed."

Gessi's reaction was surprisingly muted. He looked up at the ceiling for a moment. "So that printer broke his promise."

"You do not deny it then?"

"No," he said defiantly. "I have nothing to hide. I was simply walking off a headache and stumbled upon the scene outside Alfonzo's. I recognised Lord Celsi. I do not know who the other man was."

"A headache?"

"Yes."

"Can you talk me through that evening, the ninth?"

Gessi sighed heavily. "I accompanied His Eminence to dinner at the Celsi's vulgar home. I left early and returned here. I have a small room on the ground floor. I could not sleep and had a headache. I suspect it could have been from the repulsively rich food the Celsis served up. Or perhaps it was the company." He winced again.

"Anyway, after failing to get to sleep, I decided to take a walk."

"All the way to the Ghetto, in this cold?"

"I like walking, Sagredo. Is that against Venetian law? I entered the campo and heard a burst of noise that made me stop in my tracks. It was merely the sound from that house of sin as the whore opened the door to leave. I was about to turn back when Celsi appeared out of nowhere. He accosted the woman and then a second figure ran up and the two men started to fight. I saw the girl slip away."

"What did you do then?"

"Walked back here to the embassy."

"You have visited Venice before, Father Gessi?"

"No," he said, narrowing his eyes. "Why?"

"It's just that you only arrived here some thirty-six hours before these events and yet you seemed to know your way around the city."

The priest shrugged. "If you must know, I did not do that well in finding my way around. I had no intention of ending up in the Ghetto at that time of the evening, and did not realise I was in that district until the following day when I learned of the murder of the whore. Then, upon my return journey I took many convoluted paths and an inordinate time to reach my destination."

"I see." I paused for a moment, the room silent save for the crackling of logs in the hearth. "What I find slightly puzzling," I said. "Is why you went to the printer, Titus Rinilto exposing the fact that Lord Celsi was there outside Alfonzo's arguing with a woman who a few minutes later was murdered and mutilated. Why would you want to cause trouble for Lord Celsi?"

"It's not that hard to understand. I hate the man."

I tilted my head to the side, puzzled.

"He and his family are uncouth peasants made good. They worship money and nothing else. They are as heathen as you are, Sagredo."

"But your master, Cardinal Severina told me only half an hour ago that he and the Celsi family go back a long way."

"I cannot speak for His Eminence, heretic. He is a man of great grace, saintly. I truly believe he feels no malice towards any man."

"Really?"

"I wouldn't expect you to see it. You are an irredeemable sinner heading for the perpetual fires of Hell. But, I do not have my master's noble spirit. I wish with all my heart that I did. I am a miserable sinner, but I am trying constantly to be a better man."

I was suddenly back in the torture chamber with Gessi's demonic face in front of me, his eyes lit up red from the reflection of flames from that infernal fire.

"So, let me get this clear. You happened to stumble upon Lord Celsi in a highly compromising position. You do not like him for the reasons you explained, and decided, quite some time after the events of the 9th, to expose him to Rinilto? And yet you profess your love for Cardinal Severina."

"What do you mean?"

"Well, I thought it would be a simple thing to understand, Father Gessi. You put your personal feelings over what you knew to be best for the cause . . ."

"The cause?"

"The reason you and His Eminence are here in the first place . . . to ensure Giordano Bruno is taken to Rome in chains. The Celsi family are a close ally of the Cardinal's. Niccolo and Violetta have done their best to aid the cardinal, and through him, Pope Clement. Surely, you put all that at risk? You assumed Rinilto would publish the story straight away, Celsi would be embroiled in the murders and face damage to his social standing. And all because you think the family are 'uncouth'."

For a moment, Gessi did not react at all, then to my astonishment, he crumpled on his stool, brought his hands to his face wincing again as he touched his wound, and shook as he wept. I have to confess to feeling an odd blend of surprise and embarrassment. I had not seen a man cry for a long time and the fact that it was the person who had tortured me just a few days earlier meant his reaction came as quite a shock. I watched as Gessi's shoulders lifted and fell, his pathetic sobs muffled by a hand at his mouth. When, after a few moments, he was able to pull his hands away from his face, I could see his eyes were shot through with red veins. Tears streamed down his cheeks.

"Look at me, heretic. LOOK AT ME!"

Then I glanced up and saw the guard move his head slightly.

I stared at the priest, not really knowing what to say. Was this all an act? I wondered. If it was, the man was a fine performer.

"Don't you think I feel ashamed? I acted on impulse. I was weak and immediately after talking to the printer I felt riven by guilt. I considered telling His Eminence, but could not find the courage. Besides, it would have changed nothing. I thought of going back to the printer and threatening him to stop him revealing what I had told him, but I reasoned that such a thing would only spur on a man like Titus Rinilto. I know his type. So, instead, I threw myself into my duties with more vigour and enthusiasm than I have ever before displayed. And each day I have dreaded seeing my information in print; Niccolo Celsi exposed in Rinilto's filthy publication."

"I see," I said, and took momentary pleasure in knowing that Titus had no intention of publishing unless he could verify the information. Gessi clearly had no idea the printer needed a second witness before writing about it, and it he was quite oblivious to the fact that Rinilto had never known the identity of the other man involved in the fracas, Carlo Perugino.

"So, there you have it . . . Happy?" Gessi hissed.

I nodded. "I can't say I'm happy, Father Gessi, but I am grateful. You have been most helpful."

He frowned. "Oh, no, not intentionally, heretic. But I am used to the battering, the buffeting of my own soul. I serve the Lord, the Good Christian Lord, of whom you would have no understanding, Sagredo. His glory is all that matters, it comes ahead of my master's wishes here on this vile earth. Even the desires of His Holiness himself are secondary. Don't thank me, heathen. I'm all too used to absolving. It is my duty, my purpose."

I paced over to the door. The guard made to open it, but I stopped and turned.

"Might I ask one more favour, Father Gessi?"

His eyes narrowed. "What?"

"May I see the soles of your sandals?"

"My . . . ?"

I walked back over to my chair. "Yes, your sandals . . . if I may?"

"Why?"

"Humour me."

The priest sighed heavily, lifted a foot, pulled off his sandal and passed it to me. I turned it over and saw that the sole was completely smooth with no markings at all. "Thank you," I said, handed it back, and left.

Chapter Thirty-six: New Information

I was halfway along the corridor leading back to reception when I saw a young man talking to an attendant just inside the main doors. The attendant saw me, said to the boy something I did not catch, and the youth turned and headed along the passage towards me.

"Lord Sagredo?"

"Yes."

"I was told you would be here. I first went to your home, My Lord." He had a cream envelope in his hand and presented it to me. "I work in the household of Lord Pinelli. Here is a message for you."

I noted the fine calligraphy on the front, tore open the flap and read a typically succinct message from my friend, Gianvincenzo Pinelli. It said: 'My Dear Francesco, Could you please pay me a visit as soon as you are free? I have someone here you must meet. G.'

I was feeling weary after an early start and a succession of stressful interviews, most especially the last of them, and decided to catch a gondola to Pinelli's palace. It was early evening. I had not checked a clock for a while but guessed that it must be around five o'clock. The sun was low and as we pulled onto the Grand Canal I saw that it was busy with traffic and the banks close to the Rialto were crowded. I sat back against the rich cushions of the gondola and closed my eyes for a few moments listening to the lapping of water and the rhythm of the gondolier's pole.

The next I knew we were pulling into the quay at Pinelli's waterfront and I was waking with a start. 'Lord,' I thought, 'I must be tired to fall asleep on such a short journey.' I thanked my driver and paid him then took the broad path up to the palazzo. I greeted Ajith as he opened the doors. He gave me a smart bow and I was about to enter when the door was quickly pulled back further by a large hairy orange hand. Pius stood there grinning broadly. "Hello, Pius," I said. He made a sound that was amazingly reminiscent of a laugh, produced a low bow and waved me in.

"Pius, please," Ajith remonstrated. "Could you either do something useful or go to your cage."

The orang-utan raised a thumb to his nose and blew a raspberry before hobbling away into the shadows at the back of the hallway.

"I'm so sorry, My Lord," Ajith said.

I was laughing loudly. "Don't apologise, my friend. It's the best thing I've seen for a long while."

"I shall take you straight through to the library," he said and led the way across the echoing hall, through an antechamber, and from there, we came to the doors to the library. Pinelli and another man were seated in the wide leather chairs close to the huge window of the library, chatting animatedly. Seeing me enter, they stood. Ajith walked a little behind me as I paced towards them. Pinelli's guest was the Dutch lens-maker, Hans Lippershey, whom I had met briefly at my friend's dinner party the night Eriador was murdered. I shook hands with Gian, and Ajith lifted a third, smaller chair over for me.

"You remember Mr Lippershey, Francesco?" Pinelli asked in Spanish, the first language we Venetians use with non-Latin speakers.

I grasped the young fellow's hand. "Yes, of course," I said. "A pleasure to meet you again."

He was a short and slender man who looked younger than his twenty-two years, his face was narrow but his large dark eyes and curly black hair gave him a boyish appearance. He bowed and in heavily accented Spanish said: "The pleasure is mine, Doctor. I'm sorry we did not have a chance to speak at greater length on the tragic evening I was last here."

"Hans has just returned from the latest stage of his European tour," Pinelli explained. "He visited Trieste and Belgrade but wanted to see again the glories of our Republic before returning to Middelburg. He had not heard of the third murder, the death of the actor, Franco Andreini. We had been talking about it over a late lunch when Hans told me something I think you should hear."

"Oh?" I turned to the young man.

"Yes. I hope it will help, but . . ." He glanced at Pinelli briefly. "You may remember during our brief conversation the night of Galileo's talk that I mentioned I had visited other parts of Italy before reaching here."

"Yes indeed, Florence and Milan, I seem to remember."

"And a few other places." He waved a hand in front of him. "But, it was only after Lord Pinelli explained some of the details of the terrible murders that have occurred over the past few weeks that I remembered something that may, as I say, prove of use to your investigation. Back in the summer when I was in Rome there was a succession of murders that bear a startling resemblance to what has been happening here in Venice."

I felt a shock pass through my stomach. "This summer?"

"Yes."

"When exactly?"

"Through the month of August."

"Please, tell me everything you can remember."

Lippershey ran a hand through his hair. "It caused something of an upset at first, but then as quickly as the news broke, it seemed to be quashed."

"Quashed? I don't follow."

"I think the authorities censored any public speculation concerning the events, and well, people just stopped talking about it . . . in public at least."

"That seems pretty drastic."

Lippershey paused to gather his thoughts. "Four people were murdered within a period of two weeks. The killings had begun on 7th August a week before I arrived in the city. A second murder occurred the day I reached Rome, the 14th, and then later there followed two more horrors."

"What form did the murders take?" I felt as though the excitement would burst out of me and had to force myself to remain calm and analytical.

"A well known sodomite aristocrat, Vannozzo Riva was the first victim. He had his throat slashed and . . . well."

I said nothing but caught Pinelli wearing an expression of deep disgust.

"Riva had been castrated and his penis stuffed into his mouth."

"I see."

"Next was a visitor from Germany, a bookseller who, it was rumoured, had been in discussion with Roman intellectuals about a set of volumes containing heretical material of great value he wished to sell. This only came out after he was found with both his eyes crudely removed and disposed of. The third victim was a prostitute, dumped in the Arno, on," he thought for a moment. ". . . the 17th August. But no one is sure if she was actually killed by the same person who dispatched the aristocrat and the bookseller because she was not disfigured. Some said it was a crime entirely unconnected with the others, but there were stories circulating that the killer had been disturbed in the act and was unable to carry out any symbolic atrocity. But as I said, not long after that, people were silenced and speculation over the matter dwindled. The fourth murder happened on the 19th of the month."

"Who was the fourth victim?"

"Another aristocrat, Julius Santoni."

"Oh? What was known about him?"

"Actually, he was a rather famous man in Rome and it is believed that his family caused such trouble for the Pope over the man's murder that His Holiness immediately set up an investigation and enforced a moratorium on any public discourse over the matter."

"So perhaps the public censure was the wish of the victim's family?"

"It is perfectly possible. Julius Santoni was a well-respected and extremely wealthy patron of the Arts, a pious Catholic, a family man. He was married to Angela della Vollu, a Milanese who is said to be the most beautiful woman in all Italy. Santoni's body was found bound and gagged in a brothel, his shirt front soaked in strong spirit, an opium pipe at his side. Perhaps strangest of all, his mouth had been stuffed with playing cards, and behind these a couple of coins."

"Which implies," I said. ". . . that the murderer knew Santoni to be a man quite different to his public persona. Or else, the victim was deliberately and falsely smeared by the killer who, for reasons we shall probably never know, set him up in this compromising tableau after he was murdered. I can see why the man's family forced a censorship of the horrible events."

"And of course the Pope would not have objected," Pinelli observed. "He would not have wished Rome to be viewed in a bad light from without."

"No, naturally." I said. "Well Mr Lippershey, this is quite remarkable news. I'm enormously in your debt."

"Not at all, Doctor Sagredo. I only wish I had possessed the wits to connect sooner the events here with what I learned in Rome."

"You must not think that way, Hans," Pinelli said.

"No, indeed," I reiterated. "At the time of the dinner there had only been one murder – that of Antoinette Perugino and you were undoubtedly shocked by events later that evening."

"And how, if I may ask, is the investigation here proceeding?" Lippershey said.

I produced a pained expression. "Not as well as I had hoped when I first embarked upon the task."

"I think you are another inclined to be too harsh on yourself, my dear friend" Pinelli said, shaking his head. "You could not have done more."

"Well, it's kind of you to say so. I am just beginning to piece together a possible set of answers that may, if good fortune sides with me, lead to the man behind the crimes here. And from what you have told me tonight, Mr Lippershey, it might also finally reveal the truth behind the horrible events that unfolded in Rome during the summer."

Gian led me out of the library and we headed across the hall. "By the way," he said as we reached the front doors. "It seems you were right all along about the innocence of my servant, Bertino Magallore, at least as far as being complicit in Eriador's murder, that is."

"Oh?"

"He has been caught and confessed to me. He stole the ring on an impulse after finding our friend's corpse. A nasty crime. I find it hard to imagine how the wretch's mind works."

"A result of poverty, I imagine, Gian. I sometimes think that our wits are dimmed by comfort. Not that I'm condoning his behaviour. It's a shame the boy could not have applied his obvious intelligence and cunning to something more productive."

Pinelli sighed as he opened the door for me. "Yes, it is indeed a pity," he said and waved me farewell.

•

It was dark by the time I reached home, but as I opened the door and walked in I was met by a very pleasing sight. Tomasso was sitting by the fire reading a book while Isabella, looking quite recovered, was in the kitchen area with Teresa; delightful odours wafted my way. And, for the briefest moment, I was transported to a fantasy world in which Teresa and I were married and Isabella was our servant and all the anguish and pain, the uncertainty and fears were swept away.

"Isabella, are you sure you should be up?" I said, dropping my shoulder bag by the door and waving a greeting to Tomasso.

"I feel very well, Francesco."

I turned to Teresa. "Thank you so much for coming over, Lady Teresa," I said. "I hope I have not inconvenienced you."

"It was no trouble at all. And Tomasso insisted I start the meal to stop you serving up a ... what was it, Tom?"

Tomasso did not seem to hear her.

"Tomasso?" Teresa called.

He looked up.

"It's a curry, Teresa," I said. " A staple in India. I tried to get Tom to break away from his usual lamb, pork and overcooked vegetables the first day I was back in the Republic, but he was extremely rude about it."

"It tasted like shit, Francesco." Then he caught himself. "I'm sorry, ladies."

Isabella looked slightly affronted, but Teresa giggled and turned to lift a saucepan which she took over to the cooking tripod placed over the fire. I started over that way myself when there came a soft tap at the door.

"Who could that be at this hour?" Isabella said and started to wipe her hands on her apron.

"It's fine, Isabella. I shall answer it," I said, and pulled on the latch. A large, scruffily dressed man stood on the doorstep and it took me a moment to recognise him. "Galileo!" I exclaimed. "How delightful to see you, my friend. Please come in."

He strode in with a blast of cold air behind him. He had an old leather bag over his shoulder. I turned to see Isabella eyeing the new arrival suspiciously and I introduced Galileo to everyone. Isabella looked distinctly unimpressed and returned to preparing food as I showed my friend to a seat close to the fire.

"Galileo," I said. "This is Lady Teresa Damas, a very old and dear friend of mine. And of course you already know Tomasso Cicogna."

Galileo kept his coat on but removed his hat. I could not avoid the body odour coming from the scientist as he warmed up in the close confines of the room. I forced it from my mind and pointed to Galileo's bag. "Does that hold what I think it holds?" I asked.

"Your wonderful device, Francesco," he said. "The Shenl."

Tom and Teresa gave us puzzled looks and I explained how I had been given the device many years ago and how I had taken it with me to Padua recently to ask for Galileo's help.

"Have you had any success?" I asked.

"Of course I have," Galileo said without a hint of irony and less still, modesty. "Would you like a demonstration?"

"Indeed, I would. Come, let's take it downstairs. I have a small laboratory." I indicated that Teresa and Tom should join us and checked with Isabella that dinner would not be ready for at least half an hour.

Galileo placed his bag on a counter and I smiled seeing him wandering around the room studying my books, jars of chemicals, stuffed animals and the table upon which I had conducted Franco Andreini's autopsy.

"Fascinating," he said.

I unpacked the Shenl and placed it on the counter. Teresa was close to my right elbow. "This really can magnify objects, Francesco?" she asked staring at the device, her eyes wide in wonder.

"Sounds like witchcraft to me," Tomasso commented.

I heard Galileo make a scoffing sound and realised that he was listening to everything even though he appeared to be totally absorbed with the contents of my shelves and the objects that lay on the counters. He came over to us.

"When we met in Padua you told me you had found what you described as white particles in Eriador's hair," Galileo said. "But the best magnification you could obtain was about ten-fold and that was not enough for you to make out anything clearly or to identify the particles."

"Yes, that's correct," I replied.

"Well, I think I have achieved a magnification between twenty and twenty-five,"

I looked at him in disbelief for a second.

"You doubt me, Doctor?" he said with mock offence in his voice.

I shook my head. "No, my friend. Please, show me."

"Where are your particles?"

I pulled a small box from the shelf directly overhead. Inside, lay a piece of cloth, and in the centre were half a dozen small white dots.

"So, let me get this clear, Francesco," Tomasso said. "You found these in the

Alchemist's hair? Could they not be flecks of dry skin?"

"They might," I replied. "Hopefully we shall find out the truth of their nature with this." I nodded towards the Shenl.

"Please, you do the honours," Galileo said. "It is your device."

On the side of the counter I found a piece of clean dark cloth and with the same small French forceps I had used the night Eriador was killed I lifted one of the particles from the box and placed it in the centre of the cloth. I then positioned the small tripod used to support the Shenl over the cloth and slotted the device into the holder. It took me a moment to adjust the distance between the lenses using the control at the side, and there it was, a staggering image, crystal clear and showing the particle magnified to at least twenty times its actual size.

"That's astonishing!" I exclaimed.

"May I?" Galileo said. I took a step back and the scientist peered through the top of the Shenl. "Yes, yes, very good," he said half to himself.

Next, it was Teresa's turn. At first she had trouble staring into the device, but then closing one eye, she got the hang of it and emitted appropriate sounds of wonder and excitement. Tomasso was reluctant to even put his eye to the top of the tube and it took him several attempts before he could see anything, then he leapt back almost knocking the magnifier over.

"It *is* witchcraft!" he declared.

I caught Teresa's eye and she smiled. "It is truly wondrous," she said.

I returned my eye to the top of the cylinder of the Shenl and made a tiny adjustment using the control at the side. "If I'm not mistaken," I said. "This particle is a minute fragment of bread."

Galileo, and then Teresa, took turns. "I think you are right, Francesco," Teresa said. "You can make out a structure that is almost like a web."

"Indeed, you can," Galileo nodded.

"I would like to look at one particular piece I saved," I said and selected a mote from the flecks left in the box, replaced the original fragment and took another look through the upper lens. It was a slightly smaller piece than the others and I had to adjust the focus again, but then I had it, a clear image. I shifted the crumb slightly and saw what I was after, a discoloured patch, a speck of brown-red. I felt a shiver pass down my spine. Things were beginning to fall into place, but I knew I was still trying to formulate conclusions without a scrap of proof.

"Well, I have to thank you, Galileo. You have done a most marvellous job."

He beamed. "I'm delighted to help."

"Now, my friend, we are about to eat. You must join us."

He shook his head. "It is very kind of you to offer." He looked from me to Teresa and Tomasso. "But I'm afraid I have a prior engagement . . . with

Lord Pinelli who has asked me to dine with him and that young fellow, Hans Lippershey who was at my talk."

"That is a shame," I said. "Perhaps next time."

•

Isabella ate with us and then retired to bed. I found a fine bottle of wine in the cellar and Tom, Teresa and I sat around the dinner table with the warmth from the fire reaching every corner of the cosy main room.

"So, Francesco," Teresa said. "What have you learned from the white particles you removed from Eriador's hair? You did not tell us what you saw with the last speck and then hurried us up here."

I looked at her and realised yet again how astute and incredibly intelligent she was. I had indeed rushed us away from the laboratory, and there I was thinking I had been rather subtle about it.

"Well," I began. "The whole reason I asked you here tonight was to go through some theories with the two of you. I had no idea Galileo would turn up as he did. But what he has helped to reveal adds weight to my reasoning. Although, I must profess to still being some way from a clear resolution. To be honest, I am confused and would greatly welcome your council. Teresa? Tomasso has brought you up to date, hasn't he?"

I took a deep breath and flicked a glance at Tomasso. I did not want to be the one to tell Teresa about Celsi's relationship with the first victim, Antoinette. I was about to speak but Tom cut over me, and well . . . just came out with it. "The only piece of information I omitted to tell you was that Lord Celsi was having an affair with Antoinette Perugino."

I watched Teresa's beautiful face, her dark brown eyes, her dilated pupils in the low light from the candles on the table.

"I was not aware of that," she said calmly. "But, I am not altogether surprised by this news. I have heard that Niccolo is seen often at Alfonzo's and other bordellos and gambling dens, but I never did have him marked out as a morally wealthy man, and I think it might be troublesome for you to show me any man who has not shared a bed with a prostitute."

"This was more than a business transaction, Teresa," I added gently and told her all we knew about Celsi and the night Antoinette was murdered, including the way he accosted the girl outside the bordello, the fight with Carlo Perugino and how all this had been witnessed by Father Beringheiro Gessi.

"But, you don't think he killed her, do you, Francesco? For all his character flaws, I would find it difficult to conceive of him as so violent a man."

"He showed considerable violence towards us," Tomasso said. "Most especially, Francesco. Do not forget that only a few nights ago Niccolo Celsi had him and Bruno chained to stakes and the faggots lit."

"You are right, Tomasso," Teresa said.

I raised a hand. "I have always known Niccolo to be mendacious, but I do not believe he is well inclined to murder and I certainly do not think he killed the girl."

"But why?" Tom asked, topping up his goblet and drinking half of it in one go.

"We've been through this," I replied. "If Celsi killed Antoinette he certainly could not have dispatched Andreini."

"What if he paid someone to commit that deed, Francesco? Have you considered that?" Tom raised his eyebrows challengingly.

"It is conceivable, but I think there must be other, better explanations. Why would he wish to have the thespian killed?"

"To deflect suspicion from him committing the first two slayings?"

I nodded. "It is just about possible," I conceded. "But it does not strike me as the most likely sequence of events."

"Then you have a better idea?"

"I don't know. Perhaps."

"You have some new information, don't you?" Teresa said.

"As a matter of fact, yes, I do. As I was leaving the Vatican Embassy I was intercepted by a messenger bearing a note from Lord Pinelli. He asked me if I could drop by at my earliest convenience, so I called at his home on the way here. Galileo mentioned dining tonight with Pinelli and the young lens-maker from the Low Countries, Hans Lippershey. Well, Lippershey was there when I saw Gianvincenzo and he had a rather surprising story to tell. It appears that there was a similar series of gruesome murders to the ones we have experienced that took place this August just past . . . in Rome."

My friends looked suitably startled and I gave them the details.

"Lord Celsi has not been in Rome since we began to see each other after I returned from Paris. So that would suggest even more that he is not the murderer here, would it not?" Teresa looked from Tomasso to me.

"Yes, but you know who may have been in Rome in August?" Tom said.

"No."

"The company of thespians at the Cavalini's."

"How did you . . . ?" I suddenly remembered the young actress, Angelina Gena telling me how the troupe had rehearsed through May in Florence and headed south to Rome and Naples before returning north in late October. I felt a surge of excitement.

"One of the lads who helped me with the bier carrying Andreini's corpse back here was a cousin of one of the actors," Tom added. "I asked him a few questions on the way including where they had performed. I thought it might be useful. I'm sorry, I forgot all about it."

"I should not worry too much, my friend," I replied, suddenly deflated. "The south of Italy is a big place, Tom. We have no idea if they were within fifty leagues of Rome at the time of the murders there. Besides, no one involved with the acting company can be held responsible."

"Why?"

"They were nowhere near here the night either Eriador or Antoinette met their tragic ends. They were in Verona."

Tom made to protest. I held up a hand. "They told me when I interviewed the whole troupe."

"Someone could have been lying," Tom said half-heartedly.

I shook my head. "No. Quite impossible. If someone had lied about that in front of the others they would have been challenged over it."

Tomasso exhaled loudly and raised his hands in surrender. "So, let's face it; we are nowhere."

"Well, not entirely." I leaned an elbow on the table and placed fingers to my forehead. "I am beginning to formulate a hypothesis. But I have almost no evidence, only a further set of contradictions, so I would suggest that what I am about to say can only edge us a little closer to finding a perpetrator. I think the best thing I can do is state a list of what I do know and then put forward a tentative proposition.

"First: the particles found in Eriador's hair. They are crumbs of bread; I am now sure of that. I also found identical crumbs on Andreini's shirtfront and in his hair. Second: I found traces of wine on the floor of the actor's dressing room and the note we found in Andreini's throat." I glanced at Teresa. "It was stained with red wine."

"Yes, I quite forgot," Teresa remarked. "You said there were red wine stains in the carpet of Andreini's dressing-room, but that he had not been served wine, nor was there any trace of a bottle. You were about to say something about an idea you had . . . but then Niccolo burst in."

"Bread and wine. Fuck! More ritual," Tomasso exclaimed. He refreshed his goblet, took a gulp and wiped drips away from his chin with the back of his hand.

"Indeed. And I think it must be integral to the motive behind these murders. I would love to know more details about the killings in Rome, but as I told you, Lippershey said the authorities silenced any official talk, censoring the public."

"Pff, what do you expect? Rome does not enjoy the freedoms we have." Tomasso said.

"First thing tomorrow I shall get permission from the Doge to send an official request to the Roman government for information concerning the murders. But I cannot expect to hear back for at least two weeks."

"All right, so bread and wine, Francesco. What else?" Teresa looked at me earnestly, the candlelight casting shadows across her face.

"There is another clue but it has so far led to a dead-end."

"What clue?" Tom asked.

"Remember at the scene of Andreini's murder, I managed to get an impression of a footprint in the bloodstain?"

"I don't follow," Teresa said.

From my pocket I produced the piece of cloth I had used at the Cavalini palazzo to make a copy of the footprint in the wine stained carpet, and explained what I had done to get it.

"Ingenious," Teresa said and gave me an admiring look.

"Maybe," Tom said. "But as I remarked at the Cavalini Palazzo, it is not much use unless you can compare it to every pair of footwear in Venice!"

"I made a point of asking Gessi to show me the sole of his sandal today to see if it bore any similarity to this." I pointed to the linen. "His sandals were completely smooth.

"This looks like a boot print anyway," Tom said.

"Yes, and it is much bigger than Gessi's feet, which are actually rather small for a man.

"You have always said that two men have been involved with each murder, Francesco; and that the one who slit the victim's throats was quite tall. Taller people usually have bigger feet." Tom gave me a hopeful look.

"I know. So I'm working on the principle that this print is from the killer's boot; but that's as far as it goes. However, I got something much more important from my talk with Gessi. When he was describing his movements on the night of Antoinette Perugino's murder, Father Beringheiro Gessi lied to me."

"Little surprise there!"

"I know, Tom, but this was a subtle lie, a mistake. When I asked him what he happened to be doing in the Ghetto close to midnight so that he could witness Celsi confronting Antoinette, he claimed he was simply taking a long walk to clear a headache. However, he told me he had not realised he had even been in the Ghetto until the following day when he, like everyone else, learned of Antoinette's brutal slaying."

"That's horseshit!" Tom exclaimed.

"Of course it is," I said. "One does not simply wander in and out of the Ghetto after curfew. The gates are closed and he would have been checked in and out by one of the sentries."

"And so," Teresa began. "You are suggesting what, Francesco? That Gessi is the killer?"

"I would, except for one fact. I noted that whoever mutilated each victim was left handed. Gessi is right-handed."

"So, we *are* still nowhere." Tom looked dejected.

"I did say I had no definite answers, Tom."

Teresa stifled a yawn. "Goodness! I'm sorry."

I laughed. "No, it is I who should apologise. The hour is late."

"And perhaps the lady has consumed too much wine?" Tom chided.

"Lord Cicogna!" Teresa retorted. "How dare you!"

We all laughed, but a part of me felt an acute pain. I was reminded of wonderful, now long-gone days when we had been together on picnics or at dinner. Now, everything was so sadly different, so diminished.

"I shall escort you home, Teresa," I said, and pulled up from the table. "Tom, you are most welcome to stay again."

"Yes, I think that might be wise," he slurred.

•

It was late and very quiet, the campo and the surrounding paths, deserted. Teresa was wrapped up warm in an ankle-length lynx fur coat and matching hat, but I was content in my best velvet doublet.

"I hope you enjoyed this evening," I said. "Although I fear Tom may feel the worst for wear tomorrow."

She laughed. "I think he has a tough hide."

"Thank you for staying and helping with my efforts to work out the thorny task I've been set. I must say, I feel rather despondent."

"Don't be, Francesco. Clearly, whatever evil individual is behind these atrocities, they are very cunning. They have been covering their tracks well. But most of all, they are audacious in the extreme. The killing of Andreini was reckless."

"Yes, it was, but even then the killer slipped away after completing the act."

We fell quiet crossing the Rialto Bridge and heading west towards the Palazzo Duolo. It began to snow; large, powdery flakes that drifted down from the sky like feathers in a breeze.

"Would you mind if I saw some more of Piero, Teresa? Get to know him . . . after this business with our killer is over?"

She did not reply at first and my heart sank, but then she looked round at me and smiled. "Of course, Francesco. Piero is your son . . . and he likes you."

"That is very nice to hear."

"Why should he not? You are a perfect role model for any young man."

"Me! You mock!"

She looked puzzled. "Of course you are. In his eyes you are a hero returned from far flung lands, an adventurer who has seen the world."

"Yes, actually you are quite right of course. I can see why any intelligent boy would love me."

She laughed and slipped her hand through my arm. I must have tensed for she started to withdraw, but I caught her hand and kept it in place.

Soon, we reached the path leading down to the canal, close to Teresa's home. It curved to the right just before the water's edge and then ran straight and up a gentle incline to the main doors of the palazzo. We stopped at the entrance. "I'm so pleased you are here with us again, Francesco," Teresa said.

Our eyes met and I could not stop myself. I leaned forward to kiss her. She did not pull back and my lips touched hers, her hair brushing my face as I caught her fragrance. "No," she said softly, and drew away. "I cannot ... it is all too much, too confusing."

I straightened. "I'm sorry, Teresa. I ..."

She placed a finger to my lips. "There is no need to apologise."

The night lay still all around us, with just the lapping of the water at the canal wall disturbing the silence. I ran a finger along her cheek. "Ring the bell," I said. "I will see you soon." And with that I turned and followed the path away from the Palazzo Duolo.

Chapter Thirty-Seven: The Trial of Giordano Bruno

Giordano Bruno's trial began at four o'clock in the afternoon. As one of The Ten, I was permitted to attend the court hearing along with a select few other high ranking officials and those with useful contacts in high places. I was met at home an hour before the start, escorted across the city to the venue, the Patriarchal Palace, which is positioned opposite the prison on the Rio di Palazzo and led through the main doors of the building into a large high-ceilinged room adorned rather over-ornately with paintings by Tintoretto. Two sets of wooden benches occupied the north and south sides of the room. I was shown to a row close to the front of the southern aspect. As I took my seat I caught sight of the printer, Titus Rinilto. He saw me and pointedly turned away. Off to my left a few seats away sat Niccolo Celsi and I saw three other members of the Ten settling into their places in various parts of the room.

On a dais in the centre of the room, a semicircle of high-backed chairs stood empty. This is where the judges, a triumvirate of powerful men, the *Savii all'eresia*, Assessors of the State known as The Three would sit. These officers were elected anew each year, and at the time of Giordano's trial, The Three consisted of Laurentio Priuli, the Patriarch; Ludovico Taberna who was formerly a Venetian Ambassador to Paris, and the Very Reverend Father Giovanni Gabrielle of Saluzzo. To their left stood a chair for Cardinal Severina, the Apostolic Nuncio, there to represent Rome strictly as an observer only. To the right of where The Three were to sit stood the desk of the Assessor, Aloysio Fuscari, who had the power to halt the proceedings immediately if he believed the trial deviated from the letter of the Law.

The judiciary is one institution about which we Venetians are particularly proud and none of my countrymen gathered at the Patriarchal Palace that afternoon would have doubted that justice would not simply be seen to be carried out, but that Bruno would be given a fairer trial than he could have expected in any other state or province.

And so, at precisely the preordained hour, the trial got underway with the ceremonial arrival of the key players. Patriarch Laurentio Priuli, his white beard tumbling over a fine silk bodice and jacket, his black eyes glinting, led his two companions, Ludovico Taberna, a rotund, bald man with a dark beard and moustaches, and the Very Reverend Father Giovanni Gabrielle of Saluzzo, resplendent in his red gown, a man gangly tall and bird-faced. They walked to the chairs and arranged themselves as the Assessor, bearing a long wooden and gold staff, found his seat and a fifth figure lowered himself into the remaining seat.

And it was with something of a shock I realised it was not the man I had expected, Cardinal Severina. Instead, the Vatican Ambassador to Venice, His Excellency, Buto Testa pulled himself into the seat reserved for the nuncio. I was still trying to work out what was going on when I saw Bruno himself being escorted into the rectangular space girded on one side by the semicircular arrangement of judges and court officials and on two other sides by the benches of the observers. This latter group included government officials and important noblemen.

Bruno looked pale, nervous and very ill and there was a slight hint of madness about the way he held his mouth, the line of his chin and in the sallow hollowness of his cheeks. Before the semicircle of officials, his ankles were chained together and then his wrists bound. Four guards took up positions at the corners of a square with Bruno at the centre.

We all stood silently until the officials had arranged themselves. The Assessor stood and tapped his staff on the stone floor three times before declaring the hearing open. He gazed around the room and began: "We are gathered here today to hear the case against Giordano Bruno. As is our custom over long centuries, the pronouncements of witnesses, the prosecution and the defence offered by Bruno himself shall be heard and considered. A judgment shall then be handed down as to the guilt or otherwise of the man before us. I would like to draw everyone's attention to the fact that due to extenuating circumstances, the Vatican is today represented by the honourable ambassador, His Excellency, Buto Testa, in the capacity of observer, as His Eminence Cardinal Severina is otherwise detained." He then turned to the four others on the raised dais, nodded and sat.

'Otherwise detained?' I thought to myself. 'What possible reason could keep the Apostolic Nuncio from Bruno's hearing? It was the very reason Severina had been sent to Venice by his master, His Holiness Pope Clement VIII. I felt a knot of anxiety in my guts, but shoved it aside as Patriarch Laurentio Priuli, the Chief State Prosecutor began to speak.

"Before us today stands the man, Giordano Bruno on a charge of heresy brought by the state after the accused was arrested in May this year upon the accepted testimony of Lord Giovanni Mocenigo, a citizen of the Republic who accommodated the accused in his home from March to May and made a citizen's arrest leading to Giordano Bruno's containment at the Doge's pleasure. I call upon Mocenigo to be the first state witness."

There came a sound from the other side of the room beyond the arrangement of observers on the benches facing me, and Lord Mocenigo appeared beside an armed guard. He walked straight-backed and proud to the centre of the semicircle where he stood with his hands clasped before him, head slightly bowed. This was the first time I had seen Mocenigo since my return. I knew the man only vaguely, but from the few occasions we had met socially, I had taken a dislike to him. I thought him to be a shifty, vain and not very intelligent man. He was white-haired now, but he carried himself with ingrained and cultivated nobility as befitted a man whose family were one of the oldest and most honoured in Venetian history. But I could see immediately that a noble upbringing was really all he could still boast. For all his fine clothes, bejewelled fingers, and airs, he was the same dullard I remembered from a time now long passed.

"I am compelled by my conscience and the order of my Confessor," Mocenigo began. "To give a thorough account before you Illustrious Lords describing the vileness of the man, Giordano Bruno." He considered the judges gravely and went on: "At various times when he has talked with me at my home, the accused said that he was an enemy of the Mass; that no religion pleases him; that Christ was a wretch who worked miracles in appearance and was a magician; and that souls, created by the operation of nature, pass from one animal to another. He set forth a design to form a new sect, under the name of The New Philosophy; said the Virgin could not have brought forth a child, and that our Catholic faith is full of blasphemy against the Majesty of God."

I regarded the man with renewed interest; not because of anything about his graceless persona, but thanks to his extraordinary claims. I had read about Bruno, had spoken with him briefly, and, as of course you know, two of my closest friends had been working to rescue the man from what they were convinced was his unjust arrest and imprisonment, but I had no idea Bruno's interests and philosophies were quite so far ranging. But then of course, it was merely Mocenigo's statement of opinion. There was no reason to believe he was telling the truth. I could not conceive for a moment that Bruno would be so careless as to make these remarks to a man as clearly untrustworthy as Mocenigo. I did not perceive Giordano to be a great intellect, but I assumed he was astute; and through long hardship, a good judge of character; he must have know Mocenigo to be at best, a rogue.

"We now wish to interrogate the accused," Laurentio Priuli said.

I saw Mocenigo retreat to a row of seats in front of the set of chairs opposite without making eye contact with Bruno. The prisoner then took three steps forward, his chains rattling, the guards shuffling along parallel to him. He looked up, and before Priuli could say another word, he cried out: "I *shall* tell the truth. Often I have been threatened with the Holy Office and I deemed it a joke; so I am quite ready to furnish an account of myself." As he spoke, his voice trembled and he waved his hands before him, gesticulating earnestly. For months he had been left alone in his tiny cell to contemplate his fate and it occurred to me now, that perhaps for the first time, he had come to realise the gravity and seriousness of the situation, for the first time, he had caught the distant crackle of flames, the faint whiff of his own burning flesh.

Father Giovanni Gabrielle leaned forward in his chair and began the questioning. "You have heard the testimony of Lord Mocenigo who gives witness to your arch-heresy. You are an enemy of the Mass?"

"No, I am not."

Unsatisfied, Gabrielle's eyes darted over the man in front of him. "You doubt the existence of the One, the existence of God?"

"I never have," Bruno retorted forcefully.

"And what of Christ and the incarnation? Was that a lie?"

"I have doubted and wrestled with this matter, but I have never denied the dogma, only doubted it. And I believe the Father and Son are one in essence."

"And you have denied Christ's divinity, and declared the Son of God to be an 'evil wretch,' the third judge, Ludovico Taberna stated.

I watched Bruno's expression. He seemed genuinely shocked, almost hurt by the accusation. "I marvel that you should even suggest such a thing," he declared. "Never did I say or think such a nonsense. I believe as Holy Mother Church does about him. I cannot conceive how such things could be imputed to me. I hold that Christ was begotten, by the Spirit, of a Virgin-mother."

"And according to Lord Mocenigo's statement you do not believe in the very Catholic doctrine of the immortality of the soul" Taberna said. Then consulting his notes: "You hold the believe that souls migrate . . . from one body to another?"

"I have held that the intellectual soul does not pass from body to body, but goes to Paradise, Purgatory or Hell; but I have thought deeply, as a Philosopher, how, since the soul does not exist without body and does not exist in the body, it may pass from body to body even as matter may pass from mass to mass."

"Ah, I see . . . so you are a skilled theologian, are you?" Gabrielle asked.

Bruno was taken aback. "Not much," he replied. "I have pursued philosophy which has been my avocation."

"Have you then criticised theologians?"

"No, I have not. I have read Protestant teachings and always argued for Catholic doctrine, especially the teachings of Aquinas. I have read heretical books and dissected them."

"Have you mocked priests and monks?"

Exasperated, Bruno threw up his arms. "I have said nothing of the kind, nor held that view."

"Do you believe Christ wrought his miracles by magic?" Father Gabrielle asked.

Bruno looked bewildered. "What is this?" he cried. "Who invented these devilries? I have never thought such a thing. Oh God! What is this? I would rather be dead than have said anything of the kind."

Gabrielle was clearly unconvinced, eyeing Bruno he said: "You have mocked the faith. In a written testimony from Lord Mocenigo, he states you have said with heavy sarcasm that all the good Catholics await the Judgment, when the dead shall arise and they will get the reward for their righteousness.' Are these not your words?"

Bruno was stunned. "I have never said these things. My Lord, please read the books I have published. They are profane enough; but you will not find a trace of this; nor has it entered my head." And Bruno glared over at Mociengo. "This man is a vile liar!"

"Silence!" the Patriarch, Laurentio Priuli snapped and his dispassionate eyes bore into the prisoner's. A sudden hush fell over the room, the judges sat motionless. Bruno, his confidence clearly ebbing away, his energy almost drained, looked around the room once more, seeing the still faces, the eyes of witnesses quickly averted. "You have admitted enough to make the charges against you credible," Priuli declared icily. "You deny the authority of Rome, you question the Trinity, deny the Divinity of Christ, you dispute theology, mock the Mother Church and the priesthood, you lend support to the faithless, and you practice magic. You must take heed and make full, open and faithful confession in order to be received into the bosom of the Holy Mother Church and be made a member of Jesus Christ. But it would be a marvel indeed if persistence in your obstinate denial did not lead to the usual end. The Holy Office desires only to bring forth light to the heretic by its Christian love, to bring them from their evil ways and guide them onto the path of eternal life."

The words fell into the silence like lead in water. Bruno kept his head bowed throughout Gabrielle's statement. Then, looking up, he said slowly. "So may God pardon me."

I watched the exchange with a growing disquiet. I just could not piece together what Bruno was really saying. He seemed to be filled with contradiction. On the one hand, he was playing the role of the pious former priest keen for absolution, but on the other, he maintained still the heretical views he had written about in so many books and about which he had taught for many years. But then I recalled how he had spoken to me the first time I had met him. In his prison cell, he had told me that, all along, his plan was to be sent to Rome, and he believed that once there, he would be allowed an audience with the Pope and thereby convert the Pontiff to his ideas. It had been after that I had concluded the man was losing his mind. Priuli was speaking again. "This hearing shall now adjourn for two hours." He stood immediately and his companions joined him.

Now, you will have to forgive me for I was not privy to the deliberations of these noble fellows during the two hour break in the trial of Giordano Bruno. I know from others that the Nolan was taken to a holding cell in the basement of the Patriarchal Palace. There, he was given a crust of hard bread and a beaker of water. However, after the events that kept Venice under a dark veil throughout most of that bleak November had run their course, I was told what had transpired by someone who had been a first-hand witness and illustrious participant, the Lord Doge, himself.

They had gathered for dinner in a room close to the Doge's apartments; the three judges, Laurentio Priuli, Ludovico Taberna and Father Giovanni Gabrielle of Saluzzo, along with the Vatican's ambassador, His Excellency Buto Testa. There, they feasted on quail and hare and were served some rare wines from the Doge's vault.

"I asked Testa directly where Cardinal Severina was," Pasquale Cicogna recalled. "Of course, we all now know the answer, but at the time, it was a mystery."

"Indeed," I replied. "So, what did Ambassador Testa say?"

"That he was confined to his bed by order of the embassy doctor. His Excellency suggested Severina may have been suffering a stomach disorder from some bad oysters he had eaten as a guest of Celsi's friend, Sebastiano della Fiori who had thrown a small private dinner the previous evening."

"And oh, they were all so very pleased with themselves," Cicogna went on, a sour expression on his face as the memory from the recent past had not the benefit of time's diminishing. "None more so than Testa. He was suddenly elevated into a very influential position, for although I had insisted to His Holiness that none of his representatives were to be allowed roles other than that of observer, the ambassador knew Father Gabrielle well and I am sure he had some sway over Ludovico Taberna. Laurentio Priuli though, did, I believe, act with honesty and detachment throughout."

"So Testa tried to influence proceedings covertly?"

"Oh indeed, Francesco," the Doge told me. "He was not shy about it. Over supper, he was saying that the Republic should rid itself of the 'cancer of heresy' before it spread to ruin La Serenissima. I couldn't disagree with him, and you know that I have no love for the thoughts of Giordano Bruno. If I could have found a way to pass the man onto Rome legally and without us losing face, I would have done so long before the trial; but I did not much like the way Buto Testa was trying to foist papal opinion on us just as Severina had been doing for weeks. Of course, he had seen an opportunity for preferment and had snatched at it. Testa knew very well that if he could get Bruno to the Vatican in chains, he would acquire great kudos with Pope Clement. Or at least that's what I thought was going on at the time."

"So, he must have been unhappy when you suggested Bruno should be allowed a character witness to support his defence?"

The Doge laughed then. "He was indeed; very unhappy. But there was nothing he could do about it. It was a fair suggestion within our constitution even if it was a totally alien idea for the Roman judicial system."

I returned to my bench a good ten minutes before I needed to, and stared at the empty centre of the room where, in a short while, the defendant and the accusers would once more play their roles in this elaborate game upon which a man's fate hung, finely balanced. I could see no way that Bruno could escape a ruling that branded him as a heretic, but I knew that this was only one aspect of the tableau. The Venetian authorities had executed fewer than a score of heretics during the course of the past three or four centuries, and during that time, the Roman Inquisition had sanctioned the death of hundreds of thousands throughout Italy and beyond. Yet Bruno was a special case. He was not a Venetian, but he was viewed as an arch heretic, an activist, an extremist, a provocateur. Rome wanted him and he had confided in me that he wanted to be taken to Rome. It was clear to me that he was somehow trying to manipulate the situation so that he might get his way: be condemned as a heretic and handed over to the Roman authorities where he would face another trial in the Vatican. It was only politics that stood in his way.

The officials were almost at their seats before I came out of my reverie and the hearing moved onto its second phase. The Assessor called the court to order and Bruno was brought out to face further questioning. The Patriarch surveyed a set of notes in his lap and said: "A direct question: have you the accused been involved in occult practices since arriving in Venice?"

"Never since I have been in Venice have I taught heretical doctrine," Bruno declared. "... but have only discussed philosophy with many patricians, as they can tell you."

I knew this to be a lie. Pinelli and Tomasso had both told me that Giordano had attended meetings of occultists in Padua and in Venice during the period leading up to his arrest earlier in the year, and I knew that he had been working on having published here in the Republic some new work which Pinelli had described as the man's most inflammatory ideas yet. I looked at the Patriarch and the other two judges, then at the ambassador and I could see that they also had very strong suspicions that Bruno was not being truthful.

"My works," Bruno said, "... are purely philosophical and I hold that the intellect should be free to enquire provided it does not dispute divine authority, but submits to it. I have only ever expounded philosophically and according to the principles of Nature and its light," he announced bravely. "...And I believe that nothing can be found by which I can be judged heretical, for never have

I taught anything directly contrary to the Catholic religion."

"Tell us what you consider to be 'purely philosophical'," Father Gabrielle said, smirking.

Bruno held the man's gaze with a steady one of his own. If nothing else, he was a great performer, a teacher with a healthy ego who liked to be centre stage even if it was on such a solemn occasion. It was this egotism, I realised, that gave him the strength to overcome ill-health and the months of hellish agonies he had been subjected to. "Very well. I hold the universe to be infinite as a result of divine power," he began, ". . . for I think it unworthy of divine goodness and power to have produced merely one finite world when it was able to bring into being an infinity of them. Wherefore I have expounded that there is an endless number of individual worlds like our earth. All these bodies constitute the infinite whole. Within the universe I place a Providence whereby everything lives, everything grows, acts and abides in its perfection. And I understand this in a two-fold way: one, after the fashion of the spirit which is completely present in the whole body and in every part thereof. This I call Nature, the shadow and record of the Divine. The other manner is the inconceivable way in which God, an essence, presence and power, is all-embracing."

"Yes, all very interesting," Ludovico Taberna interrupted, looking round at his companions. "But, what of your Catholic faith? Do you deny it?"

"I believe that there is a distinct Godhead in the Father, in the Word and in Love, which is the Divine Spirit; and in Essence, these three are one; but I have never been able to grasp the three really being Persons and have doubted it."

"And the Holy Incarnation?" Gabrielle asked. "The very essence of our Faith, the meaning of the Holy Communion? What of that, heretic?" Gabrielle let the word escape and made to correct himself, but realised that none of his colleagues had noticed the unprofessional slip even if some in the audience, myself included, had.

"I cannot understand how the finite flesh of humanity could be fused with the Word, an infinite essence, but I respect the Church doctrine of transubstantiation."

Rising, the Patriarch said. "Enough." And he indicated to the guards that they should return the prisoner to his place a few paces back. "We have been in discussion during recess," he went on, ". . . and have agreed to allow the accused a prominent Venetian citizen to speak on his behalf, to offer us insights into the character of the prisoner. I therefore call upon Lord Gianvincenzo Pinelli."

I must say I was rather stunned, but as the shock faded, I could see the logic of it. My dear friend, along with others of the Resistance, had tried and failed to snatch Bruno, so it was logical that they should now attempt to aid his release by using the legal system. The Republic permitted character witnesses, and no one could have effectively denied this right to such a powerful and esteemed figure as Pinelli.

My friend looked weary, but I believe that I was probably the only one to notice it, for I knew him far better than did anyone else in that room and I was quite aware of the pressures he was facing at the time. To others though, he must have offered the sort of image he intended, the very embodiment of wealth and sophistication, a man known to consort with kings and popes, but also to hold non-conformist views on many things: a man of culture and learning who discussed philosophy with the most elite minds and gave succour to mystics and shamans. Dressed as elegantly as always, Gian walked into the room with the air of a man who was deigning to grant the judges a few moments of his precious time. He glanced at Bruno and with his back turned momentarily towards The Three and Buto Testa, he gave the man a gentle smile before taking up his position before the semicircle of officials.

"We are very grateful to you for attending this hearing today, Lord Pinelli," Laurentio Priuli said and held Gian's eye with a guarded professionalism. I knew that the two men enjoyed a cordial relationship and held a genuine respect for one another. I noticed though that the other three kept their heads bent for the moment. On more than one occasion, Pinelli had mentioned to me that he considered Testa to be an upstart who had risen too far for his limited abilities. "According to the laws of the Republic, any prisoner, no matter how vile his crimes, is permitted one spokesman who may offer the court his opinion of the accused. We understand you know Giordano Bruno well and would wish to offer us your observations and insights."

I could detect in the Patriarch's words a subtle hint of accusation. Behind the polite phrasing, he was making an implicit suggestion that Pinelli was himself a man too keen on esoterica and that it was somehow beneath him to associate with such lowlife as Bruno. Gian, I knew, had caught the hidden meaning also and I saw a glint of amusement in his dark eyes. For he, and everyone else in the room, knew that the three judges could never touch him; that he was, by virtue of his high station, completely immune from persecution by the Church, and that no officials of the faith would dare to claim that Pinelli was connected with anything other than orthodoxy.

"I do know Giordano Bruno well," Pinelli began. "And I have been interested in his work for a long time. I first met him when he visited the Republic very briefly in the mid-'70s. I realised then that here was a man of unusual vision, a man of learning, but an individualist, not bound by rules or manacled by trivial constraints. In other words, a free-thinker." He looked confidently around the room. "But of course, the very notion of freedom of thought is frowned upon in some quarters." His eyes levelled on The Three and the ambassador.

"Are you condoning heresy, Lord Pinelli?" the Patriarch asked, meeting Gian's gaze.

"I believe it is merely a question of definition."

"What does that mean?" Taberna asked.

"In some lands, far from here, our orthodoxy would be considered heresy."

"But we are not living in those lands, Lord Pinelli, are we?" Priuli stated flatly.

Gian appeared to ignore the retort. "Anyway," he said. "Unless I'm mistaken, we are not here to discuss my views, but to speak of the *philosopher*, Giordano Bruno and his works." The room was very quiet. "I am of the opinion that the man has been hounded and is a convenient scapegoat. What Bruno discusses, teaches and proselytises in his published works are theoretical concerns. He has stated repeatedly that he is a devout Catholic, that he believes in a Christian God, the divine wisdom of Christ and the teachings of the Bible. He has merely expressed doubts about some aspects of theology."

"Cherry picked," the Patriarch declared.

"If you wish to call it so, Lord Priuli. But aside from these differences in ideology, Bruno confines himself to Natural Philosophy. There is nothing within accepted doctrine that precludes the notion that the stars have planets that are perhaps inhabited by living things, and although it has become a convenient custom of the Vatican to place Aristotle and his ideas on an insurmountable pedestal, as far as I am aware, Aristotle is not believed, even by the most devout Catholic, to have been blessed by Christ's light. He is not a prophet."

Gabrielle looked up at that, outrage burning in his eyes. "You speak heresy, Lord Pinelli."

"No, merely common sense, Very Reverend Father Gabrielle. Besides, even if I were, what do you propose doing about it?" And I caught an expression on Pinelli's face I had never seen there before, a fierceness that chilled even my heart. It was at that moment, I realised what were Pinelli's intentions. He was trying to deflect sentiment from Bruno, have the judges shift some of their spite and pious enthusiasm from Giordano to him. I looked at the five men on the dais. The Assessor, Aloysio Fuscari was writing assiduously, the Patriarch was wearing a neutral expression while Taberna's flabby features and the avian lines of Gabrielle's face had morphed into self-righteous shock. But, it was Testa's face that was the most interesting. He alone reflected Pinelli's strength and steeliness, but it was leavened not by anger or any vulgar display of outrage. No, he looked almost amused, as though he knew something no one else was aware of, some secret weapon that he might unleash at a moment of his choosing.

"Are we not straying again from the point?" Gian asked.

"Please continue, Lord Pinelli," Priuli said.

"I will reiterate my central concern; which is this. It is my contention that Giordano Bruno is being unfairly hounded. The Vatican, in its wisdom, seeks to make an example of him. In the eyes of the Faith, his crimes are more symbolic than actual. Bruno has harmed no one, he has merely taught unorthodox philosophy. He has never tried to damage the core tenets of the Faith. I do not trust the word of Lord Giovanni Mocenigo. I have observed him for decades and seen that he is not a man of honour."

Mocenigo, seated in the front row of the audience the far side of the dais started to pull up out of his seat, but with a single black glare from Priuli, he lowered himself down again looking like a cowered dog.

"He betrayed the accused and entrapped him in his palazzo after inviting him into his home. Can a man who would do such a thing be trusted?" Pinelli gazed around the room, his eyes roving over the judges. "Are those the actions of a gentleman?" He paused. "No. But it is clear, is it not, that this man." And he stabbed at finger at Mocenigo. ". . . has been a stooge of the Vatican all along? Bruno has been the victim of entrapment. Mocenigo was persuaded to pose as a man interested in the occult, in order to flatter and to intrigue against Giordano Bruno and to make him risk returning to Italy. The prisoner believed, as we are constantly being reminded here, that the Republic is a place in which we cherish freedoms that we have spent centuries gathering unto ourselves and about which we are justly proud. Bruno was tricked by such a liar as Mocenigo, a man who defames the good name of Venetian nobility."

Giovanni Mocenigo was now red-faced and beads of sweat had broken out on his forehead. I almost felt sorry for him. But then I turned away to consider the judges.

The Patriarch took a deep breath. "Thank you, Lord Pinelli. If you have nothing more to add, I shall call a second adjournment so that we may deliberate on what is to be done with the accused. Accordingly, we shall return here two hours hence to announce our verdict."

It was a repeat of the previous adjournment. Bruno was made to shuffle away into a dark hole while the Lords and noble clergy of The Three and Testa removed to the palace. They again met the Doge in the same room as they had been in earlier that day, and again, the Doge presided over a discussion he later recounted to me.

"They were all fired up," the Pasquale Cicogna told me. "I had no idea why at first, because having not attended the court, I was reliant on third-hand accounts. But I soon learned of Gianvincenzo's scathing attack. It was bold of him."

308

"Was it though?" I asked. "Lord Pinelli is untouchable."

"He is personally, of course. But he has business concerns, distant family, friends; the vindictiveness of some within the Vatican should never be underestimated. But, all that is by-the-by, there was an atmosphere of quiet seething, mainly engendered by Gabrielle and Taberna. Priuli seemed to have risen above it all, but then he has always appreciated Pinelli."

"What of Testa?" I asked.

"He was late to the palace, delayed by another meeting, which as you know, turned out to be of crucial importance."

"With the lawyer, Episcopo?"

"Yes, clever scheming with Fredorico Episcopo turned round the whole case. And even though Pinelli had angered the judges, successfully deflecting the bitterness away from Bruno, the degree to which he achieved this was at best, partially. I am fond of Gianvincenzo and consider him one our Republic's very finest, but in some ways, he made The Three hate Bruno more."

"I suppose nothing Pinelli said could deflect their belief that Giordano had lied and seemed to be constantly contradicting himself. He had claimed to be a good Catholic, but argued vehemently against orthodoxy, something the Vatican absolutely loathes. He is an occultist and a mystic. And for all our friend's fine words about how Aristotle's ideas should not be conceived as doctrinal, they are: and Bruno has constantly abased Aristotleianism."

"Indeed, Francesco," the Doge said. "All this is a correct view of how it was. They considered Bruno to be a disgusting, anti-Christian, a danger, a man who could not be trusted to tell the truth, a man who's rightful place was chained to a burning stake."

"They would view me as a candidate for the fire too."

The Doge waved away the remark. "So, they were biased in the extreme. However, the central problem remained. Bruno may be the most repugnant heretic who ever lived, but what were we to do with him? Hand him over to Rome and we would look weak and hypocritical; set him free and we could expect to incur the wroth of the Holy See. So, I have to say that in some ways, certainly from my perspective, Testa offered us the solution we were all looking for. He appeared with Fredorico Episcopo in tow, apologised for the breach in etiquette, but claimed that he had only brought the lawyer along because he and Episcopo believed they had a way to solve the political conundrum we faced. You have to understand, Francesco," the Doge explained earnestly. "I was utterly exhausted by the whole issue. Bruno was one problem I really wanted to have removed. It was a terrible time."

"It was indeed, sir."

"I knew of Episcopo, but he had not worked closely with the government for some time and had travelled extensively, returning only recently from a sojourn in Florence and Pisa lasting some two years. Anyway, he was invited to sit and to offer his council. Episcopo had sifted though the testimony, the witness statements and the background to the Bruno trial, as well as the material in dispute: Bruno's heretical writings. It was clear, he said, that Bruno had consorted with heretics, and had apparently led a licentious and diabolical life. Bruno had, the lawyer admitted, a mind as excellent and rare as one could wish for, but his heretical offences were very grave. The lawyer suggested that the judges, myself and my counsellors had, perhaps by religious zeal and bigotry, overlooked glaringly obvious facts. First, Bruno was not a Venetian citizen, and therefore should not have expected the protection of Venice in the first place; second, and most importantly, Bruno had been selling his books in Venice without paying taxes. But, above all else, Episcopo stated, Bruno had continually asked to be accepted back into the bosom of the Church and had declared his intention to petition His Holiness directly. Why should this state," he said. ". . . prevent him in this avowed desire?"

I studied the Doge's face as he told me this and he seemed to be reliving a fondly-remembered moment - when a huge weight was lifted from his shoulders. For a few seconds, Pasquale shed ten years before my eyes and produced a broad smile. "It had been staring us in the face all along," he said. "It was so beautifully obvious!"

And so, I returned to the brief third and final instalment of Bruno's trial and arrived with the main body of observers shortly before the dignitaries and the accused returned to their respective places. Bruno looked even more bedraggled now than he had been during the early evening. I suspected that he had been given little nourishment - there was a sickly pallor to his cheeks - and he stood hunched, his head bent.

We all stood as The Three and Testa, along with the Assessor, took their seats and sat in expectant silence while Priuli shuffled some appears, studied the top sheet and then cleared his throat before speaking.

"Due to the exceptional circumstances of the case," he began, ". . . we, assigned by the Republic to pass judgment on the actions and expressions of the man, Giordano Bruno, rule that he shall be delivered over to the Vatican judicial authorities."

The observers, the guards, the accused and the accusers were, for a moment, bonded by silence. Then I caught a slight movement from Bruno, a mere nod of the head. But, I knew that for all his own confused desires, he had succeeded in manipulating events to suit him. He did not look up, perhaps he had no energy left for even such a simple task. The Patriarch nodded to Bruno's guard and the prisoner was shunted away, his chains rattling dully.

310

Chapter Thirty-eight: Crucifixion

We all rose with the judges and stood as they egressed from the building. I caught a final glimpse of Bruno as he was shoved from behind, almost tripping over his chains before I followed the rest of the observers to the main doors and the chill night beyond.

Stepping on to the cobblestones, I nearly crashed into Tomasso who had rushed towards the doors as the small crowd emerged.

"Tomasso!" I exclaimed.

"God's cock, Francesco! I thought it would never end. Tell me, the verdict."

I shook my head and Tomasso threw up his arms and let them slap against his sides. "Fuck!"

"Did you really expect anything else?"

"Yes, Francesco, I did," Tom snapped.

I glanced round uneasily, aware that we were in a throng of people.

"It's an outrage," Tom shouted. "A fucking outrage."

"Tom! Sssh,"

He glared at me and I could see that he had been drinking. I caught the whiff of spirit on his breath. "I'm not tolerating this," he yelled. I took a step towards him and went to grip his arm. He looked down at my hand and shook me off, belligerently.

"Tom, perhaps we should go somewhere quiet to talk . . ."

"No! Not this time. I'm going to my father about this."

I sighed. "You're not thinking straight."

"Don't talk to me like that." He was red-faced, his voice far too loud. People around us were turning. I glimpsed a palace guard standing close to the doors leading back into the Patriarchal Palace.

"Tom!" I reached for him again. He turned and started to push his way through the people still clustered around the small square in front of the judicial building. I made to follow him, but within seconds, he was lost from view. I stopped, I had no energy left to chase after him. "Don't do anything stupid," I said under my breath.

There was one more job I had to do before retiring for the night. I caught a gondola to Alfonzo, the Spaniard's bordello and asked for the gondolier to stop some distance from it. It was the busiest time of the evening and I found myself confronting a line of hopeful patrons at the door. I was thinking of trying the side entrance when Alfonzo himself appeared at the doors and caught sight of me. "Feeling horny, Traveller?" he asked with a sly smile, his eye patch twitching slightly as his face creased.

"I've come to ask a few questions, actually.'

"I feared as much. You've great timing."

"I'm sorry, but it's urgent."

He showed me in and we crossed the main room. The dwarf, Jimito who took care of customer's cloaks and coats waddled across the room with garments draped over each arm. He was on his way to the tiny booth that was his personal fiefdom. The establishment had been transformed from the one time I had visited here before. The windows were shuttered and the room lit dimly by dozens of candles in tall holders. A small group of musicians played in the corner. It was strange music and it reminded me of what I had heard at Turroro's palazzo the night Tomasso had almost killed himself. Couples lay on sofas in various states of undress, while others danced intimately. A separate area served those more interested in drinking and watching the antics of the other clientele.

Alfonzo strode confidently across the room and we were soon ensconced in his office with the door closed. It was a spacious room with a view through the open slats of dark wood shutters onto the central room and another out to the street. I could imagine Antoinette standing approximately where I now stood on the night she was killed explaining to her boss that she was heading off to a party and trying to make excuses for her father who had just made such a dramatic entrance. It suddenly occurred to me that Alfonzo must have seen something of what happened on the street outside the bordello.

He shook his head as I asked the question. "I wish I had, Lord Sagredo. I would certainly have told you. Do you know who accosted the girl outside?"

"Her father came back, and there was another."

He looked at me expectantly.

"But I cannot say who that was."

"All right. So, how can I be of assistance? I have heard of the latest murder, the actor. He was here you know, the night before he died. He'd just reached Venice and had come from a dress rehearsal."

"Really?"

"With his boyfriend. I have no problem with that. We cater for all tastes here, but, well, you don't bring your own wine here do you?" He laughed. "I saw them arrive and hoped they might at least have hired a couple of girls or boys, or any number of each." He waved a hand in the air. "Nah ... stayed for a couple of drinks and a bit of a dance and that was it. Sorry to hear what happened to him. He was a good actor by all accounts."

"Indeed he was," I said. "I wanted to ask something about yourself and the staff."

He held my gaze. "Go ahead."

"Your male staff . . ."

"I only have a handful. Stefano, two casual workers, Marino and Luigi, Jimito who takes the coats, and a couple of black fellas who clean the place. Mind you, the casuals have become a bit if fixture recently. We're booming." He turned to face the main room. "As you can see."

"How long have they worked for you?"

"Jimito came with me from Spain, many years ago. The two lads started in September. Before that I made do with one assistant for Stef, a bit of a tearaway, Juno. He was here for about a year."

"And Stefano?"

"Oh, I've known him for years. Wandered into the place when he was thirteen. Worked here ever since. He'll be nineteen next month."

"And has he been here since then?"

"Yes. Why? What do you think Stefano has got to do with anything?"

"I don't, specifically," I said.

"He's a good worker and honest. I really noticed it when he had to go away."

"You just said . . ."

"It was for two months. I forgot. Last summer."

"May I have a word with him?"

"Certainly, I'll get him here."

"Could I speak to him in private?"

He shrugged and pulled up. "I'll find him."

"Just a moment . . . one other question. You mentioned that Franco Andreini was here the night before he was killed. Did you sell him and his boyfriend refined poppy?"

Alfonzo was taken aback, then he screwed up his one good eye. "Do you really expect me to answer that?"

"Yes, I do actually, Alfonzo."

"I thought you were investigating Antoinette's murder."

"That's correct, but I know she was an addict, and that Andreini was probably also a user. The second victim, between Antoinette and the actor, was Eriador, the Alchemist. You would know him of course."

Alfonzo said nothing.

"He supplied Antoinette."

"I knew the man. He is . . . was one of the main suppliers in the Republic. I think that was widely known about. But no, I did not sell Andreini any drugs. Now, do you want to speak to my lad?"

He was away for at least ten minutes and I was left outside the office to watch the comings and goings. Alfonzo had not been exaggerating when he said it was the busiest time of the night, but even so, I was approached by three different girls asking if I was lonely. Stefano came down the broad, ornate staircase that opened out into the centre of the room and sauntered over, an insouciant expression carefully applied.

"*Lord* Sagredo."

"Is there somewhere we can talk?"

He flicked a glance across the floor to a corridor. I remembered it from my last visit; it led to the back entrance. We found a small storeroom and he closed the door muffling the sounds of voices and music.

"I only have a minute," he said and gave me a defiant look.

"More than enough. Your boss mentioned that you were away last summer, for two months."

"Yes, what of it?"

"Where were you?"

"Why?"

"Could you just answer my question?"

"Rome."

"Was that in August, September?"

"Mid-July to mid-September, including the journey there and back."

"And what was the reason for the trip?" I asked.

"If you must know, my mother was dying."

"You would have heard of the series of murders there."

He gave me a blank look and then started to realise what I was driving at. "You think..?"

"I don't think anything. That's why I'm asking you questions. My next one is this: Where were you on the night of 7th August?"

"Oh, fuck you!" He made a move towards the door.

I stepped in his path. "I think you should answer my questions."

"Do you now? And I think you should get out of my fucking way."

"I know you have been dealing refined poppy. Would you like me to mention it to Alfonzo?"

"I work for him, you idiot."

"Oh, I'm sure, but you've been cutting yourself a little extra portion of the pie, haven't you, Stefano?"

He brazened it out. "Proof?"

I had none of course. It had been a guess and he probably knew it. I felt exhausted and could sense my patience fading. "I also know you have been abusing some of the girls. Now, I'm really certain, Alfonzo would not like to hear about that, especially if Antoinette's name was to be mentioned, I understand he rather liked her."

The young man's eyes blazed, and for a second, I thought I was going to

314

have a fight on my hands. I sized him up. He looked like he could do well in a brawl and he was almost certain to have a concealed weapon. "The night of the 7th August?" I asked.

"My mother died on the 9th," Stefano said deliberately. "I was at the farmhouse for three days before then. She had slipped into her own world and lost her speech and sight almost a week before . . ." He swallowed hard. "I have four sisters, Sagredo. My father died three years ago. I have been supporting them. Our farm is ten miles beyond the city walls. There . . . any more fucking questions?"

•

"Francesco! Francesco . . . Master . . ." I came to and jolted upright almost hitting Isabella in the face.

"I'm sorry sir," the woman said. I tried to focus and gradually her face emerged from distortion. "Isabella . . ."

"Two men, sir, at the door. From the palace."

I pulled out of bed and tugged on my boots, ran my fingers through my hair and beard and stood. "Thank you, Isabella," I said and paced out to the main room. The front door was open and I could feel the freezing air. Two palace guards stood in the opening. They snapped to attention as I came into view.

"Lord Sagredo," one of the men said. "Apologies sir for disturbing you so early, but you are needed urgently."

"What is it?" I asked, a sudden snap of anxiety in my guts.

"I'm not permitted to talk about it, Doctor Sagredo. We have orders directly from the Doge. Please ready yourself with haste and follow us . . . by your leave."

My mind was racing as I returned to my room. It must be a development in the case, I mused. If I was in any official trouble I would not have been greeted with such civility. But then, I caught myself. I was becoming paranoid, surely, and I realised again just how badly scarred I was from my recent ordeal. I changed clothes, pulled on a jacket and ran a comb through my hair, catching a glimpse of myself in a mirror. I had looked better.

It was barely light, nothing more than a maroon tinge to the sky, and sleet fell hard, stinging my face. In the dim light I lost track of the twists and turns we had taken. I knew we had crossed into the San Polo district, but I only recognised the Chiesa di San Rocco as we turned into the square and I saw the church's squat structure ahead through the streaming icy rain. Two more

315

guards stood at the door, soaked through. They remained there and the men who had escorted me from home showed me in and retreated without a word.

I walked from Nature's dark to a hazy grey, mere patches of illumination created by rows of wax candles running the length of the nave. Starting towards the altar, I could just make out a few shadowy shapes. Three steps along the nave, I was startled by a figure rearing up out of the gloom and it took me a second to recognise him as one of the officials from the Vatican embassy, the thin, well-dressed fellow who had shown Tomasso and me into Cardinal Severina's rooms the day before yesterday.

"Lord Sagredo? Martino della Secco. I'm a secretary at the embassy."

I stared at the man. "Yes," I said. "What's going on?"

"Please follow me." I noticed then how his voice was shaky. "There has been a terrible tragedy."

I kept two paces behind della Secco and we came to the chancel. I took the steps up, my path lit by more rows of large candles casting a dull light about the space. Two men dressed in black robes, heads bowed, stood to one side. I looked up and noticed that the black outside the church windows was beginning to lighten. In the east, the sun was rising.

Della Secco walked towards the font. We passed round it. To left and right ran benches where the choir sat during evensong; they were cast in deep shadow. Above these, I glimpsed paintings, their colour, theme and meaning lost in the Cimmerian shade. Ahead, a life-size Christ clung to a cross. Crossing the apse, we were almost at the altar when I saw another tall figure dressed in black hose and a long cloak. Della Secco stopped and in the fresh light I could see that both men looked drawn and pinch-faced as though they were struggling to cope with some unnamed horror. I approached the second man. Half-recognising him as another of the embassy officials, I nodded. "You're name?"

"Senior Secretary Giovanni Juventi."

"Could someone please explain what this is all about?" I said and turned from Juventi to della Secco.

The senior secretary said nothing, just turned and pointed a long finger towards the crucifix. And, as I took in the horrible truth, I felt a tingling shock pass the length of my body. What I had thought to be the figure of Christ on the cross was no crafty representation wrought by human hand; it was a person, a once-living, once-breathing man. Dressed in a bloodied loincloth, he had been nailed to the wood, a crown of thorns jammed down onto his head, and there was a deep, blood-caked gash in his side. I could only just make out the opening at his neck and the Latin word *proditor*, 'traitor' cut into his forehead. It was the Apostolic Nuncio, Cardinal Santoro Severina.

"Who found him?" I asked Juventi. He waved a hand back to the doors and the two robed figures I had seen. "The priest, Father Mancello."

"When?"

"About two hours past. He did not know what to do and was terribly shocked . . . as you can imagine. He alerted the palace guard. A captain recognised . . ." He stopped, unable to say any more.

I looked up at the cardinal pinned to the cross, and now that the initial impact of the sight had begun to subside, I realised what an utterly surreal thing it was. Cardinal Severina, a man to whom I had spoken less than thirty-six hours earlier; a man I had loathed and someone who, I was quite aware, hated me; a man who had attempted to kill me; a man who had colluded with Niccolo Celsi against the Doge and was determined to have Bruno dragged to Rome in chains. Well, he would have been pleased with the outcome of the trial, I thought; and wondered if he had lived to know of it.

"I need all hands to help lower the cross," I said. Senior secretary Juventi looked at me mutely and I could tell that the man was still in deep shock, functioning with mechanical professionalism.

"Yes," he said snapping out of a reverie. He flicked a glance along the nave and the two embassy officials headed towards the doors of the church.

It took them no more than a minute to return with four guards and a young cleric in tow. The boy was barely past puberty by the look of him, his face as pale as flour. I noticed that the boy conscientiously avoided looking at the monstrous sight. I pulled him to one side. "What's your name?"

"Brother Clemento," he said, his voice little more than a whisper.

"Brother, I would like you to run an errand for me." He gave me a confused look and when I told him I would like a message delivered to Tomasso Cicogna, an expression of relief passed across his face; he was to be excused the onerous task of helping with the crucifix.

Lowering the cross turned out to be far less arduous than I had imagined it would be. The entire structure was anchored to the floor using a lever mechanism, the base of the cross was sunk several inches into a rectangular hole cut into the altar. I supposed it had been built this way to help clean it. Bringing down the crucifix, removing the statue of Christ and replacing it with Severina's body before hoisting the cross back into position could, I realised, have all been done by two men of average strength working together.

We lowered the cross to the stone floor carefully and I asked for half a dozen large candles to be placed close to the corpse so that I might study it in detail. By the time this was done the sky had started to lighten noticeably and early morning sunlight soon began to filter through the stained glass above the altar.

Rigor mortis was pronounced. I knew that meant he had been killed about eight hours past, around eleven o'clock last night, some three hours after the Bruno trial had concluded. The cause of death was the same as all three previous murders, a fatal slash wound to the throat, carried out in identical fashion to the earlier slayings, from behind, a left to right movement from a right-handed man; in this case someone a little shorter than the victim. The cuts into the forehead had been made, I ascertained, by the same knife and crafted without hurry. From the relatively sparse amount of blood I surmised that the crucifixion had been carried out post mortem and a fair while after death.

The cardinal had a well-toned and youthful physique for his age; his strong chest was covered with a fine down of white hair. I leaned in close and saw the now familiar flecks of white I now knew to be bread, and there were red wine stains on the dead man's white skin. The loincloth was streaked with blood, but also with a lighter red staining reminiscent of the red discolouration in the carpet of Franco Andreini's dressing-room. Glancing back at the soiled loincloth, I noticed another smudge. It was a bloodstain, but very different to the others. I pulled over a candle and bent down close, positioning the candleholder to get the most light falling onto the red mark. I could see the curved lines, the arcs and parallel markings produced by a fingertip wet with blood. I had almost forgotten the forensic method of using a person's fingerprints to identify them. It was a criminal detection technique first shown to me over a decade before by a great Chinese thinker, Tung Hu who lived in the magnificent city of Cambaluc, the great northern capital of China.

I withdrew my dagger from its sheath on my belt and cut away a small piece of the cloth with the mark approximately at its centre. Folding it carefully, I placed it in a leather pouch I kept on the same belt. Pulling up, I ran a hand over my forehead feeling suddenly very weary, a black cloud of disquiet heavy on my mind. As Tom, Teresa and I had discussed at my home, the murderer was clearly a religious fanatic who was performing some bizarre pseudo-religious ritual. But, what confused me was that the first three victims had fitted a pattern – a prostitute, an occultist and a sodomite who also had the temerity to be a thespian; but a cardinal? And one of Clement's closest advisors to boot? I considered the word cut into Severina's flesh: 'proditor' and the implication was inescapable. The cardinal had, in some way, let down the killer, betrayed them. The murderer then was someone whose religious proclivities were even more extreme than the nuncio's.

I looked at the hole in the stone altar. More than any of the others, this murder proved to me that at least two men were involved. A single killer could not have created this grim tableau. It reaffirmed what I had suspected from the start. And this thought led straight back to Father Berlinghiero Gessi, First Assistant to Cardinal Santora Severina, the man who had almost been my nemesis. He had been at the scene of the first murder, and had lied about

318

why he was there. He had no clear explanation for his whereabouts when Eriador and Andreini had died, and he fitted the description, the only witness description I had – a small, hooded figure. Perhaps this latest evidence - a fingerprint - could prove his culpability in the murders. I needed to find him and match the print.

Gessi had been absent from Bruno's trial. When I had last seen him he had been in a very bad mental state, either that, or he had given a worthy theatrical performance. I saw his sweaty, scarred face again as he peered at me squinting, half-demented. What was it he had said? Something about the glorifying of the Lord's grace being his true vocation. "Don't thank me, heathen," he had said. "I'm all too used to absolving. It is my duty, my purpose."

I felt a stab of excitement. 'Of course!' I said under my breath, 'Of course.' I turned at a sound from along the nave and saw that the young cleric, Brother Clemento had re-entered the church, his silhouette in the doorway, the sunlight of a new day about him. He took a few steps inside, and I walked down between the line of pews. He was out of breath. "You saw Lord Cicogna?" I asked.

The boy shook his head. "No sir, I'm sorry, I did not. He was not there. I asked the neighbour on the ground floor and they claimed they did not see him return home last night."

Chapter Thirty-Nine: Tomasso

Tomasso had not heard the sound from behind him until it was too late. A stinging pain was all the awareness he had of being attacked and then the cobbles had reared up before him. He hit them hard and darkness descended.

A drop falling into liquid. Another, then another. At first they were part of dream, a cloudy collection of thoughts and images that made no real sense. Events were out of sequence, effect before cause. Then, the clouds started to dissipate and he felt as though he was rising up through water, cold black water. Coming round, he was face down in an icy puddle pooled in a rut in the floor. For some time, he had no idea for how long, he felt numb, the only clear sensation, the freezing liquid against his skin; but then the pain roared through his brain, an agony so intense, he started to pass out again.

He opened his eyes to almost total blackness. Moving, a new pain screeched, low in his back. He shifted to abrogate it and realised he was bound by chains at his wrists and feet. He saw the movement of the chains like black snakes in the dark. Hearing the metal clang, he picked up other sounds; the tapping of water from his dream, the snuffling and scratching of rats, and close to his cell, a human sound, a whimpering.

He strained to listen. It came from beyond the room, he could tell by the way the sound echoed and reverberated. He heard what he guessed to be the jangling of metal, keys. This was followed by the creaking of a rusty door hinge . . . a voice.

"Thank Jesu."

Tom almost recognised the voice, but not quite.

A second voice, low, muffled.

"Wait . . . What are you . . . ?"

Tom knew who's voice it was: That loathsome scum, Cardinal Severina.

A stifled word: "Stop . . ."

A third voice. "Hold him tight."

Tom tried to move silently. He held his breath, listening, listening. A muted, truncated scream that seemed to die in the air was followed by a sound he could not identify at first; a gurgle. He had heard that sound before, the noise made by someone choking on their own blood, the airless rasp from a slashed throat as the mortally wounded who knew they were just moments from death tried in vain to make themselves understood: But they were always too late, they could never again form a word. He had heard that sound at

Lepanto, had stepped back as men fell to their knees grasping at their necks senselessly, their flesh ripped open by the tip of his sword. In the next cell, he knew, Cardinal Santoro Severina was being murdered.

Chapter Forty: Inside the Embassy

"Are you absolutely sure, Francesco?"

From across the large desk that dominated his office, I looked at the Doge's earnest expression. The release brought to him by the outcome of Bruno's trial could be heard in his voice. "Well, no, My Doge. I cannot be *absolutely* certain that I have found our killer," I replied. "But all the evidence points to Father Berlinghiero Gessi."

"And as evidence, you have the fact the man was at the scene of the first murder and lied about the events surrounding the death of the prostitute, Antoinette Perugino?"

"Those facts, and because he has no verifiable explanation for where he was at the time of Eriador's murder or the slaying of the actor, Andreini."

"Tell me about what you found at Chiesa di San Rocco."

"The cardinal was, I believe, killed somewhere else and his body brought to the church."

The Doge narrowed his eyes. "How can you possibly know that, Francesco."

"Because there was so little blood at the scene, sir. There were drips along the nave and some around the corpse, but nothing like the amount there would have been if he had been dispatched there. Blood had dried and become encrusted around the wound in his neck and the cuts in the forehead, which implied that he had been killed several hours before I was there, furthermore his body showed the degree of rigor mortis that would fit with this."

"And you have no idea where he was murdered?"

"No, sir."

"Going back to Gessi. Is there anything to link him to this latest outrage?"

"I must admit, I was really thrown by it. I knew that Gessi was a very loyal companion to the cardinal. The last time I spoke to the priest he made a great show of his devotion to his master."

"And that does not make you doubt your theory?"

"No, it does not."

"And what is his motive?"

"I cannot pretend to understand it entirely, I believe that Gessi is acting out some strange compulsion. I think he is an extreme zealot. No, more than that, much more, he is actually insane and his madness is expressed in a distorted view of the world and the way he perceives his fellow man."

"Explain."

"He kills in the name of cleansing, cleansing the evils of the world, and he believes that he can absolve those he murders, but at the same time make examples of them.'

"So, Antoinette Perugino, a prostitute, Eriador, an occultist and possibly a heretic. The actor?"

"Some zealots," I said. ". . . believe thespians to be heretics or certainly immoral; that the depiction of a false persona is somehow irreligious."

"That's incomprehensible."

"To normal people, yes, My Doge. But Gessi is far from normal. There is also the fact that Andreini was a drug user and, based on hearsay at least, a sodomite."

"I see. But, Severina? He hardly fits the pattern."

"Indeed, sir, but, the word 'proditor' cut into his flesh suggests very strongly that the murderer felt betrayed by Cardinal Severina. I can only assume that Gessi had been led to believe that the Nuncio was more of a religious zealot than he proved himself to be. Perhaps they had a row, a falling out. Or else, it is possible the acolyte learned something damaging about the man he idolised, something that destroyed the image he had of him. It is even conceivable that somehow, Severina learned that the killings here in the Republic were Gessi's work and confronted him over them. Gessi would then have been forced to shut him up."

"A little speculative, isn't it, Francesco?"

"Yes, it is, until we have some firm evidence. But there is also the series of very similar murders this past summer in Rome. As far as I am aware both Father Gessi and Cardinal Severina were there at the time. I have had no hint to the contrary, as I only learned of those murders after I last spoke to each man."

"Yes," the Doge said, nodding. "And the stains you have found?"

"I discovered traces of wine and crumbs of bread on the three most recent victims. Antoinette was dragged from the canal, so all evidence of this type was lost, but I have every reason to believe that if I did found her body as I had the others, the same traces would have been there. I believe they are the remnants of some strange ritual. Father Gessi is either posing as, or really is, a Sin Eater."

"Forgive me," the Doge said. "I am not familiar with the term."

"It is a suitably archaic name, sir, for an anachronistic concept. A Sin Eater is a priest who volunteers to absorb or 'eat' the sins of the dying, thus absolving them and allowing them to enter Heaven. The priest carries the burden of these sins until he is absolved by another Sin Eater."

"Yes, I recall it now," Cicogna said with a frown, clearly dredging up a piece of his education almost lost in some dark recess of his memory. "A very peculiar notion. But you have no proof that Father Gessi is one such 'Sin Eater'?"

"Sadly, not, My Doge."

"And what of this strange art of studying finger marks?"

I gave him a gentle smile. "Fingerprinting, My Doge. It is an ancient technique first used a long time ago in China. But I think it is perhaps new here in Europe. Philosophers in the court of Emperor Qin Shi Huang some two centuries before the birth of Christ realised that the fingerprints of every human being are unique to them. The skin forms whorls and curls in individual patterns. If their imprints are left behind at the scene of a crime and can be matched to a suspect, it may point to their guilt."

"But how could you try to match it with vast hoards of people?"

"Well, you cannot, but the philosophers of the Qin dynasty realised that records of prints of known criminals could be kept, and if prints were subsequently found during the investigation of a crime they could be compared to those on record."

The Doge thought for a moment. "That is very clever, Francesco, but we have no records."

"No we do not, sir," I said a little downbeat. "That is quite right, but I have to gather any fragments of evidence I am left by our murderer. You never know if any scrap might be useful at some point."

"And so you wish me to grant you permission to enter the Vatican embassy and be allowed to search Father Gessi's room, even if the Ambassador objects?"

"Yes, I do, sir."

"It is asking a lot of me, Francesco."

"I realise that, but it is the only way I can see that I may have any chance of finding incontrovertible proof. At the very least I would like the chance to talk to Father Gessi again."

"Yes, I do see that." Doge Cicogna paused and a heavy silence lay between us. "Very well, he said after an agonising few moments. "I will grant you permission, and I know I have no need to ask you this, but I shall in any case. Please tread lightly."

"My Doge, I shall," I promised.

It was early evening before Doge Cicogna could gain official permission for me to enter the embassy. The ambassador himself could not be reached and his assistant claimed he did not have the authority to sanction such an extraordinary request; the embassy and its grounds were, after all, as good as Vatican soil. But the Doge realised the importance of there being no further delay and by five o'clock, with the sky darkening and the temperature dropping, he sent for me and I was escorted to the Vatican Embassy by a troop of heavily armed palace guards.

In the meantime, while I had been waiting for permission, I had called on

Tomasso, but found no one home. I had then taken a gondola to see Teresa and asked if she could repeat the favour of calling in on our friend if I had not contacted her by six o'clock with news that I had found him. Next, I conducted a tour of all Tomasso's favourite watering holes in the city. It was still early and I knew Alfonzo's would be closed up still for several hours, so I called in at the Palazzo Londisi to see if by unfortunate chance he may have been induced to call in on Lord Mario Turroro.

A young man had opened the door. He struck me as being anxious, too delicate a soul to be employed by Turroro. He had a slight lisp and explained slowly, each word measured, that his master and the entire household had removed to the warmer climes of Naples to see out the winter.

"And Caravaggio?" I had asked.

"He returned to Milan two days ago, sir," the boy had said mechanically.

From the Palazzo Londisi, I travelled the fairly short distance to Pinelli's palace. Ajith had answered the door and beamed his radiant smile when he saw me before explaining that after the Bruno hearing His Lordship had spent the night in Padua but was due back in the Republic within the hour. I brought Ajith up to date and expressed my concerns for Tomasso. He said he had not seen him for a few days and that his master had not mentioned seeing him either. I asked him to pass everything onto Pinelli as soon as he saw him.

A government messenger caught up with me soon after I had returned home. He had the note from the Doge informing me that an armed party awaited me at the palace. Isabella was not home and I surmised she was perhaps at the market. I washed quickly and changed, found a hunk of bread in a cupboard under the chopping counter and headed for the palace. From there, I walked to the embassy feeling very well protected.

We were stopped by a pair of guards at the entrance; they each held a pike. I handed over a letter the Doge had signed granting me unhindered access to the building and the grounds. One of the troops withdrew with the missive and returned a few minutes later with Senior Secretary Martino Juventi. He was dressed in the same black ensemble he had worn this morning in San Polo and his narrow face was contorted with a pained expression.

"Is this really necessary, Lord Sagredo?"

"I'm afraid it is, Senior Secretary. You realise the urgency, surely?"

"Of course I do." He looked offended. "But this is Vatican soil. We will conduct our own enquiry."

"You're most welcome to do that," I replied, my voice steely. "But I have my own investigation to conduct. Cardinal Severina was murdered on Venetian soil, as were the three earlier victims."

"You can't possibly believe the slaying of the Nuncio is in any way linked with the..'

"I don't believe it," I said coldly. "I know it. Now, if you will please step aside."

I made to advance and the two embassy guards crossed their pikes, blocking my way. I felt the four soldiers behind me bristle and then adopt a defensive stance.

I looked into Juventi's face. "I really don't want anyone to be hurt."

"Nor I."

"And I assume you would like to know who killed your countryman, the cardinal?"

"I would."

"Then let me do the job I have been assigned to." I nodded to the official letter in his hand. "Permission has been granted from the very highest authority."

Juventi sighed deeply, then he took a step back. "You may conduct your search, but your guard stays here."

"That is fine with me," I said.

"And I will escort you throughout."

Father Berlinghiero Gessi's room was a bleak affair. It befitted his calling, I mused as Senior Secretary Juventi showed me in. He lit a pair of candles and these swept away the shadows. A narrow bed lay against the far wall, a small window to one side of it. A table stood against the wall opposite the bed. The room was exceptionally neat, the floor clean, the bed well made. The table was bare apart from a candle in a wooden holder. I lit the candle to provide us some extra light.

"What are you expecting to find here?" Juventi asked watching me poke around in the corners of the room. Without answering, I lowered myself to the wooden floorboards and peered under the bed. The floor was clean there too. I pulled myself up. "Could you please help me with the bed, Senior Secretary?"

The man gave me a puzzled look, produced a shrug and stepped to one end of the bed. Between us we managed to shuffle it into the centre of the tiny room and I slipped into the space close to the wall against which it had rested. I crouched down and inspected the wooden boards starting at the end closest to Juventi. Two thirds of the way along, just a few feet from the corner, I saw it, a rectangle of wood slightly raised and chipped around its perimeter. I unsheathed my dagger, slipped the blade along one edge of the rectangle and levered up the panel.

"What in the Lord's name?" Juventi exclaimed.

I lowered my hand into the space under the prised open section of board and lifted out a leather bound notebook. Coming round the bed, I placed the item carefully on the table. "We'll see, shall we?" I untied the thong around the

326

book and turned back the cover.

The handwriting was very neat and the contents extremely ordered. It was a form of diary, but with only key dates listed. The first clutch consisted of four entries: 7th, 14th, 15th and 19th August, in which Gessi described in some detail the succession of murders in Rome. He had a formula for his entries, date, name of victim, details of the murder, and in each case in conclusion, he had written: *In nomine Patris, et Filii, et Spirtus Sancti. Amen*: 'In the name of the Father, and of the Son , and the Holy Sprit . Amen.'

I flicked through the pages with Juventi looking over my shoulder. The first Venetian entry was 10th November. Below this was the name Antoinette Perugino. Gessi had written: "Very early on 10th day of November. First venture in the Republic. A whore in the Ghetto. We were fortunate not to be spotted by two men with whom she had argued. She struggled, but was, in the end, easy meat. It was an exquisite pleasure to take her soul unto me and I know that she will have been completely absolved."

I moved on to the next entry the same date, 10th. Below this: "Late evening. The arch heretic, Eriador, the Alchemist. Such a foul smell as the man died. He was filled with evil. Saviour was delighted with this catch, his face full of mirth as the vile creature breathed his last, his life blood shooting into the air. We were quite drenched by it. I then conducted the necessary mutilation."

'Saviour?' I said under my breath. Juventi gripped my arm. "What is that?"

I turned to him. "This is a confessional, although I feel Father Gessi sees it more as a record; little more than bookkeeping for his nefarious activities."

"I don't understand," the Senior Secretary said.

"Your pious friend, Father Berlinghiero Gessi has murdered many. He has described here a series of crimes perpetrated in Rome last summer and also itemises the more recent atrocities."

"That can't be true."

"Look here," I said. "He has an accomplice. He names him." I pointed to the page. "Saviour."

"Saviour?"

"Any idea who that could be?"

"None."

I turned back to the next entry, the 18th November. Gessi had written: 'Franco Andreini, sodomite, drug user, thespian. It was an audacious murder. Saviour is a genius and I love him unconditionally. That fool, Sagredo is nowhere close to catching us and he never shall; we are far too clever.' I turned the page, but that was the last entry. 'Well that was interesting,' I thought. 'Gessi has not been here since killing Severina.' I closed the book. "When did you last see Gessi?"

Juventi thought for a moment. "Yesterday afternoon. As far as I am aware, he was here most of the day. He barely emerged from this room and had asked not to be disturbed as he wished to spent time in contemplation and prayer."

Surveying the bleak little room, I walked back to the hole in the floor. Kneeling down, I put my hand back inside the opening.

"What are you looking for now?" Juventi asked.

I ignored him and stretched down further into the secret compartment, groping blindly. My fingers caught on a loop of wire. I felt around it carefully, then, lying flat on my front, I tried to see into the hole. But it was to no avail. I clambered to my knees and decided to take a chance by pulling on the loop. It was resistant, so I tugged harder. It gave, and I almost fell backwards as a much larger section of floor levered up and away from me. By the time I got to my feet, Juventi was already at the opening in the floor and looking down, his face creased into an expression of disbelief. We could just make out a very narrow flight of wooden steps leading down into darkness.

"Did you know this was here?" I asked.

The man turned and shook his head. "Absolutely no idea, although I have heard stories of strange hidden passages and hideaways that had been included in the design of the building."

Could you please hand me one of the large candles?" I said.

Juventi paused for a moment. I could almost see his mind working. A large part of him was terrified by the prospect of entering the hole, but another part knew it was his duty to do just that.

"Please wait here," I said and before he could protest, I had taken from him the candle in its holder and started to lower myself into the hatch.

I only just managed to squeeze inside, my shoulders rubbing against the stonework, fraying the mortar and sending dust and small stones downward. I noticed a loop of rope a few inches above my head and realised it was a means by which to close the trap door. I left it open. At the bottom of the steps, the entrance broadened to a narrow passage in which I had to crouch almost double in order to avoid banging my head. The floor of the passage was wet and the subterranean crevice stank - a blend of mossy damp and stale air. I shuffled along perhaps a dozen yards with nothing but a puddle of candlelight to guide me. I took it slowly, careful of each step forward until, much to my relief, the corridor widened again and I could straighten with perhaps an inch to spare.

The passage ran straight before curving gently to the left, what I determined to be approximately west. A pale luminescence appeared. I edged towards it and as I approached I realised it was an opening to the outside covered by a rusted metal grill. I peered through the distressed latticework and saw a stone canopy. As my eyes adjusted, I was able to make out a few details, dark, wet

328

bricks, their edges crumbling and covered with lichen. Straining, I could just about hear the dripping of water and realised that the passage opened under a bridge close to a canal. "So, this is how Gessi managed to get in and out of the embassy unnoticed," I said, my words falling flat in the dead air.

Chapter Forty-one: Visitors

Tomasso had lost all sense of time. In the unremitting blackness and with no sound apart from the rats and the dripping of water, it was impossible to know whether it was night or day.

He occupied himself trying to work out what could possibly have happened. He was sure the man in the next cell had been the monster, Cardinal Severina and that he had been murdered. But who might kill him? And why? Given half the chance, he would have happily been the one to commit the crime. Who else though felt so strongly about the cardinal? Who would kill him, here in this dungeon?

Had it been Niccolo Celsi? Tomasso mused. He knew the Celsi family were associates of the Nuncio. Indeed, he would not have been at all surprised if he had learned that the family was working with the cardinal to further their business plans in exchange for Niccolo's assistance in his entrapment of Bruno. But murder? Were any of the Celsis really capable of that?

Why not? He thought to himself. Niccolo had doubtless wiped out business rivals and those who had betrayed him in the past. Niccolo thought only about Niccolo. Then, his mind drifted to the trial that had just been concluded. The cardinal had won, the Celsis had won . . . they had won the battle at least. Then Severina had been slaughtered . . . like an abattoir pig.

He slept fitfully out of sheer boredom. There was nothing he could do. He had been clamped in chains attached to two sturdy rings in the wet, mossy stone floor; he could barely see his own hands held up close to his face. There was nothing to do but conserve his energy, to pass the time and to fantasise about what he would do to his captors if he were to be given the slightest opportunity.

The sound awoke him immediately, his senses primed to react to the slightest disturbance. It was the creak of a door opening at the end of a passage. Repetition . . . it was the same as before. A spasm of fear shunted along his spine and he was as alert as he had ever been.

A key was slipped into the lock and the door of the cell opened. Torchlight flooded the room dazzling him and he raised an arm to shield his eyes. He could see only vague shapes approaching him, two hooded figures, faces shrouded within black holes circumscribed by folds of cloth. One of the men grabbed him, pulling him to his feet. Tomasso yanked his arm back and it slipped from the man's grip. He heard a snigger from the other person in the room and his arm was grasped again, nails digging into his flesh. Tom sensed the second figure come round behind him. He stumbled backwards and found his head clamped in a strong grip, a forearm under his chin.

'So this is where I die,' Tomasso thought as his head was yanked back, a fistful of his long hair in the jailor's free hand. A surge of viciousness and strength pulsed through him and he propelled himself forward bringing his forehead down on the man in front of him, smashing into his nose. The man yelped in agony and fell back out of the torchlight.

Tomasso felt the grip on his hair tighten and there was hot breath on his neck, a fug of body odour assailing his nostrils. He caught a glint of metal in the hand of the man clambering to his feet. The creature was hissing with fury, but still Tomasso could see nothing of his features. Taking a deep breath, convinced it would be his last, Tom shoved himself back hard into the man behind him and writhed. But it was a futile gesture. The metal touched Tom's skin and he braced himself ready for the onslaught. A hand moved up to his lips, rose to his jaw and roughly forced his mouth open. Fingers slid across his teeth and he snapped at them, caught on one and bit down hard. Prising open Tomasso's jaws, the man smashed a pair of pincers against Tom's incisors. Tomasso jerked backwards with a desperate, pained cry. The man managed to shift his grip, edging the pincers round and clamping them about a tooth. It cracked and Tom's mouth filled with the iron taste of his own blood. Feeling the pressure from behind suddenly release, he collapsed to the stonework, grabbing at his throbbing mouth.

Chapter Forty-Two: Fire

By the time I arrived home, it had passed ten in the evening. There was a message from Teresa waiting for me. She had gone to Tomasso's rooms but had found no one home. I laid aside the note with a heavy sigh. Isabella had stayed up and was full of questions, but I made it clear I was in no mood for conversation. She could see the anxiety in my face.

"Is there anything I can do for you, sir? A meal?"

"Thank you Isabella but no," I said with all the kindness I could muster and started towards my laboratory, Gessi's notebook under my arm. I stopped. "Actually, there is one thing," I added. "The young man who lives across the campo, the German family."

"Edgar Schrimmel?"

"Do you think he would he be willing to drop a message in at Lord Pinelli's for me?" I held a grossoni coin in my opened palm. "I would like Lord Pinelli to come here as soon as he can.

"Francesco, I would deliver it for a tenth of the price!" Isabella said with a sigh. "You must have money to burn, My Lord!"

Gessi's leather bound diary lay on a counter in my laboratory. I had lit every torch, and the room was positively aglow. Which was just as well, I thought to myself, for I would need as much light as possible. Sifting through a collection of bottles on the shelf above the counter, moving aside two or three vials, I eventually alighted on a small bottle made from green-tinged, Murano glass. It was filled almost to the top with a grey substance. I found a small porcelain dish and poured into it some of the material from the bottle. It was fine powder, silvery in the light, a compound that had travelled halfway around the world with me. A blend of finely-ground iron and some carbon which had been produced from the purifying of burned wood, the substance was called magnetic powder. From a cupboard to the side of the counter, I withdrew a wooden box and placed it on the dissection table just behind me. It did not take me long to find what I was looking for, a fine brush made from fox hair. I blew across it to remove fluff and accumulated dust and laid it on the counter. I then took a liberal pinch of the powder, brought Gessi's book directly under the nearest torch suspended on the wall and sprinkled the cover with the magnetic powder. Next, I picked up the fox-hair brush and swept it over the powder in the way I had been taught during my forensic studies in China. Finally, I lifted the book and poured the excess powder back into the dish. Bringing the notebook closer to one of the candles, I could see several ovoid shapes on the cover; but they were indistinct. From a drawer, I removed a magnifying glass that was capable of creating an image in the eye almost double the size of any small object under observation. I hovered the glass over the marks.

There were three quite different sets of prints. From long hours of work with Tung Hu in Cambaluc years earlier, I knew that one of these was mine. Of the other two sets, one struck me immediately as being similar to those I had seen in the church earlier that morning. I found the piece of loincloth in the pouch on my belt, lay it on the counter and flattening it out. Comparing the whorls and curls on the cloth with the marks on the cover of the notebook I could tell immediately they were not merely similar, but absolutely identical. The print must have been Gessi's as he was almost certainly the owner of the book which meant he had at least been present at Severina's murder.

I found a sheet of paper and a sliver of charcoal and had just started to make a drawing of the fingerprint when I heard glass smash, a thump, and then Isabella's taut scream. I dropped the charcoal and sped up the stairs, through the door and into the main room. Isabella was standing close to the opened front door, a rock lay on the floor just inside the room, glass from a smashed window was scattered next to the door. Isabella had a hand to her mouth and was making a strange sound at the back of her throat. I ran over to her and saw she was pointing to a figure speeding across the icy cobbles of the campo.

"Wait here, Isabella," I said quickly, and as I ran out, I noticed an envelope on the stoop. I grasped at it and set off as the man disappeared into a lane off the south-eastern corner of the square.

I lost sight of him as I entered the narrow alley. Running as fast as I dared, twice I almost fell flat on my face. Reaching a bend in the lane, I caught a flash of black cast into sharp relief against a whitewashed wall of a building. I stumbled onward, catching hold of a railing as my feet slid from under me. At a junction of two passageways, one directly left, the other a wider path that joined a short bridge over a canal, I picked the latter and then followed a bend towards the Grand Canal. Emerging onto a broader laneway, I found it deserted.

"Damn it!" I cursed and bent forward, hands on knees catching my breath. And there, clasped between the thumb and fingers of my right hand, was the envelope; I had quite forgotten about it. Straightening, I ripped it open and withdrew a sheet of paper. It contained just three words: 'Calle del Cortesia'.

I knew where it was; no more than a minute away. I sped off, heading northeast along Calle della Caffetiere. A pair of shutters above my head swung in the breeze, the rusted hinges creaking. Turning right, I still had not seen a soul since leaving home. A left and another right brought me onto Calle del Cortesia. The houses were silent, shutters closed, doors locked. I ran as fast as I could, and there, close to the end of the street, stood a house different to the others. It looked like a derelict, its front door flapping in the brisk easterly wind.

I approached warily, listening, waiting for any flicker of movement. I stepped over the threshold. The hall was cast in darkness. Taking one slow, steady step after the other, I edged along the hallway, reached the opening into the front room and was thrown off my feet by a burst of orange flame and the boom of an explosion. Crashing backwards my ears rang and my eyes stung with smoke and debris.

I picked myself up and hurtled back down the hall almost reaching the front door when I saw through the smoke something on the wall to my left; three more words, the letters painted a foot tall. It was a second address: 'Via del Monte'.

Gasping for air, I felt the freezing cold hit me like a bare fist and I slipped on the doorstep, landing, arms and legs spread-eagled across the frost-sprinkled cobbles. Coughing and spluttering, I managed to pull myself up to my knees. People were emerging from their houses and running towards me. From behind came the hot, dry air sweeping around the crisp flames, biting and chewing their way through the rooms.

Two sets of strong arms helped me up. "Water," I gasped. "Fetch water. Alert the palace guard and the Night Watch. There's a madman on the loose." I realised only half my words were coming out coherently. Turning, I set off immediately for Via del Monte, just two lanes away south-east in the direction of San Marco. I could hear shouts as I ran, the district was waking up, the ingrained terror of fire driving men from their beds to grab pails and to rush for the nearest canal. Two turns and a long straight stretch of passageway swept clear of the worst of the ice and I was emerging onto Via del Monte.

The house could be seen from the end of the lane, a red glow visible through shutterless windows. I sped over and peered inside. The fire was small and localised in a metal brazier standing on a stone ledge. I could see immediately that it was a trap. A cord ran from the brazier along the floor to a table in the centre of the room. A glass dome such as was used to cover cakes or other delicacies at a banquet stood close to the nearside edge. A second envelope lay under the glass.

Easing open the front door, I tried to stop too much air blowing into the house and snapped shut the door behind me. I was in a darkened hallway, the only illumination a devilish red glow from the room off to my left. I took it carefully, all senses alert, and turning left, through the doorway, I could see the workings of the clever mechanism set up in the room.

334

The glass dome was positioned such that if it were lifted to remove the envelope, a lever would be released. This was connected to a string that opened the brazier holding a small collection of burning coals. They would fall into a large bowl containing a colourless liquid. I could smell it from close to the doorway . . . pure spirit, instantly flammable and quite deadly.

I tried to get to the envelope without disturbing the dome and tripping the mechanism, but it was impossible. I pulled down the sleeve of my tunic so that it covered my hand and quickly jerked away the glass dome feeling a sudden scouring heat pass through to my fingers. The dome crashed to the floor and shattered on the stones. Snatching up the envelope, I span round and dashed back into the hall as the brazier tipped and a fistful of red hot coals tumbled into the bowl of spirit. I felt the surge of flame skitter across the room faster than an arrow, bolted for the front door and pulled on it with a maniacal strength. Seconds later, I was once more emerging into the shattering cold. The front windows and the front door exploded. Glass, wood and stone flew all about me. I dived to the ground and crawled away as fast as I could. Reaching the end of the street, I ripped at the envelope. A small white and red object slid out and slipped through my fingers to hit the cobbles. Crouching, I plucked it from the ice. It was a human tooth. The envelope held another single sheet of paper. In fine calligraphy was written: 'A little personal gift from your good friend, the Doge's son.' Beneath that was a single word. 'Londisi'.

From all around me came sounds of panic and terror. Half of Venice, it seemed, had been awoken by cries of 'Fire'. The smell of smoke and soot from the burning houses clung to my clothes and my own singed hair produced a repulsive stink. I could taste sulphur on my tongue. I felt bedraggled and ached all over. But I could not stop. The shock produced by the words written on the piece of paper and the horror of realisation that Tomasso had been captured and disfigured, could, I knew, propel me through the very flames of Hades. For the first time in many years, I was filled with hatred and an almost uncontrollable terror. Londisi? Mario Turroro's palace? What in God's name was going on? Even in the dungeons of the Doge's palace, not so long ago, I had not felt this rage, nor this fear. And so, I ran on, paying no attention to the pain, caring nothing for the stabbing agony in my sides, the rasping of my lungs and the dryness in my eyes that caused each blink to feel like a thousand needles were puncturing my eyeballs. None of it mattered.

I reached San Marco and saw a troop of guards leaving the palace. Without a second thought, I ran up to the captain. It was the man I had seen the morning Antoinette Perugino's body had been dragged from the canal. That now felt like a lifetime ago. I stepped in front of him, holding up a hand. For a second he looked outraged and then he recognised me, halted his company and gave me a curt bow. "Lord Sagredo," he said. "There is an emergency in the west of the district."

"Yes, I know Captain and I won't hold you up. Could I please borrow one of your men for half an hour? It is another emergency, I'm afraid." He was about to argue. "The life of the Doge's son depends on it," I snapped.

He gave me a hard look and called out a name. A young soldier appeared and saluted. "Please have him sent on to the fires, Lord Sagredo. We need every man we have."

"I understand," I said and watched as the troops marched off across the square.

"Your name, soldier?"

"Guillianno, sir"

"I need you to run to my home on Campo S. Maurizio. I'm hoping Lord Gianvincenzo Pinelli will be there. You know who he is?"

Awestruck, the soldier, a young boy little more than sixteen or seventeen, simply nodded.

"This is what I would like you to tell him."

The Palazzo Londisi looked little different to the way it had presented itself earlier that day when I had come here in search of Tomasso. Now I knew that he must be held captive here or else already dead.

The windows of the palace were shuttered. A boat was moored at the front. That had not been there when I had called before, I noted. Along the path, old footprints in the ice had frozen over and there was a light sprinkling of frost and snow over them. Clearly, no one had entered or left the building by this route for several hours. Halfway along the path I stopped and crouched down. A piece of blue paper lay stuck in the ice. I pulled it away and tried to see if there was anything written on it, but there was nothing, it was some sort of wrapping, I surmised. Approaching the main doors, they appeared to be closed, but as I came near, I realised one of them was ajar and pulled close to the other. I eased it towards me, unsheathing my dagger with my spare hand.

The vast hall was brightly lit by torches in holders, clusters of half a dozen lining the back wall and in wall brackets. At my feet lay a body, face down on the marble, a pool of dried blood around it. I turned it over and saw the face of the young man who had answered the door to me that afternoon. There was a long strip of red down his front giving his torso the look of a stuck pig ready for the spit. I looked up and it was only then, as my eyes adjusted to the light, that I began to realise what a scene of Dantesque horror and devastation I now found myself facing.

The floor was strewn with bodies and bits of bodies. Most of the dead appeared to be servants. A head had been driven onto a candleholder, the tongue rigid between blue-black lips, eyes gouged out. It took me a few moments to absorb the full wickedness of it. Just hours earlier, an orgy of violence had taken place here, in the heart of Venice, and no one had been aware of it. No one had escaped, no one had been able to raise the alarm; defenceless, unarmed innocents had been scythed like wheat.

I took two steps into the building, leaving the front door wide open. The stench of blood and entrails was almost overpowering and I nearly lost my footing on the blood-smeared marble. Then, turning to the staircase, I saw them. Three naked men had been nailed to the wall running alongside the stairs. They hung there like paintings following the slope of the steps. Each of the men had gaping throats wounds and their left sides had been split open above the pelvis, their guts dangling from the gashes.

I strode across the hall to the broad step at the base of the staircase. The first man, a slender, middle-aged fellow with long grey hair stared back at me blindly. Next to him was a young boy about the same age as the page who lay gutted close to the front door. I ascended carefully, watching my footing and sidestepping a severed hand. Close to the top, I drew parallel with the last of the three crucified victims. It was a grossly obese man in his sixties, bald and bug-eyed. His severed left hand had been stuffed into his mouth, the stump of his wrist nailed to the wall. It was Lord Mario Turroro.

I felt a strange numbness. It was the nonchalance of it all that struck me as being almost inhuman. I expected and understood many of life's cruelties, it was the rightful order of things. Seeing a man, a woman, even a child ravaged by disease or their bodies torn to shreds by the wild forces of Mother Nature was a thing hard to bear, but at least it was part of the normal order of things. This . . . this was an abomination.

And did I feel afraid? I have to be honest and say that I did not. It was only later that I was afraid, petrified in fact. On cold nights for years after the events I now describe, I would be drawn back to the memory of those moments and I would feel inflamed with an existential terror, a bewilderment really, a suffocating confusion, unable to comprehend how such things could be wrought, how any human being could descend into such abject savagery.

I was not sure what to do. I had been summoned here, led by the nose; but where were the killers? Where was Tomasso? I was terrified that at any moment I might stumble upon his mutilated corpse. I reached the landing and gazed down at the carnage, my mind racing.

"Francesco?" The voice was barely audible. I stood rigid, holding my breath. "Francesco?"

It was coming from along the passage leading off the landing that led towards the eastern wing of the palazzo. I walked slowly along the richly ornate carpet, blind to the incredibly valuable tapestries and ornaments lining the corridor.

"Francesco?" The sound was coming from up ahead. I walked on, reaching a doorway to my right. Leaning into the opening, I saw a steeply ascending flight of stone stairs.

"We are up here, Francesco." Now that I was closer to the source, I could recognise the voice; it was Gessi. There was no mistaking that voice with its vaguely effeminate edge and ill-disguised smugness. "Do please join us."

"Where is Tomasso?" My voice sounded shrill, the words seeming to collapse in upon themselves.

A pause. "Won't you join us, Francesco?"

I gripped the knife between sweaty fingers and felt my heart pounding in my chest. Stepping onto the stairs, I crept upward slowly. It was a narrow stairway girded by stone. I could feel fresh air streaming down to me and realised that this must be the entrance to a tower. Approaching the top, I could see a parapet and the stairs opened out onto some type of platform. I took the opening with the knife held before me, sweeping clockwise then anticlockwise as I had been taught long ago in naval training. I stepped out. The sky overhead was sprinkled with stars and the misty thread of the Milky Way swept directly above me. To the northeast I could see red orange and yellow flames, spirals of grey smoke rising from the burning buildings of San Marco.

Dressed in a monk's robe, his head cowled, Father Gessi was standing three yards in front of me. He held a sword in his right hand and with his left hand, he pulled back his hood to allow tessellated shadows to fall across his features, his burned flesh was still raw and weeping and I could tell that his nose had been broken very recently. Behind him, I saw Tomasso seated on a rough wooden stall, his wrists were bound behind him, his ankles roped together, his mouth gagged. I saw the fear in his eyes and could only guess at the agonies he had endured. Leaning over him, with his back to me was another black-robed figure. He turned, his head covered by a hood, his face in deep shadow. His Excellency Buto Testa pulled back the fabric and stared into my eyes.

It seemed so obvious after the event. The man who had remained so calm at Bruno's trial, the man I had watched carefully and who's facial expression had rarely changed from impassive confidence. He had bent events to his will in the Patriarchal Palace and he had been running the crazed game that had occupied my every waking hour since arriving back in the Republic three weeks ago.

"Did you enjoy my tableau downstairs, Lord Sagredo?" Testa said, taking a step forward. In spite of the chill breeze up here, the man's face was lathered with sweat.

"What do you want from me, from Tomasso Cicogna?"

338

He turned towards Tom. "Him? Oh, he was simply bait. You are the fish I wished to line."

"And you are here to cleanse La Serenissima, is that right?"

"Of course." Testa said and took another step forward. "It is my destiny, my calling. We are here to continue with the work we began in Rome."

"You were there during the summer."

"Yes, it surprised me that you did not ascertain that rather important fact earlier. If you had, well . . ."

"And you have taken it upon yourself to decide who is a sinner and who is not, is that it?"

Testa laughed and flicked a glance towards Gessi. "I, we, have been guided in all that we do by the Divine Light of the Holy Spirit, something you could not begin to understand."

"Oh, I can understand it," I said. "I have encountered people before who have maladies of the mind."

Testa produced another laugh.

"Sounds a bit hollow," I said.

"Sssh!" the ambassador brought a finger to his lips. "Hush, you know not what you say. I wish to tell you what is now about to happen."

I span on Gessi. "You are being very passive, priest. Always the servant, are we not? Never the master."

Father Gessi stared back at me without the faintest flicker of emotion.

"First you were Cardinal Severina's lap dog," I went on. ". . . and now . . . who's whipping boy are you tonight? This pathetic man before us? It is for him you will bend over, like some little male whore from the Roman slums?"

He merely grinned. "Carry on, Francesco. You are an entertaining fellow, I'll give you that."

"Shut up, both of you," Testa said. He stepped to one side. "Sagredo, you have been concentrating on your friend here, Lord Cicogna. That is commendable, but I would like to draw your attention to this." He waved towards the wall behind Tomasso. In the shadows, I could just discern the shape of a row of barrels, their tops covered with a blue paper pasted to the lids. Gunpowder. The blue paper was identical to the fragment I had seen on the path leading to Turroro's front doors.

"The boat. You transported the gunpowder here this afternoon."

"Oh yes, the servants worked hard."

"You are insane."

"Perhaps, by some definitions, Sagredo. But to others, you and your kind are the mad ones. You run around sodomising, whoring yourselves, playing with occult forces, speaking all sorts of vile heresies."

"And Cardinal Severina? How does he fit into that collection?"

In some ways my old friend was the worst of them. He betrayed us. He was once a noble man. He loathed heretics and detested the libertine values of you Venetians."

"But he was planning a drug deal with the Celsis?" I offered.

Testa raised his eyebrows. "So you have not been completely useless then, heretic." He laughed. "But then of course, you have every reason to hate the Celsis . . . and Severina, come to that."

"And you believe yourself to be the supreme arbiter; deciding who should live and who should die? Oh, no sorry, it's your fanciful Divine Holy Spirit, is it not?" I laughed and for the first time, I caught a flicker of anger in Testa's eyes.

"There is enough explosive here to destroy this building and to start a conflagration that will make the little disturbance in San Marco tonight look like a stray spark in Beelzebub's inferno. Venice will burn and its evil shall finally be expunged. This running cesspit of a city with its whores by the thousand, its addled heretics and seers, its arse-fucking thespians and its drug lords will sample the flames of Hell. And you had better get used to it, Sagredo, because you and your kinsmen shall soon face an eternity in the fires." He reached into his pocket and withdrew a tinderbox.

Gessi snapped to attention, his smirk had slipped. "Sir, should we not first place ourselves at a safe distance?" His eyes slid from Testa's face to the tinderbox. Testa said nothing but opened the lid of the box to check the flint and firesteel. He then withdrew the flint.

"Master! We need to set a fuse from over there," Gessi pointed to a spot the far side of the platform from the gunpowder. That was always the plan, was it not?"

Testa struck the flint against the firesteel, sending out a spray of yellow sparks.

"Saviour!" Gessi screamed and Tomasso started to groan through his gag, struggling against the ropes.

"Be still, vile creature," Testa snapped at Tom, and went to strike the flint again. "I shall enjoy setting you alight and making you my human fuse."

"No!" Gessi hollered and brought his weapon round in a shallow arc. I dashed forward. Testa's attention was drawn by his acolyte. I dived at the ambassador, got my fingertips around the tinderbox and wrenched it from his grasp. It fell to the floor, the flint bouncing on the stone floor and kicking up small sparks, the charcloth tinder landing silently beside it.

Gessi's sword scythed the air and whistled past Testa's left ear. He lost control of it and it clattered to the floor. I brought my dagger round, the tip aimed for Testa's face, but Gessi grabbed my upper arm, bending it backwards with surprising strength. The dagger fell from my fingers, but Gessi lost his balance and stumbled backwards towards the top of the stairs, his head smashing hard against the stone parapet.

Testa stood hunched forward, his hands at his sides staring at me and panting. Sweat was running into his eyes and he looked utterly insane. He made to dive forward for the tinderbox. I smashed my knee up under his chin and heard his jaw crunch. His head jolted upwards. He opened his mouth and coughed up blood, spraying it all around us. I steadied myself, leaning back to centre my weight and swung an arm round. Testa saw it and lifted his arm to block me. I dodged his right fist as he lunged for me. But he had left himself exposed. I shot out my leg, my boot slamming into his guts. He doubled over and I punched him hard, square in the face, shattering his nose. He fell forward unable to break his descent, his head hitting the flagstones, he crumpled.

Swinging round, I saw Gessi scramble to his feet, my dagger in his hand. I braced myself and eyed his sword where it lay too far away for me to reach in time. Not hesitating for a second, the priest dashed for the stairs and shot down the narrow opening. Plucking up the tinderbox, I sped after him. By the time I had reached halfway down, Gessi was at the foot of the stairs. I caught the glint of armour and a flash of bright colour ahead of him. Gessi did not break his stride but charged forward, slashing the dagger before him. I heard a cry and a confusion of bodies.

Hurtling to the bottom of the stairs, all before me was confusion. Pinelli was there with three soldiers. A man lay on the floor at my friend's feet. To the right stood two more soldiers, they had Gessi cornered at the point of their swords. He was pressed back against the wall, a look of sheer terror on his face. I saw him drop the dagger and raise his hands.

"Francesco," I heard Pinelli cry, his voice a shrill rasp. "It is Ajith. That animal has stabbed Ajith."

Two soldiers carried the injured man into one of the bedrooms along the hall while another group ran up the stairs to arrest Testa and unbind Tomasso.

Ajith was in great pain, but still conscious. His face was a mess of sweat running in the creases of his worn skin. He was clutching his abdomen with bloodied palms and I eased them away as he lay back. At my instruction, Pinelli lifted his servant's head and settled it onto a pillow.

"Take long, slow breaths, Ajith. Fetch hot waster and towels, quick," I barked at a soldier.

I opened the man's tunic and to save him moving too much I cut away his leather jerkin and shirt to expose the wound. There was a lot of blood. I used some sheets to soak it up and to try to clean it enough to get some idea of how serious it was. Ajith cried out in agony. On a counter to my left I found a

341

long, narrow wooden box. I ripped off the lid and tossed it to Pinelli. Place it between Ajith's teeth, Gian," I snapped.

Pinelli's face was ashen and I could read the fear in his eyes. "Please save him," he said so that only I could hear.

I leaned in to inspect the wound and looked up to Ajith's face. He was passing in and out of consciousness and moaning incoherently. The soldier arrived with a slopping bowl of steaming water and an armful of towels and rags. I nodded to him to place them carefully on the bed.

Soaking a towel, I plunged it into the wound. Ajith screamed. I could see the servant's bowel was damaged, an opening of about a hand's width ran laterally along the large intestine.

"I need my medical kit," I snapped. "Gian, please tell a soldier how to get to my house. He must make all haste."

Pinelli took a man aside and within a few seconds he was gone. I cleaned the wound as best I could and kept pressure on it to contain the bleeding. Ajith made a few more moaning sounds and finally fell unconsciousness, his breathing shallow.

"What can you do, Francesco? Please tell me you can save him."

"I will do my best. He has been badly cut, right through to his gut. I will need to sew him up. If he survives the night, the next battle will be against infection."

"My, God," Pinelli said. "What has become of us when such things happen?" He nodded towards the door and the horrors that lay beyond.

"I cannot answer that, my friend. I think evil has always been with us, and so it shall always be. Some rare individuals become obsessed with a new cause and their diseased minds propel them to commit unspeakable evil."

We turned at a sound from the door. It was Tomasso. I pulled up from the bed and we embraced. "You had me worried," I said, gripping his shoulder. "Are you hurt at all?"

He opened his mouth and I saw the gap in his teeth. "Apart from this, I got off lightly."

The door opened again and the soldier who had been sent to my house appeared and handed me the bag containing my medical equipment. I opened the bag and pulled out everything I need, laying a set of needles, thread, a collection of bottles and soft bandages on the bed.

"It might be best if you two left me to it for a while," I said, looking from Tom to Gian. With the door closed behind them, I turned back to Ajith laying still on the bed, picked up a needle and set to work.

Chapter Forty-Three: Memorial

Two Days Later.

The church of St' Mark's was filled to capacity and outside, ten times this number crowded the square and spilled onto the streets feeding into San Marco.

The church was lit with a beautiful lemon glow and the air resonated with the mournful strains of Palestrina's *Missa Papae Marcelli Sanctus*.

I stood in perfect stillness absorbing the moment, soaking up the sound, and the smell of incense, the sensation of the ground pushing back on my feet and the air passing around me; and for just a second I was transported back almost a decade to Nepal and the voice of my old master, Tenzin. 'Nothing is real,' he was saying. 'All things must pass, both the good of the world and the bad.'

Next to me stood Tomasso, his face rapt. He looked better than I had seen him since my return to the Republic and that at least was one good thing to have come from the ordeal we had lived through. Although we had caught the killers, I felt as though I had actually failed. So many had died, four victims and then the slaughter at Lord Turroro's home. Three citizens had lost their lives to fire and Ajith had only just turned the corner and started on the long, painful road to recovery. How much could have been saved? How many families could have been spared bereavement if only I had solved the crimes sooner?

So much, I mused, had escaped me. As Testa had said: 'I did not think to see who, out of all the possible suspects, had been in Rome in August. I had missed so many clues and had been distracted by my feelings for Teresa and my old feud with the Celsis; and to top it all, I had allowed my loathing for Cardinal Severina to obscure my sight from the real demons, Gessi and Testa.

Finally, I had overlooked the single piece of the puzzle that could have helped me to resolve the crime sooner. I had followed the forensic evidence as I had been taught to do, but this had been the first real crime I had ever been called upon to solve, and I had let the evidence overwhelm any other lines of thought. I was convinced that one of the two killers was left-handed. Because of that, I had pondered Celsi and his assistant, Luca as being involved long after it was clear they could not have been the killers. But the mutilations of the victims had been carried out by Gessi, who was right-handed. It was only after I had realised the priest's role in the atrocities - a Sin Eater, who performed a version of the Mass over the dying victims with bread and wine - that the truth had finally come to me. He could not use the same hand to do both jobs. Instead, he had conducted what he believed to be the purification of souls with the right hand, and sliced into their flesh with his left. It was just such small details, just such phobias and compulsions of the sick of mind that could, I knew, identify a criminal, and I had missed it. My teachers, I thought, would have been ashamed of me.

I glanced around and saw Teresa and Piero standing close to the front of the crowd across the nave from Tom and I. I caught her eye and she produced a faint smile. I glimpsed, some way along, towards the north transept, the Celsis, Niccolo, Violetta and Sofia. And then a procession led by the Bishop of Venice began to walk slowly from the altar. We watched it pass us and turn left at the vestibule. The congregation started to relax and dissipate.

Tom and I walked out of the church and found a path through the crowds thronging San Marco. Slipping away to the side of the square, we weaved a path through to the western edge and the relatively quiet streets beyond.

"You are very quiet," Tomasso observed.

"Am I?" I said.

"Yes, my friend, you are. What's troubling you?"

"Oh, I cannot define it really, Tom."

"All right, let me try for you. You feel distressed because, since your return, all you have experienced is pain and sorrow, death and destruction. You don't know where you are with the lovely Teresa, and to add a further turn of the screw, you feel you made a fucking great mess of the investigation and could have done a lot better."

"How well you know me," I said and grinned at him. "You forgot the painful knee."

He laughed. "Stop kicking yourself, Francesco. Stop placing such impossibly high standards upon yourself. You did the best you could. The barbarity that has befallen La Serenissima this past month has not been any fault of yours, and if you had not been here, the murders may have continued longer; more innocents would have perished and Testa could have seriously damaged my father's Dogeship, not to mention the city itself.

"And Teresa?" I said steadfastly looking at my feet as we walked. "I have caused nothing but turmoil for her."

"Oh, utter bollocks, Francesco! Do you honestly think Niccolo fucking Celsi would make your beloved happy? And the boy? Piero hates the bastard. Your return came in the very nick of time."

"Perhaps, but ..."

"No buts," Tom insisted and slapped me on the back.

We reached Campo S. Maurizio and crossed the cobblestones to my little

344

house. Inside, it was warm, a roaring fire in the hearth. Isabella was there to greet us. "How was the memorial?" she asked.

"Far too long," Tomasso said.

"Beautiful," I said. "You should have come, Isabella."

"Oh, it's all very well for you fine Lords and dignitaries," the servant admonished. "I did not much fancy standing in the freezing sludge for two hours to catch the odd line of a psalm."

"Fair enough," Tomasso said, throwing himself into my favourite armchair close to the fire.

There came a tap at the door. Isabella stepped over and peered through the pane of new glass that had been fitted yesterday. Straightening, she pulled on the door and held it wide. "Come in," she said cheerily, and turned to me. "If that is all right with you, sir."

Teresa and Piero stood on the doorstep. I paced over. "Come," I said, make yourselves at home and get warm, for goodness sake." I turned to Isabella. "My servant has just been telling us she skipped the memorial because of the cold outside in San Marco, but I can testify to the fact that there were many red noses and a pant of steamy breath inside the church."

"Some ale?" Isabella asked.

"How about heating some mulled wine, Isabella? I think we deserve a treat."

"Fuck, Francesco," Tom exclaimed, don't push the boat out too far . . ."

Isabella tutted at the profanity and retreated to the scullery.

"So what brings you here?" I asked.

"I . . . we." Teresa looked towards her son and then back at me. "We wanted to make sure you were well. After all that . . ."

"I'm absolutely fine," I said with a smile. "Everyone seems to be worried about my state of mind!"

Isabella returned with a large pot. I could smell the wine even before it was heated. She pushed past us, busied herself with the cooking tripod and arranged it over the fire. With experienced hands, she levered the pot onto the holder refusing any help from either Tom or I.

"I was concerned," Teresa said.

"As was I," Piero added.

I smiled at him. "That is kind of you both," I said. "But really, I am . . ."

"You're a fucking clod, Francesco!" Tom bellowed. "For all your so-called brains, you're a clod."

"What?" I looked from Tom to the others, arms opened out in supplication.

"Isn't it mind-numbingly obvious that we are all worried you will be so upset by what has transpired that you will upsticks and leave us?"

I was so stunned, I stood there with my mouth open, unable to speak.

"You'll catch flies," Tomasso quipped and Piero laughed.

"I can assure you," I had begun when there came another knock at the door. I sighed heavily and walked over to open it. Two guards snapped to salute. "Sir," one of them said. "Your presence is required at the palace . . . immediately, My Lord."

I took a deep breath. "Very well. Who?"

"The Lord Doge, sir."

"I see. I'll get my robe." I turned to the gathering. "I am sorry," I said. "I hope this won't take too long. Isabella, can you make dinner for us all?"

"Of course."

"Then, please, enjoy the mulled wine . . . and save some for me."

I caught Teresa holding me with a steady gaze, and as I went into my bedroom to fetch my official robe I was not too surprised to see her follow me in.

"Francesco," she said easing the door almost closed.

"Yes."

"What Tomasso said. It is true. We are . . . I am . . ."

I stopped a pace in front of her and put a finger to her lips. "You have nothing to fear, My Lady," I said. "I'm here to stay." And I leaned forward to plant a chaste kiss on her cheek, but she moved her head and her lips found mine.

•

"What the devil are you doing here, Sagredo?" It was Niccolo Celsi seated outside the Doge's apartment. The guard who had escorted me there bowed and retreated.

"I could ask the same of you." I replied and was about to sit when the door next to us opened and an assistant appeared. "Please," he said and indicated for us to enter.

Doge Cicogna was seated at his desk. He was dressed in red silk and had recently been attended to by his barber who had trimmed his beard. He looked rested and relaxed. We took seats opposite him.

"Lord Celsi, Doctor Sagredo, thank you for coming. You probably realise why I have called you here. We need to deal with Gessi and Testa. Their diplomatic immunity means that we cannot try them in the Republic."

"Which means they will escape prosecution," Celsi said.

"That is a possibility," the Doge replied. "It will be in the hands of the Pope."

"Who will not relish the idea of embarrassing both the Church and the

Roman government." I turned from the Doge to Celsi.

"He may hold a secret trial," the Doge offered.

Celsi scoffed. I looked at him for a moment and realised what a complex situation this was for him. He could not let Gessi and Testa get away with their crimes because they had the power to expose the Celsi family over his and Violetta's nefarious plans discussed with the late cardinal. Their attempt to corrupt Severina into helping them to secure an inroad to unlock the lucrative drug market in Rome would not go unmentioned, and Clement for one, would not be best pleased.

"Their identities have been kept from the public?" I asked the Doge.

"So far, yes."

"Could we not simply release them to the mob?" Celsi said.

"Do you have any ideas, Doctor Sagredo?" Cicogna asked.

"Diplomacy is not really my forte, Your Serenity."

"Is that so?" Celsi said.

The Doge threw Niccolo a black look. "And the best *you* can offer, Lord Celsi is to hand the killers over to the mob?"

"It served our ancestors well enough. And, until either, you, My Lord, or my esteemed colleague here has a better suggestion, it would seem the most practical solution."

"We are not barbarians!" the Doge snapped. "Do you have no pride in Venetian values at all, Lord Celsi?"

Niccolo blanched. "I have every pride in our nation, but this appears to be an intractable problem."

The Doge looked down at the papers on his desk, lifted the uppermost sheet and waved it at us. "No sooner do I resolve one problem with the Vatican than I have another just as thorny. This is Bruno's deportation document. He was shipped away from the Republic this very morning, while the city was distracted by the memorial to Gessi and Testa's victims." He sighed heavily.

"May I suggest a radical alternative, sir?" I asked.

Celsi exhaled noisily.

"We cannot execute the two of them and it seems unlikely that Clement would like their identities revealed in a show trial in Rome. He may decide to hold a private trial or simply have them eliminated once they step over the border into Vatican-controlled territory, but I would be very surprised if Testa had not protected himself against such an eventuality."

The Doge raised a hand and took a deep breath. "That is indeed the case," he said. "The men have been threatened with torture . . . shown the instruments. Testa has made it very clear that he has hidden documents that would expose secrets concerning the papacy that Clement would not want to have made known. That is how the two of them escaped prosecution over the Roman murders. Testa knows that we certainly cannot put him on trial here. The priest is more vulnerable, and of course ,Testa has said nothing to help Gessi."

Celsi sighed and shifted in his seat. "Filth."

"So," I said. "We have the weapon of knowing the identities of Testa and Gessi, do we not? They have the weapon of holding information that could damage the Vatican, and the Pope would not allow us to put the two men on trial in Venice, let alone execute them. So, we need to find a way to use these threats."

Celsi was staring at me with his usual look of contempt. The Doge had his elbow on the desk and was fingering his newly-trimmed beard.

"Perhaps we should contemplate the consequences of freeing the two men on the condition that they act as spies for us in Rome," I said.

"What!" Celsi exploded. "Are you quite mad?"

"I don't believe so, Niccolo."

"Letting mass murderers go free, Lord Sagredo?" the Doge commented.

"Not free really, My Lord. They would be our servants for the rest of their lives and could be very valuable."

"What's to stop them betraying us at the first opportunity?" Celsi said, shaking his head. "Do you really think you can trust such repulsive scum?"

"I could trust them if I was convinced they could not manoeuvre out of our trap. Think on it. If they betray us to Rome, they have to admit to their crimes here and in Rome last summer. If they do not serve us, we have the threat of exposing them to the Vatican."

"In which case they will make public the secrets they have concerning the Holy See," Celsi commented.

"Assuming they have the chance, Lord Celsi," the Doge said. "If they fail to keep their side of the bargain we could quickly report them to Clement who would see they did not live long enough to act upon their blackmail threat. And of course we can make Testa and Gessi very much aware of this."

"So then, why don't we simply tell the Pope now anyway?"

"And pass up the opportunity to receive high quality Intelligence from a Roman ambassador?" I replied. "We can expel Testa from Venice with a reason that will increase Clement's respect for him, and the ambassador will be relocated, perhaps many times. Each new assignment offers us valuable opportunities."

"It's absurd," Celsi declared. "How do we know they will no go on another killing spree in whichever city they are posted to?"

"For all the reasons I have stated." I gave him a withering look and Niccolo held my eyes for a moment as the Doge peered down at his papers, lost in thought. In those few seconds, I could tell that Celsi realised I knew that Testa and Gessi not only held secrets concerning the papacy, they possessed dangerous information about him and his family.

"I think this is a promising idea," the Doge declared, looking up. "It is a dangerous and audacious plan; just what I would have expected of you, Doctor Sagredo," he added, smiling at me.

"Excuse me, My Lord," Celsi said with surprising force. "But, you cannot seriously consider this a possible solution? It is utterly preposterous."

"Is it?" Cicogna asked and interlinked his fingers on the desk. "Explain."

"Do I really need to? Celsi exclaimed, exasperated. "They are mass murderers, for God's sake! What more needs to be said?"

"I did not say I was happy with Doctor Sagredo's proposal," Cicogna replied. "But I think it should be given serious consideration. Do you have a better idea, Lord Celsi? If you do, this would be a apposite time to voice it."

Celsi said nothing, just stared back at the Doge.

"No, I thought not," Cicogna concluded. "I shall inform you both of my decision."

Chapter Forty-four: Solution

Lord Niccolo Celsi left the Doge's apartment with a controlled fury that, through long practise he had become very skilled at hiding. From the meeting, he was escorted one flight down to his office by a silent guard. Celsi nodded and watched the man retreat to his post before returning to the stairs and descending to the dungeons.

"Lord Celsi," said the new chief jailor, Mario Lippitti, a thug of a man in his early twenties with a pink scar running from under his left eye around the orbit and up to his temple. He had been Fabone's assistant and promoted upon the death of his predecessor.

"I have a proposition for you, Lippitti," Celsi said and placed an arm about the jailor's shoulder.

The younger man peered down to where the nobleman's hand lay and then back into Celsi's eyes. "Yes," he said uneasily.

"There is no need to be afraid." Niccolo gave the man his most reassuring smile. "It's more a favour actually, one for which I am happy to reward you most handsomely."

Lippitti brightened and waved towards the door to his small, malodorous office. Once inside, he did not walk around to the seat behind his tiny bare desk but stood close to the exit.

Celsi withdrew a small leather pouch and bounced it in his palm. "Ten ducats," he said watching as the jailor followed the motion of the money bag with a steady gaze. "It's yours, Lippitti. All you have to do is look the other way for thirty minutes."

Lippitti took the pouch with a satisfied smile and nodded.

"No, I actually mean you need to look the other way, literally." And Celsi made a circular movement with his hand.

The jailer produced a momentary look of confusion and then spun slowly on his heel to face the wall.

"Thank you," Celsi muttered. Withdrawing his dagger, he slipped it between the young man's ribs with shocking force. Lippitti slid down the wall, blood gurgling from his mouth and streaking the stonework as he went.

Celsi pocketed the bag of coins that had slipped from the jailer's dying fingers, wiped the dagger on a piece of cloth he found on the man's desk and sheathed the blade. He knew his way around the dungeons. He had been here many times, always as a master, always in control, and today was no different. He would have his way whatever it took. He descended a flight of stone stairs, the way lit by a torch he had snatched from Lippitti's wall. He knew which cell he was looking for, the third on the left on the second level. Reaching it, he stopped, moved the torch and peered through a grill in the door. All he could see was what appeared to be a pile of rags close to the centre of the tiny cell. In the lock, he turned a key from a bunch he had been given and opened the door outwards.

Stepping inside, the shape on the floor moved, and in the faint light from his torch, Celsi could see the face of the bedraggled prisoner, Carlo Perugino. His beard had grown straggly and he had lost ten pounds. His face was filthy, and with a dirt-streaked and veiny forearm he shielded his eyes from the burning brand. He recognised the visitor and pulled back, scrambling across the excrement-stained floor kicking up a fine cloud of crumbling straw as he went. "You!" Perugino croaked. "Come to torture me yourself, have you?" His voice was barely audible.

Celsi produced a smile. Perugino misinterpreted it and spat in Niccolo's face. "Do your worst. I no longer care."

Niccolo's smile vanished, and he raised a fist to strike the prisoner, then stopped himself, lowering his hand slowly. "I am not here to harm you, Carlo Perugino," he said through gritted teeth. "Quite the opposite, in fact."

The man looked away. "Oh yes! And I believe you!"

"The men who murdered your daughter . . .'

Perugino's eyes narrowed.

"They have been caught and arrested."

"Who?"

"You would not know them; Buto Testa and Father Berlinghiero Gessi."

"A priest!" Perugino exclaimed, disgusted.

"Testa is the Vatican ambassador to Venice, no less!"

Perugino took a deep breath, wheezing as he did so. "When is the execution? I may still be rotting in here, but at least I can celebrate that moment when it comes."

"I'm afraid you shall not, Perugino."

The man peered into Celsi's eyes. "My hanging will be first?"

Celsi shook his head. "Not if you do exactly what I tell you to do."

"You make no sense."

Celsi lifted the bunch of keys with which he had opened the door, found the correct one, bent towards the shackle holding Perugino's foot to the wet stone floor and unlocked it. "Stand," he said, and pulled himself up, shoving the keys into a pouch at his belt. He offered the prisoner his hand. Carlo Perugino rose unsteadily and started to fall, but Celsi caught him. "It will take a few moments," he said. ". . . but you will be fine." Then he pushed his hand inside his cloak and withdrew a dagger. Perugino flinched.

351

The man was so short, he had no need to bend, the low ceiling stretched close to his bald pate. Celsi handed him the knife, handle-first. Perugino stared at it and then up into the face of the man who had caused him to be here in the first place. He took it. "What's to stop me slicing you open with this, Celsi?"

"It's *Lord* Celsi, Perugino. Nothing. Except that if you do not, I can help you escape. I have a boat waiting to take you beyond the boundaries of the Venetian state."

Perugino stared at him. "Why?"

"His Excellency Buto Testa and Father Berlinghiero Gessi are no more than fifteen yards along that corridor from here." Celsi turned and pointed to the blackness beyond the cell. He could see the light from his torch reflected in the black pools of Perugino's eyes. "And, of course," Celsi added holding up the bunch of keys. "I have these. I assume you would like to avenge the murder of your little girl, Carlo?"

"This is a trick."

"No trick, my friend. I have paid the jailor Mario Lippitti more than a fair price to keep his face to the wall and his door closed for precisely thirty minutes. That will give you time to bring some justice to this world and be gone before the guards are alerted."

"Why?"

"Oh, I have my reasons. But if I were to tell you, your life would be forfeit and you would never even reach the boat I mentioned."

"And what of yourself, Lord Celsi? Why do you not wish to do the deed?"

"Oh, I do, I do. But, I have always taken pleasure in watching. And besides, one has to consider the poetic justice of it all, don't you think?" He grinned and waved towards the door, handing the gondolier the torch.

The two men had been put into the same cell. It was higher-ceilinged but not longer or wider than the one in which Perugino had been imprisoned. Gessi and Testa were chained to the far wall two feet apart, their hands manacled to the stonework, their feet gripped by iron anklets secured to the floor. The room stank of shit and piss.

Perugino stepped inside, the torch aloft, and he saw the faces of the priest and the ambassador. The pair had been here two days and they were already wild-eyed, their faces lathered with sweat. The wound on Gessi face had become a weeping, stinking abscess that covered one side of his face. His eye was closed and puffy.

"Gentlemen," Carlo Perugino said, his voice still weak and husky. "*His Excellency* Buto Testa and Father Berlinghiero Gessi, apparently." He looked from one to the other and bowed exaggeratedly. Testa was still struggling to maintain some dignity and gave the newcomer a contemptuous look. Gessi was too far gone to care about appearances and simply stared at Perugino mutely, his lips cracked and bone dry. Then both men noticed the dagger in the squat figure's right hand as he lifted it into the circle of light about the torch.

"Who the fuck are you?" Testa managed to squeeze out, his voice unrecognisable as the man who had once been the Pope's ambassador to the Most Serene Republic.

"Me?" Perugino said. "Oh, I'm ain't nobody. Just a peasant. But I once had a beautiful daughter, skin like a baby's. I remember her as a tiny bundle in my arms, 'er big, dark eyes and lovely smile. The most beautiful thing I ever did see, she was. Antoinette was her name. You met her once."

Gessi produced a little giggle, the sound of a man on the verge of madness.

"And I suppose," Testa rasped, ". . . you've come to exact your revenge?" He paused, eyeing Perugino as though he were a pile of vomit. "Fuck off, little man. As you said, you're a peasant. I am the Vatican's ambassador to Venice."

Perugino grinned. "You *were*, Buto Testa. 'but ere and now things are different to up there." And he flicked a glance towards the ceiling. "Peasant, ambassador, priest. None of that matters. You're just a couple of cunts who are about to die." He glanced at Gessi. "You're half-mad already, *priest*. I'll dispatch you first, so your friend 'ere can watch."

Gessi stood completely still, watching, speechless as the knife came level with his face. "I saw what you did to my little girl and many a man in my position now would cut little pieces off you, torture you slowly. But, I'm not a sadist, *priest*. An eye for an eye, the Bible tells us." And slowly, Perugino slipped the dagger into Gessi's neck drawing it left to right, cutting down deep. The dying man's eyes rolled up, blood showered from his neck, splashing into Testa's face, half-blinding him. Perugino took a step back. Gessi shook, the chains rattling. Then he stopped moving abruptly and slumped, his life all drained away. There was a vacuous silence in the cell, the last ring of the chains fading to inaudibility.

Testa did not move a muscle. In the torchlight, Perugino could see now the terror in the man's face; his partner's blood dribbled down his cheeks. Perugino stepped forward to wipe the gore from his eyes. But Testa's terror was not all-consuming, not yet. He had been a powerful man and still, even now, even here, he could not fully accept that his power had ebbed away just as Gessi's life had left him moments before. "You know I'm not the real villain, don't you?" he said. "I killed one of the men responsible – Cardinal Severina."

Carlo fixed him with a cold stare. "I have no idea what you're talkin' about."

"And Niccolo Celsi. I know you know him. He runs the drug trade in Venice. He had been arranging a deal with Severina to get the poppy into Rome."

"So? What's that got to do with anythin'?"

"Celsi supplied your daughter. The drug would have killed her before too long."

"But you made sure of it, didn't you? You . . ." Carlo's words caught in his throat. "You cut her throat."

"I saved her. Gessi . . ." He nodded towards the corpse hanging from the wall beside him. "He's a Sin Eater."

"What in God's name is that?"

"He takes the sins of the dying. Yes, I did kill your girl, but she is now with the Lord. If, thanks to Lord Celsi she had died from the drug, she would not have been saved."

"You're talking shit!"

"I'm not. If you hadn't killed the priest . . ."

"I would know?"

"Yes." Testa was nodding frantically.

Carlo produced a deathly version of a laugh, and said very quietly: "I'm going to kill you now."

"I could make you rich," Testa said desperately, sweat streaking his bloody, filth-spattered face. "You know they cannot execute me here, don't you? The Holy Father loves me, supports me. He sent me here to do his work, God's work. The Doge and his men will *have* to release me; the pope will forgive me. No . . . more; he will reward me and he shall . . ."

Perugino raked the sharp dagger across Testa's throat so fast his hand was a blur. Testa's lips continued to move but no words came, just animal grunts that were soon swamped with gurgling blood. Perugino's face was red and wet, his front drenched, and he looked into the eyes of the former ambassador, watching as the light faded from them. It was the last thing Testa saw.

For a few moments, Carlo Perugino could not move. His arms lay at his sides, the dagger gripped in his blood-smothered hand, the handle sticky. He felt strangely empty, hollow. As he had sliced and stabbed, a tiny irrational part of him had almost believed that by murdering these two men he could somehow bring back his beloved daughter. Now the mania was passing he stared at the slumped bodies and what was left of their blood dribbling like red spittle from gaping ragged wounds. He knew that nothing on earth or in Heaven would have stopped him killing Gessi and Testa, but he also understood it had achieved nothing. Antoinette would be forever dead.

He turned and shuffled towards the door to the cell. Celsi was standing in the opening. He had seen and heard it all. He held out his hand and Perugino passed him the bloody dagger, handle first. Niccolo simply nodded towards the end of the corridor. "Follow me. The boat awaits, as I promised."

They ascended three flights of narrow, winding stone stairs, and at the

354

top, Celsi leaned on a wooden door that opened onto the freezing noon, the brightness so intense, Perugino was almost physically pushed back by it. They were on a stone walkway running beside a slender ribbon of dark water. An old gondola knocked against the bank secured to a pole by a length of rough rope. Perugino stepped forward and stopped a foot from the edge of the bank before turning back. Celsi swept a hand towards the boat, and with a sudden, black realisation, Carlo Perugino ducked and felt the air rush over his head as Celsi slashed with the bloodied dagger.

It was the third time the two men had fought and now Perugino had the measure of him. He charged like a wild boar. Celsi crashed backwards against the wall of the prison and yelled in pain as his spine slammed into the stonework, the dagger spinning up into the air. Carlo grabbed for the knife on the cobbles. Celsi was too quick and reached it first. But before he could bring it up, Carlo kicked Celsi in the face, shattering his teeth. Niccolo tumbled back again and lost the dagger. Perugino plucked it up and took two steps towards Celsi. He went to thrust with the blade, but felt his legs give way as a boot caught his knees. Carlo tumbled forward, lashing out with the dagger as he fell and sliced Celsi's arm, making him scream.

Niccolo was up first, blood gushing from a deep wound just above the elbow, his shirt sleeve already soaked red. He could see Carlo still had the knife. He made a dash for the door, diving back into the darkness of the prisons and quickly yanking the door closed behind him.

Carlo, pulled himself up. He felt battered and bruised, but not seriously injured. Celsi had come off far worse. The door was locked. He glanced around at the boat, dropped the knife on the cobbles, detached the rope and jumped confidently into the bottom of the gondola. Tugging on the pole, he pushed away from the bank, turned in the canal and followed his nose north to the exit that would take him to Laguna Veneta and onwards from there to Mestre, and freedom.

The End

61877227R00219

Made in the USA
Charleston, SC
28 September 2016